HOSTILE EXTRACTION

HARRISON KONE

SEVERN RIVER
PUBLISHING

Severn River Publishing
www.SevernRiverBooks.com

ISBN: 978-1-64875-856-0 (Paperback)

ALSO BY THE AUTHOR

David Shaw

Into the Valley of Death

Saber Down

The Defection Protocol

Invictus

Unlawful Combatant

Hostile Extraction

The Second Directive

To the men who have walked in life beside me—you know who you are. Thank you for your devotion and friendship. King's to you.

"In this life we are either kings or pawns, emperors and fools." — Napoléon Bonaparte, *The Count of Monte Cristo*

PROLOGUE

Principality of Monaco

The ceiling of the luxurious suite spun as the man slumped into the pillows and his lover rolled off him, panting and grinning broadly. Anderson Stovall let out a long exhale before breathing deeply, his muscular chest rising as his partner played with his thick, dark chest hair. The silk sheets were cool with sweat against his back, but he paid them no mind. Had he ever experienced such pleasure?

Sofia Vitori, her long, dark hair falling in waves over her bare shoulders, propped herself up on an elbow to gaze at Stovall's face. He glanced down and chuckled before wrapping a strong arm around her and pulling her closer to him.

"We are breaking all the rules," he muttered, still breathless and bewildered.

"The most powerful people in the world are above rules," Sofia replied coyly. Stovall smirked and draped his free arm over his eyes as he continued to catch his breath.

"The rules have kept order for decades," Stovall countered.

"An old way," Sofia remarked, lightly as if knowing some secret. "This is the dawn of a new world."

Skeptical and curious, he watched her slip from the bed, dress in a black, satin robe, and head to the bar. She returned with a dram of Scotch for Stovall and a glass of wine for herself.

"The world has changed," she said, her hazel eyes gleaming with desire. "The balance has shifted, and alliances are the only way forward. Barakat's territory is open for the taking, and war is coming."

"What war?" Stovall probed, suddenly more interested in what she had to say since she mentioned Barakat's assassination. Though no one knew who had pulled the trigger, Stovall and Sofia both had their suspicions, but the fact that they couldn't find out with certainty unnerved them.

First Rykov, now Barakat, Stovall thought. There was the obvious candidate, and Stovall knew David Shaw was capable of the deed. However, neither his people nor Sofia's could connect a motive, other than knowing that Barakat had wanted to eliminate Shaw from the moment he learned about him.

The recent lovers had followed closely the events after the devastation that was Operation Taskmaster, which culminated in the sinking of an Iranian tanker off the western coast of Egypt. Though unproven, it was easy to speculate that Barakat had tried to take things into his own hands concerning Shaw, and the results had proved disastrous.

Stovall had never seen a slip-up quite like it at their level. It was a reminder of how fragile the balance of power was, and now he, as Sofia had suggested, could see that the balance was shifting after the sudden and violent deaths of both Rykov and Barakat.

The peasant is once again trying to elevate himself, Stovall thought, *or am I missing the truth entirely? Is that what Rykov had thought? Such arrogance would be fitting.*

"The world is changing right before our eyes. The Global War on Terror is ending, Chinese and Russian aggression is mounting, Iran continues to bring tension to the Middle East, Africa is ripe for plunder, only war follows such developments," Sofia explained.

Stovall raised an eyebrow before taking a sip of his Scotch. *She's not wrong*, he reasoned.

"I'm no fool," Stovall replied, adding a stern strength to his voice. "You are attracted to me on account of my power."

"I do like your eyes," she quickly countered. Stovall couldn't have stopped his chuckle if he had tried.

"You and I both know that this," he continued, pointing at her, then himself, "is transactional for power and leverage at the most and simple fun at the least."

"Oh, I have more power than you, dear Anderson," Sofia jested as she bit her bottom lip. Stovall laughed.

"Wealth, perhaps, but power? I don't think so," he stated. This intrigued her.

"You have no power here, with me, right now," she countered.

Smirking, Stovall reached out with his hand and caressed her cheek, and she nestled into his warm palm. He dropped his hand downward, tracing her jaw, before gripping her neck. He squeezed slightly and watched as Sofia's eyes widened in sudden surprise. He increased his pressure around her neck, and Sofia blinked rapidly in response and gasped even as a smile played at the corners of her plump lips.

"No, sweet Sofia. I have all the power here," he said before he released his grip. Sofia sucked in air and brought her fingers to her throat. His actions had warmed her blood, and her desire for him skyrocketed. No man could treat her in such a way and live, yet she permitted this American to do so and even relished it; its rarity fueled desire and thrilled her.

"Make love to me again," she pleaded, breathless. Stovall laughed and rubbed his face.

"What is your angle?" he pressed. He did not understand why she acted so infatuated. Surely, it wasn't genuine. "I'm an old man, Sofia," Anderson said, taking a large gulp of his whiskey. Sofia only smiled, leaned forward, and nibbled at his ear.

"Russia is mobilizing. War is coming again to Europe," she breathed as she bit down hard on his earlobe. "There is wealth and power to be gained, prestige and glory, legacy beyond reach until now."

In the presence of Sofia's seductive words and actions, Anderson felt himself arouse, and Sofia grinned again.

"Not as old as you think," she praised. "Together, we can rule the world, shape Europe, the Middle East, and Africa to our benefit. Instead of segmenting the world among few, let it be all ours."

"And what of Oza?" Stovall asked, his body suddenly, surprisingly, tingling with desire.

"He cannot stand against us if we are united together," Sofia countered.

"I've come to know of a man who does not take kindly to what you are proposing," Stovall said.

"David Shaw, yes. I owe him a great debt," she replied with a laugh, pulling away from Stovall's ear. "But I've figured him out, and he won't be a problem for us."

"I'm sure Rykov and Barakat thought similarly. Normally, I could have handled such threats with a phone call, but I'm not so sure about this one. Should Shaw prevail, which history suggests he will, then I would be his next target," Stovall stated.

"Yes, to move against Shaw is death, but to leverage him, *that* is the real challenge."

"What are you saying?" Stovall asked. "I've already tried to secure him as an asset."

"You cannot throw money at someone like David Shaw. You need my expertise: optics, manipulation, story crafting. You must make him believe he is acting of his own free will, but in the shadows, we will control the strings."

"And you know how to do this?"

"Dear Anderson, I'm doing it right now."

"With Shaw or with me?" he probed.

"David Shaw is exactly where I want him to be," she said, intentionally ignoring his question.

"And where's that?" Stovall asked, his alarm eroding his pleasure.

"Syria. Moving on Abdur Rajeev el-Shahan."

"The terrorist?"

"One of Barakat's men," Sofia replied proudly. Stovall's mouth hung agape as he realized her brilliance.

"You're feeding him intelligence?" he asked. Sofia nodded, her smile never fading.

"I can craft Shaw into our perfect weapon to point at whomever we choose, Oza included. With Invictus under our indirect control and Red Horse at your disposal, there is nothing we cannot conquer."

PART I

THE TAKEN

1

Off the Coast of Syria
February 2, 2022

As dawn crested the horizon of the rugged landscape rising ahead, its radiance surged in vibrant warmth, arcing across the water and turning the churning black into shimmering gold. The sudden burst of light warmed David Shaw's face, and he squinted, though he didn't deny the scene its beauty. However, the thrum of helicopter rotors above him and the operational chatter in his ears kept his mind focused on the mission before him.

General Tom McCoy, the commander of Joint Special Operations Command, had held true to his promise to the Secretary of Defense just hours after the tragedy that was Operation Taskmaster, and the United States military had responded with vengeance against the terrorist organizations that had killed so many of their men. What had started as an unprecedented victory for Islamic jihad had become a literal bloodbath as the United States brought a new wave of war—a war where politics didn't intervene, a total war against terrorism.

Gone were the conventional forces and the delicate political considerations. SOCOM had been turned loose, and there were few to scrutinize this action, as nearly all Western nations had suffered at the hands of Faatin

Radi and were equally eager for payback. No one was concerned with rebuilding, only killing those responsible.

Invictus International had found itself a cornerstone asset in this retribution. In the last three months, Shaw had conducted operations across the world, gaining notoriety with his enemies and recognition from military officials and politicians alike. With Natalie's skill in tracking targets and Shaw's battlefield expertise, Invictus had already brought many to justice, and today would be no different.

Two nimble MH-6 Little Bird helicopters transported Shaw and his team while the two accompanying AH-6 attack variants thundered in formation just ahead. Behind them, two UH-1Y Venom helicopters carried JSOC's Detachment One. The Marine Corps staffed Special Mission Unit was never far from Invictus' side in each operation, and as a result, the two units functioned and flowed with unrivaled fluidity. After their joint success in taking down Radi, SOCOM had paired Det One with Shaw until further notice.

As the battlefield commander, Shaw was privy to all communications as the operation commenced. Dressed in full M81-camouflaged combat gear and toting a M4A1 rifle fixed with a M203 grenade launcher, Shaw checked his watch before pressing his PTT. "All callsigns, thirty seconds."

"Payback One-One, this is Crusader Two-One, flight of two Harriers, four HARMs for the section, standby for SEAD, over."

"Solid copy, Crusader Two-One, your lead," Brent Dawson replied while piloting the Little Bird on which Shaw found himself.

Once again, Shaw peered forward as their target took shape.

"Assad's not going to like this," Tāne Pikari remarked on Invictus team's private channel.

"The gloves have come off," Shaw replied gravely.

"You can say that again," Owen Bray added with a chuckle. Under different international optics, Bray knew they would have assaulted this compound under the cover of darkness, without air support, and likely from watercraft or SCUBA, but now, after all that had happened, the full might of the United States' Joint Special Operations Command was awe-inspiring to witness.

Flying below radar, the two AV-8B Harrier IIs raced beneath the pack of helicopters, their formation perfect as their afterburners brought grins and shouts from the warriors watching with glee.

"That never gets old!" Bray shouted.

"That's a first for me!" Pikari replied, grinning from ear to ear as he watched the two fighter aircraft pass below his dangling feet. Even Shaw couldn't hide his smile as the two fighters surged forward.

Within seconds, the fighters released their payloads, and the AGM-88 High-speed Anti-Radiation Missiles ignited under their wings and soared forward as the Harriers banked north, leaving a trail of exhaust in their wake.

Shaw watched the missiles as they followed their radar guidance forward. The white fumes from their burn left visible streaks in the air as the missiles spun, maneuvered, and pitched before slamming into their targets, the ensuing explosions catapulting black smoke and flame high into the air.

"Nectar, this is Invictus One-Six, confirm SAM status, over," Shaw called into his radio.

"Invictus One-Six, surface-to-air capabilities are destroyed," Natalie Shaw answered. "Crusader Two-One, good hit, I repeat, good hit," she added from her location at MacDill Air Base in Tampa, Florida.

"Affirmative, Nectar," replied Crusader Two-One. "Invictus One-Six, you're clear all the way in," came the pilot's additional confirmation. "Good luck, out."

"Good copy, Crusader," Shaw replied. "All callsigns, we are cleared ahead."

The ensuing rounds of confirmation brought another smile to Shaw's face as the squadron advanced toward the coast. The black smoke thinned as they neared, and enemy combatants swarmed in the chaos, unaware of the advancing threat.

"Payback Two-One, commencing attack run," said the squadron commander of the AH-6 attack helicopters.

"Alright, gents, here we go," Shaw called into his radio. In response, his men settled into their seats and readied their weapons for immediate engagement.

Payback Two, in their Little Bird attack variants, soared over the coastal fortress compound as they unleashed a violent barrage of rockets and minigun fire. The 12.7mm slugs spat from the GAU-19 mini-guns at a near constant rate, the weapons snarling down upon the unsuspecting enemy, cutting apart bodies and destroying defenses with sheer power.

The two helicopters buzzed in circles around the compound, its ancient, high stone walls doing little to protect those inside from the violence raining upon them.

As Payback One neared with its squadron of two Little Birds, Payback Two continued to swarm.

"Pick your targets," Shaw called into his radio as those of his men carrying light machine guns and a marksman rifle commenced engagement. Though the enemy combatants attempted to regroup and respond with gunfire, most retreated into the fortress as those staying to fight were mercilessly cut down.

"Invictus One-Six, Payback One-One, LZ secure, standby for infiltration," Dawson stated.

"Good copy, One-One. Bring us in," Shaw replied.

The two helicopters with their cargo of four Invictus warfighters each descended upon the circular fortress as Payback Two continued to mop up the remaining resistance. After the Venoms made their drops on the northern and southern rampart walls, Payback One-One and One-Two touched down in the courtyard to offload the entirety of the Invictus operators.

"Nectar, Invictus One-Six, we are on the ground, how copy?" Shaw called into his radio microphone once he had found a secure position and the helicopters had departed.

"Copy, Invictus One-Six, we see you. Happy hunting," Natalie replied as she watched the events unfold in real time through a UAV feed. Once her husband and his men descended into the bowels of the ancient citadel, she knew she would lose visual.

"Krulak One to Invictus One-Six, ramparts secure," Det One notified from their position on the southern wall. "We're moving on the upper keep."

"Copy, Krulak One, we're making our way to the lower," Shaw replied. "Nectar, how are we looking?"

"All clear, One-Six," Natalie replied.

"Invictus One and Two, on me," Shaw commanded as he stood from his cover and proceeded toward the massive metal doors that led into the citadel's interior. The limestone courtyard lay strewn with blood, bodies, and debris from Payback's assault, and Shaw stepped over a detached torso as he led his team forward.

"One-Seven, Two-One, you're up," Shaw ordered. Pikari trotted forward alongside Bray, and the two men prepared breaching charges. "All callsigns, prepare to breach."

2

SOCOM Headquarters,
MacDill Air Base,
Tampa, Florida

Natalie chewed her cheek as she stood shoulder to shoulder with General Tom McCoy. Dressed casually in rugged attire—jeans, leather boots, and a tucked-in red flannel—she stood in sharp contrast to McCoy's official visage, his Marine Corps Service Alpha uniform impeccable with its abundance of ribbons, badges, and cords. He stood taller than she did, taller than her husband, but his face held that same firm resolve that she appreciated. To her, he appeared kind and unassuming. If out of uniform, she might never guess his lethal past or current profession.

Regardless, Natalie appreciated his unrelenting attitude toward those who had perpetrated Operation Taskmaster, and he, in turn, was impressed with how quickly and thoroughly she had dealt with Radi. Though he didn't care much for contracting out operations, he felt better knowing that Invictus brought a caliber of war-fighting experience, expertise, and morality he found extremely rare in the world. How David and Natalie Shaw had managed to build such an organization was a testament to their ability.

With his reduced forces spread thin across the globe, he grew to value Invictus more and more, even though he was constantly bothered by Red Horse Global representatives. They weren't without their uses, but certain missions required a precision the Shaws had mastered, and McCoy felt confident in the current operation.

"Any word on the identity?" McCoy asked Natalie.

"No, our source doesn't know," she replied, never taking her gaze off the UAV feed that dominated the massive, wall-mounted monitor. She watched as Captain Tyson Thornton led Detachment One's Krulak One element eastward atop the southern ramparts while Staff Sergeant Cade Boerkircher led Krulak Two's tactical element across the north wall. "But el-Shahan is holding one of ours in there," Natalie finished.

McCoy nodded and rolled his lips inward. He wished they had a map of the compound's interior, but the Shaws had assured him whatever lay inside wouldn't be a problem. Still, in the wake of Operation Taskmaster, McCoy, though aggressive, still fought against the concern that they were walking into a trap. However, Natalie was confident in Reza Afshar's intelligence. She and her husband had abducted the Iranian in Istanbul a few months ago to aid in their search for Radi. The threat against him and his family was one that he knew the United States wouldn't hesitate to deliver, and this kept their working relationship transparent and Afshar cooperative.

Natalie now hoped against hope, wishing the identity of the captive was who she longed for it to be. However, she knew how wishful her thinking was, and she reminded herself that their primary objective was killing or capturing Abdur Rajeev el-Shahan, one of the world's most wanted terrorists and an integral player in Barakat's crumbling empire.

She was constantly amazed at how well the terrorist network was connected. Most of what had been believed to be "lone wolf" attacks had been revealed, through Radi's intelligence, as structured within a much larger network of which el-Shahan was at the top.

That was the reason the previous raid against the terrorist leader during Operation Taskmaster had garnered so much attention, and now they had kept all operational planning as close to the chest as possible. In truth, Natalie was relieved they had located him so quickly after the previous, catastrophic failure. She knew they had gotten lucky and that they couldn't afford to let him slip away again.

"I know what you're hoping for here, General," Natalie said.

"A forlorn hope, but hope nonetheless," he replied. Natalie chewed her cheek and nodded.

"Krulak Two, this is Krulak One, we're preparing to enter, check your fire," Sergeant Carlo Galinato called through his radio as he and the rest of his tactical element stacked up on the narrow entry that led inside the upper levels of the stone keep. Just ahead of him, Sergeant Salvatore Barone prepared to enter at his commander's order.

"Good copy, Two," came the reply.

"All callsigns, breach on my mark," came Thornton's order through every headset.

Barone set to work priming his breach charge and fitting it to the door in the location that would yield the most devastating results to those on the other side while minimizing effects on his team. It was a careful calculation the breacher had made in seconds upon seeing the door for the first time.

"Five, we good?" Master Sergeant Ratliff asked as he and the other Det One operators watched Barone work.

"All good, Seven," Barone replied through his radio, which connected him only to his immediate team. He stepped back from the door and double tapped his helmet with his support hand fist to indicate ready to breach.

"Krulak One ready," Galinato, the team's radio operator, said into his microphone as he pinched his PTT.

"Krulak Two ready," Boerkircher replied.

They waited in a brief silence, their bodies tingling with anticipation to continue the fight. However, they knew what danger might lie across the threshold. How many friends had caught a bullet passing through the fatal funnel? Too many, they knew.

"All callsigns, mark," Thornton ordered.

The ensuing detonations buckled the doors inward, sending the heavy metal slabs careening across the entries and startling all inside.

"Flash out!" came a number of shouts as the second men in the stacks pulled the pins and tossed the nine-banger grenades through the smoke and into the rooms. Sergeant Jimmy Hogan waited patiently opposite Barone in the stack with his carbine ready until he heard the quick succession of the grenades' bright and sharp reports.

Hogan aggressively inserted across the threshold, his rifle in line with his eyes and his finger poised over the trigger. He absorbed the scene in an instant—the dead men who had perished from the breach and the remaining who coughed and recovered from the flashbang with weapons still in hand.

Noticing he had space to his left, he ran the rabbit laterally down the length of the wall, firing his weapon at the insurgents as they shrieked in terror. Barone followed closely behind him, and knowing he couldn't go right, trailed Hogan as he made space for the rest of their team while firing at the same targets as Hogan, their bullets chewing through tender flesh.

Within seconds, the room stilled, but no one spoke. Their Team Chief, Master Sergeant Ratliff, stormed by them, taking point with Captain Thornton close on his heels. Hogan and Barone took up the rear as the lethal MARSOC element engaged new targets in the next room.

3

While both tactical elements of Detachment One made their entries from the upper ramparts, Shaw, with Pikari and Bray leading point for Invictus One and Two respectively, pressed through the smoke from their own breach charges and flashing grenades and entered a wide stone hall. Shaw's rifle joined the breathy chatter of his team's weapons as they cut down the disoriented and frightened insurgents. Only a couple managed to cut loose a shot, but no enemy rounds found their targets.

Silent, the team fanned out and dominated the open interior of ancient stone. Shaw wondered who had built the relic he and his team were now destroying on their mission to bag el-Shahan and rescue their unknown compatriot.

Instinctively, team two peeled left as Bray led them through an opening on the far right wall while Pikari led team one down the left wall to press deeper into the structure.

"We're inside," Shaw said as he pressed his PTT, alerting Natalie and the other callsigns of their progress. Shaw's eyes followed the cables bolted to the stone walls as they ran from light fixture to light fixture, illuminating the dusky space in soft yellow. The team illuminated dark corners with their white lights as they cleared the next room before stumbling on a set of stairs that descended deeper into the earth.

A cold, damp scent rose from the depths, and Pikari glanced at the operator next to him, a former Green Beret named Eric Rakestraw. The stairway would only allow their descent in single file, and each knew a dangerous death trap when they saw one. A sole enemy combatant could cut them all apart at the base of that stairway. They wouldn't even have to aim.

As they covered their sectors, they saw shadows dancing on the floor at the base of the stairs, confirming their suspicions.

"One-Six, we've got tangos down these stairs," Pikari whispered into his mic. Shaw moved forward in the line and observed the route that had given his point men pause.

"That's a Charlie Foxtrot," Shaw muttered over Pikari's shoulder as the Māori kept his carbine pointed down range.

As a veteran of the famous New Zealand SAS, Tāne Pikari knew a bad route when he saw one.

"There's at least three if you count the shadows," Rakestraw added quietly.

"But there's got to be more than that," Shaw replied.

"All it would take is one," Pikari said. Shaw nodded, understanding the threat as well.

"If they've got an LMG set up down there, they'll cut us apart before we even see them," Rakestraw remarked.

"That's if one of us doesn't trip down those stairs," Pikari said, glancing at the crude, modern addition.

"Two-Seven, sitrep," Shaw said into his mic. Rick Reeves, a former Navy SEAL and Ground Branch paramilitary officer, led his team just behind Bray as they cleared another room beyond the wide, stone foyer.

"We've cleared the right wing," Reeves replied.

"Copy, do you see a way deeper in?" Shaw asked.

"Negative," Reeves answered. "We've got a dead end."

"Regroup on me," Shaw ordered. Reeves double-clicked his PTT in the affirmative and rerouted his team back the way they had come. Shaw, activating the command radio on the right side of his plate carrier, addressed the tactical elements outside of his eight-man team. "All callsigns, Invictus One-Six, we've come across a tunnel leading east.

It does not look to be part of the original structure. We're going to proceed."

"Good copy, One-Six," Natalie replied. "Proceed with caution."

"One-Six, this is Krulak One, we've linked up with Krulak Two and cleared the top floor of the keep. We've got a tango here who said el-Shahan has escaped through a tunnel. Might be what you're looking at," Thornton said.

"Copy, Krulak, regroup with Payback One and provide overwatch," Shaw commanded as Reeves and his team arrived.

"Roger, Invictus, we're Oscar Mike," Thornton replied. As the Raider's hand dropped from his PTT, he signaled to Barone and Hogan to bring the captive before they funneled out of the keep and reunited with their helicopter squadron.

Shaw turned from the entrance of the stairs, the shadows at the bottom now stationary and waiting. His eyes found Tyler Aston—a former dog handler with the 10th Special Forces Group—before dropping his attention to the Dutch Shepherd standing obediently at his side. Roman, his dark brindle coat catching the yellow light, appeared alert and focused despite subtly panting, which exposed his glinting, titanium-capped, canine teeth.

"Two-Four, we'll lead with a multi-banger then send in the MWD, how copy?"

"Ready when you are, sir," Aston replied.

Turning around, Shaw addressed Rowan McEwen, a former E Squadron trooper with the UK's Special Air Service, "Cut those wires before we go in." He pointed to the cables that connected the lights.

With only a nod in reply, the Scotsman offloaded a set of heavy-duty bolt cutters from their position on his rear plate bag. The entire team fitted their helmets with their stowed night vision binoculars, with Shaw and Bray helping Pikari and Rakestraw so they were still able to keep their watch down the stairs, rifles ready.

"Check your fire for friendlies," Shaw whispered as he assumed a position behind Aston. He draped his rifle across his chest and dug into the assaulter's back panel mounted to the rear bag of Aston's plate carrier. He produced a cylindrical flash bang grenade and extended it out over Aston's shoulder so the operator could see it. After receiving a nod, Shaw retracted the device and looped his finger through the ring.

Pikari and Rakestraw parted as much as possible, creating a gap between them, while they kept their rifles downrange. Aston then moved forward between them with Shaw following closely and Roman leading at his feet. Aston kept his rifle in low ready as he focused on his footing. One wrong step could spell disaster for the assaulting force.

Gauging the angles, Shaw halted Aston halfway down the stairs. The ceiling still hung low enough to hide theirs and Roman's bodies from an ambushing force. It was a suck situation, all knew, but at least one life was depending on them. Shaw carefully calculated the drop of the ceiling and when he would need to release the banger so that it didn't bounce back toward them.

Confident, he pulled the pin and bowled the device past Aston's legs and over Roman's back. The flash bang cleared the low ceiling and bounced down the hallway, traveling farther than Shaw had hoped.

Suddenly, the passage's lights failed as McEwen cut the cable, plunging them into relentless darkness. Shaw and his men flipped down their night vision binoculars just as the flashbang detonated in a concussion of sequential blasts and blinding light far down the tunnel.

On cue, Aston released Roman, who bolted into the darkness with frightening aggression.

4

The prone insurgent shouted in alarm as the lights failed all around him. The rising, fearful babbling everywhere near him only further ate at his nerves. He reminded himself that he didn't need to see in order to kill anyone coming down the corridor, but he still called back for a flashlight.

Before his comrades could reply, a clinking sound reached his ears, followed by a series of deafening blasts and blinding light which immediately disoriented him. His mind screamed that he had been shot, but he didn't feel any pain other than in his ears and eyes. He quickly withdrew his firing hand and rubbed his eyes vigorously as he shouted his fear and frustration. The ringing in his ears masked the pounding of small paws on the concrete floor, and the insurgent suddenly shrieked in terrified agony as a snarling beast slammed into him.

He had never experienced such horror, much less imagined it. What demon had his enemies summoned against him? He attempted to fight off his assailant, but the snarling only preceded searing pain as the creature tore into the insurgent's throat, thrashing back and forth and ripping away chunks of flayed flesh.

The insurgent seized under the onslaught, and his body shook as the shock of the damage overtook his senses and functions. Seeing only blackness with pulsing rings of white, he gurgled through his death throes as the demon continued to rip at him.

In the chaos, the other insurgents shouted and raised their rifles to fire down the hallway, but the chirps of precise and deadly suppressed fire dropped them quickly to the ground as Invictus team advanced down the hallway, revenants from the shadow.

At his handler's command, Roman released his hold on his target's throat. Shaw's eyes fell on the insurgent the Dutch Shepherd had killed, and he thought that death by burning might be the only way worse than that.

"We're clear. On me," Shaw whispered into his team radio. McEwen and Reeves, who had been pulling rear security, moved down the stairs to regroup with the rest of their team.

With Roman on point just ahead of Aston, the animal led them forward, but after a few yards, he stopped and dropped low.

"Hold," Aston whispered, lifting his support hand in a tight fist. Under the glow of their helmet-mounted IR lights, the team paused all forward movement at the signal. "Roman has indicated." Stooping low, Aston placed a hand on Roman's harness as he peered toward what he had indicated. Meanwhile, Shaw kept his rifle aimed down the hallway over Aston's head.

As he began his sweep, Aston quickly noticed a wire running laterally across the hallway about a foot from the ground.

"Got a tripwire," he said into his mic while pressing his PTT. He followed the wire to an explosive device mounted low on the wall. The familiar *FRONT TOWARD ENEMY* greeted him, and he sighed. "It's a claymore," he said.

"One of ours?" Shaw asked, keeping his attention down the tunnel.

"Looks to be," Aston admitted, his southern accent subtle and classic without a hint of twang. "Probably from the Afghan withdrawal," he added as he effortlessly disconnected the trip wire and removed the blasting cap. "A lot easier to deal with than IEDs, that's for sure," he continued as he stowed the inert explosive in the dump pouch hanging from the rear of his belt.

"We good?" Shaw asked.

"Yep," Aston replied as he rose. Shaw raised his rifle into high port as Aston took back command of the forward space and ushered Roman onward.

"I need lights now!" Abdur Rajeev el-Shahan shouted as his men scrambled around him, their flashlights frantically darting back and forth. He hadn't heard any gunfire from the tunnel nor an explosion yet. His men covered the tunnel entrance to their compound with flashlights pointed into the darkness, but they only reached so far. El-Shahan gripped his AKM with one hand as he shouted for everyone to move faster.

His black beard was short but thick around his face, appearing to roll outward from his cheeks and curl sharply beneath his jaw. He was not immune to fear, though he taught that doctrine to his followers. Even now, he began to doubt if houris awaited him in paradise. Terror had that effect, especially knowing he would lose all he had built here: his power and his influence.

Surely, paradise will be worth it, he told himself, but he wasn't willing to give in to death just yet. *I still have more to accomplish!*

Having orchestrated countless attacks against the West and brilliantly organizing them to appear as single, isolated strikes—to include the 2017 Manchester Arena Bombing—el-Shahan thought of the numerous operations currently in development. Without his directives, they would surely be discovered and thwarted.

This was too soon, and he now recognized Faatin Radi's fatal flaw. In Radi's effort to ambush Western special operations during Operation Taskmaster, he had to use real and vital intelligence to make that happen. At first, it was fine, as el-Shahan and others believed they could relocate in time, but they never expected the vengeance of America to be so swift and decisive. This old adversary applied new pressure that they had not anticipated. The lumbering, gluttonous giant had become a swift and lethal eagle far beyond that which they thought it capable.

Operation Taskmaster had changed his enemy, and for the first time in his leadership, el-Shahan was one step behind. The reality frightened him even as the Americans closed in around him. What Radi strived to accomplish for the cause might very well be the catalyst that doomed them all.

"Emir," came a call from up a ladder that led to the surface. El-Shahan glanced into the darkness and scowled when a flashlight blinded him. The beam quickly darted away as the owner realized his mistake.

"What is it?" El-Shahan called, his voice irritated and strained.

"There are helicopters coming this way! It's the Americans!" the voice from above shouted. El-Shahan cursed, despite it being forbidden to do so. His men teetered on the edge of panic.

"Do not be afraid, my brothers!" El-Shahan called out, mustering a benevolence to his voice. "Bring the prisoner to me!" Within seconds, two insurgents dragged a badly bloodied man and dropped him at their commander's feet. "On his knees," El-Shahan ordered. The two men wrenched the prisoner up and balanced him as ordered. The man hardly made a sound, but his head lolled atop his shoulders before he coughed and spat blood.

El-Shahan seized hold of his short hair, there was barely enough to grip, and wrenched his head back before jabbing the muzzle of his rifle into the man's clavicle, which drew a wince and sharp inhale from the prisoner.

"What of our reinforcements?" the terrorist leader asked one of his lieutenants who stood next to him.

"They are on their way from the northern and eastern tunnels," he replied, his voice soft and laced with fear. El-Shahan forced a smile, hoping they would arrive in time now that they were cut off from the surface. He glanced down at his captive and mustered his anger.

"Your friends are coming for you, but you will die with them," he sneered quietly.

5

Billy Bratcher relished the stiff wind on his face as Payback squadron thundered eastward toward a small compound not far away. Remaining on overwatch, the former SAS sniper had not entered the compound with the rest of Invictus team. It was fine with him. He didn't care much for confined spaces. Though he could fight through it, he would much rather not.

The sun had fully crested the mountains to the east and bathed the desert landscape in painful brilliance. Bratcher eagerly palmed the grip of his designated marksman rifle and glanced across the landscape to view one of Krulak's Venom helicopters thundering alongside.

One of the MARSOC Raiders waved at him, and Bratcher squinted to see who it might be. He grinned and waved back upon recognizing Sergeant Jimmy Hogan.

He's a good kid, Bratcher thought just before Payback Two's call clipped in his headset.

"Payback One, Payback Two-One, we've got a visual on the compound preparing to engage."

"Solid copy, Two-One. We're on your six," Dawson replied.

"Here we go," Bratcher remarked excitedly as he checked his lanyard harness one last time. Satisfied and locked in, Bratcher readied his rifle to engage the enemy.

As Payback Two's guns spun up, Bratcher raised his rifle, fired, and dropped the first of many enemy combatants.

Insurgents preparing vehicles scrambled and darted in all directions while only a few stood and returned fire with their weapons. A few rounds popped against the bottom of Krulak One's Venom helicopter, cutting a path through the fuselage and embedding in the ceiling. Curses spilled out of the Raiders' mouths as they recoiled from the unexpected fire.

"Get us on the ground!" Thornton growled.

"Roger," their pilot replied as he banked south. Hogan and Barone gripped the lip of the fuselage above them to keep steady in their seats. "Hold on!" the pilot called before he reoriented his craft toward the outskirts of the small compound.

The sand whipped up around them, stinging their cheeks and scratching against their protective lenses as the team disembarked and advanced in an arrowhead formation toward the compound. Hogan led as the grenadier, and Barone paced just behind him and to the right a few meters, while their machine gunner, Sergeant Jason Kitts, covered the left flank opposite Barone. Their SARC—Special Amphibious Reconnaissance Corpsman—Petty Officer Third Class Phillip Zane, followed behind and to the right of Barone. Captain Thornton and Galinato brought up the rear.

As the small force advanced, their helicopter returned to the air to provide close air support for the assaulting Raiders. Krulak One adapted their formation as they found an opening in the compound's decrepit mud walls.

"Get topside," Thornton urged Kitts and Hogan as he covered their move across the exposed alley while the rest of the team held down the other direction. Kitts entered the flat-roofed structure first, sweeping the entry with his light machine gun as Hogan rode on his heels. Barone entered next with Thornton and the rest following.

Kitts' keen, dark eyes sought every nook and crevice, anywhere an enemy might be waiting in ambush, but the room was clear. As gunfire raged outside and the helicopters continued their deadly assaults, Kitts led Hogan up the plaster stairs that melded into the wall made of the same natural material.

The two men moved fluidly and carefully with their weapons ready while Barone and Ratliff checked the courtyard through the north-facing windows. They peeped around the edge of sun-bleached, decorative curtains.

"How we looking?" Ratliff asked quietly into his radio.

"Moving onto the second floor now," Hogan whispered back just as Kitts advanced with aggression and swept the space. He met the gaze of a startled and horrified young man who clutched an AKM rifle as he hid in the corner. Under normal circumstances, Kitts might have issued a call to surrender, to throw down his arms, and lie on the ground, but he had lost friends in Operation Taskmaster. He snapped his machine gun toward the youth's torso and squeezed the trigger. The heavy weapon bellowed, its concussion pounding through the small space as it chewed through the cowering insurgent, cutting apart his body.

"Clear," Kitts said coolly.

"Clear," Hogan echoed after surveying the room as well, locating steps cut into the wall that led to a thatch-like cover.

"Eight, status on the roof? Is it clear?" Hogan called to Galinato. The radio operator hailed their helicopter and received the all clear.

"That's an A-firm, Six," came Galinato's reply.

"Good copy. Be advised, we're advancing onto the roof," Hogan informed.

"Understood, Six," Galinato replied. He addressed their pilot, "Be advised, friendlies on the roof of the square, two-story building on the southern end of the compound."

"Copy all, Krulak. We see them," the pilot answered.

Within seconds, Hogan and Kitts found suitable firing positions and swiftly cut down their targets. Barone and Ratliff added their fire to the chaos, selecting their targets quickly and engaging with deadly accuracy.

From his perch high up on Payback One, Bratcher's eyes darted over the courtyard. He noticed an insurgent brave the withering fire from the Marines and the helicopters to reach the well. Just before he dove in, Bratcher blasted a hole through both lungs. The man gasped as his body jerked to the right and tumbled to the ground. Blood quickly pooled around him. The former SAS sniper followed up with another shot that ceased the man's squirming.

Another insurgent raced toward the well before he was cut down by Krulak One. This behavior puzzled Bratcher, and he gazed at the well through his scope, noticing the rope ladder descending on the inside.

"Payback One-One, Invictus Overwatch, there is a ladder on the inside of that well," he called into his secondary radio that served his role as Invictus Overwatch, connecting him with Dawson and the other Payback One pilots.

"I see it, Invictus Overwatch," Dawson replied. "Could be the tunnel exit."

"I was thinking the same thing," Bratcher agreed.

"All callsigns," Dawson began, addressing all team and squadron commanders, including command at SOCOM HQ. "The well looks to be the tunnel exit. How copy?"

"Good copy, Payback One," Natalie replied as she peered at the well broadcast from the UAV on the monitor before her. She glanced at McCoy, who wore his usual firm expression.

It made sense, Natalie thought, to use an already existing well, a dry one at that, to link underground tunnels. If there were no concerns for an assault, they wouldn't have needed to expand or build a structure over it. Perhaps, it merely served as a crossroads for additional tunnels that extended to other compounds to the north, south, and further east. However, she also knew that having ground forces descend into an entry point like that was particularly challenging, and she was not keen on the unknown risk.

"All callsigns, let's secure that entry point," she ordered. Every commander confirmed the receipt of their orders and pressed the attack.

6

"Hold," Shaw commanded quietly as he and Aston saw the flashing lights ahead and the beams bearing down the tunnel toward them. Though the tunnel had widened to accommodate two men shoulder to shoulder, it was still the worst fatal funnel in which Shaw had ever found himself, but there was no second-guessing his decision. Up ahead and aided by his night vision, he made out the bloodied figure kneeling before a thin, bearded man. Though he couldn't discern the identity of the captive, he knew he was their guy.

Figuring he wouldn't be able to connect with command or other elements from within the tunnel, Shaw analyzed his options. Seeing the muzzle of the terrorist's AKM shoved into the neck of the prisoner boiled his blood, and thus he knew he couldn't retreat. Still, though veiled by the darkness as they were, pressing forward proved perhaps even more problematic. It became clear that the only option was to release Roman, run the rabbit, and pray they came through on the other side.

He wondered briefly if Bratcher and Det One had located the compound in which they now found themselves. Shaw figured they must have hiked two kilometers from the citadel, but he soon received his answer as the dull reverberation of rocket fire rolled down from the surface and startled the insurgents. The man holding the rifle on the prisoner glanced toward the ceiling, while the lights pointed toward the tunnel snapped upward. Seeing this, Shaw issued the order.

"Go," he urged.

Aston released Roman, and he bolted forward with impressive acceleration. Invictus team followed quickly, but the canine easily outpaced them. Shaw watched the animal as he raced forward, appearing only as a dark blur under the glow of his night vision. Still, he anticipated Roman's time on target, raised his rifle, activated his IR laser, and watched as the glowing green dot fell on the terrorist who held the prisoner at gunpoint. Shaw squeezed the trigger several times, each time allowing the invisible green dot to resettle on the insurgent before firing again.

Following his commander's lead, Aston opened up; his rifle's suppressed shots thundered in the confined space as he prioritized the targets who posed the greatest threat to the team. Shouts of alarm followed, and flashlights swirled in confusion, while Invictus team funneled out of the tunnel, each man cutting either left or right depending on the direction the man ahead of him took.

Roman slammed into an insurgent attempting to orient his RPK light machine gun. His momentum sent Roman careening past the terrorist, but his bite held true, and he catapulted the lightweight combatant around him as the two tumbled across the concrete floor. He released his hold on the man's arm and dove for the tender, exposed flesh of his throat. After tearing away chunks of meat, Roman spun quickly—his agility awe-inspiring—and rushed toward the downed POW, circling him and snarling as he formed a protective wall of fur, muscle, and sharp teeth.

Small arms and heavy weapons fire bellowed from the surface and echoed down the circular opening to which a ladder ascended. The sun poured in a bright beam directly over Roman and the prisoner, and Roman's brown eyes darted from adversary to adversary as his human counterparts engaged with ferocity that equaled his own.

Though a few insurgents fired back, the chaos was so complete, so overbearing that they didn't know who or what they were aiming at, as every shadow appeared to harbor death.

As the final insurgent fell, Shaw and Invictus Two joined Roman in forming a protective barrier around the prisoner while Invictus One secured the room and set up defensive positions ready to repel any threats from the intersecting tunnels.

"We've got to get out of here, One-Six," Pikari stated as he trained his rifle down a long, dark corridor.

"Understood, One-Seven," Shaw replied as he reached for the prisoner. He gripped a bloody shoulder and turned the shirtless man over. Immediate shock widened his eyes as he recognized the individual.

"Sod Buster?" he called, but the man's ears rang too loudly from the gunfire to hear. However, Sod Buster recognized that these men were there to save him, and he reached out with his arms in immense gratitude, gripping their sleeves and uttering his thanks over and over again as tears came to his eyes.

Shaw looked at Reeves, who, equally as dumbfounded in rescuing a Delta Force legend who they all believed dead, couldn't hide his grin as he patted Sod Buster's hand that held his shoulder.

"Let's get him up," Shaw urged Reeves as he reached under Sod Buster's arm. The two men hoisted him upwards, and the grizzled warrior found his feet with ease, knowing he was being rescued. Hope propelled him forward. "Two-Seven, get me a PID on Haman," Shaw ordered, referring to el-Shahan by his assigned callsign.

McEwen left his position in the circle and commenced Shaw's request. The former E Squadron commando hurried from body to body, running facial ID until he got a positive hit on the insurgent Shaw had first shot.

"PID on Haman," McEwen declared as the smart device logged the photos on internal storage while awaiting open air to transmit confirmation via satellite to operation headquarters for Natalie and General McCoy.

Shaw handed off Sod Buster to Reeves and neared the rope ladder that descended from the circular opening. As he pressed his PTT, he hoped the radio signal would clear the hole. He did not want to endanger himself or his men further by exposing themselves to an enemy force.

"All callsigns, Invictus One-Six, Haman is KIA, and we've secured Greyhound. How copy?" Shaw called into his radio, relaying el-Shahan's death and the rescue of their unknown POW. Shaw waited a moment for a reply. When none came, he inhaled deeply before ascending the ladder. He paused halfway up and tried again. "All callsigns, Invictus One-Six. How copy?"

"Solid copy, One-Six, sitrep?" came Natalie's relieved reply.

"Haman is KIA, and we've secured Greyhound. We're looking up at some kind of circular opening. We heard Payback and Krulak overhead. Can you confirm area secure?"

"Affirmative, One-Six," Natalie replied. "Krulak and Payback are right outside. Area secure. You're looking at a well."

"Good copy, Nectar. I see it now." Before Shaw could proceed, blasting gunfire echoed down the eastern and northern tunnels, followed by shouts of *Contact!*

A bullet struck Shaw in the back, and he spiraled off the ladder and hit the ground hard. Wheezing from both the bullet and the fall, Shaw blinked his eyes rapidly and fought through the pain.

Pikari, Bray, and the others returned fire down the two tunnels as they hunkered down behind their cover. The husky thundering indicated heavy weapons as the slugs tore through the space. Shaw crawled toward the westward tunnel as he wrestled back control of his faculties.

"You alright?" Rakestraw shouted at him as he rushed to Shaw's side and checked him over.

"Yeah, I'm good," Shaw called back over the incessant bellowing of enemy fire.

"They've got some big guns," Rakestraw said as he helped Shaw to his feet. He took a minute to get his bearings.

Shaw's six men took cover and returned fire from the corners of the tunnels, keeping close to the rounded walls. As he thought through his options, Shaw knew immediately that returning down the tunnel through which they had arrived would only get them killed. With two kilometers to sprint, they wouldn't make it in time before their enemies opened fire after them. There was nowhere for those bullets to go except straight after them.

"Looks like we've only got one option," Shaw said to Rakestraw, and Rakestraw knew his commander's thoughts immediately. "Let's get some forty-mike-mike down those tunnels."

Shaw and Rakestraw moved in concert, keeping out of sight of their enemies' fields of view. Shaw prepped the M203 grenade launcher mounted underneath the barrel of his M4A1 as he advanced toward Pikari. Standing over the Māori, who knelt at his feet and returned fire down the tunnel, Shaw peeked around the corner—only exposing a sliver of his head and torso—and aimed his weapon with the aid of his night vision binoculars. He depressed the trigger, felt the familiar thump, and waited for the detonation.

The concussion rolled over them as the grenade detonated downrange in a sharp flash of light.

"Get topside," Shaw ordered as he stepped back to reload, allowing Rakestraw to take his place. Shaw skirted right to line up down the eastern tunnel, where Reeves laid down heavy suppressive fire with his M249 light machine gun. Shaw sent a second grenade down that tunnel before quickly reloading.

As the enemy gunfire paused, McEwen urged Sod Buster up the ladder, and the man, renewed with sudden vitality, climbed as swiftly as he could, reaching the top of the well with McEwen quick on his heels.

"Two-Four, you're up," Shaw commanded. Aston hurried from his position. Once at the base of the ladder, he clipped Roman's body harness into a special rig he wore over his shoulders that suspended Roman across his lower back. He then began his climb.

Shaw returned his attention down the eastern tunnel as enemy fire surged toward them again. A round smacked into Reeves' machine gun, and the operator instinctively turned his prone form away from the impact. Shaw fired another grenade down that same tunnel, and though the enemy bullet had ripped away Reeves' side-mounted IR laser, the gun remained operational, and he quickly returned fire.

"Two-Five, get up there!" Shaw shouted as he reloaded again. He was halfway through his grenades. "You get clear once topside!" Shaw added.

"Copy," Bray replied, but before he left Shaw's side, Shaw grabbed his plate carrier and shook him briefly.

"You get Sod Buster and the rest of the boys back. You load up on Payback and get him out of here. You understand?" Shaw pressed.

"But sir!" Bray began in protest. He knew the legend that stood before him, and he couldn't fathom that he would be asked to abandon him.

"Listen to me," Shaw growled, giving the younger man a quick shake.

"I can't leave you here," Bray interrupted.

"Look, if I planned on dying, I'd be giving you my pistol for Nat. You get topside and exfil. We don't have comms down here, and I need you to relay that order. You understand?"

"Yes, sir," Bray answered reluctantly.

"Good. Now go," Shaw said, thrusting him toward the well.

Bray rushed to the ladder. The enemy bullets zipped and popped around him. Halfway up, he slipped on one of the wooden pegs. He caught himself, but the sun highlighted him as a beacon for all enemy fire.

Enemy bullets snapped as they broke the sound barrier, flying past Bray as he trudged upward.

"I'm clear," he called down once he crested the surface.

"What's the plan, One-Six?" Pikari asked as he picked his targets down the tunnel. He and Rakestraw had managed to prevent any advance from the northern tunnel, but he knew they couldn't hold. Their ammunition would run dry soon enough, and there was no way they were all making it up the ladder before the enemy cut them down.

Who's making the sacrificial play? he wondered as he continued to fire.

Shaw, impressed by the enemy's persistence, lobbed his final grenade down the eastern tunnel followed by accurate small arms fire, while Reeves reloaded his light machine gun. Once Reeves had his weapon back up and running, Shaw keyed his PTT and said, "We've got to blow the tunnels. As assaulters, we've got all the C4."

Now it made sense to Pikari why Shaw had selected the four of them to remain.

"We'll blow the northern tunnel first. Once it's caved in, we'll move to the eastern tunnel and do the same. How copy?" Shaw relayed.

"We could drop the entire ceiling down on us," Rakestraw countered.

"We don't have much of a choice," Shaw replied grimly.

7

Natalie watched Bray climb from the well, search for a moment with his weapon high, before he received a radio call from his teammates directing him toward a building to the east. She waited impatiently for her husband to rise from the well, but after a few moments, it became clear no one else was coming. She unfolded her arms and keyed the communicator in her hand that connected her to Bratcher.

"Invictus Overwatch, this is Nectar. What's going on?" she asked, her voice strained and concerned.

"Two-Five says we still have men down the well. They're taking heavy fire, but we've secured Greyhound and are evacuating him now. Invictus One-Six has relayed orders to evacuate the compound," Bratcher explained.

"We don't leave our people behind," Natalie quickly scolded.

"I understand, ma'am, but One-Six is planning on collapsing the tunnels to cut off the enemy reinforcements they're currently engaged with," Bratcher said, relaying the information he had just received from Bray.

Natalie chewed her cheek before taking a deep breath. While she had the utmost confidence in her husband, she was not keen on his course of action. Thinking quickly, she rushed to one of the operations personnel arranged at their workstations within the room.

"Krulak One-Six Actual, this is Nectar, how copy?"

"I copy, Nectar, go ahead," Captain Thornton replied.

"I need an accurate layout of that tunnel system," Natalie said into her mic.

"I don't have that," Thornton responded.

"Then give me your best guess, Captain," Natalie snapped back. "Patch it through your ATAK."

"Yes, ma'am," he said before he consulted with Bray, drawing up the lines over the grid map to indicate the tunnels' best possible trajectories. After confirming with both Bray and McEwen and receiving their approval, he patched the information to HQ.

"Pull it up," Natalie urged the operations officer over whom she hovered. Referencing the grid pattern and the estimated trajectory of the tunnels provided by Thornton, Natalie formulated the fire mission protocol in her mind. "What ordinance are those Harriers carrying?" she asked, turning to address General McCoy.

Catching the gist of Natalie's plan, the general smirked.

"Each is carrying a pair of GBU-39s, which are quite capable of collapsing those tunnels," he replied, moving to her side and reviewing the information. Approving, he stood to his full height and peered at the UAV feed. He engaged his microphone and called, "Crusader Flight, this is Chaos, how copy, over?"

"Chaos, this is Crusader Two-One, we read you, over."

"Crusader Flight, go ahead and push into the overhead at flight level one-eighty to two-hundred. No threats at this time. Go with CAS check-in," McCoy said.

"A-firm, Chaos. Crusader Two-One/Two-Two. Two AV-8B Harrier II's. Mission number: Alpha-Bravo-Zero-Zero-One. Ordinance: two GBU-39s, one GBU-54, two AGM-88 HARM, two AIM-9 Sidewinders, three hundred rounds twenty-five mike-mike."

"Chaos copies," McCoy replied. "Say when ready for situation update."

"Send it," Crusader Two-One answered, his voice digitized by the transmission.

Natalie watched McCoy's expression harden in focus as he prepared his update for Crusader Flight.

"Crusader Flight, situation update. Threats: as briefed. Targets: enemy PAX. Friendlies are located in the village center, east of your ECHO point. Clearance will be Chaos. Ordinance and restorations will be per nine line."

"Copy all. Crusader Flight is visual friendlies and established in the overhead," Crusader Two-One replied.

McCoy turned to Natalie and asked, "You're sure you want to do this?"

"They may not make it out otherwise," she said gravely. McCoy rolled his lips inward and nodded.

"All callsigns," he began over the open operation channel for all players to hear. "We are currently troops in contact, receiving fire from the tunnels to the north and east. I've got a nine line for Crusader Flight and Payback. Say when ready."

"Crusader Flight ready."

"Payback ready."

"Going to be a type two control bomb on targets. Lines one through three from the overhead. Elevation: three-eight-two. PAX hidden underground at Target Reference Point Bravo. No mark. South two hundred meters. Egress back to the overhead," McCoy stated. Natalie tried hard to decipher the code but was unable to. The general continued, "Say when ready for remarks and restrictions."

"Crusader Flight ready."

"Payback ready."

"Remarks and restrictions are as follows: looking for flight clearance. Crusader Flight, requesting two GBU-39s, one per tunnel. Payback, you're on squirter control, clean up with rockets and guns. Crusader, final attack heading will be southeast to northwest using the corner of the citadel as your boundary. All effects must remain to the north and east of the village.

"Payback, your final attack direction will be west to east after impacts from Crusader. This will be Danger Close," McCoy said gravely, pausing for effect. "Read back four, six, and restrictions."

Both Crusader Two-One and Payback Two recited back the requested portions of the close-air-support fire order to General McCoy's satisfaction.

"Good read backs, Crusader push immediate," he ordered.

"Pushing," came Crusader Two-One's reply.

"Payback, call when set," McCoy instructed.

"Payback set."

"Crusader Flight is in from the southeast," Crusader Two-One stated as they lined up their approach.

"Crusader Flight is cleared hot," McCoy informed.

"Copy, cleared hot. Two away. Time of flight: twenty seconds," Crusader Two-One replied.

Natalie held her breath and endured the longest twenty seconds of her life.

As Shaw primed his C4 breaching charge, Rakestraw did the same but was skeptical about their chances of survival. He kept glancing at his commander while he worked to arm his own explosive and inhaled heavily to steady his nerves. He did not fancy well the idea of being crushed by heaps of dirt, rock, and concrete, but he also didn't see an alternative.

As Pikari kept up his cover fire, selecting his shots carefully to conserve his ammunition, the entire chamber shook with extreme violence before a wave of dust hurtled past them, blinding them and their enemies. Shaw and Rakestraw both fought to keep their balance and pressed their backs against the wall to keep themselves from falling.

"What was that?" Reeves shouted as he coughed through the dryness assaulting his throat. Even through their ear protection, their ears rang from the explosion.

"The tunnel is collapsing!" Pikari roared as he watched the support beams along the northern tunnel snap under the pressure. Cracks in the ceiling surged toward them with frightening speed.

"Let's go!" Shaw shouted, reaching down and ripping Reeves up by his drag handle just as a chunk of rock slammed down where the former SEAL had been lying. "Up the ladder now!"

The enemy assault ended as abruptly as it had begun, and their terrified shrieks could barely be heard over the tunnel system as it groaned in an effort to remain intact.

Shaw backpedaled suddenly as a torso-sized rock smacked into the ground in front of him. Keeping his eyes up, he sprinted forward and watched as Rakestraw reached the ladder first and began his ascent. He had never seen a man climb so quickly. Reeves started his climb as soon as there was enough room for him on the ladder.

"Tāne, you next!" Shaw commanded, shoving the New Zealander toward the ladder. Knowing better than to protest and that climbing fast would be Shaw's best chance of making it out, he slung his carbine out of the way and seized hold of the swinging rope ladder.

Once Pikari had cleared six feet and Reeves had crested the surface and vanished into the sunlight, Shaw gripped the eye-level peg and hauled himself onto the swinging ladder. Debris fell in a constant, thunderous roar as Shaw focused on placing one hand in front of the other, huffing in his exertion and rising fear. He thought of how John Wyatt had appeared to him in the depths of the Mediterranean only a couple of months ago.

Will I see him again now?

Pushing the thought from his mind, Shaw focused on his climb. He glanced upward to keep his NODs from catching on the ladder and saw a multitude of hands pull Pikari out of sight. Shaw increased his effort and stretched for the hands reaching down for him, his men shouting encouragement to him, but he couldn't hear their words over the clamor echoing around him.

He reached upward toward the many hands, but before he could seize hold, an unsettling sensation hurtled through his stomach as he felt himself falling. He realized only then that the ladder had failed.

Shaw snapped his arms out wide, his palms finding firm pressure on the walls of the ancient, stone well and suspending himself in midair, though he had slid down a meter or so. His muscles strained under the pressure as he fought to find secure purchase for his feet.

"Come on, David!" Pikari shouted as he reached as far as he could. The others with him all shouted the same encouragement, stretching for their commander as they did so.

Shaw shimmied his way up even as he felt the stones loosening under his hands. Realizing what was happening, he glanced up and shouted back,

"It's all collapsing! Go!" No one moved; they only strained harder to reach their commander.

Seeing that the well structure was failing, Pikari pivoted over the lip of the well at his waist.

"Grab my legs!" he called back. The others immediately complied as Pikari committed fully, headfirst, into the well. Shaw continued his climb, but the walls crumbled around him. Just before his feet fell free, he jumped upward in one last effort to clear the looming death that awaited him.

His flailing hand found Pikari's, who fastened his grip like iron around Shaw's wrist.

"I got him!" he shouted. "Pull us up!"

With his other hand, Pikari seized the shoulder strap of Shaw's plate carrier as Shaw grabbed his. Locked together, the two men rose as their teammates hoisted Pikari upward. Feeling strong hands grip the back of his belt as he rose, Pikari could only loudly hoot his exhilaration in defiance of death's claim over them.

"What happened?" Shaw asked once he was back on his feet. They hurried away from the well to clear the collapsing area. Once reunited with Captain Thornton and Krulak One, Shaw glanced back to watch the well and the surrounding ground crumble inward, swallowed up in a large plume of brown dust.

"Your wife collapsed the tunnels," Thornton replied, clapping Shaw on the shoulder and laughing.

"Sounds like her," Shaw said, laughing with him. "Thank you, boys," he added, turning to address those who had risked their lives in remaining behind to save his. Rakestraw, Reeves, and Pikari all grinned and patted a very tired Shaw on the shoulders.

"Nectar, this is Invictus One-Six. Thanks for the assist," Shaw called into his radio.

A world away, Natalie exhaled her great relief in hearing her husband's voice.

"Zero-Six, this is Chaos. What is the identity of Greyhound?" General McCoy asked, his voice stern yet hopeful. He knew he shouldn't have asked, but the anticipation was too much to bear.

"It's Sod Buster, sir," Shaw replied as he and his Invictus operators made their way back to their waiting Little Birds.

General McCoy sank into the chair behind him and exhaled his profound disbelief before chuckling as the relief and joy swept over him. He still mourned the loss of Rebound, Bone, Moose, and the other members of Viking Team, but he was beyond grateful to hear that Shaw had rescued Sod Buster. He looked up at Natalie as she approached him.

"It's better than I could have hoped for," McCoy said solemnly.

"It is," Natalie agreed, placing a hand on his shoulder. He patted her hand before rising again.

"Good copy, One-Six," McCoy replied after keying his radio. "All call-signs, this is Chaos. Let's get you boys home."

8

Off the coast of Syria,
Aboard the USS Arlington,
Task Force 61,
Kearsarge Amphibious Ready Group,
United States 6th Fleet

Private First Class Christian Sapp stood among his fellow Marines with the 22nd Marine Expeditionary Unit as they joked to pass the time. While waiting for the order to respond to any crisis that might arise during Operation Granite Mountain, the force remained vigilant and ready near their V-22 Osprey aircraft.

The operation had commenced earlier that morning—pre-dawn—and Sapp, sporting his full combat gear and rifle, had watched the seasoned operators depart aboard their helicopters, even as Harriers took to the skies from the neighboring USS *Kearsarge*. As a young Marine, Sapp couldn't help but idolize the men he watched. They reminded him of his older brother, Hunter, who served as a MARSOC Raider, an ambition he, too, shared.

Sapp was the fourth of six brothers, two of whom were still at home with their widower father. The three ahead of him—Hunter, Stetson, and

Forrest—had also joined the Marines; therefore, he had chosen to as well. Coming from a poor family of fifteen children, Sapp knew—as his older brothers had—that the only opportunity for him lay in the military. Though he had only been in less than a year, he had loved every minute of it. The adventure was far beyond what he could have expected, and now, deployed on a ship to respond as a QRF for a joint Marine Corps-SOCOM operation was even more thrilling than he would have believed. Even the more seasoned NCOs brimmed with excitement.

Sapp inhaled the cool, salty air and scanned the eastward horizon before pointing and exclaiming, "There they are!"

The Marines around Sapp, who reclined against their packs, jumped to their feet and shielded their eyes from the sun with their hands as they focused out over the ocean.

As the force watched the helicopters approach, the Harriers screamed overhead on a low fly-by, appearing suddenly and unexpectedly, their engines booming. Feeling the reverberation in his chest, Sapp hooted and celebrated with his fellow Marines, pumping his fists into the air alongside his squadmates.

They really didn't know what they were celebrating other than the simple glee of seeing such might on full display, but they all immediately quieted as medical personnel rushed onto the landing platform.

"What does that mean?" A Marine named Hanson asked. Sapp focused his gaze on the medical team as they prepared to receive the incoming helicopter squadron. Diverting his gaze back out to sea, he watched as two Little Bird attack helicopters peeled off from formation and lined up their approach to a different vessel within the Amphibious Ready Group.

"It means someone's hurt," another Marine named McDonald replied.

"You don't know that," Sapp interjected. "Could just be procedure."

They didn't know all the details of Operation Granite Mountain, but they knew enough to comprehend how dangerous the mission was. Though they didn't possess all the details surrounding the kill/capture mission, they knew these men had hunted a high-level terrorist target. Theirs was not to know, only to respond to crisis, and it looked like they wouldn't have to today.

As the helicopters touched down, all held their breath as they watched for the unloading of any wounded. However, their relief grew and grew as they watched the seasoned operators disembark, all seemingly fine. Finally, a group helped one man from one of the Venom helicopters. The bloodied, yet imposing, individual clutched a mylar blanket tightly around his broad frame and seemed to walk without assistance before relinquishing himself into the care of the medical team.

"Alright, gather around!" came the call from his platoon sergeant, a gunnery sergeant named Daly. Sapp couldn't pull his eyes from the group of hardened men as they congratulated and shook hands with each other.

Feeling eyes on him, Shaw turned and met the gaze of the young Sapp. He grinned and nodded, and in that moment, Sapp welled with pride to be part of something so incredible. He smiled back and nodded.

"Sapp!" Daly roared. Sapp turned quickly and joined the rest of his platoon. Though as Daly addressed them, Sapp's mind remained fixed on the operator with whom he had made eye contact, and in that moment a greater ambition bloomed within him.

"Knock, knock," Shaw said, rapping his knuckles on the steel frame of the bulkhead door. Sod Buster glanced up at him and grinned a tired smile. The ship's Medical Corps Officer, Lt. Jonathan Hudson, glanced at Shaw and nodded his welcome. Truthfully, he didn't know how to address the contractor, but Shaw didn't pay him any mind.

"How you doing, brother?" Shaw asked Sod Buster as he neared the bed. Sod Buster lay in a typical hospital gown, and his face was adorned with numerous Steri-Strips. With the blood cleaned up, Shaw now saw the extent of the bruising on his face. "I thought you were ugly before," Shaw added as he gripped Sod Buster's outstretched hand. The man's blue eyes showed deep appreciation and gratitude as he chuckled.

"Not all of us can be as pretty as you," he replied, gripping Shaw's hand with what strength he had left. Shaw laughed. "I suppose we're even now," Sod Buster added, but Shaw shook his head.

"No one's counting, brother. I'm honestly so glad you're back with us. We thought the worst. Your wife..."

"How is she?" Sod Buster asked, his tone wavering.

"Generals Wood and McCoy are on their way to see her now. They'll break the news to her. I'm sure she'll be devastated," Shaw replied. Sod Buster laughed, even though it hurt, appreciating deeply the humor shared between warfighters.

"She was almost free of me."

"Going to be awkward to pull your headstone from Arlington," Shaw said, but Sod Buster was already shaking his head.

"Not until I get a selfie with it!" Both men laughed following the comment, Shaw even wiping tears from his eyes. It wasn't that the joke was overly funny, but it was the deeper communication woven through their words that struck them deeply. Under the guise of humor, both men connected in a profound way, both saying *thank you* and *you're welcome* at the same time.

For Shaw, he was glad to see Sod Buster so relieved. He didn't have to imagine what three months of captivity was like, and in that way, the two men shared an exclusive bond not truly known since the Vietnam War.

"Seriously though, thank you," Sod Buster finally said, refusing to let the humor speak what he felt he was man enough to voice.

"You're welcome," Shaw replied, his tone warm yet growing somber, "and I'm sorry about Rebound, Bone, and the others."

"Yeah," Sod Buster huffed, fighting through the tender wounds.

"I wanted you to hear from me, all of it, why it happened, and what we did about it," Shaw explained as he scooted up a chair. "Only if you're ready for it."

"I've been waiting for those answers for too long," Sod Buster replied, his voice growing quiet.

Dr. Hudson realized the moment and said, "Alright, I'll be back in a bit to check on you, Master Sergeant."

"Thanks, Doc," Sod Buster said. With that, Lt. Hudson departed, and Sod Buster turned his attention to Shaw as he shared everything that had happened with Operation Taskmaster, the how, the scope and scale of the tragedy, and Radi's demise. When he finished, Sod Buster sat in stunned silence.

"I have so many questions," he said before choking on his grief. Shaw reached out a hand. Sod Buster allowed Shaw to grip his palm, and through firmly pressed lips, he nodded several times. He sniffed even as his lips and face fought to contain his emotions.

"It's alright, brother," Shaw said, feeling his own loss well up within him. He thought of his friends, his son, and grunted through his own pain.

"Yeah," Sod Buster said again, nodding sharply. He inhaled deeply and exhaled forcibly before looking Shaw in the eye. "They're taking me to Landstuhl for a full workup before sending me home."

"I've been there," Shaw replied.

"How was the food?"

"I couldn't tell you," Shaw replied with a laugh. "I was out cold the whole time."

"I never can count on you," Sod Buster chided. Both men again broke out into laughter.

9

Invictus HQ,
Eastern Shore,
Virginia

With Shaw safely back aboard the USS *Arlington*, Natalie could breathe easier. Life had grown hard amidst their high operational tempo. She thought constantly about her lost son, Nathaniel, even though she didn't want the pain. But the pain kept his memory alive, and without it, she feared she might forget him forever. Her mind was plagued by an inability to picture the face of her boy, and her imagination concocted different complexions, sometimes favoring her, other times her husband. It was enough to drive her mad.

However, her work kept her stable, focused, and calm. Without the work, she feared she might spiral into insanity. When she wasn't running an operation for Invictus, she was busy searching for connecting ties between Anderson Stovall, Red Horse Global, Sofia Vitori, and Vayun Oza. All besides Red Horse were ghosts, and the only traces of their existence lay in a web of corporations that proved almost impossible to unravel. However, the information provided by the late Hasan Salameh proved helpful.

She almost regretted his death.

Almost.

Hunting terrorists was a skill Natalie had perfected; however, hunting elites so deeply buried within their layers and layers of corporate veils proved a new challenge, and one that frustrated her greatly. She sighed and rubbed her forehead, leaning over the keyboard as her braided hair fell into view.

Natalie inhaled her frustration and gently took hold of her hair, losing herself for a moment searching for split ends. Frowning, she noticed far too many, and taking a pair of scissors from the center drawer in her desk, snipped off a centimeter of hair at the end of her braid. She exhaled as she dropped her scissors onto the desk and shook her braid over the small trash can nestled next to the desk.

She rose from her leather chair and turned toward the French doors, which led to a wide balcony that overlooked the property, the view extending all the way to the Chesapeake Bay. Throwing open the doors, Natalie relished the winter chill and allowed the refreshing air to cool her lungs. She placed her hands on the balcony railing and watched the excavators and bulldozers work to move earth and prepare the foundations for the additional facilities planned.

Things are coming together, she thought.

Money had long since become a nonissue. Their investors were more than pleased with their dividends and investment returns, and the company had far surpassed the million-dollar gifts those two men had given them for eliminating Francisco Silva. Invictus had made more money than Weber's illicit dealings, an irony that was not lost on either Natalie or Shaw.

Quickly becoming cold, Natalie returned inside to again face her greatest frustration. In hindsight, Rykov and Barakat had been easy to mark as enemies. Their organizations had targeted the Shaws for death, and the Shaws had responded in kind. There was a reason, a justifiable reason, for their retaliation. Stovall, Vitori, and Oza were only guilty by association, and even that, she couldn't prove outside of Salameh's word.

By all accounts, these individuals weren't threats, nor could Natalie prove they were involved in nefarious dealings. She sighed at that last thought. The odds were high that they were, even if she couldn't find proof. However, she hoped that if she kept looking, kept searching, she would find what she was after.

With each dead end, she began to wonder if this hidden council—as Salameh had described it—was in fact evil. Though she hated the idea of select elites controlling the direction of humanity, could she actually put a stop to it? Like a mythological hydra, would they just be replaced? Kormann's warnings about global upheaval rang in her ears. Would the chaos and destruction created by the vacuum left in the council's wake be worth it? How many more would die on account of turnover?

Are we just hurting things? Natalie asked herself. *What if these others are decent?*

Again, she doubted their morality, but she couldn't prove any of the three had done anything like Barakat or Rykov had. In that moment of desperation, she wished her husband was with her now, so she could fall into his arms, close her eyes, and focus on his steady, beating heart.

There were more credible and immediate threats to deal with—threats similar to el-Shahan—and with Reza Afshar feeding her viable intelligence to confirm that which she had recovered from Radi's cache, Natalie felt nearly unstoppable. Still, she couldn't let this council go.

In that moment, she felt an agitation she couldn't quite describe. All her cells vibrated, creating a sense of discomfort she couldn't place. Was it the weight of monotony? Boredom? Impatience? As she thought through her feelings, she felt the quick thrust of procrastination, likely what had driven her to cut off her split ends. She inhaled deeply once more and exhaled, hoping it would bring relief, but the agitation remained.

What is this? she asked herself, her frustration mounting.

Before she could contemplate further, her cellphone rang, the encrypted Signal feed showing the caller's identity. She scooped up the device and received the call.

"Hey, Reggie," she greeted.

"Hi, Natalie," Reggie Ramirez, the Director of National Intelligence, replied. "You sound upset. Everything okay?"

"Yeah, I'm fine. Just tired from work. You know the post-operation valley," she explained.

"That I do," he replied with a chuckle.

"What can I do for you?" Natalie asked. With their long history, she had no issue getting straight to the point with her old Navy commander.

"SecDef has called a meeting for an update on the state of our special operations post Taskmaster. He's requested you attend," Ramirez explained.

"When's the meeting?"

"Friday," Rameriz replied. "I know it's last-minute."

"It's fine. Pentagon?"

"Yes."

"I'll be there."

10

Kalorama,
Washington, DC
February 4, 2022

The brisk wind whipped down the pristine avenue of proud old hardwoods and perfectly manicured neighborhood landscaping. The swirling winter air bit through Diego de la Vega's wool coat as he exited the Bentley Continental GT Mulliner, immediately chilling his ears and nose. He handed the keys to the red-jacketed valet without a second thought as he proceeded at a slow trot up the stone steps leading to the entry of the impressive brick manor. The entry's conical tower drew his eyes, and he wondered how many United States Presidents had been hosted within the famous estate.

Nestled in what was probably considered the most prestigious neighborhood in Washington, the manor was legendary among the circles in which De la Vega found himself. Though more annoyed than excited, he still looked forward to greeting his host and his colleagues who made up the nation's military industrial complex. It had been a few years since they had last congregated.

Something big must be happening, De la Vega thought.

The dark wooden door opened upon his approach as if his ascent up to the landing was carefully watched and timed. Upon seeing the man behind the door, De la Vega inclined his head with great respect.

"Mr. Peter, it is good to see you again," De la Vega said as he stepped across the ornate threshold.

"A pleasure, Mr. De la Vega," the butler replied. "I'll take your coat," he added, extending his hand to receive the guest's garment. De la Vega doffed his Italian leather, cashmere-lined gloves and exhaled the comfort the manor's warmth offered. After stowing his gloves in his coat's interior breast pocket, he shrugged it off and folded it over his arm before presenting it to Mr. Peter.

"Thank you," De la Vega said, turning to marvel at the massive chandelier and the extensive collection of colonial art that decorated the foyer.

"You are welcome, sir. Everyone has gathered in the study. Shall I escort you?"

"No, thank you, Mr. Peter. I remember the way," De la Vega acknowledged with a grateful nod. The stoic butler, his face wrinkled and his hair a glossy white, inclined his head before turning to stow the coat as the guest's dress shoes clacked against the polished marble floor.

De la Vega heard the buzz of numerous conversations as he approached the French doors that led to the study. Another man, whose name De la Vega didn't know, greeted him with a nod before reaching to open the right side door.

"Thank you," De la Vega said quietly as he strode inside.

He couldn't hide his frown as he joined the elite congregation, bringing the average age down considerably. His dark, keen eyes scanned the faces even as he observed the hunter green walls, mahogany wainscoting and crown molding, and supple leather furniture, all while searching for a secondary point of egress.

Old habits die hard, he thought as he inhaled the sweet smell of pipe smoke and whiskey, which only elevated the antique, hunting club atmosphere. He recognized most individuals—major players in the military space—which included former generals in consulting roles as well as CEOs of companies that made their profits from Department of Defense contracts.

De la Vega's keen eyes quickly located Anderson Stovall, the estate's owner and the host of the event. They made brief eye contact as Stovall happened to gaze over the shoulder of the man to whom he was speaking. His bright blue eyes gleamed with approval upon seeing De la Vega. He raised his glass in welcome, to which De la Vega responded with a respectful nod.

"Excuse me," Anderson Stovall stated, offering his guest a closed-mouth smile before maneuvering his way toward De la Vega. His impressive height and athletic build only added to his presence as guests stepped back to let him pass. With his suit perfectly tailored and his tie knot accentuating a muscular neck, Stovall's taut face betrayed a youth he did not possess.

"Diego, welcome, my friend," Stovall greeted as he extended his hand. The shorter Latino gazed upward into Stovall's eyes and smiled as he gripped his employer's hand. He applied a courteous amount of force, not enough to overpower Stovall's, but enough to remind him of his strength and lethality. Stovall received and appreciated the veiled message.

"Mr. Stovall, always a pleasure. Thank you for welcoming me into your beautiful home," De la Vega returned. Stovall laughed and clapped his guest on the shoulder.

"The pleasure is mine," Stovall replied. "Can I get you a drink? Pappy's?"

"That would be great, sir," De la Vega replied. Stovall led De la Vega to the expansive mahogany bar that stretched nearly the entire length of the left-hand wall.

"George," Stovall called to the bartender dressed in a classic waistcoat. "A Pappy's for Diego here."

"Of course, sir," George replied before quickly moving to deliver the order.

"How are things at Red Horse these days?" Stovall asked, leaning on the bar and turning his attention back to De la Vega.

"Not without its challenges, but things are going well."

"Challenges?" Stovall echoed, his interest piqued. "I know we didn't land the el-Shahan bid."

"Yeah, unfortunately," De la Vega sighed. He received his dram from George and offered the man a soft *thank you*.

"Invictus International beat us out," Stovall stated, drawing raised eyebrows from his guest. Stovall chuckled and clapped De la Vega on the shoulder.

De la Vega didn't understand what was so funny. Invictus International was growing at an alarming rate and was outbidding Red Horse Global at nearly every turn. Most of De la Vega's operations were now serving as a quick reaction force or fire support element to David Shaw's operations. He had never seen a paramilitary defense contractor grow so quickly or secure operation contracts at the rate the Shaws had.

Red Horse had not seen the action he had hoped for in the months following Operation Taskmaster, and the CEO was sour about it. It went beyond company profits. Shaw was avenging the deaths of De la Vega's friends while De la Vega's staff sat on the sidelines guarding merchant vessels and serving as general war zone security forces.

"Never mind all that," Stovall finally said as he took a sip of his Scotch. "Africa and Eastern Europe have opened up for us. I'm sure those opportunities have been quite lucrative."

"I don't know if lucrative is the right word," De la Vega admitted, still annoyed about losing critical special operations missions.

"Ah, but Eastern Europe is about to become much, much more exciting for us," Stovall admitted. De la Vega tilted his square head in contemplation, but Stovall only smiled. "Come on, there's someone I want you to meet."

De la Vega took a sip of the fine bourbon before turning and following Stovall back into the crowd. Again, all attention was reverently gifted to Stovall as he passed. Guests paused their conversations in order to offer regards to their host, but De la Vega paid it no mind. They were all like him with Stovall owning their companies either outright or holding the majority ownership share.

Stovall *was* the American military industrial complex, and all the guests knew that they possessed their fortunes and opportunities on account of Stovall's legacy, influence, and wealth.

The Global War on Terror had been particularly profitable, but now that troops had been withdrawn from Afghanistan, many in the room looked to Stovall for what would come next for them. They wouldn't admit it, but they all feared a military drawdown. They knew the branches, all save the Marines, were missing their recruitment numbers, and history was clear on what would happen to their enterprises if the American public turned against military spending.

They needed something, and needed it quickly, in order to achieve their projected profits and accomplish the growth metrics which would result in insurmountable bonuses across the board.

De la Vega wasn't as concerned. His company wasn't bound by the government to only serve the United States. While many of the technology-based and weapons-based enterprises were dependent on US government funding to grow, he had plenty of income from Foreign Internal Defense contracts across Africa, South America, the Middle East, and Oceania.

We'll always need men to pull triggers, De la Vega thought.

"Here we are," Stovall said as the two men approached the rear wall. A woman turned to greet them, and De la Vega's eyes split wide in wonder. Had he ever seen a woman so beautiful? He couldn't say, but he quickly collected himself. "Diego, may I introduce you to Ms. Sofia Vitori?"

"Ma'am," De la Vega greeted, inclining his head and gently gripping her outstretched hand.

"Sofia, this is Diego de la Vega, CEO of Red Horse Global," Stovall added.

"A pleasure, Diego," Sofia replied, her accent as alluring as her looks. Upon hearing it, De la Vega glanced questioningly at Stovall.

"The pleasure is all mine, Ms. Vitori," the former Green Beret replied. Sofia grinned at him before sipping her martini, her hazel eyes gleaming with what De la Vega could only describe as desire, maybe ambition.

"Ms. Vitori and I are working on a joint project that I think you will find very interesting, and now that you're here, we can proceed," Stovall explained. De la Vega nodded and stepped back as Stovall took a position centered on the back wall. Sofia stood close to De la Vega, too close, but the CEO only sipped his bourbon as he waited for Stovall to address the congregation.

"I understand you have met David Shaw in person," Sofia said quietly, leaning closer to him, her eyes fixed on his face, though he kept his gaze forward. In truth, he recoiled from her statement. How did she know David

Shaw? More so, what did she know of David Shaw, and why was she so interested?

"I have," De la Vega answered hesitantly.

"What's he like?" she immediately asked. De la Vega swore he detected a sense of desire behind her question.

"I don't know what you mean," De la Vega answered quietly. Sofia smirked and sipped her drink.

"Oh, Deigo," she began, slipping her arm underneath his and curling her fingers around his thick bicep. De la Vega immediately thought of his wife but knew better than to offend the woman whom Stovall had so intentionally introduced to him. "I think you know what I'm asking."

"He's like any of us: dedicated, hardworking..."

"Us?" Sofia interrupted.

"Yes, special operations community," De la Vega clarified.

"You are a member of this community?" she asked, intrigued.

"Yes, ma'am," De la Vega answered, not providing any information beyond what was asked.

"Well, Mr. Shaw is clearly counted among the best," Sofia stated before taking another sip and returning her focus to Stovall. De la Vega inhaled his frustration and drowned his rising anger with a swig of bourbon.

"My friends and colleagues," Stovall began as all attention focused on him. He clinked his glass lightly with the stainless steel band of his wristwatch. The clinking grew, echoing as all joined in. De la Vega found himself tapping his wedding band against his glass without realizing it at first. "For the last twenty years," Stovall continued once silence spread through the room, "we have enjoyed record profits while driving the force for freedom across the globe. Because of your joint efforts, the terror of Islamic Jihad is but a shell of its former self."

A round of applause followed, but most knew better, so did Stovall. Still, such things were expected to be said.

"We now have to turn our attention to rising threats in the East. I have it on good authority that a Russian invasion of Ukraine is imminent," Stovall continued. Whispers surged all around. Only a fool wouldn't have heard of the Russian build-up in Belarus and on Ukraine's northern and eastern borders, but how that translated into invasion was still very much unclear.

No one, however, dared question the validity of Stovall's statement. If he said it, they all knew it to be true.

"A war in Europe represents an unprecedented opportunity for all of us here, and for many of us, a fight long overdue," he added with a grin. All applauded, many from the older generation more excitedly than the rest. "I trust all of us will rise to the occasion to support and supply the cause of freedom with the latest in war-fighting technology." Another enthusiastic round of applause circled the room. "I look forward to working with each of you toward that end!" Stovall finished, raising his glass.

All answered his toast, even De la Vega, who, unlike the rest, was disturbed by the sudden news. While technology was replaceable on the battlefield, his men were not, and he feared what Stovall might ask Red Horse to do in the wake of war on European soil.

11

Pentagon,
Washington, DC

Director Ramirez met Natalie at the designated entrance to the Pentagon wedge that housed the Secretary of Defense's office suite. After leading her through security, the duo made their way down the wood-paneled, oddly-tiled corridors toward 1000 Defense Pentagon, where a congregation of military leaders and officials mingled and waited for the meeting to start. Natalie met eyes with Generals Wood and McCoy, and the three of them exchanged cordial nods.

"Hi, Natalie," Mari Sosa, the CIA's Deputy Director of Operations, greeted.

"Hey," Natalie replied warmly as she embraced the woman who had become a close friend over the last year and a half. Together, they had found her predecessor's body—James Caldwell—slain by Connor Roark at his personal residence. The following events had solidified, not only an understanding of each other, but mutual respect.

"How are you?"

"I'm doing alright," Natalie said, knowing the woman referred to the recent loss of her and David's son. Sosa's coffee-colored eyes showed immense compassion against her dark complexion.

"I'm glad to hear it," Sosa replied.

"Hey, Natalie," came a raspy voice behind her, a voice she knew well. She turned to regard Scott Lincoln, the CIA's Associate Director of Operations and Chief of Ground Branch—the CIA's elite, land-based fighting force.

"Good to see you, Scott. How are things?" Natalie asked.

"Things are better," he replied. Ground Branch had taken the worst of the damage dealt by Radi last November. "But it's hard to recruit from the communities we need on account of a renewed fervor to rebuild. It's going to take years to recoup what we lost."

"I understand," Natalie replied.

"Unless you want to give me some of your people. I could use Rick back," Lincoln said with a laugh.

"The choice was always his," Natalie countered with a grin. "Still is."

"That stings a bit," Lincoln admitted, though jokingly. "Anyway, your competition's here. Thought you'd want to know." Natalie's face scrunched in confusion before clarity dawned on her.

"Where?" she pressed eagerly, searching the faces.

"He's the short Latino standing by himself in the corner. Blue suit, red tie, holding a sparkling water."

"I see him," Natalie said, making no effort to hide her gaze or suppress the fire behind her eyes.

Diego de la Vega, feeling eyes on him—a sixth sense honed from years in USASOC—quickly located Natalie and held hard her stare. Stoic and firm, he still offered her a respectful nod. How could he not respect her and her husband? Their success nagged at him. He swallowed his pride and headed her way.

"Mrs. Shaw, I heard about Sod Buster, and I wanted to personally thank you and your husband for his rescue. He and I served together in Fifth Group many years ago before he transitioned to CAG," De la Vega said, extending a muscular hand.

Without hesitating and giving De la Vega the honor his military service was due, Natalie shook his hand and kept her eyes set on his.

"We're beyond grateful to have played a part," she said. De la Vega smiled, and Natalie was startled by the sadness she witnessed behind the act. Though hard, his expression appeared strained and sorrowful.

"I appreciate your humility, but everyone knows the full extent of the *part* you played. Again, you have my sincere gratitude," De la Vega said.

"You're welcome," Natalie replied, feeling uncomfortable with his unanticipated sincerity.

"Please, allow me to treat you to lunch as a show of my gratitude," De la Vega stated. "My flight departs this evening."

"I'm free right after this," Natalie replied. De la Vega issued a professional smile.

"Excellent," he said. "I'll find you after." He inclined his head toward the others present before taking his leave back to his corner.

"What are you up to?" Lincoln asked slyly as he cut his eyes toward Natalie.

"Answers," she replied with fiery confidence. Sosa and Ramirez exchanged wary glances, but before anyone could question her further, the call rang out for the meeting to commence.

At the end of the long, wooden conference table, the Secretary of Defense sat with a hard expression, his dark skin gleaming in the fluorescent lighting. His lips were pressed flat and thin beneath a wide nose and unamused brown eyes. His salty hair lay closely cut to his scalp, rounding his head despite the asymmetrical positions of his long ears. In his black suit and despite his age, he appeared imposing with his sloping, broad shoulders. His massive hands lay comfortably coiled on either side of the black leather portfolio situated on the table before him.

The most prominent and important officials held a seat at the table, while others, including Natalie, Lincoln, Sosa, and De la Vega, sat in chairs that lined the walls. Generals Wood and McCoy sat together, their differing green uniforms showcasing their impressive careers. Ramirez sat to Wood's left—closer to SecDef—and intelligence community officials, generals, and admirals representing clandestine operations, Army Special Operations,

Naval Special Warfare, and others gave SecDef their undivided attention as they waited for him to begin the meeting.

"Thank you all for being here," SecDef began, making a deliberate attempt to make eye contact with all seated at the table. "It has been almost four months since the disaster that was Operation Taskmaster, and I'd like to begin by extending our heartfelt gratitude to Mrs. Natalie Shaw and her husband of Invictus International for the rescue of a Delta Force operator known to many of you as Sod Buster," he said. He turned to Natalie and said, "Mrs. Shaw," raising his hand to indicate she should stand.

Natalie stood, clutching her portfolio at her waist as she offered all a nod and a smile. SecDef led the group in a round of applause which echoed loudly through the small room. Unaccustomed to such recognition, Natalie rolled her lips inward and nodded again before quickly returning to her seat. Sosa clapped enthusiastically beside her, and Lincoln nudged her with his shoulder. In response, Natalie curled stray strands of her dark hair over her ears, clearly uncomfortable.

She met the SecDef's gaze as he continued to clap while rising from his seat.

This is really not necessary, Natalie thought as the rest of the room followed suit by standing. She wanted nothing more than to melt into her chair upon receiving the standing ovation. She dropped her chin, nodded again, and forced another smile.

As the clapping subsided and everyone again found their seats, SecDef said, "We needed such good news. Again, Mrs. Shaw, our thanks, and please pass our gratitude and praise on to your husband and the rest of your team at Invictus International."

"I will. Thank you, sir," Natalie replied.

"Very good," SecDef answered. "Now," he continued, turning to face the center of the table, "let's start with our progress toward recovering what we lost. General Wood, please update us on SOCOM replenishment overall."

"Certainly, sir," Wood replied, opening his portfolio and proceeding to relay the requested information. Natalie listened intently as Wood detailed their recruitment of new operators, the reinstatement of previous warfighters from their private sector careers or retirement, and the anticipated timeline to return to previous operational capacity.

Natalie knew already it would take years to replace the experience and skill lost, but hearing it confirmed out loud only made it hurt worse. That seemed to be the sentiment in the room as she glanced at the faces around her. Even De la Vega seemed upset by the official report.

When the CIA's executive director finished his report, concluding the long string of despair, the SecDef remained composed and nodded before saying, "Thank you all for your updates. It is my understanding that we've been able, through the use of our private military companies, to fill the gap rather well. Is that correct?"

"Mostly, sir," replied General Wood, to whom SecDef had directed the question. "However, there remain certain challenges, particularly monetarily, to extending those contracts."

"We hardly seem to have a choice," SecDef countered. "Besides, as I understand it, at least one of our contractors is punching above their weight class." He glanced at Natalie as he said this, and Natalie didn't know whether to acknowledge his statement with a nod, a smile, or what. She decided to remain stoic, and he soon returned his attention to General Wood.

Natalie couldn't help but glance at De la Vega. His stoic expression revealed nothing, and he didn't notice her attention—or was at least very good at hiding it as he continued to focus on SecDef.

Ramirez took over, providing a brief on current intelligence efforts to track down those responsible for the global ambush that was Operation Taskmaster, and, pleased with the report, SecDef appeared more relaxed as Ramirez listed the individuals who had been either killed or captured as a result of Invictus' work alongside SOCOM's and the CIA's Special Activities Center's operations. Particular praise was given to MARSOC Detachment One under the command of Captain Tyson Thornton. Efforts were now underway to expand the Special Mission Unit further, something of which the Shaws were immensely proud.

With a healthier understanding of the status of the nation's special operations regrowth, SecDef concluded the meeting with his gratitude, praise, and expectations. As everyone rose, Natalie followed suit, but before she could join the crowd, a deep voice called for her.

"Mrs. Shaw, a minute, if you can spare it," the SecDef said as the crowd shuffled toward the exit.

"Of course, sir," Natalie replied. She turned to Sosa and Lincoln and nodded her farewell.

"How are things going for you all?" SecDef asked once the room had cleared.

"Going well, sir. We're glad to be of service and to do good work," Natalie replied.

"That's hardly an answer, Mrs. Shaw," SecDef said. Natalie smirked and looked down as she thought about how best to answer.

"The operational tempo has been challenging," she explained. "In just three months, we've run countless ops across the world, from the Philippines to Sudan, and all across the Middle East. And that's with the remaining fifty-five or so percent of SOCOM and Ground Branch. There's a lot of work to go around."

"I understand. Thank you for your candor, but you've managed to deliver consistent results above expectations, especially with this last mission against el-Shahan," SecDef shared.

"Lady Luck has her part to play, sir."

"Not too big a part," he said. "I've not found luck to be consistent. Like the Goddess Nike, she's never in one place for too long."

"Well, neither are we," Natalie countered. SecDef laughed.

"Well said." SecDef took a minute to study her freckled face. Her glowing green eyes were framed by a head of sleek brown hair woven into a single braid draped over her left shoulder. "Well, I only wished to inform you that the DOD and other offices are grateful for your contributions and that Invictus has a permanent home here. You've proved yourselves to be immeasurably valuable. I've even heard rumors of your work to dismantle international crime."

"Only rumors, sir," Natalie said, though she felt the twisting in her stomach.

"All legends start first as rumors," he said, winking at her. Natalie forced a smile.

"I look forward to your continued work. Thank you, Mrs. Shaw." He extended his hand, and she gripped it politely.

"Thank you, sir," she replied.

"You didn't have to wait for me," Natalie said to Lincoln when she found him leaning against the hallway wall.

"What did SecDef want?" he asked as he returned his full weight to his feet. Natalie inhaled and rolled her lips inward in contemplation.

"I'm not quite sure," she began, "but I have a feeling Invictus will have some new opportunities coming in the near future."

"What makes you say that?"

"Just how SecDef was talking to me in there."

"Did it feel right? You look a little unsure," Lincoln probed. Natalie chewed her cheek as she considered his question.

"Well, with all we've been through, it's hard not to feel like everything is part of a larger manipulation," she answered.

"I get that," Lincoln replied. "Speaking of manipulation, I don't think I'm feeling too good about you having lunch with Red Horse over there," he answered. Natalie turned and looked at De la Vega, who waited patiently for her farther down the hall. Catching her gaze, he offered her a disarming smile and nod.

"Well, then keep an eye on me," Natalie responded, nudging her forearm into him as she left to join De la Vega.

Lincoln sighed and looked up at the ceiling before shaking his head. He watched Natalie shake De la Vega's hand and blew out an annoyed exhale.

David would never forgive me...fine.

12

De la Vega held open the gold framed door to DC's historic Colorado Building and extended a hand for Natalie to enter. Before following her inside, he turned, located the white Toyota Tacoma, and offered the driver a mock salute. Seated behind the wheel, Lincoln sighed heavily before scratching his forehead and wondering if he was losing his touch. Then again, perhaps De la Vega was simply very skilled at counter-surveillance. He was a former Green Beret after all, who undoubtedly had hefty experience with recognizing and losing tails.

Perhaps his intentions are innocent, Lincoln thought. Still, he felt better knowing that De la Vega knew that someone was just outside, likely armed, and there for Natalie. He found comfort in that thought.

"Welcome to Ocean Prime. Do you have a reservation?" the young, dark-haired hostess asked with a simple smile. Natalie looked at De la Vega, but he didn't return her gaze.

"Yes, De la Vega. For two," he replied. Natalie hummed her intrigue at his assumptive preparedness.

"Certainly, Mr. De la Vega. If you'll follow me," the hostess said, producing two menus from the stand and turning toward the restaurant interior.

"After you, Mrs. Shaw," De la Vega said warmly. Natalie inclined her head and followed the young woman deeper into the luxurious establishment.

With dark walls and golden, sheer curtains hanging from the high ceiling, the atmosphere pleased Natalie, and, noting the exposed wine room, unique light fixtures, and expansive bar, she felt her husband would like the place—if the food was good.

As their hostess guided them to their table, Natalie wasn't surprised at all that De la Vega had advanced reservations for two.

"This looks to be more than just a simple show of gratitude," Natalie stated as she slid into their booth. She figured it was specifically requested since from both seats, one could observe the exit and the kitchen entry. "Shake Shack probably would have sufficed."

De la Vega chuckled as he took his seat across from her.

"Wine menu," the hostess said, handing him the folded leather booklet.

"Thank you."

"Your server will be with you shortly," she said before leaving.

"Shake Shack," De la Vega mumbled as he perused the wine list. "Not had it."

"You're kidding."

"I am not," he said, his voice carrying a light honesty that Natalie appreciated.

"Well, you'll have to before you leave.

"We have them in Miami," he said, looking up from the menu and grinning. "But when the company is paying, I like to get my money's worth."

"Ah, so it is a business lunch then," Natalie countered.

"Everything is business at my level. Maybe you're just not there yet," he said, keeping his smile.

"Perhaps not," Natalie admitted as she reached for the water glass slick with condensation. "You going to offer to buy us out again?"

"No," he quickly replied, a short laugh following. "I think we both know that things have moved beyond that. I'm impressed with what you've built,

Mrs. Shaw. It's quite unheard of, and I must admit that I am fighting a bit of jealousy."

"Because of the money?"

"Because of the results," he countered quickly, almost offended. Natalie found his response quite interesting and far from what she had expected. "Operation Taskmaster hit us all hard. I lost friends. Not being the tip of the spear in the retaliation operations is a hard pill to swallow. Many of my guys feel similarly."

"I didn't realize you were so personally affected," Natalie admitted.

"Yeah, well, I'm still happy the work is getting done," he replied. "The fact that Sod Buster is back with us and el-Shahan is in the dirt brings great relief and comfort, even if Red Horse didn't get the op, or the one before that, or the one before that..."

"I get your point," Natalie said with a smile. De la Vega returned it and exhaled as he scooped up the menu.

"Ever been here?" he asked.

"No."

"I'm partial to the fixed lunch. Love the fish tacos and the clam chowder. Also, the cookie dessert is to die for," he explained.

Natalie studied the menu, finding it difficult to decide between the enticing options.

Do I want the Sushi or the Sea Bass? She asked herself, remembering the Sea Bass she had had with Shaw in Grand Cayman. She then sighed as her eyes fell on the Maryland Crab Melt. De la Vega, catching on to her dilemma, chuckled.

"It's why I go with the fixed lunch," he said. Natalie smirked. "But, let's get a bit of everything for the table."

Their server, Felicity, arrived, and Natalie attempted to keep up as her host rattled off a plethora of appetizers, entrées, and sides, getting particularly excited for the Lobster Mac & Cheese and Jalapeño Au Gratin.

"Do you have a wine preference?" he asked her.

"No," she replied. He then ordered something with a long title that didn't mean anything to her.

Once the server had confirmed the order and departed, Natalie asked, "Did you learn all this in USASOC?"

"No," De la Vega answered with a chuckle. "Something I had to learn fast, though."

"Because of Anderson Stovall?" Natalie probed, her tone now icy. De la Vega's face twisted in amusement before he scratched his upper lip with his index finger. He tilted his head as he considered her position. Though unexpected, he praised her ingenuity—however bold—and he now began to suspect how capable she truly was.

Stovall was a name known only to a few, and all who knew it held power because of Stovall's direct involvement in their lives. The fact that Natalie—an outsider—knew of him increased his admiration and complicated the relationship greatly.

"I believe you said it's always business?" Natalie added, wearing what De la Vega believed to be a confident yet slightly smug expression.

Or is it agitation? De la Vega thought, reconsidering his initial assessment. He wondered how much he dared share, but the game had changed so much, so drastically, that he had to suppress his instinctual response toward damage control.

"I believe I may be outclassed," he admitted.

"Is that so, Zorro?"

De la Vega laughed heartily, nodded, and said, "Very much indeed. I see you've done your homework on me."

"As you should expect," Natalie countered. De la Vega only nodded while keeping her hard stare. Those green eyes held a fire he had only seen in the eyes of his brothers-in-arms.

She is something, he thought.

He wondered how he should proceed, and he knew that his silence had a time limit. If he kept quiet too long, that would certainly send signals to his guest that he was sure she would be able to decipher accurately. If he denied the existence of or of knowing Stovall, how might that be received—if he could even be convincing enough?

At the same time, if he admitted to Stovall's existence and she was only bluffing to get information out of him, how might that jeopardize his and Red Horse's future? What interest did she have in his employer?

I'm running out of time.

He thought back to Stovall's personal interest in David Shaw. Certainly, the woman across from him played a large role in unnerving his employer, and he clearly saw that she was the surgeon and her husband was the scalpel.

"Even now, you're not only wondering if you should confirm or deny Stovall's existence but attempting to determine to what extent," she finally said just before Felicity returned and presented De la Vega with the bottle of wine he had ordered. The Red Horse CEO was grateful for the interruption, but he couldn't deny he was intrigued by his new and quite formidable competitor.

De la Vega tasted the wine, nodded, and directed Felicity to pour a glass for Natalie, which she did with a smile on her narrow face full of sharp features. Ever cordial, Natalie lifted the glass to her lips and tasted the dry white, but she failed to understand the complexity the expensive bottle provided.

"Good, thank you," she said.

"Wonderful," Felicity replied. "Your appetizers will be out in just a moment."

"Thank you, Felicity," De la Vega responded.

"Certainly," she said, her high, blonde ponytail bouncing as she nodded and departed.

De la Vega inhaled as he leaned forward and braced his weight on his forearms along the edge of the table. Natalie watched him, studied him, and he felt the weight of her scrutiny.

"Look, it's clear you're good, truly, and so is your husband. You've spooked some powerful people," De la Vega began.

"Tell me something I don't know," she said, sipping her wine with an air of satisfaction. De la Vega chuckled and looked around the restaurant before bringing his attention back to her.

"What's your interest in Mr. Stovall?" he finally asked, studying her expression for a hint of whether or not she was already aware of his existence or their professional relationship.

Her countenance offered nothing.

Man, she's good.

"I must admit, I wish I had you at Red Horse," he said.

"What if I told you that Stovall is complicit in a global conspiracy that extends beyond national borders?" Natalie said quietly, daring to probe.

"I'd believe you," he replied simply. For the first time, De la Vega witnessed a flash of surprise across her face. It was there only an instant before fleeting away, but he had seen it, just barely.

"Would it bother you?" she asked.

"Depends," he replied. "Why share this with me?" Natalie's stare told him everything he needed to know. "You're hunting, aren't you?"

"Depends," she echoed, her voice mirroring his own inflection just moments prior. Again, De la Vega chuckled and shook his head. He knew he was better at leading and fighting than he was espionage.

I have sorely underestimated her, he thought. Still, he pondered her motive. The only reason he could determine was that she was probing him, perhaps testing his loyalty or what he might know. He couldn't say that he had fared well, and he knew that Stovall would be displeased if he found out how poorly at that. However, he found himself admiring her more than scolding himself.

"To Sod Buster," he said, lifting his wine.

Natalie smiled in her victory, clinked her glass against his, and said, "To Sod Buster."

"Well, Mrs. Shaw, thank you for your work. I look forward to the next time our paths cross," De la Vega said, his tone sincere and cordial.

"Thank you for lunch, Zorro," Natalie replied as the two stepped outside.

De la Vega offered her a closed-mouth smile and a nod before saying, "I trust you can secure your own transportation?" He glanced over her shoulder at Lincoln's vehicle, offering the man a knowing nod. Natalie turned, following his gaze, and smiled.

"Yes, I don't think that will be a problem," she replied. De la Vega extended a gloved hand, which Natalie took professionally.

"Give my best to your husband," he said.

"Give ours to Mr. Stovall," she countered. De la Vega smirked and looked down before meeting her eyes again.

"Should I be concerned?"

"Depends," she said. The Latino laughed, inclined his head a final time, and turned toward the valet. Natalie, taking the cue, headed toward Lincoln, who she saw put his truck in gear.

Once she closed the passenger door, Lincoln asked, "How did it go?"

"Fine," Natalie replied as Lincoln merged slowly into traffic. She turned her gaze out the window to meet De la Vega's stare one last time as they passed the valet stand. His expression appeared grim and sour as if all professional courtesy had departed with her.

"Just fine? He doesn't look happy," Lincoln pressed.

"I suppose not."

"That was risky," Lincoln scolded. "I hope you got what you were after."

"Me too," Natalie replied, her tone pensive and wary.

13

Joint Base Andrews,
Maryland

Natalie waved happily at the C-17 Globemaster as the massive jet landed on the runway before her with thunderous noise. Natalie only smiled at the industrious display of military capability, knowing that her husband and her staff were aboard.

When the plane came to a stop, Natalie waited impatiently for the rear ramp to lower, and as much as she wanted to race from the hangar, across the tarmac, and leap into the arms of her husband, she fought the urge, knowing it was better to maintain the professional image her leadership at Invictus required. She had already broken radio etiquette on the Radi mission last fall, but she knew the guys didn't judge her for it. They all had feared Shaw lost even before she cried out personally for him.

Regardless, best to keep up appearances, she reminded herself. Dressed in a pair of dark jeans that hugged her legs and a waxed-cotton Blakeley jacket from Tom Beckbe over a wool sweater, Natalie didn't mind the cold even as the chilly breeze tossed the loose wisps of hair about her face.

A wide grin broke across her face as she watched the eight warfighters disembark at a distance. She waved proudly and happily at the camouflaged group toting their weapons and gear.

Shaw, apparently less concerned with professional image, broke into a jog as his blue eyes fell on her. The action warmed her heart, and she never tore her gaze from him until he dropped his duffel, wrapped his arms under her rear, scooped her into the air, and spun her around. He lowered her enough so that he could kiss her.

"They're watching," she said.

"Let them watch," he replied before kissing her again. The comment made her swoon, and she kissed him all the harder.

"Get a room!" Bray shouted as he approached. Pikari shared Bray's smile.

"Owen, Tāne, welcome back," Natalie said, once her husband set her back down on her feet.

"Good to be back, ma'am," Pikari replied, offering her a respectful and grateful nod. He couldn't believe that this was his life, that he was working with such high-caliber professionals on missions that really mattered.

Natalie greeted the rest of the team, shaking hands with Reeves and McEwen while the others offered her respectful nods as they passed by her.

"Good work, gentlemen," she said to each man.

"Grateful for the opportunity," McEwen said before bouncing the heel of his fist off Shaw's shoulder. "Besides, I gotta stick around if I want to keep this Mk3 Hi-Power," he joked.

"I think you've earned it," Shaw replied with a grin, remembering how McEwen's accurate shot had turned the tide against Radi.

"Well, if that's the case," the Scot said, "I'll be submitting my resignation." He laughed heartily.

"Come on, you idiot," Reeves said, grabbing the trooper by the arm and leaving Shaw and Natalie alone.

Shaw smiled as he watched them leave. While McEwen was rough around the edges, he bore the spirit and integrity they valued for the work that they had shouldered. Dropping his gaze back to his wife, he asked, "How are you?"

Natalie smiled at the tenderness and sincerity in his voice.

"I met Diego de la Vega," she said, watching as his eyes popped wide.

"Why?" he asked, trying to keep his concern hidden, but Natalie saw through his efforts.

"The opportunity presented itself at a Pentagon meeting. I wanted to confirm what we know about Stovall and his relationship with Red Horse, as well as size up our competition."

"That's dangerous, Nat," Shaw pressed, his tone disapproving.

"That's what Scott said," she countered.

Shaw sighed and reminded himself how proven his wife was, both in spycraft and combat. Still, if De la Vega wanted her dead, he doubted she would have been able to stop him.

"Did you find out what you wanted?" he asked.

"Somewhat," she replied, reaching for her braid. Shaw recognized that motion and sighed again.

Natalie knew she had taken an unnecessary risk, perhaps playing her hand too early, but after all her digging into Stovall and finding nothing that connected him to Rykov or Barakat, much less the others, she had grown impatient. She saw that now. Perhaps, floating on a high from their success against el-Shahan had clouded her judgment. "You're right," she finally said. "I gambled and, though I didn't come out empty-handed, I didn't get enough."

"What did you get?"

"De la Vega definitely knows Stovall personally. I'd bet my life on it," she answered.

"That's something," Shaw replied. "If Stovall controls Red Horse, that's valuable intel for us. Our guys are good, but we don't have the numbers if Stovall can send Red Horse after us. Nat, they have their own AC-130 as well as an entire fleet of weapon-capable UAVs."

Natalie easily heard the strain in his voice and didn't care for the thought of a UAV sending a missile into their bedroom, though she doubted it would happen.

"De la Vega doesn't seem to be that type of man," she said with finality.

"I hope you're right," Shaw replied gravely.

Invictus Headquarters,
Eastern Shore,
Virginia

The fire crackled pleasantly and spewed its glowing sparks high into the cold night air. The flames danced hypnotically across the full breadth of the wood ringed by a low stone wall. Laughter rolled from lips whose owners, bathed in the warm light, reminisced on stories previously known and those heard for the first time. More than once, it became clear to all how gifted and hilarious storytellers McEwen and Bray were. While they often celebrated successful missions in such a manner, this one felt deeper as they celebrated the rescue of Sod Buster, who still remained in Germany for recovery and evaluation.

Natalie, holding her bottle of Blue Moon ale, sat nestled into her husband's side and beneath the thick warmth of an old, military-issued, wool blanket. Her single braid, glossy in the firelight, snaked from underneath a cream, knit beanie. Her green eyes, more than any present, reflected the flame's glow with bright appeal, making her eyes appear wolf-like in the darkness.

Seated next to her, Shaw laughed hard before clutching his side as a cramp set in his muscles. He winced and hissed through the pain, drawing howls of heavy laughter from his men. McEwen took great enjoyment in making his employer laugh so hard. He, standing before the fire with a boot planted on the stone wall of the pit, roared in deep bellowing while pointing at Shaw, but his face suddenly twisted as his own cramp seized his abdomen.

Realizing that the older of their group suffered horribly, the team could only laugh harder, with Reeves attempting with great strength not to join his older counterparts.

"I need a banana," Shaw grunted as the pain subsided. He settled back into his chair after attempting to stretch out his body. McEwen still hobbled around, straightening his left leg repeatedly as he clutched his side. Finally, the muscles relaxed, and he let out a long sigh.

"You alright there, Highlander?" Bray teased.

"Shut your geggie!" McEwen snorted before taking a swing of his Tennet's Lager and returning to his vigil by the fire, peering deeply into the pulsing embers.

The group settled after that, and Pikari, leaning toward the fire, cradled his beer bottle by the neck, rotating it around and around while enjoying the heat on his face. Seated next to him in a matching Adirondack chair, Bray nursed his own brew while propping both booted feet against the ring of the fire pit.

"Would you go back?" Bray asked Pikari quietly, dropping his feet and leaning forward while new conversations spread among the teammates. Pikari glanced at him with a surprised expression on his dark features.

"What do you mean?" he asked, his voice low and matching Bray's. The two had formed an unexpected bond, being around the same age and having found that their deployments had overlapped regularly, though they had never before met. Also, being inaugural Invictus staff—plank owners as their leadership called them—the two had formed a confident friendship and trust in facing the same near-death threat onboard the *Shahla* while hunting Faatin Radi.

"The NZSAS," Bray clarified quietly. "Would you go back?"

Pikari licked his lips and took another sip before answering, "No, man, not by a long shot."

"Why not?"

"For starters, the pay and benefits are way better here, but more than that, we're really on the tip of the spear with Invictus, and I trust them," he said, looking at Natalie and Shaw as they sat together, the firelight highlighting the happiness on their faces as they watched their staff enjoy themselves. "Why do you ask?"

"The Teams asked me back," Bray said somberly. "I got the message this afternoon when we touched down." Pikari straightened and looked at Bray with a new seriousness. "With all we lost, they're requesting me for DEVGRU."

Pikari sighed and nodded several times. Development Group was the Navy SEALs' most elite unit, often referred to as SEAL Team Six. It was an honor about which he understood the deep significance.

"You'd have to put up with all the bureaucracy again," Pikari stated warily. Bray chewed his cheek and nodded.

"I know," he said, "but it's the dream I always wanted. All I have to do is say yes."

Pikari nodded again, unsure how best to pose the question forming in his mind. If he said it wrong, he knew he could offend and disrespect his new friend. He settled for as simply as he could manage. "Is this how you wanted to earn it?" he asked, watching Bray wince as the question reached his ears.

"But does that really matter?" he countered.

Before Pikari could respond, he heard Shaw call his name. He glanced around as all eyes fell on him. He realized he had no idea what the context of their stares was or how he was expected to respond.

"What?" he asked.

"Have you been ignoring the conversation?" McEwen accused with a laugh. Pikari grinned back.

"You guys are so boring, can you blame me?" the Māori retorted. Laughter again erupted all around.

"We're asking about radio designations," Shaw said.

"What about them?"

"David's way has got too many numbers," McEwen said. "Too much to keep track of. Not sure what he was thinking with it all."

"I was just modeling after JSOC standard recommendations," Shaw replied. "I think it's the Ranger model."

"Zero-Six this, and One-Five that. A bunch of bullocks," McEwen joked. The others laughed.

"Well, there's not really a set standard where I'm from, but I'm the minority here," Pikari answered. "It'd be easier for me to adapt to the American way than for all of you to try and adopt something we changed all the time. How did you do it in MARSOC?" he asked Shaw.

"Well, there's a little bit of that in what we do. We'd have a designated directory we would use, and we would use each letter of that callsign to differentiate between components. So, using that in our case, we use the *I* in *Invictus* for one team, then the *N*, then the *V*, so forth and so on. From that, you get Invictus team, Nectar for Natalie, and we would grow that out as the company grows," Shaw explained.

"Why Nectar?" McEwen asked.

"Went well with Hummingbird," Natalie admitted with a shrug from underneath her blanket.

"Ah," McEwen answered. He swapped his feet on the fire pit before continuing, "Look, I understand, but that's too complicated," he continued, his rugged countenance illuminated by the dancing flames.

"Everything's too complicated for you, Rowan," Reeves teased with a grin.

"That's not funny," McEwen stated, raising a finger. Reeves met the challenge with a confidence in his bright eyes, but then McEwen laughed a hearty, deep laugh and lowered his finger.

"How'd you guys do it?" Shaw asked Aston, turning to address him. Aston, with Roman lying at his feet, looked around at his USASOC brother, Eric Rakestraw. The more senior Green Beret nodded, and Aston then sat forward to answer, causing Roman to perk up and look at him.

"It's simple. A team is made of different roles, right?" Aston began.

"Yeah," Shaw replied.

"On the ODAs, we would have a senior and junior for every role: a senior medic and a junior medic, a senior weapons sergeant and a junior weapons sergeant, and so forth and so on. We would simply use our MOS to communicate with each other. So, before I got into canines, I was an Eighteen Delta medical sergeant. I would be Delta One or Two depending on my seniority. Eric here would be Bravo One or Two, depending on his seniority. Engineers would be Charlie One or Two. You get it?"

"Sounds boring," Bray blurted. "You didn't have any cool names for yourselves?"

"Sometimes," Aston replied with a chuckle. "And we had specific callsigns for the specific ODA. I was with ODA 5411, and we were Snake Eyes 11. ODA 5412 was Snake Eyes 12. ODA 5413 was Snake Eyes 13. All the way to 5416, but that was only for external comms."

"Sounds like an HR nightmare," Natalie interjected.

"How's that?" Rakestraw asked.

"We'd have to assign you all specific job titles, update job descriptions, do a comparative analysis for salary, all sorts of stuff," she jested.

"Will that mean our salaries would increase?" Bray asked.

"Yours would decrease," Natalie quickly countered to hoots of laughter. Bray laughed along, unfazed.

"Rick," Shaw began, turning to face his longtime friend. "How did you guys do it on the Teams?"

"Oh," Rick started, glancing at Bray, who had also served in Naval Special Warfare. "We did whatever we felt like," he finished before taking a long swig of his beer. Bray voiced his agreement and raised his beer while the rest of the team grinned and shook their heads.

"Just give every man their own number," McEwen stated loudly. "Simple and easy to remember." He cut a bladed hand out in front of him to stress his point. With his thick accent and broad frame highlighted by the fire, it had a convincing effect.

"What happens when we grow and a man moves to a different team?" Shaw countered.

"Then they get a new number, in order. Do it by seniority, for all I care. One for commander, Two for team chief, Three for the next guy. Or do it by role: all breachers and assaulters are one, all medics two, on and on like Tyler suggested. Plain and simple."

"So we're after the simplest blend, then," Bray added.

"I'd say so," Natalie admitted. "I didn't realize it was so different across the different branches. It's giving me a headache."

"If you want it as simple as possible, then every guy—and gal," he said, nodding toward Natalie, "gets their own callsign. I've got dibs on Star Lord. Tāne can be Moana."

"Hey! Watch it!" Pikari retorted, snapping a pointed finger toward his friend, but everyone laughed.

Natalie rolled her eyes.

"Still got to have team designations for the battle space, Owen," Shaw said.

"Callsigns goes the same for the teams. You can standardize it with your MARSOC way. Doesn't matter," Bray replied.

"I don't hate it," McEwen added.

"We'll think about it," Natalie responded. "Thank you all for this helpful and informative staff meeting. We'll have a pizza party on Friday."

"Yes!" Bray shouted, the beer finally getting to him.

Everyone laughed again, enjoying the warmth of the fire and the caliber of the company.

14

Odéon Tower,
Principality of Monaco

Anderson Stovall inhaled deeply the mild, yet cool air gliding off the Mediterranean. The salty fragrance was almost sweet and uniquely European. He didn't know why, but the sea air simply smelled different to him here. It wasn't as coarse as in the New World, not as sharp or pungent. It held a softness he enjoyed, a fragrance he wondered if Julius Caesar had noticed and enjoyed, or perhaps Alexander the Great.

Obsessed with such men, Stovall couldn't help but count himself among them; however, he knew he would likely never share their fame, not unless something shifted.

The threats were too real.

Vayun Oza was too real.

But the checks had failed, and the game was open like it had not been for over a hundred years. Not since the great Robber Barons of the Gilded Age had such an opportunity lay before one man, and Stovall intended to seize it for all its worth. Perhaps then—when his conquest was complete—he could reveal himself to the world, sweeping change and directing the course of humanity openly, receiving praise he never knew he coveted.

It's funny how things can change so quickly, he thought to himself as he braced his weight against the balcony railing. His blue eyes beheld the beauty of the sparkling sea before him. *I mustn't squander this opportunity.*

"Sir," came a stoic greeting behind him. Stovall turned in response, his eyes falling on the young aide. "They are ready for you."

"Thank you," Stovall said before proceeding by him and into the conference room where he had hosted the council last fall.

All rose as he entered, and Stovall's eyes lingered on Sofia Vitori, who, though not part of the committee he had summoned, held important information crucial to their war effort against Oza.

"Mr. Stovall, we are ready to begin," greeted Ross Barton. Stovall inclined his head and took his seat at the head of the rectangular wooden table.

"Thank you, Mr. Barton," Stovall said once settled. "Please proceed." He extended his palm in a respectful gesture.

"Of course, sir."

Stovall pressed his fingertips together in a steeple before his mouth as he awaited recent reports and the recommended strategic direction. He cut his eyes toward Sofia, who grinned as he met her gaze. Though seated in the corner with a mimosa in her hands, he knew she was more eager than her calm demeanor indicated.

Barton, the sole individual standing, addressed his employer and his counterparts as he began to speak for them all. "The effort to secure the First Arab's assets and enterprises is going well, but not without obstacles. Both of Mr. Oza's kinetic and acquisition entities are pressing hard against us, but we are edging forward."

"Break that down for me specifically," Stovall instructed, pleased with a report of emerging victory.

"Certainly, sir," Barton replied. Managing strategic asset collaboration for all of Stovall's enterprises, Barton could only describe his work as consulting and reporting. He met, consulted, and cast Stovall's vision for the many enterprises and endeavors under Stovall's ownership. He was solely responsible for the entire mechanism that was Stovall's power grinding forward. Though he couldn't confidently say he was Stovall's second, he wouldn't be surprised if he truly was.

"We've made great progress in securing entities directly responsible for operations at the Suez Canal. With continued effort, I suspect we should have complete non-governmental reign over the asset by the end of the quarter, that's if our competition's efforts to thwart ours are not successful. Already, we've had to activate and leverage assets from Mr. Scalco's area of expertise to deal with some unsavory attempts at corporate espionage and sabotage," Barton said, addressing the younger, dark-haired, and very fit Josh Scalco, who inclined his head toward Stovall in assurance.

His beard is longer than last I saw him, Stovall thought, and he returned the nod. Stovall couldn't begin to list the illicit accolades of Scalco's dark career, but he was grateful to have such competent kinetic leadership. He wondered then who might prevail if pitted against each other, David Shaw or Josh Scalco; he honestly couldn't say, only that he hoped he would never find out. However, he figured a duel between the two most dangerous men he knew would prove extremely entertaining.

"I trust everything was handled with care, Mr. Scalco?" Stovall asked.

"Absolutely," he said, his voice light and confident, yet somehow fitting for his angular features and muscular neck, made to look larger by a wide Windsor knot. "I can confirm that we eliminated a number of both Barakat's assets and Oza's as they attempted to eliminate our own. While not difficult, we are tracking and countering our own ghosts. They are well-trained and capable," Scalco added.

"You said Barakat's and Oza's?" Stovall questioned.

"Yes, sir," Scalco replied. He shifted his gaze to Barton to continue.

"Sir, Mr. Oza does appear to be more persuasive in securing the loyalty of those previously in Mr. Barakat's employ."

"And why is this?" Stovall asked in both curiosity and frustration.

"We'll call it cultural incompatibility," Scalco answered for him, wearing a grin that exposed his overpronounced canine teeth. Stovall always thought he looked like a vampire, his teeth appearing more like fangs than what was certainly more common.

"The Global War on Terror has made it difficult to secure the trust of Mr. Barakat's people. It appears that the fears Mr. Barakat held permeate his network with great fervor. While not unexpected, we've found workarounds," Barton interjected.

"What workarounds?" Stovall asked, though he suspected the answer.

"Let's just say it's easier to remove them than convert them," Scalco added with another grin.

"I trust Red Horse has been a valuable asset in that endeavor?"

"Yes, but most of what we're discussing takes place in the shadows. It's close, personal, specialized—not really Red Horse's specialty," Scalco explained.

"I see," Stovall replied. "It does make sense that Oza would have better success on a cultural level, but he knows he can't compete kinetically."

"That is true, sir," Barton replied. "With Ms. Vitori securing and maintaining Mr. Rykov's holdings and operations in Africa and Eastern Europe and allying her operations with our own, we are more than a match for Mr. Oza. It is only a matter of time."

"That's what I like to hear, Mr. Barton," Stovall said. He turned his attention back to Scalco. "Thank you for your diligent and thorough work." Scalco nodded confidently.

Stovall looked at Edward Guiette, his chief strategic advisor on outcomes, data, and analytics, who sat tall and proud in his chair. Perhaps one of the most ingenious data engineers in the world, Guiette's brilliance was supplemented by a broad team of analysts all over the world working as fund managers, economists, and partnership consultants who reported data and intelligence the CIA would salivate over.

"Mr. Guiette, please paint a picture of our current trajectory and strategic outcomes," Stovall asked him.

"My pleasure, sir," Guiette stated, rising from his seat and activating the device in his hand to begin his digital presentation.

Scalco's eyes glossed over as the older man spoke about timelines, objectives, key results, and the impact specific initiatives had on their war for dominance over Oza. He knew that these reports and initiatives were crucial to secure victory, but he also believed a well-placed shot could end the entire thing.

"As you know, Mr. Stovall, it is not enough to defeat Mr. Oza, but we must either render his operations inoperable or draw those enterprises under our umbrella," Guiette said. Stovall nodded his understanding of the elementary concept. "Thus far, and with Ms. Vitori's assistance, we've managed to keep casualties low on our side, having leveraged connections in the United States military and intelligence communities to eliminate the terrorist infrastructure responsible for Operation Taskmaster, which coincidentally makes up a large portion of Barakat's operations."

"We suspected this for a long time," Stovall interrupted. "Is it as ingrained as we originally thought?"

"Yes, sir, perhaps more so. Our reports indicate that over twenty-five percent of Barakat's wealth is directly linked to terrorist activity. He was able to indirectly motivate operations through funding that facilitated events which increased his wealth, power, or standing. There is a pattern here that, while not alarming or novel, does indicate that we should abandon any efforts to woo, if you will, any previously under Barakat's leadership."

"Is Oza working with these terrorist entities?"

"There is no indication of that. The data suggests that Mr. Oza either has great disdain for terrorist activity or knows that direct confrontation might lead to entanglement with either ours or United States forces."

"That is smart of him," Stovall admitted. "And I would expect nothing less. My instinct is telling me it is the latter, that he wishes to avoid entanglement, especially with the success of Invictus International." Out of the corner of his eye, he caught Scalco's quick sneer.

"I would agree with that assessment, Mr. Stovall," Guiette said.

Stovall listened as his council continued to detail the developments in the move toward their global domination, and he found humor and irony in the fact that he might succeed in the shadows where so many had previously failed.

Perhaps it is only possible now in this Age of Information, he reasoned.

Barton reclaimed everyone's attention by explaining in greater detail the scope of their progress. While it was difficult to know with certainty the fullness of Barakat's enterprises, they had made what they believed to be accurate hypotheses based on their expansive network of corporate spies in various fields of law, politics, military, intelligence, and countless others. With a stronghold in Israel, Stovall was primed to dominate the Middle East in a way Oza was not. From Turkey to Egypt, the entire Fertile Crescent was open for the taking, and Stovall wanted it all.

"We anticipate nearly forty percent of Barakat's holdings are now under our control, representing over four hundred billion in revenue and assets, the majority of which is oil and banking," Barton said. "While we face challenges in the government sectors on account of recent history and our connections to Israel, we have made great progress," he finished, concluding the committee's report.

"Well done, all. Truly, well done. This endeavor could not be in more capable hands, and you have my gratitude," Stovall said. Disregarding their nods, he turned to Sofia and beckoned her forward with a hand.

Barton watched her suspiciously, not knowing why she was there, but knowing very well her new position in the world. In truth, he had to admit that things appeared tighter under her leadership, not that he had personal experience with The Czar's Brotherhood, but new reports evidenced a cohesion that he had not expected in the fallout of Rykov's death.

"You are all aware that war is coming to Europe," Stovall said, rising as Sofia came to his side. "I alerted you as such earlier this month, but I inform you now that this is a joint venture for the mutual benefit of both our enterprises." He turned to Sofia and nodded.

"Ukraine is harboring former colleagues who have refused to acknowledge my accession and place as Rykov's successor. They've proven extremely resistant to my efforts thus far. With the Russian president's desire to reclaim as much of the old Soviet territory as he can, I am opening the gates to him for Ukraine. He will dispose of those troublesome actors, or, at the very least, will drive them from their security where they will be more vulnerable to me," Sofia explained.

Barton looked at Guiette with a concerned expression. Scalco appeared neither surprised nor worried; rather, a hint of excitement tugged at the corner of his mouth and gleamed in his eyes. However, all already knew the benefit open war in Europe would provide to their employer and his enterprises, but now they knew the catalyst, and Barton found himself wondering about these holdouts—who they were and what power they possessed to be worth so much trouble.

"There is more," Stovall said, drawing all eyes, including Sofia's, which glittered with gleeful excitement. "We will work to invoke NATO Article Five." Stovall watched each man closely to surmise his response, and each reacted in the way he suspected—Barton and Guiette with trepidation and Scalco with excitement. "Through Article Five, we will move in our national influence for the deployment of ground forces to Ukraine by wielding the power of the President's administration while seeking a declaration of war with our sway over Congress. This will fuel financial opportunities for both Ms. Vitori and us. Think of the industry born from World War Two? War breeds opportunity, and fighting rats in the desert, while permitting a certain degree of innovation, has not brought the same scale of growth as world war has in the past. Our grandfathers showed us the way, our fathers had their chance, now we must push the mantle forward and reap the unparalleled benefits."

"Is it wise to undertake such a momentous endeavor while we're in the process of eliminating Barakat's influence and combating Oza's?" Barton asked.

"We've an ace up our sleeve there," Stovall said, grinning. Barton stared at him inquisitively, wondering what asset or opportunity his employer possessed of which he was unaware. "Invictus International is perhaps the world's most effective special operations force," Stovall continued.

"We've been watching them for some time," Barton responded, confused. "We've attempted to acquire them in the past through Red Horse, but we met strong opposition."

"Ms. Vitori has found a way to leverage Invictus to our gain, and soon Oza will no longer be a problem for us, leaving us free to take advantage of all that Article Five will allow."

"How?" Guiette asked, impressed and wary.

"Even now, my agents are meeting with an asset that will direct Invictus after Oza. Past experience suggests that once the Shaws have a target in their sights, it won't easily escape them," Sofia answered.

"Is this a false-flag type thing?" Scalco asked.

"Of sorts," Sofia answered. "Let's just say that we have tested our Trojan Horse in their intelligence network to satisfactory effect. I am able to direct them as we need."

"I like it," Scalco stated with a grin. Sofia's own smile gleamed with satisfaction.

"As I understand it," Stovall said, "Ms. Vitori's agents are making contact now with the appropriate instructions and protocols to facilitate the operation. I expect Mr. Oza to be dead in seventy-two hours."

15

Istanbul, Turkey

Reza Afshar, his girth spilling over the wooden chair, checked his watch and licked his lips. His unexpected guest was taking far too long. Afshar glanced back up at the Macedonian. He certainly looked Greek to the Iranian, but he knew that the man would never identify as one. With his thick black hair and trimmed beard, the Macedonian possessed dense, flat eyebrows over squinted, dark eyes, and if his complexion was only a shade or two darker, he might have passed as Arab or Turkish.

Regardless, the man was overstaying his welcome; however, Afshar couldn't find the courage to force him out of his hookah and tea house. His life had become far more complicated than he could have possibly imagined since he first met with Faatin Radi last November. As a result, he now held less power with his contacts in Iran due to the botched mission and the loss of six nuclear suitcase bombs. He didn't mind that so much as he would have time to repair and regain that standing, but what proved more troublesome was this Natalie Shaw, whom he was committed to assist.

He didn't like it, but he knew she was not one to give idle threats. If he wanted to keep on living, enjoying his hookah and tea, as well as watching his children have children, he knew he could not afford to offend, much less betray her. What complicated matters further was the sudden appearance of this Macedonian.

He had approached Afshar with bags of euros for contracted employment. Already, Afshar had made over two-hundred-fifty-thousand euros from his relationship with the mysterious man by feeding Natalie the provided intelligence on el-Shahan, and he now suspected that that was a test somehow. Either way, he was more than inclined to continue the relationship.

However, this next job was different, and Afshar knew that if Natalie caught wind of the deception, she would come for his head.

But the lure of wealth was still too great to pass up.

One million euros for a single mission. Never before had he faced such a financial opportunity.

Besides, Natalie is still getting what she wants. I've made no breach in our arrangement, Afshar thought. The target she wanted dead was being handed to her on a silver platter, courtesy of the Macedonian.

All this deception between the parties ruling over him had left him beyond wary, fearful even. Already, he had replaced his security with Turks who held no loyalty to Iran. He had restricted his patrons to eliminate the threat of leaks. He had taken all the precautions he could think of in order to benefit handsomely from these complicated relationships.

Despite the threats from all sides.

Still, the Macedonian needed to leave. He was cutting it close.

How to tell him, though? Afshar thought. He was careful and knew better than to schedule meetings with conflicting parties on the same day, but the Macedonian's unexpected visit couldn't be ignored. Afshar then considered the chilling notion that the Macedonian was up to something sinister that might jeopardize his security under Natalie Shaw.

"Is there more business to discuss?" Afshar dared to ask. The Macedonian cut his eyes upward before exchanging glances with the two men standing behind him.

"Are you kicking us out, Reza?" the man asked, his accent smooth and pleasant, but not without strength.

"Of course not," Afshar replied, perhaps showing more fear than he intended. The Macedonian grinned, his teeth very straight yet off white.

"I noticed you keep checking your watch," the Macedonian said as he reached for his tea. "Are you expecting someone?"

"I do have an appointment," Afshar said, mustering his courage. The Macedonian chuckled as he focused on the fat Iranian.

"I envy your life, Reza. I truly do," he said, rising from his chair. Afshar forced a smile and inclined his head respectfully. "However, it is interesting how swiftly one might fall from grace. Don't you think?"

"Yes, indeed," Afshar answered quickly. The Macedonian smirked and nodded his head several times.

"Well, our business is done. You have the next target and corresponding intelligence to relay to your American contact. All is good?"

"Yes," Afshar answered. He fought the urge to check his watch yet again. What would happen if his American contact and the Macedonian ran into each other? *Surely nothing*, he told himself.

"We shall go," the Macedonian said, donning his brown leather jacket with thick lapels. He fastened the buttons and the belt around his narrow waist before flipping up the collar high on his neck. By his physique alone, Afshar knew he was a formidable and dangerous man. He had the look of those who had raided his tea house just a few months back.

The men who had worked for Natalie Shaw.

Afshar rose to escort his guests out of the second-story lounge when a knock sounded at the door they now faced.

"Your appointment?" the Macedonian asked, raising a dark eyebrow. Panic set within Afshar at that thought.

"Perhaps. One moment," the Iranian said. He began to sweat upon realizing there was no other exit for the Macedonian and his men, should it truly be Natalie Shaw's contact. Everything was handled outside of digital spaces, a condition Natalie had set forth and one to which Afshar had readily agreed.

Afshar reached for the handle and opened the door, using his girth to hide the room and its occupants from view.

"Mr. Afshar, your appointment is here," said Musa Ozal, Afshar's receptionist, but Afshar didn't hear him. His brown eyes gazed past Musa and met the stare of the Spider of Kandahar.

Laila Malik's blue eyes squinted as she noticed Afshar's unnerved expression. Sweat beaded at his temples, so Laila centered her weight over her feet, prepared for anything. Feeling a strong pull from her gut to flee, Laila shifted her weight down the stairs, but before she could descend, a voice stopped her.

"Laila?"

Startled, she snapped her gaze over Afshar's shoulder to meet the dark eyes of a man she knew all too well. The astonished expression on his olive countenance quickly turned hard, and holding his stare, she inhaled deeply and discreetly, filling her lungs with oxygen for the fight she knew was coming.

As the tension mounted, both Laila and the Macedonian remained locked in hard contest as they considered how the presence of the other affected their objectives. It was clear to Laila that Afshar was compromised. The dread on his face that she noticed in her peripheral vision was evidence enough of that.

"You're working for the Iranians now?" the Macedonian reasoned, his tone holding faint disappointment. Laila heard the threat and swallowed her fear.

"What happens now, Troske?" she asked, her eyes never leaving his.

"I think you know," he said. "Let's not make a mess of things here. Come with us, and we can talk through this with civility."

No chance, Laila thought.

She watched as Troske raised an inviting hand, his fingers beckoning her into the room. In that moment, Laila attempted to calculate how many men he might have with him. With a steady exhale, she felt her entire body teeming with anticipation, as if some energy vibrated every cell in her body.

In a flash, Laila tore her gaze from the Macedonian and raced down the stairs. Troske and his men immediately bolted after her, shoving Afshar aside, who stumbled and fell into a shelf hosting a collection of rare vases and china.

Laila didn't look back, gritting her teeth when a man emerged at the bottom of the stairs to block her route. Her honed senses rapidly deconstructed his intent, her options, and the best route forward. Her leading foot hit the fifth stair from the bottom before she launched her body toward the man. She whipped her trailing leg forward at the precise moment, driving her knee at the man's chest.

His eyes widened, and he attempted to shield his torso with his arms, but Laila's flying knee slammed hard into his sternum. She rode him to the floor, rolled forward, and popped to her feet before continuing her sprint toward the front entry.

The small gathering of patrons jumped from their cushions in alarm and protest as they watched three men chase after the red-headed beauty they had all previously admired. The fourth man, who had received Laila's flying knee, groaned as he rolled on the floor and attempted to recover.

Laila, dressed in a short, black leather biker jacket, jeans, and lace-up leather boots, raced out the front door and into the hard arms of two more of the Macedonian's men. As they attempted to secure her, one caught a swift elbow to the chin in a textbook uppercut that rattled his brain and sent him sprawling backward. The other man seized a handful of Laila's hair and wrenched downward, drawing a cry from the woman.

Keeping her cool, Laila fished her hand into the opening of the man's coat and seized the pistol holstered just under his right arm. It was a gamble, but she remembered Troske's SOPs.

Pulling the gun free, she angled the muzzle toward the man's chest and fired three times. The suppressed pistol chirped as it sent slug after slug through the man's heart.

He screamed, released her, and fell back, clutching his wounds. Wrenching her torso to the right, Laila dropped her sights on the second assailant before squeezing the trigger three times, performing a flawless Mozambique—two to the chest, one to the head.

The door to the teahouse crashed open. Picking up her sights again, she fired quickly, sending a round thundering through the first man's face before she scurried away and cut into an adjacent alley.

Keeping her stolen pistol in her strong hand, she fished her phone out of her jacket pocket. Using the virtual assistant feature, she said, "Call Ed Burroughs."

"Calling Ed Burroughs," the female voice replied as the software initiated the call to a secure emergency line at Langley. The name served simply as a cover in the event her phone was subject to prying eyes, but the recipient of the call was prepared for the contingency Laila now faced.

"This is Ed," came a generic, male voice. He sounded just over middle-aged and unassuming.

"This is Firefly—Seven Echo Four Two November One Eight," she huffed. She glanced back just in time to see her pursuers, weapons ready, follow her into the alley using advanced tactics.

"Understood, Firefly, stand by for confirmation," the CIA personnel replied. Laila instinctively dipped left as she heard the snap of suppressed, subsonic fire behind her.

She grunted as pain scorched through her upper back, a bullet tearing into her left trapezius. Stumbling, she regained her footing before another round pounded through her thigh, bringing her to the ground. Her phone clattered against the cobblestone and slid out of reach.

Keeping her wits, Laila rolled over and took aim, the iron sights appearing hazy through her agony, but she couldn't see her targets.

"Drop it, Laila. Don't make me kill you," Troske called from the darkness ahead. Laila attempted to crawl, but the Macedonian's words stopped her. "Toss the gun!"

"What do you want with me, Stefo Troske of North Macedonia?" Laila called, loud enough for the phone to pick up her voice. Troske smirked, realizing what she was doing.

"Don't do that, Laila Malik of Afghanistan," he scolded with a grin, appreciating her wit. "It's been a long time," he added.

Laila winced through the agony pulsing in her shoulder and leg. Her eyes darted in search of her phone, but though she held the pistol pointed in Troske's direction, she didn't feel confident in moving too much for fear he might actually shoot her again, this time fatally. With the alley entrance blanketed in darkness, she couldn't make out her targets anyway, but the alley light directly above her highlighted her to her enemies.

"I should kill you for what you just did!" Troske shouted, though his voice sounded more amused than angry.

Laila suppressed her fear, but she knew she had experienced worse. She thought about trying to get away, sending rounds down the alley to cover her movement, but she also knew how good a shot Troske was. Had he wanted to kill her, he could have.

"But there are standing orders to bring you home. The Czar may be gone, but the Brotherhood remains," Troske replied. Laila's mouth dried.

"Who's running things now?"

"Put down the gun, and you'll find out," Troske answered.

"I have a shot," his companion whispered from his position behind an adjacent dumpster. At his angle, he had a clear view of his target, and his PDW afforded him greater precision than Troske's pistol.

"Take it," Troske ordered.

In the darkness, Laila never saw it coming.

PART II

RUMORS OF WAR

16

Singapore,
Republic of Singapore

Vayun Oza peered over the expanse of his city as he stood on the balcony of the luxury high-rise hotel. The wind tousled his wavy, black hair streaked with silver. And his pensive eyes bore a fatigue and a longing as the city twinkled below him, going about its nightly business and pleasure as every night, completely naïve to the struggle that waged around them.

The entire world is naïve, Oza thought as he rolled his lips inward. Wearing a black, collarless dress shirt, the thin, quiet man inhaled deeply, keeping his hands laced at his waist. So much had changed, the balance of power upended by a new player. The irony, Oza believed, was that the Shaws possessed no grasp of the weight of their actions, and if they had, he couldn't rationalize why they had done what they had done.

While not perfect, the system had worked, and the understanding between Rykov, Stovall, Barakat, and Oza had brought a semblance of peace.

To an extent.

Now, Oza was forced to contend with Anderson Stovall and his new ally, Sofia Vitori.

How things have changed, Oza lamented. Everyone had known their place over the last thirty years, and now, ambitions were stirring.

Oza, however, was tired.

Though not an old man, he felt it, and he glanced down at his knuckles as his hands mated together, noting the wrinkles and prominent veins. He sighed again before reminding himself of the stakes.

Perhaps I am old.

He inhaled deeply and nodded toward the city he called home—a promise to fight to the end, to oppose Stovall's ambition, and to secure his family's future. However, he knew that could not happen while Stovall's and Vitori's ambitions lay unchecked.

"Mr. Oza," a soft, curt voice called from the doorway. Oza turned and smiled warmly at his chief of staff. The Japanese man bowed his head in respectful duty before drawing his dark eyes back upward and finishing his thoughts, "The update you have requested is prepared."

"Thank you, Mr. Takuma," Oza said. Takuma bowed swiftly before departing, and Oza took one last glance at the city glowing in its evening reverie before turning and following Takuma inside.

All rose from the conference room table as their employer entered. Oza took the time to acknowledge each individual with a nod of gratitude for their hard work on what all knew was a losing front. Still, all returned the honor with a deeper bow.

When assembling his cabinet, Oza had taken careful consideration to ensure proper representation of the strategic Asian nations, though first requiring absolute loyalty to his dynasty and mission above national ties. His generosity had made that demand easy for those in the room. Each hardly identified ethnically or nationally, but each viewed themselves as part of an endeavor greater than themselves, and one from which they had all received much honor.

"Please, begin," Oza instructed politely as he took his seat in the middle of the conference table. Takuma rose from his chair, as all expected, and activated the projector while simultaneously dimming the lights. Singapore sparkled all the brighter through the massive, corner windows.

"I will be brief," Takuma began as the first slide showed a series of data points and revenue actuals. "We have not made the progress as we had originally projected. Mr. Stovall's and Ms. Vitori's combined efforts are causing a great deal of concern, and all of us here are afraid we cannot hold, much less push into the territory previously held by Mr. Barakat. We have compiled the data for you to review and a list of possible directions to salvage the situation."

"Thank you, Mr. Takuma," Oza said as he studied the data projected on the screen. His heart sank, but he kept a stoic expression. "What are the proposed opportunities?"

Takuma mustered a smile at his employer's optimism, though he knew the severity and direness of the moment.

"We have excluded the options, though they may be most effective, that do not align with the core values of your enterprises," Takuma began. Oza nodded approvingly.

After outlining the different proposals, Takuma inhaled deeply and awaited his employer's response.

Oza, fingertips pressed together in a position of deep contemplation, finally looked up at Takuma, then to those seated around him.

"Mr. Stovall has brought war to our doorstep. It is not the first time the West has dared to do so, and by all accounts, Mr. Stovall appears to be among the ranks of those who have succeeded. However, the story has not been finished, and the world is ever-changing. There are pieces at play that we previously have not accounted for, and perhaps have not considered in a long time."

"What pieces?" Takuma asked, knowing his employer well enough to justify the clarifying question. Oza smiled.

"The will of a single man or a single woman," Oza replied. All looked puzzled, which brought a chuckle to Oza's lips.

"Forgive me, sir, but I believe we find ourselves in this position because of the unchecked will of a single man and woman," a counselor named Jatayu Jayavant stated.

"Indeed, and something tells me that the Shaws will have an important role in finishing what they started. We will hold our front, pause all endeavors to take what Barakat has left," Oza explained.

"But that will give Mr. Stovall and Ms. Vitori a permanent advantage over us," Jayavant countered. However, Oza saw the understanding flash across Takuma's stoic expression.

"Permanent?" Oza questioned with a grin. "The Shaws have shown us that nothing is permanent, only complacent."

"You wish to make allies of them," Takuma reasoned.

"Before our enemies do," Oza confirmed.

"Our intelligence suggests that might not be possible," Sukarno Sumadi, Oza's head of intelligence, stated.

"Yet we know that the Shaws are reasonable people," Oza replied.

"Do we know that?" Takuma countered. Oza smirked.

"I believe that," Oza corrected. Takuma frowned. "Mr. Stovall will either leverage them or attempt to remove them."

"What makes you certain of that?" Sumadi pressed, his eyes focused on his employer.

"Mr. Stovall's ambition has only ever been checked by Mr. Rykov's, who I believe he secretly feared and with good reason. If the Shaws' past actions tell us anything, it is that they will oppose Stovall's ambition."

"How can you be sure? They are all Americans," Jayavant interjected.

"General Linus Weber," Oza said simply. "Was he not also an American?" Only silence answered him, and Oza nodded at their understanding. "The Shaws do not tolerate tyrants, regardless of their form or position. Stovall's ambition has the makings of a tyrant. He rejects contentment as a value, and he will suffer for it. We only need to be ready to support the Shaws when it is time. Meanwhile, we will shore up our defenses, build a bulwark around our assets. We have lost too many already trying to play Mr. Stovall's game, and now we must pray for them and the families they have left behind."

The respectful nods all around were laced with admiration and loyalty, and Oza returned each one with gratitude.

"We have work to do," Oza said as he stood. His cabinet rose and bowed as he took his leave.

17

US Capitol Building,
Washington, DC

De la Vega sighed at being in Washington again so soon. He lived in Miami for a reason, and every time he had to drag out his winter wear for a trip to DC, he grew instantly annoyed. However, he embraced the suck and tightened his peacoat collar around his neck after stepping from the SUV Stovall had sent for him at Reagan International's private terminal. With his black hair styled in a slick fade, the former Green Beret stepped off the street and began the short climb up the famous stone steps of the US Capitol Building.

"Mr. De la Vega," a young staffer greeted. She stood at just over five feet with her light brown hair pulled into a tight, professional bun. De la Vega wondered if she was former military by the way her hair was so meticulously styled—flat and tight against her scalp. Regardless, it was clear she had been waiting for him.

"Yes, hello," De la Vega greeted as he pulled off his leather gloves and reached for her extended hand.

"My name is Brittany Rorrer, and I'm here to escort you during your visit to the Capitol," she said.

"Thank you, Ms. Rorrer," De la Vega replied.

"We'll first get you through the visitor center for your security screening, and afterwards I will see to your schedule."

De la Vega only nodded and allowed the staffer to lead him through security, providing all the proper clearances for his visit. Surprisingly, she whisked him through far quicker than De la Vega expected, and once on the other side, she checked her leather-clad iPad and nodded to herself as she made sure there hadn't been any last-minute changes to the meeting schedule or locations.

"Right this way, Mr. De la Vega," Brittany said.

"If we have time, I'd like to see the Rotunda," he mentioned. Brittany grinned in reply.

"Our route will take us right through it," she promised.

"Excellent."

Though he tired of visiting DC, De la Vega never tired of seeing the inside of the Capitol. He believed it to be the most exquisite building in the city, though he had not yet visited the White House. Still, he doubted the White House would evoke the same awe as the architecture, paintings, and statues arrayed within this historic building.

They took an elevator to the fourth floor after giving De la Vega time to marvel at the Rotunda. Brittany then led her charge down the elaborate halls of the northern wing.

"Here we are," she said, stopping at a wooden door marked with nothing more than a room number. "I'll return at the end of the scheduled time," she promised before knocking on the door. It opened immediately, and, knowing the process, De la Vega entered the hideaway—one of nearly a hundred secret offices situated around the building and assigned to various senators based on seniority.

"Ah, Mr. De la Vega," Stovall said, standing from the velvet couch and moving to shake his hand.

"Mr. Stovall," De la Vega greeted professionally, a nod accompanying his handshake.

"Welcome," Stovall replied. "We were just about to have food brought. Are you hungry?"

"No, sir, I ate on my flight."

"We'll have something brought for you anyway," Stovall said with a laugh. "Come, join us."

Stovall offered De la Vega his seat on the couch, an honor all present recognized, even De la Vega, who wondered why. Stovall took a seat in one of the French-style, velvet chairs at the head of the meeting space.

Though the room was decorated with an attractive French inspiration, De la Vega kept his professional attention on the meeting instead of taking in the decor, which he found impressive.

"Everyone, this is Mr. Diego de la Vega, the CEO of Red Horse Global," Stovall said.

"It is good to see you again, Mr. De la Vega," Senator Jim Hobart said, extending an aged hand.

"You, too, Senator," De la Vega replied.

The CEO knew most in the room and realized quickly how important the meeting was based on the attendees alone. Retired Four-Star General Henry Tamerius nodded to De la Vega, which he returned. He knew the retired Air Force general had commanded United States Europe Command and served as the Supreme Allied Commander of Europe. To De la Vega's knowledge, he was the most recent individual who had held the post who was also retired. He knew his presence would weigh heavily on the topic of the day's meeting.

War in Europe.

"Gentlemen," Stovall began as he sat comfortably in his chair with one leg draped over his knee. "We know that recent intelligence confirms that a Russian invasion of Ukraine is imminent. To catch De la Vega up to speed, we've been discussing all morning the different avenues to secure military support for Ukraine."

"Which brings up the question as to why he is here," General Tamerius stated, his voice monotonous yet firm.

"As you all know, we cannot put anything in writing until the coming events motivate that action. However, we can pre-deploy deniable assets to combat this threat and give Ukraine a fighting chance," Stovall replied as he turned his gaze toward De la Vega.

Suddenly realizing his employer's intent, De la Vega did his best to hide his surprise.

"You would leverage Red Horse Global to defend Ukraine?" Senator Hobart asked, drawing the eyes of the other lawmakers and consultants.

"In a training and support capacity only," Stovall assured. He returned his attention to De la Vega. "Isn't that right, Diego?"

De la Vega suppressed the anger rising in his chest as he nodded. Just as surprised as the rest of the room, he wondered why Stovall had withheld this information until now. The only reason he could discern was to secure commitment before an audience, an audience powerful enough to force De la Vega to follow through.

"Red Horse Global is always prepared to meet the needs of the nation," De la Vega stated, though he felt utterly deceived.

Since Stovall had informed him of the coming invasion of Ukraine, De la Vega felt he had reached a new confidence with his employer; however, that new standing came with an unexpected manipulation that he just couldn't rationalize. It was not how he himself led men, and he couldn't understand it.

"In what way?" General Tamerius probed.

"Red Horse has the ability, flexibility, and most importantly, the readiness to support Ukrainian forces with command assistance and training," De la Vega answered. "Many of our top-tier personnel have advised generals and battalion commanders in Iraq during GWOT. We would be able to provide the same support as a private military company on contract with the Ukrainian government and thereby providing our government with access while permitting a certain degree of military distance."

"Well said," the general replied.

"And Red Horse personnel are American heroes. Who better to sway public opinion for Ukrainian aid than America's finest?" Stovall added.

So that's the play, De la Vega thought angrily.

"And the risk to your people?" another senator asked.

"We've always been ready to risk everything for the cause of freedom, sir," De la Vega dutifully replied, though it certainly was not a lie.

"It is extremely clever," Senator Hobart admitted, his grin sharp and cunning despite his age.

Stovall appeared smug and satisfied as De la Vega turned his attention toward him. A nod showed his approval of De la Vega's performance, and De la Vega returned it respectfully.

"So," Hobart continued, "Red Horse staff will insert in strategic positions to ensure Ukraine does not crumble under Russia's first wave. That buys the world time to mobilize if necessary, should Russia's actions invoke Article Five. And it will provide our nation with a bit of skin in the game from the start—something for us to continually feed the media with. I do like this plan very much. I've wanted to go toe to toe with the Soviets my entire life."

De la Vega found great irony in Senator Hobart's statement. At his age, he would have had every opportunity to enlist and bring the fight to the Soviets during the Cold War, but De la Vega knew the man had not done so. Distaste manifested on his tongue like bile, but he kept his expression stoic and firm, as expected of a man with his history and capability.

Though the meeting continued to outline strategic objectives in the areas of politics, military response, and propaganda campaigns, De la Vega struggled with his growing anger toward his employer. Had he been briefed ahead of time for what was expected of Red Horse, De la Vega would have done his duty, but this manipulation was something new and unfamiliar.

He did not like it.

Trust is everything.

18

Bucharest, Romania

Stefo Troske sipped his coffee as he rode in the rear passenger seat of the charcoal Mercedes-AMG SUV. He glanced out the window briefly to admire the architecture of the old city.

"I wish Skopje looked like this," he lamented, sighing and shaking his head. He turned to the passenger next to him, who sat with her hands bound in her lap. Her copper hair shimmered with ringlets, and Troske reached to touch her cheek, relishing the memory of her recent nakedness.

Laila Malik pulled away with as much authority and disdain as she could muster, her mind replaying him stripping her and forcibly bathing her by cuffing her to a chair and dumping bucket after bucket of cold water over her. She had endured torture before, but that didn't make it any easier.

"Think of what we could have been, you and I, if you had not left us," Troske lamented with a sinister smile. His dark eyes gazed upon her, falling on her bosom as he licked his lips. He had wanted so desperately to have her but had withheld per the instructions sent out from the higher leadership should Malik be captured.

"There was never a *you and I*," Laila snapped, her bright eyes cutting toward him with fierce anger.

"There could be now," he said, reaching over and dancing his fingers over her breast. Quicker than he could anticipate, Laila shot her right elbow outward while driving her torso in the same direction. Her powerful core twisted at the last minute, slamming her elbow into Troske's face, blood splattering from his nose.

Laila withdrew herself back to her seat and raised her hands, cuffed at the wrists, with her palms facing the front passenger who now trained a pistol on her chest. A stream of curses flowed from Troske's mouth in his native language.

"Are you alright?" the passenger asked his leader, though he didn't take his gaze from his captive.

"Yeah," Troske replied as he sniffed repeatedly while blood drained from his nose and over his leather jacket and pants. He pulled a white handkerchief from his jacket pocket and attempted to stem the flow. He turned to Laila. "You're going to regret that," he sneered.

"Are you going to shoot me again?" Laila snapped.

"Careful, Malik," the front passenger warned, jabbing his suppressed pistol forward with intentional warning.

"He touched me first," she countered, satisfaction curling her lips into a smile. He didn't need to be reminded how lethal she was. She had killed three of their men in Istanbul in nearly as many seconds. The fact that Troske antagonized her did not sit well with him.

In truth, he admired her greatly, and her exploits were well known throughout The Czar's Brotherhood. Even though she had been shot three times—through the shoulder, thigh, and forearm—humiliated, and faced a hopeless situation, she still possessed a fight that he commended. He wondered if he would have the courage to face such direness so well.

"We're here," the driver alerted in his thick accent. Troske cursed again as he wiped his nose, embarrassed at how Laila had so swiftly bested him. He was most angry that he could not retaliate in the way he wished.

Soon, he hoped.

The driver parked along the street, killed the ignition, and stepped from the vehicle before taking in the area around them. Bald with a beard and dressed in a suit, it was clear to all who laid eyes on him that he was not a man of legitimate enterprise. Receiving nods from a few of their men posing as pedestrians, he turned and opened Laila's door before reaching in with a large hand and grabbing her by the left bicep. He roughly pulled her from the vehicle, but not so roughly as to draw attention. Regardless, she got the message: *Don't try anything.*

Laila glanced around the narrow street, taking in the unique blend of Western and Eastern architecture, while seeking an escape route. Her trained eyes easily found the men stationed and posing as bystanders at various points along the avenue.

The driver ushered her around the back of the SUV while keeping a vicelike grip on her arm. Though her green wool overcoat kept her body warm, her face, neck, and ears suffered from the sudden winter cold. However, in less than a minute, she was directed into the lobby of an apartment building that was clearly reserved for the elite earners of the city. Though exhibiting a gilded interior in an Art Deco style, Laila saw none of the beauty, only the exits, as well as additional adversaries watching her as they approached the elevators.

Seeing no outlet, Laila swallowed her fear—though she hid it well—and boarded the elevator with Troske and his men.

Though the ride felt slow—like the passage of age—Laila controlled her breathing and wondered who she would see on the other side of the doors. What advantage could she gain, or what information could she leverage over them? Was it Dolzhikov Ilyich?

They had not found him on the *Anastasia*, so it was possible that he was now in command. However, the Brotherhood was flourishing too well.

Before she could contemplate further, the doors opened, and Laila's eyes widened. Before her stood Sofia Vitori, a woman she had revered and admired, but whose savagery she knew all too well.

"Hello, Laila, welcome home."

19

Invictus Headquarters,
Eastern Shore,
Virginia

Natalie sipped her coffee as she sat in front of her computer. Sitting in the dark, the bright monitor irritated her eyes, and she realized she should have turned on a lamp. But it was early, very early. Her head hurt just slightly, and her body felt off after the night of drinking and celebration. Regardless, she couldn't sleep. She often didn't after too much alcohol. For some reason this morning, she couldn't shake the urge to continue her hunt.

The Shaws' residence—the first of the scheduled buildings to be constructed—sat proudly on a small rise that overlooked the expanse of the property. Turning from her seat, Natalie gazed out the bay windows of their shared home office and took in the westerly view. Though the sun still slumbered underneath the eastern horizon, Natalie could see all the way to the water, her eyes falling on the impressive construction effort that dominated the center of the property approximately two hundred yards west of her home.

She envisioned what the final product would look like: a two-story, concrete structure to serve as the company headquarters, which would house various conference rooms, classrooms, and shared office spaces for the current and future staff. More exciting for her husband, the building would also house an indoor, ventilated shooting range, an expansive armory, a fitness center, and a large garage. The investors and owners had spared no expense in making the main building all they needed it to be.

Next door and connected by a covered walkway would sit the residential dormitory for single staff, which would provide single-occupancy rooms complete with full bathrooms and a kitchenette. A larger community area would host a plethora of activities and amenities such as a movie theater, video game consoles, billiards, darts, ping pong, cold plunge, sauna, and more.

Natalie couldn't believe how far they had come in what seemed like so little time. Their success in bagging el-Shahan and rescuing Sod Buster had only cemented their status as a premier special mission and intelligence provider. She could only imagine the ways in which they would impact the world for the better, and she hoped that what she could conceive, she could achieve.

Taking one last look at the stars and the soft glow of the moon, Natalie spun back around to stare at her computer. She sighed and dove in, attempting to find actionable intelligence on any of her three targets. Vitori was nothing but a ghost, and Natalie began to suspect that the name was an alias. Stovall was the easiest to dig up information on now that she knew what to look for and had cataloged his enterprises into a Rolodex of sorts. Still, she would have a hard time proving his involvement in anything illegal, much less anything that warranted the type of elimination she desired.

The words her husband had spoken in Turkey last fall rang in her mind, *I can't kill those men if I don't know that they're against us*. All her intelligence and experience told her that her three names were against her, but she knew she had to prove it. If two of their colleagues had already tried to kill her, her husband, and had successfully murdered her son, then these remaining three had to be equally as ruthless, evil, and guilty. How could she reconcile it any other way?

After an hour of searching, checking and cross-checking entities, and delving into criminal activities across the globe, searching for any connection, Natalie dropped her head into her hands and quietly grimaced out her frustration. She lowered her hands so that she exposed her eyes while still covering her mouth with her fingers. Taking note of the time, she sighed and dropped her head onto the wooden desk.

I've got to keep going, she told herself, *for my baby boy.*

With a new resolve and a steely green gaze, Natalie leapt back into her dizzying work only to be interrupted by her ringing cell phone minutes later.

"This is way too early," Natalie remarked as she checked the caller ID. She answered and greeted the caller, "Hey, Scott."

"Good, you're up," Lincoln replied, his voice curt. Natalie picked up on his concern immediately.

"What is it?"

"Laila missed her check-in, and we can't get a hold of her," he answered. Natalie rolled her lips inward as she considered the implications. After securing Reza Afshar as an asset, Laila Malik was assigned to keep tabs on him and relay analog data so as to keep his cover intact.

"You don't think she's turned on us, do you?" Natalie asked. She heard Lincoln sigh.

"While it's possible, neither Director Sosa nor I think so based on the video evidence we received. We fear something more sinister," he replied.

"Video evidence? You think Afshar is responsible?"

"We don't know."

"What do you know, Scott?" Natalie asked, her tone indicating her frustration at losing access to her most crucial asset.

"I don't know anything more than I've told you. We've got people looking into it now. Thought you would want to know," he retorted, his tone indicating that Natalie's abrasiveness was unappreciated.

"Sorry," Natalie said, blowing out an exhale.

"Forgiven," Lincoln replied.

"I'll be there in a couple of hours," Natalie added.

"That's not necessary," Lincoln replied.

"I'm coming anyway."

CIA Headquarters,
Langley, Virginia

Scott Lincoln extended a hand in a casual wave as he observed Shaw and Natalie enter through the main entrance. Striding forward to cross the CIA seal emblazoned on the checkered floor, Lincoln gripped Shaw's palm with firm respect before shifting his attention to Natalie.

"Hey, Scott, appreciate you calling," Shaw said, clearly upset at Laila's disappearance.

"Yeah, sorry to be the bearer of bad news," he said as he escorted them toward the turntables.

"Learn anything new?" Natalie asked quickly as she fished out her identification.

"Let's get upstairs first," Lincoln said, his voice hushed. Natalie nodded.

All three swiped their badges and proceeded to the waiting elevators. Shaw couldn't help but think about how normal it had all become to him since his first visit with the late Director James Caldwell.

As they stepped into the elevator, Lincoln waved away a staffer to ensure he and the Shaws would ride alone.

"Is it foul play on Afshar's part?" Natalie asked once the doors closed, her voice woven with fiery anger.

"We don't know. Anything is possible at this point," Lincoln answered.

"Any word on Laila?" Shaw interjected.

"None," came Lincoln's curt reply. Natalie got the message, and despite her eagerness, she resolved to save any additional questions until they could speak more securely. Natalie heard her husband's swift inhale, indicating his own frustration.

The elevator doors chimed open, and Lincoln led the Shaws into a suite they'd been to several times before. Mari Sosa sat at the head of the conference room table while two others, whom Natalie recognized, prepared their reports. Upon their entry, Kara Bivens and Regan Pompeo stood and welcomed the Shaws.

"Good to see you, Kara," Natalie said after embracing the young woman.

"You, too, Natalie. How are you?"

"I'm managing," she replied.

"Mr. Shaw," Regan greeted, offering a hand.

"David's fine," Shaw said as he gripped the younger man's palm. "Good to see you." He turned to Kara and gently shook her hand as well.

"Hi, Mari," Natalie said, moving to embrace the woman.

"Hi, Natalie," Sosa replied, warmly hugging her back. "David," Sosa added, moving her gaze to address Natalie's husband. "Good work on el-Shahan," she said as she offered her hand.

"Thank you, ma'am," Shaw replied, taking her hand in his and offering her a firm pump.

"Now that everyone's here, let's begin," Sosa stated, returning to her seat. Everyone took the cue and directed their attention to the monitor fixed to the wall. "Scott," she urged.

"Yes, ma'am," Lincoln responded. He nodded to Regan, who began the presentation. Standing by the monitor, Lincoln began, "At eighteen-thirty local time, Laila Malik missed her scheduled check-in after planning to meet with Reza Afshar. As you know, she's been working Afshar as an asset on behalf of you guys since last fall, given her knowledge of the city and history with the criminal enterprise Radi was working with. From the surveillance equipment we set up to monitor Afshar's teahouse, these are the events we captured the night we lost contact with her."

With a nod from Lincoln, Regan played the video, and all watched the dark street before seeing Laila enter the establishment after eyeballing two men smoking and laughing at the corner of the house.

"Who are they?" Shaw asked.

"We don't know, we're running their IDs based on the partials," Kara answered. Shaw nodded and turned his attention back to the screen.

"Regan, you can speed it up here," Lincoln instructed.

"I don't like this," Shaw mumbled as he watched the two men, their actions exacerbated by video settings, move to cover the entry. "They look to be running some type of EP detail."

"I thought the same thing," Lincoln confirmed.

Natalie just watched intently, her green eyes narrowed and focused on every action.

Regan, following his timestamp markings, reduced the video to normal speed, and the audience watched as Laila slammed through the door and into the arms of the two men. None spoke as they watched her make short work of her two opponents before taking the life of a third man. She then sprinted out of view as two others bounded through the doorway with weapons drawn.

Shaw exhaled forcefully. While impressed by Laila's brutality and effectiveness, he was still concerned for her. "She's outgunned," he noted, seeing the small carbine one of the two men carried.

"What else do you have?" Natalie asked Lincoln, Sosa, and the team.

"Laila attempted to make contact through secure channels, relaying her authentication, but her contact was not able to converse with her," Lincoln explained. "But we did get this," he added, nodding toward Kara, who played the recording picked up by the phone.

The gunshots popped oddly through the audio, but the dialogue—though faint—came through clearly enough.

"Who is Stefo Troske?" Natalie asked, her eyes darting between the four CIA employees.

"It definitely seems like she knows him," Shaw interjected. Natalie nodded her agreement.

"Regan," Lincoln encouraged.

The next slide showed a portrait of a man in North Macedonian military dress. His subtle smile was a far cry from the scowl on the same face in the adjacent photo of him emerging armed from Afshar's teahouse.

"Stefo Troske," Lincoln continued, glancing down and reading from the file in his hand. "A former officer in the Army of North Macedonia with the Special Operations Regiment. From Laila's work over the last several months, we have a full dossier on him."

"He was one of Rykov's?" Natalie reasoned.

"Yes," Sosa answered, speaking for the first time since watching the video again. Regardless of whether justified or not, she always found it difficult to watch people die.

"So, either this is all a coincidence or The Czar's Brotherhood is still in play," Natalie stated gravely.

"We believe the latter," Sosa replied. Natalie exhaled swiftly through her nose and nodded again.

"You think someone has filled Rykov's shoes?" Shaw asked.

"It's not so hard to believe," Sosa countered.

"With the buildup of Russian forces on Ukraine's borders and in Crimea, we figured we were witnessing the beginning of the fallout Kormann predicted," Shaw said, "the evidence of the chaos Rykov's demise would bring."

"It still may be," Sosa said, "or even factions vying for control of his enterprise."

"That seems the most likely," Natalie said. Shaw chewed his cheek.

"Do you have any idea where Laila is now?"

"We're working on it," Lincoln promised, but that did not comfort Shaw. He looked at his wife, and she met his gaze.

"I'll get on it," she said, seeing the question in his eyes.

"Laila saved us all on that bridge in Zürich," Shaw reminded them, his hard voice filled with conviction. "We owe her everything."

20

Bucharest, Romania

"My dear Stefo, what happened to your nose?" Sofia asked as he emerged from behind Laila. The young man scoffed and cut his eyes toward Laila. Sofia chuckled and shook her head. "Go get cleaned up, and let's get these restraints off our beloved sister."

Directing her attention back at Laila as one of Troke's men freed her hands, Sofia extended a hand, which Laila did not take. Upon seeing Laila's hesitation, Sofia offered her a warm smile and curled her fingers in rapid succession to stress her invitation.

"The Spider of Kandahar, we have much to talk about, and I've called for brunch on the patio. Please join me," Sofia urged, her tone holding a jovial flair that Laila believed deceptive.

Though wary, Laila reached out slowly with her left hand and took hold of Sofia's palm. The two women walked as if old friends toward the open French doors that led to a marble-floored patio decorated with a variety of greenery and sculpted, iron decor.

Aching from her wounds, Laila was grateful to be seated once more. She took subtle notice of the armed security all around, and short of throwing herself off the high balcony onto the street below, she knew she was trapped.

"Champagne?" Sofia offered as she nodded to the attendant to her right, who quickly approached and poured two glasses.

"Thank you," Laila replied, but she did not readily reach for the bubbling crystal.

"Now, I'm sure you have questions, just as I do," Sofia said after setting her glass back on the table. "I've heard troubling rumors." Her voice sounded like a mother chastising a child for an act she found wrong, yet also humorous.

"What rumors?" Laila asked. Her mind flowed with clear direction on how to survive the conversation, but she also reminded herself to glean important intelligence. Sofia smirked at the recognition of Laila's attempt, and both women realized there were no games to be played between them.

"To the point then," Sofia said, her smile shifting slightly. "I've heard rumors that you're working with American intelligence. That you were captured in that audacious raid on Washington, DC and only released after you agreed to a deal."

"That's quite a rumor," Laila replied, keeping her expression stoic.

For a moment, Sofia marveled at how beautiful Laila was as the midday sun graced her freckled face. With tanned, imperfect skin, glowing blue eyes, and a head of curly, long copper hair, she sat in stark contrast to Sofia's sophisticated, mature beauty. There was a childlikeness to Laila that provoked disdain within Sofia, though she knew how lethal the young woman was.

"It's a logical conclusion when you consider that the Americans targeted and killed The Czar, not to mention that mess with Barakat last fall. I believe Reza Afshar had something to do with all of that, and now Brother Troske catches you meeting with him. You must admit that it is all quite curious," Sofia said before reaching for her champagne again.

"The Czar is dead?" Laila asked, convincingly.

"You might fool most, Sister Laila, but you cannot fool me. I'm sure you helped the Americans as part of your deal," Sofia said.

Is that it? Is that why I've been brought here? Laila wondered. She knew the answer to the question might very well be the only reason she still breathed.

"Otakar is dead," Sofia stated. Her plump lips curled into a satisfied smile, but Laila remained expressionless. As a result, Sofia couldn't determine if Laila had known that information or not. It was frustrating, but she knew the conversation wasn't yet over. "Brother Kozár may be dead, but his rogue sect is still causing great problems for us. I could use your unique talents in quelling such opposition," Sofia said. "That's if you're freelancing and not..."

Laila watched as Sofia's eyes suddenly widened, her expression seeming to fall as if her skin had been dragged down by an unseen hand. Laila's eyes narrowed, and her body tensed, curious and alarmed by her host's sudden shift. At that moment, Laila realized that her capture was a sheer coincidence, that none of this was planned. Troske had seized an opportunity presented to him and hadn't yet considered the consequences.

"That is like Stefo, isn't it?" Laila dared to ask. The comment drew sharp and hostile eyes from Sofia. "To not consider the consequences or nuance of a situation."

"So you do work for the CIA," Sofia accused.

"You said it yourself, I'm just freelancing. Trying to survive in this big, scary world," Laila replied, her confidence brewing.

How did I not see this? Sofia thought, scolding herself. *We've broken the very lifeline upon which we depend. Laila was managing Afshar. Of course!*

"A minor setback," Sofia assured Laila, her tone returning to its usual dignity.

"Is it?" Laila dared. Sofia's eyes flashed with anger while Laila's mind raced at Sofia's words. *A setback? I was part of a plan and didn't even know it?*

The reality dawned on her suddenly and frighteningly. Afshar was compromised, and Sofia, somehow, was wielding Afshar to command Invictus International's lethality. Now, because of Troske's carelessness, the chain was broken with Laila's abduction.

"Troske will be disciplined for his oversight," Sofia said quietly, not taking her fierce gaze from Laila. "However, he can hardly be blamed. I have been looking for you after all—Otakar's protégé—and how could we have known that you were the link between Invictus International and Reza Afshar."

"You would willingly admit this to me?" Laila asked.

"There is no hiding what you have already discerned. I can see as much in your eyes," Sofia answered, gambling she would reveal a hint of truth to her assumption.

"What happens now? You should kill me for killing our brothers, as the code demands," Laila said. Sofia's face scrunched in disgust.

"An ancient barbarism. We should not discount opportunity for the sake of traditions that no longer serve us," Sofia replied.

"What opportunity?" Laila asked warily.

Sofia, having regained her composure, simply smiled as she settled deeper into her chair while taking another sip of her champagne. "I owe the Shaws a great debt. Their thirst for vengeance has elevated me to my new station, and now that I see your involvement, the mystery of their success becomes clearer."

Laila didn't know how to respond.

"People think assassinations are easy; Hollywood is to blame for that. They would be right, of course, if the target was an unwitting politician or a paranoid dictator, but you and I both know that those who really control things are not so easily taken. It's why The Czar's and the First Arab's demises are so startling. And now, I have the missing piece to the puzzle sitting before me. How many confirmed kills do you have on your record?"

"I stopped counting a long time ago," Laila replied, her tone icy. However, it had little effect on her host, who merely sighed and drained the rest of her refreshment.

"No matter," Sofia said lightly. "The fact that the Shaws were successful with el-Shahan proves that we had successfully infiltrated their intelligence process. The larger problem with which I am now faced is preventing the Shaws from targeting me for my role—inadvertently as it may be—in abducting you. My allies very much wish to avoid the Shaws' attention, as do I." She paused, searching Laila's expression for any hint that might give an edge or a lead.

"Why are you telling me this?" Laila asked, alarmed that they had been deceived so well.

"I am simply attempting to uncover a mutual benefit for the two of us that does not lead to unnecessary bloodshed," Sofia answered.

"But necessary bloodshed," Laila countered.

"Which is, of course, unavoidable," Sofia replied, smiling again.

"I'm not an assassin anymore," Laila stated, her tone firm. Sofia scoffed before laughing lightly.

"Don't be foolish," Sofia chided. "Ah, here's brunch."

Sofia did not speak as the meal was served. The platters held a variety of quality cold cuts and fine cheeses, thin sausages looped and bound with twine, fried eggs, thick-sliced toast cooked in egg batter and served with jam and butter, but the feast did not stop there. Laila wondered about the excess as the waitstaff placed cabbage rolls, cheesy polenta, seasoned and grilled liver, and braised pork knuckle.

"Please," Sofia offered, motioning over the wide round table. Laila took a slice of toast and placed it on the plate before her, but she did not feel like eating. "Now, how do we rectify this misunderstanding?"

Laila saw that Sofia was relinquishing some power in the conversation, and that made her believe there existed within her a truly healthy fear of the Shaws and the current situation, which Laila viewed as wise.

"I don't see what options are available to me," Laila admitted.

"You could come home," Sofia replied. Laila chewed her lip and looked down. What was home? "You could again shape the world with us, your family."

"Family doesn't shoot each other," Laila said, her voice firm and her wounds burning.

"Truly regretful, but if I recall the tale, you drew first blood," Sofia scolded. "Let me give you your options," she continued, her aura of power returning. "You can do the job I need you to do, return to the fold, and all your transgressions will be forgiven."

"Or?"

"Or we could proceed with justice right now. The choice is yours."

"And if I try to escape?"

"There would technically be nothing stopping you, but should you do that, I will dedicate all my effort into hunting you down, and any protection or courtesy you might enjoy as part of our family would be voided. Is that clear enough?" Sofia answered, her voice as hard as tempered steel.

Laila only nodded.

21

Miami, Florida

"Hey, Zorro, you wanted to see me?" said a casual voice from the office entry. De la Vega looked up from his computer and grinned.

"Yeah, Ricochet, come on in," he replied, standing and moving around his desk to shake hands with the powerfully built man. The two former Special Forces soldiers, both dressed in high-end tailored suits, offered each other a respectful nod. "Can I get you anything? Sparkling Water?" De la Vega asked, motioning for his guest to take a seat on one of the leather sofas in the spacious office suite.

"Yeah, that'd be great," Ricochet replied. De la Vega smiled again and moved to access the mini fridge situated within the lower portion of the bookcase behind his desk. He handed his employee a San Pellegrino before taking a seat on the opposite sofa.

While not the penthouse lounge on the floor above, De la Vega's working office was as nice as they came. With sweeping southward views of Miami and the coast, it hosted an expansive library filled with books on military leadership, history, tactics, and field manuals, alongside many others on business leadership and professional development.

"So, what's this about?" Ricochet asked after smacking his tongue, the crisp refreshment pleasant. Though only in his late forties, his beard was stark white, long, and styled in an impressive outward flair that only appeared to widen an already stout jaw. The two men had known each other for a long, long time, having served together at the start of Operation Iraqi Freedom in the Army's Long-Range Reconnaissance Patrol before making a later move to Special Forces.

"A new assignment. Last-minute thing in Ukraine," De la Vega said, but Ricochet frowned as he noted his employer's expression.

"How last-minute?" he asked.

"Departure is tonight. Oh-nineteen-hundred," De la Vega answered, his voice stoic, serious, and slightly apologetic.

"The missus isn't going to be happy about this," he remarked, rubbing his bald head as his blue eyes fixated on De la Vega's light brown irises.

"Yeah, I know. You're my top choice, Paul, but all you have to do is say the word, and I'll move on to the next."

"Your top choice?" Ricochet remarked with a laugh. "What is this? P.E. dodgeball?" Though he wouldn't admit it, his employer's use of his first name had slightly unnerved him.

De la Vega forced a smile, then glanced down at the metal coffee table separating them. Seeing the reaction, Ricochet's humor departed.

"What kind of op are we talking about here?" he asked, his tone growing serious and concerned.

"Foreign security and training contract," De la Vega answered. Ricochet didn't like the way De la Vega's voice sounded.

"That all? Then what's all the fuss I'm seeing here?" he asked, waving his hand over his own face to indicate De la Vega's evident mood.

De la Vega knew better than to say he had a *feeling* about the assignment from Stovall, though he knew it was likely only because of how manipulated he felt.

"Ah, nothing. Just thinking about how I break it to my wife as well."

"Wait!" Ricochet exclaimed, rocking forward and setting his bottle on the coffee table with slightly too much force. He then looked up and stared at his boss. "*You're* going? You haven't been in the field in, geez, I don't know how many years. What's going on?"

"I've still got it," De la Vega replied curtly, hiding his offense.

"I didn't mean it like that," Ricochet quickly voiced with a chuckle. "Just odd, is all."

"Yeah, but if I'm going, I'd like you and your team to come with," De la Vega said.

Ricochet just stared at him, blinking rapidly as he attempted to discern the situation. He didn't feel any unease around it, but he couldn't deny how weird and unusual the request was.

Maybe I'm just overthinking things here, Ricochet reasoned with himself. "You know you can count on me and my guys," he said, his voice quieting with sincerity.

"That's why I'm asking you."

"Yeah, but if there's anything up with this, you'd tell me, right?" Ricochet asked.

De la Vega sighed and nodded to himself. *Trust is everything*.

"Look, I'm privy to some sensitive information that goes way above my station here," De la Vega began. Ricochet's blue eyes grew intently focused. "We're to assist the Ukrainian military forces with the repulsion of a pending foreign invader. This is sensitive information to the highest degree. Am I clear?"

Ricochet barely heard him, reeling as he was from the news. He suddenly blinked rapidly as he processed the information.

"Wait, wait, wait," he said, throwing up his hands. "You're saying we're going to be helping fight the Russians?"

"I didn't say that. We'll be serving strictly in an advisory and training capacity for public optics," De la Vega replied. The conversation was an uncomfortable one, knowing how Stovall had twisted his arm.

"How did you land this gig?" Ricochet asked.

"There are things happening in the far reaches above me that sometimes dictate the company's actions. This is one of those things," De la Vega explained.

"I don't envy your job, bro," Ricochet stated.

"So, what do you say?"

"Oh man, you had me at fighting Russians. You know how badly I've wanted this? Like literal decades, bro. My old man was MACV-SOG, and you know they tangled with the Soviets," he said, "*Unofficially,* of course," he added, curling his fingers into air quotes.

"Look, this isn't a volunteer thing, but it kind of is. If this doesn't sit well with any of the boys, then they are free to withdraw. There will be no penalties or anything."

"What about bonuses?" Ricochet probed, grinning. De la Vega chuckled and nodded, having expected the question.

"Yes, there will be hazard pay and all the usual expectations with a six-figure bonus upon completion of the assignment."

"Right on," Ricochet said with a grin as he nearly leapt from his seat, extending his hand across his employer's desk. De la Vega stood and gripped the man's palm. "Don't worry, Zorro, I'll make sure you get home safe."

"I have no doubt," De la Vega replied.

"Alright then, I'll get the boys spun up."

22

Bucharest, Romania

Sofia steadied her nerves as muted ringing from the speaker indicated the encrypted signal was attempting its connection. Unsettled as she was from her conversation with Laila Malik and angry at the unexpected turn of events, she believed she had done her best to salvage the situation.

Though she was angry with him, she did not blame Troske for the mishap and the setback. He was following standing orders to bring Laila Malik in just like the rest of The Czar's Brotherhood. No one could have anticipated that Laila was serving as the link between the Shaws and Reza Afshar. The odds were so minuscule that it only infuriated Sofia further. What good was the scope of her intelligence apparatus if they hadn't uncovered that to begin with?

Still, she felt she had stumbled upon an unexpected solution. Sending Laila, who was perhaps the most gifted assassin she had ever worked with, into Kyiv to eliminate her opposition would also provide Stovall a blackmail opportunity to leverage over the CIA. She only hoped he would go for it. The invasion would then commence as planned, and she would, alongside Stovall, nearly double her wealth from NATO intervention. The plan was ambitious, the risks high, but the reward was simply too sweet.

If Stovall could convince his network to enact NATO's Article Five, then the world would change forever, and she and Stovall would be enthroned at the highest level of wealth and power.

The secure video call finally connected, and Sofia smiled warmly, albeit lecherously, at Anderson Stovall, whose expression carried an unexpected annoyance. Sofia dropped her smile and raised her chin just slightly in a display of power.

"Sofia, to what do I owe the pleasure?" he asked, his light blue eyes nothing but professional.

"Our friend in Turkey is compromised," Sofia replied, matching his expression and vocal tone. She was fully capable of ruthless business as well and hoped Stovall hadn't forgotten that fact.

"Is that so?" he asked, his tone shifting toward disappointment and, at the same time, curiosity. "And how did that happen?"

"Our link was severed," Sofia replied. She knew there was no way to fool her colleague, and so there was no point in lying. However, that did not mean she intended to provide a full account with all the details.

"So, Oza is still in play for the time being?"

"Yes," Sofia answered, knowing better than to promise a solution. To do so would be to admit some level of fault in the mishap, something she was not prepared to do. Their professional, as well as intimate, relationship required a delicacy that demanded all her focus. She knew that one slip-up could spell disaster.

"I see," Stovall answered, less than pleased.

As much as she had hoped, giving her body to him had not produced the effect she had desired or anticipated—something she would have to remedy at their next meeting. She needed him wrapped around her finger, and, though she had not underestimated the difficulty of such a task, she had not expected him to be so resistant to her wiles.

"However, I have some good news," she said. She watched as Stovall's eyebrows arched in surprise and interest. Without waiting for his reply, she continued, "I've located a CIA asset that I have leveraged to take care of my problem in Kyiv."

"What of the invasion?" Stovall immediately asked, alarmed slightly. Sofia grinned. She had phrased her statement in such a way as to draw forth that response, reminding Stovall how invested he was in the enterprise she had brought to him. She watched him rein back control and scowl at himself. Every expression was subtle, invisible to the untrained eye, but to Sofia, he might as well have shouted out his frustration.

"Everything will proceed as planned," she said, seeing in Stovall's eyes his quick processing.

"You said a CIA asset?" Stovall pressed, now very much intrigued.

"Yes, I have discovered I possess certain leverage over this individual, leverage I believe will be beneficial to both of us," Sofia replied. She watched Stovall's hand dart to his chin in a contemplative gesture.

"So, the CIA conducts an unsanctioned assassination on prominent Ukrainian leadership ahead of the Russian invasion," Stovall reasoned, grinning.

"Information that might prove rather valuable," Sofia added.

Stovall's grin widened as the fullness of the opportunity unraveled before him.

"And you're confident in this asset?" Stovall asked. "I can't leverage blackmail over the world's most powerful intelligence agency if the...how did you say it? The *link* is severed?"

Sofia's expression hardened into ice as she met Stovall's intentional stare through the video screen.

"Do you need me to spell it out for you?" Sofia asked. Stovall chuckled, and his smirk bore an air of superiority.

"If they call our bluff, it could cause my government to abandon the Ukrainian cause. How does that help?" he questioned.

She could tell he was toying with her, and she found it quite annoying.

"There is no world where the Americans abandon a cause for freedom against the Russians," Sofia stated confidently. She knew that Stovall knew she was right. "This opportunity with the CIA asset allows you to wield the agency as you see fit. The scandal that would erupt from the knowledge that the CIA carried out an assassination on behalf of the Russians would cripple the United States Intelligence Community. To avoid that, they would do whatever you ask, up to and including deploying troops to Ukraine."

"Very clever," Stovall praised, a genuine smile stretching across his lips.

"This is very good work, Sofia. I look forward to celebrating this in person at the first available opportunity."

Perhaps I am making progress, Sofia reasoned after seeing his desire for her.

"Wielding the CIA is a nice consolation prize for no longer being able to wield Invictus as we would like."

She dared not tell him the danger of leveraging Laila Malik. Though she didn't know the full extent of Laila's relationship with Invictus—if any truly existed at all—she knew well the consequences of harming someone for whom the Shaws cared. It was a lesson learned in blood, and both Barakat and Rykov had paid dearly for such an oversight.

I need to find out how close Laila is to them, she thought. She knew that information would provide great clarity as to her next move.

"It does appear to be the greater prize," Sofia replied. Stovall smirked.

"We will see," he countered. "Still, things appear to be coming together nicely. With every increase in our leverage, we take one more step toward our goal."

"I look forward to celebrating with you," Sofia said.

"Likewise."

23

February 22, 2022
Romanian Airspace,
En Route to Kyiv

Laila drew her gaze back from the window as Troske approached with two empty glasses in one hand and a bottle of liquor in the other. Laila eyed the bottle before casting her gaze up toward Troske, who, throwing his arms wide, shrugged and grinned.

"We are still friends, no?"

Laila scoffed and returned her gaze out the window. Not interpreting that as a rejection, Troske took a seat across from Laila and placed the glasses and bottle on the small table between them.

The private jet was filled with luxuries that Laila had been accustomed to while traveling on The Czar's business; however, she never thought she'd be doing so again, especially so soon. The fact that Sofia Vitori had salvaged Rykov's enterprises sat sour on her tongue. It had not been an easy decision to betray The Czar, even more difficult to betray Kozár, but now she felt as if it were all for nothing.

"Hey, no hard feelings," Troske stated as he presented her with a glass filled halfway with the liquor. Laila stared at him long and hard. She only relented when he urged the glass closer toward her. He grinned as she took it from him. "This is Rakija, the spirit of North Macedonia herself," he said proudly as he turned his attention to the bottle. "This label is particularly special as it..."

Laila wasn't listening. She threw back the dram and swallowed the fruity liquor in one gulp. She did relish the immediate calm the alcohol provided before forcefully setting her glass on the table and smacking her tongue in her mouth. She glared at Troske, daring him to question her actions and enjoying the disapproval that stretched across his dark face.

"As I was saying," he began again, disgusted with her lack of appreciation for his culture.

"It's brandy," Laila said with a certain degree of apathy.

"It's not," Troske protested. "It's much more than that, more complex, cultured."

"Whatever," Laila snorted. She couldn't deny the relaxation she felt in her shoulders from the liquor, and she was grateful for the sensation.

"I was hoping we could toast Gregor, Proteo, and Noskov—may they rest in peace," Troske said, his voice edging on anger. Laila sighed.

That stung.

"I'm sorry," Laila finally said. She nodded toward the glass, and Troske eagerly refilled it. She gently raised the glass and said, "To Gregor and Proteo, but Noskov can burn in hell." She threw back the dram just like the last and relished the burn and the additional relaxation it brought.

Troske frowned, scratched the side of his face, and chewed his top lip to calm his rising anger. He glanced up at her, his eyes full of fire. Laila, catching his gaze, pursed her lips in a show of apathy, which sent him over the edge.

"I could have had you, you know!" he hissed, fighting the temptation to do the very same now. He didn't care if his team watched. He'd allow them to have a go when he was done.

"Why didn't you?" Laila dared, her voice cold. Troske rolled his bottom lip inward at the taunt. "You think I haven't endured worse?" she stabbed.

Troske looked away, but he couldn't shake the memory of strapping her naked to that chair and hosing her down in Istanbul before they departed for Romania.

"I want you to understand something very clearly, Stefo," she said, leaning forward. She didn't need the liquid courage but enjoyed its presence nonetheless. "I am going to kill you. Whether it's after we're done in Kyiv or many years from now. I will come for you."

Troske forced a laugh to build his confidence, but Laila's hard stare—those blue eyes that had endured so much in such a short time—unnerved him. He exhaled and took a sip of his Rakija.

"I believe you," he said, thinking that to be the only reply that could give him some leverage or control of the conversation.

The comment had its effect, and Laila relented, exhaling her disdain and frustration with her entire predicament. What did it mean that she would be forced to kill again—contractually, with no emotion or remorse? Could she even do as she had before so willingly, now that the Shaws had shown her a different path? The thought troubled her more than she could admit.

She knew already the main details of her mission—the target, his lack of a standardized routine, anticipated vices—everything provided by Sofia and her own history with the target. After learning all of it, she wondered why Sofia needed her to do this.

There has to be something else at play here, Laila thought. *If I do this, what ramifications will arise that I can't see?* At the same time, she was only twenty-six, and she did not fancy the idea of being hunted for the rest of her life, regardless of how long or short it might be.

Ihor Savych Dudka, she thought to herself, remembering the man. He had been close with Kozár and was perhaps The Czar's most loyal commander—after Dolzhikov Ilyich, whose whereabouts Laila was still uncertain of. She was beginning to think he was dead.

After Dudka came Otakar Kozár, who lay in his grave in the Gulf of Finland, but unlike Dudka, Kozár had betrayed The Czar. If Dudka had known the truth, Laila wondered if he would have joined Kozár in his crusade. She found it humorous how easily men were manipulated, and at the same time, sad, for she knew that was precisely what was happening to her now.

She had never met Dudka, but she had known the name. It was feared for he commanded The Czar's most lethal and capable operators—akin, she knew, to the CIA's Ground Branch or JSOC's Special Mission Units. It was his men who had ambushed them in Zürich after Noskov's failure. Dudka was not a man anyone ever thought about crossing, much less killing. Laila now understood why Sofia was having such difficulty and why he was such a thorn in her side. He would never submit to her leadership when he likely believed the seat belonged to him.

Laila had never cared to meet Dudka, and her skin crawled with merely the thought of carrying out her new mission. She now knew more about him than she ever cared to, and at the end of that information lay either his death or hers.

She knew the game well enough.

24

February 23, 2022
Kyiv, Ukraine

Still dressed in her hunter green overcoat, Laila walked the route she was instructed to meet with the advance elements who had been stationed in the city for weeks. To avoid suspicion, Troske and his small team—what was left of it—followed Laila and observed at a distance or matched her stride for stride on the other side of the busy street, which clamored with autos and people alike.

Her blue eyes, glowing in the rising bloom of an icy dusk, sought out every CCTV camera she could, staring at it just briefly and hoping Troske's team wouldn't notice. In order to avoid being seen getting out of the same car, Troske had mapped out their route using public transportation and walking routes that would bring them to the apartment complex to rendezvous with the advance team.

She stared intently at the last CCTV camera she spotted before turning into a parking lot surrounded by towering apartment buildings constructed of concrete and painted an unflattering light brown. Though the buildings all touched and formed a ring around the parking lot, Laila noticed the color variation, ever so slight, between them, and the difference in balcony design and those that didn't have balconies at all. Industrial air systems ran up each building in wide, silver pipes, and smaller protected electrical wires snaked across the outsides of the buildings.

Typical Eastern Europe, she thought.

She dropped her eyes to locate the target apartment building before glancing back to see Troske pausing for a smoke at the parking lot entry. He looked casual enough, but even without knowing his true purpose, Laila would have singled him out. The Macedonian was good, but not as good as her team had been.

She suddenly frowned as she thought of Gregor—the imposing and faithful Dane, who perhaps even loved her. She had unknowingly led him to his death in Washington, alongside Proteo. She felt strange now being in league with their killers, but she didn't fault Shaw or Wyatt for doing what they had. She was even more grateful not to be dead, as they could have so easily killed her.

Pushing her thoughts aside and hoping her discreet efforts at discovery would pay off, Laila entered the apartment complex's lobby and headed toward the elevators.

Stepping off on the seventh floor, Laila checked the brass placard mounted to the drab wall and turned left toward her final destination. She stopped at the correct apartment number, but before she could knock the signal, the chipped, dark brown door swung open, and a laugh echoed before a form engulfed Laila in a tight hug.

"Laila!" came the high-pitched squeal. "They said they were sending in a team. I didn't know it was yours!"

Reeling from her fight or flight response, Laila relaxed and exhaled a smile as she met the gaze of a longtime friend.

"Hi, Basira. It's good to see you," Laila admitted, though she was concerned Basira's outburst drew too much attention.

"Come in," the young woman bade, nearly dragging her by the arm before shutting the door.

"I didn't know you were here," Laila admitted. Basira shrugged, her long, wavy brown hair bouncing as she did so. Her olive skin and large, honey eyes were embellished by make-up applied better than any professional. Compared to Laila's earthy and imperfect complexion, Basira might be the most beautiful woman she knew. Her eyes were delicately shaped underneath finely manicured dark eyebrows, and her narrow, straight nose drew the eyes pleasantly to a set of full, mauve lips. Though full-figured, she kept a narrow waist, which her high-waisted, belted jeans only accentuated further.

"I didn't know you were coming either, just that Stefo was bringing in a professional. You've been gone for months. Where have you been?" Basira probed, but Laila didn't readily answer, and Basira took the hint. "Later then," she said, whispering.

"Stefo is right behind me," Laila said. Basira rolled her eyes and blew out a long exhale.

"I guess we'll wait for him before introductions," Basira replied as she pulled Laila into the living room. "Look who it is!" she called out. Laila winced as Basira's grip stretched the skin around the stitched gunshot wound on her forearm.

"This is a pleasant surprise," one of the group said. Laila immediately recognized him, though she didn't know him that well. Zdenko Jarak, a tall Croatian, smiled widely at her, his once black beard now sporting patches of gray even though the short and wild black hair on his scalp showed no trace.

Laila knew immediately he was in charge. Jarak held a legend nearly as weighty as her own. "Everyone, may I present to you The Spider of Kandahar," he said, his accent deeper than she remembered.

"Zdenko, it's good to see you," she managed, reminding herself that the Brotherhood still was home for people who might otherwise be considered good.

"Ah, we knew of the orders out for you. I feared something must have happened to you during Kozár's uprising," Jarak admitted. His dark brown eyes appeared almost black as his gaze narrowed on her.

"It's a long story," Laila replied.

"How long?" Jarak asked, intrigued. Laila sighed and glanced at the two others she didn't recognize.

"I'll let you know," she answered. Jarak smirked and nodded.

"Fair enough," he said, catching her meaning.

"Can I get you anything? Tea?" Basira asked. She stood nearly a head taller than Laila, and the Pashtun looked up at her and nodded, forcing a smile.

"Tea would be great," she said. Basira left her side without saying a word and headed to the kitchen.

"When we were told they were sending in someone to assist, I didn't imagine it would be you," Jarak said.

"I didn't know I would be sent," Laila countered. Jarak chuckled again before he turned to his two companions.

"This is Laila Malik, Pashtun by birth, Afghan by nationality, spider by necessity. You're standing in the presence of a legend," Jarak said, his voice carrying a certain reverence Laila found uncomfortable. Then again, she always felt that way concerning praise for killing people. She suddenly longed to eat ice cream in Washington again, perhaps even join in the intramural sports she had seen on the National Mall.

Refusing to look at her hands, Laila kept silent, and Jarak realized the discomfort he caused her. He found it curious.

She's changed, he reasoned, somewhat alarmed.

"You up for this?" he asked her, his tone firmer than before. Laila nodded as she set her determination on her face.

It's this or be hunted the rest of my life, she thought, the reminder unpleasant and grave.

"Good, because Dudka isn't going to go down easy," Jarak added.

"They said that about Naser and Bazzi, too," Laila replied. Jarak's eyes widened slightly.

"That was you?" he asked. Laila nodded, but not with pride. "Well, maybe we can pull this off," Jarak added.

Basira returned with Laila's tea. "Here you are."

"Thanks," Laila replied, taking a sip. It wasn't too hot, and it was filled with the minty fragrance and taste of Basira's home. "This is great," Laila added, enjoying the warmth as it repelled the last of the cold onto which her extremities held.

She had first met Basira Agha on assignment in Baku, Azerbaijan, just over three years ago. From Algeria, Basira had swiftly connected with Laila over their similar pasts. Though not as seasoned despite being a couple of years older, Basira held a respectable catalog of successful assassinations, and it made sense to Laila why she was here. Specializing in seductive avenues, her specialty would have to be explored as an option, but Laila already feared it would be suicide.

The coded knock at the door drew all attention, and Basira, scooping up a suppressed Glock 19 from a small table at the entry, checked through the peephole before opening the door to Troske and his men. The mood in the room instantly soured as all beheld the Macedonian.

What had always comforted Laila about the Brotherhood was that there were some, like Barisa, herself, Gregor, and even perhaps Jarak, who held to a certain code. Then there were others, like Troske, whose moral compass couldn't quite settle in a specific direction.

Perhaps, Laila realized, she only now saw it that way after experiencing another path. Kozár's evil had been revealed to her, but she still mourned the loss of the man, even though he had manipulated her and molded her into the weapon she now was.

"Clock's ticking," Troske stated loudly with a certain air of pride. He smiled as his eyes fell again on Laila. "Legends don't create themselves," he added, a gleam of ambition flashing in his dark eyes.

25

Langley, Virginia

"She's in Kyiv!" Natalie nearly shouted as she burst into Lincoln's office. The loud slam of his door against the wall made him jump as his mind unwillingly leaped back to his near-death on Little Roosevelt Island on the nearby Potomac. He remembered the loud pop before the searing heat through his throat, the sudden difficulty to breathe, the wheezing, the gurgling, the darkness...

He shook his head, and Natalie realized she had startled him in the way one shouldn't startle warfighters.

"I'm sorry," she said quickly and quietly.

"No, it's okay," Lincoln assured her, shaking his head to clear his thoughts. "Laila's in Ukraine?"

"Yes," Natalie answered, racing to his desk and handing him a manila folder piled with warm, recently printed photographs. "Caught her on CCTV. She's not hiding," Natalie added gravely.

Lincoln dragged his bottom teeth over his top lip as he opened the file and met Laila Malik's direct gaze. The unexpected action caught him off guard.

"She's looking directly at the camera," he said. "Man, she looks rough," he added, noting the dark circles under her eyes and the general fatigue plastered across her usually vibrant countenance.

"She's looking directly at all of them on her route to this apartment complex," Natalie said, shuffling through the photos to a map of Kyiv where she had circled Laila's destination. Though annoyed with the action, Lincoln allowed her to proceed.

"Why, though?" he asked. "It doesn't make any sense."

"That's what I thought, too, but look here," Natalie said, sweeping through a series of photographs until she settled on the last one of Laila entering a parking lot. Lincoln observed what looked to be Laila sweeping her hair from her face with the knuckle of a closed fist.

"What?" Lincoln asked. The expression on Laila's face, a hidden plea, concerned him and enraged him at the same time. He looked up at Natalie as he felt her hands move and gazed upon Natalie's outward-facing fist. Her thumb lay against her palm with her fingers curled over it. "What is that?" Lincoln pressed, his voice showing his irritated confusion.

Natalie sighed.

"I'm not surprised you don't know," she said, drawing a scoff from Lincoln as he sat behind his desk holding the photos.

"Enlighten me then," he jabbed.

"It's the international women's signal for distress," Natalie said.

"The what?"

"I'm sure Laura knows about it," Natalie replied with another sigh, referring to Lincoln's wife.

"And Laila knows this?"

"Look, why save the signal for the last camera?" Natalie asked. Lincoln thought for a moment and inhaled as his suspicions grew.

"She's being followed," he said.

"That's my thought as well. Here," she said, pointing to the opening of the parking lot behind the apartment complex. "I think she knew she had cut line of sight just enough to risk the signal. Making eye contact with the cameras was a surefire way to gain our attention. It's clear she isn't hiding, and with her background, she could if she wanted to."

"That makes sense," Lincoln replied, "but I'm sure she could lose a tail. We teach that at Farm on day one."

"I think she's being tailed, but that they're all headed to the same place. I'd wager she has expectations to uphold in order to survive whatever this is," Natalie shared.

"Okay, but why Kyiv?"

"I don't know," she replied. Lincoln reclined in his chair as he chewed his cheek.

"Kyiv is easier to play in than Zürich, that's for sure," Lincoln admitted. "But we need to find out what's going on first. Have you told David yet?"

"Yes," Natalie replied. "You're not giving this op to anyone else," she stated firmly.

"No, I suppose not," Lincoln replied, sighing and shaking his head.

"And that's not all," she said. "Red Horse Global just landed in Kyiv."

Lincoln perked up in surprise. "What for?"

"I don't know, but this has got Anderson Stovall written all over it."

26

February 23, 2022
Sikorsky Kyiv International Airport
Kyiv, Ukraine

As the Gulfstream G6 rolled to a stop in the designated hangar at Kyiv International, De la Vega peered out his window to behold the delegation waiting for them. A host of dark suits finished their side conversations and turned to regard their visitors. Several wore dark green, Ukrainian military uniforms which bore only a conservative number of ribbons and awards, something De la Vega appreciated.

However, his eyes widened briefly as he recognized the Ukrainian President standing among them, his white dress shirt popping from behind a black wool overcoat, dark suit, and navy tie.

“Look alive, boys,” Ricochet called out cooly. “You’re about to meet the President of Ukraine.”

“He’s about to meet some of America’s finest,” De la Vega countered, glancing back from his forward-most seat. Though the youngest among them was late into his thirties, a chorus of excited agreement echoed all around, and De la Vega grinned.

While most on the team wore flannels, jeans, boots, and a variety of differently styled jackets, from leather to wool to waxed cotton, De la Vega maintained his image as CEO, wearing a black polo with Red Horse Global's logo stitched over the breast: a red knight's chess piece towering atop a minimalist globe emblazoned within a black diamond. The phrase, *EX BELLUM, ORDO*, lay inscribed in plain white script on the top left edge of the black diamond: *From War, Order*. De la Vega covered the logo with a black wool peacoat.

The thirteen men—the CEO and the twelve warfighters that made up Operational Detachment-Mustang—disembarked the aircraft, the cold European winter instantly chilling them. De la Vega stepped confidently up to the president with an extended hand.

"Mr. President, it is an honor to meet you and certainly a pleasant surprise," he said.

"Welcome, Mr. De la Vega, to my country. It is an honor to have men of your talents and expertise here with us," the President said. De la Vega smiled.

"The honor is ours. With your permission, my men will offload their equipment."

"Certainly," the President replied, extending a welcoming hand toward several waiting SUVs. "These are yours for your use while you are here. I trust everything will go smoothly for our mutual benefit."

"We're here to assist in whatever way we can," De la Vega assured him, not knowing if the man was aware of an imminent invasion. *He had to be, right?*

"That is good," the President said with a brief grin and even briefer nod. "May I introduce you to General Ihor Dudka. He serves with distinction as the Commander-in-Chief for our entire armed forces."

A man stepped forward wearing a military overcoat and dress cover. He inclined his head and reached forward with a gloved hand.

De la Vega felt the man had the face of a farmer. He was thin, yet fit, with dark eyes that gleamed keen with sharpness and wit. Though he didn't appear overtly dangerous, De la Vega knew how deceptive a seemingly harmless, pensive countenance could be. He'd seen it enough in his own time in the military.

"A pleasure, General," De la Vega said, offering the Ukrainian commander a welcoming smile while he grasped his palm.

"The pleasure is all mine, sir," General Dudka replied in a heavy accent that betrayed the nationality his countenance appeared to conceal. After a single pump, the two men released their greeting, and De la Vega returned his attention to the Ukrainian President.

"Given the nature of your contract to assess and advise on the readiness of our Special Operations, the General will accompany you throughout the duration of your work and stay," the President stated.

"That's excellent," De la Vega said. "Mr. President, I'm sure you've heard the rumors as well as seen the intelligence concerns presented by my government in regards to a potential Russian invasion," he dared to add, watching the President's expression sour with each word.

"Mr. De la Vega, the Russians invaded years ago."

"I'm not talking about Crimea," De la Vega interjected, hoping his credibility would draw grace from the leader. Correct in his assessment, De la Vega watched the President chuckle before rubbing his lightly bearded chin.

"Not all of us are protected by oceans," he countered.

"I have it on good authority that invasion is imminent," De la Vega repeated, adding additional weight to his voice. The Ukrainian President nodded several times as his lips pressed tightly together in what De la Vega could only discern as annoyance.

"Then it is good you are here to assess our readiness to respond to such an *imminent* threat," the President replied before he turned to General Dudka. "General, I leave our guests in your capable hands."

"Yes, sir," General Dudka replied, his tone brisk yet holding obvious weight.

After exchanging pleasantries with the other Ukrainian officials in attendance, De la Vega ordered his men to offload their gear into the waiting column of SUVs while General Dudka and his various aides waited for them in the warm interiors.

Ricochet slammed the rear door of the middle SUV closed and moved to De la Vega's side as he prepared to enter the SUV.

"If you wouldn't mind," General Dudka stated softly, motioning his chin toward Ricochet. De la Vega understood his meaning and leaned to whisper to his employee.

"I get it," Ricochet replied dutifully, though he didn't like being excluded. De la Vega smirked and patted him on the shoulder as he moved rearward to take a seat in the trailing vehicle.

As De la Vega closed the door and turned to face General Dudka, the man's overtly stern expression gave him pause. It was a look he had seen countless times during the length of his military and defense contracting careers.

"Mr. De la Vega, what can you tell me about this invasion?"

Laila Malik, seated just behind Troske astride a black Honda CB1000 Hornet SP motorcycle, had swapped her wool overcoat for a black leather riding jacket, black jeans, and dark boots. Through the open visor of her black, full-coverage motorcycle helmet, she peered over Troske's shoulder. With a black backpack strapped across her back and a black duffel slung at her side, she waited for visual confirmation of her target.

The hasty operation was one of opportunity, and though rudimentary, it provided a quick solution and one that the different members of the team had conducted countless times on separate operations. It was even a method the CIA had used on several occasions, though they would never admit their sources or methods. Having worked in the underworld as long as she had, Laila knew the subtle difference in methods between criminal and state actors, regardless of how minuscule.

"Target is moving," came a voice in her ear. She knew better than to look at the rooftop to the north where her overwatch kept eyes on the meeting.

"Do we know why they are here?" Laila asked as she settled her weight on the bike, trying to keep as much distance between her groin and Troske's rear as possible.

"Don't be afraid to slide up nice and close," he muttered. Laila sharply inhaled her frustration before violently thrusting her hips forward into him. The unexpected action smashed Troske's testicles between his pelvis and the rear of the raised gas tank. Troske grunted as the agony surged from his groin.

"That close enough?" Laila replied, taking great satisfaction in his pain. He dropped his helmeted head onto the handlebars and cursed repeatedly until the sickening pain subsided.

"Looks like they were meeting a new arrival," Basira answered as she continued to peer through the high-powered spotting scope from her elevated perch several hundred meters away.

"Any identifiers?" Laila asked.

"The tail has a logo. Looks like a red knight chess piece against a black diamond. Sound familiar?" Basira asked.

"Yeah, I know of them," Laila huffed.

"I don't like the sound of that. Are they going to be a problem?"

"Maybe," Laila said.

"Who are they?" Zdenko Jarak asked, his concern sounding more like anger.

"Red Horse Global. They're American paramilitary."

"That doesn't sound like coincidence," Basira said.

"No, it doesn't," Jarak agreed.

"It doesn't change anything," Troske cut in, his voice sounding strained. Laila watched him raise his torso off the bike and back into a full seated position. She imagined his anger, but she didn't care. He activated the ignition and, without much fanfare, the engine whined to life before dropping into a shallow rumble.

"Okay, well, the target is in the third car of the second column, rear seat, driver's side," Basira shared.

"Copy," Laila replied as Troske directed their motorcycle through traffic, following casually so as not to arouse suspicion.

"Forward team is in position," Basira noted.

"We'll have eyes in the sky once they exit the airport's restricted airspace," came Jarak's addition. "Let's keep this tight. This is our only opportunity before the invasion begins."

"Understood," Laila replied.

"Let's not mess this up, Laila," Troske added, not turning back to regard her.

"You worry about yourself," she retorted with just enough annoyance to make him scowl.

"My life's not on the line here."

Basira frowned upon hearing that statement.

"Cut the chatter," Jarak interjected, equally concerned, but not showing as much in his vocal inflection. If anything, he sounded agitated. Whether that was for Laila's sake or for the talk unrelated to the operation, Basira wasn't sure.

"We're in pursuit," Laila said after Troske cleared their present traffic pattern and fell in some distance behind the target convoy.

"Very good," Jarak replied. "Hold your course."

Laila inhaled deeply as she prepared herself for the task ahead. She had volunteered for the kinetic element to ensure she had the utmost control over the outcome. If she did it, she knew there would be no mistakes, and she couldn't afford to chance the outcome on another teammate's ability. To her surprise, Troske had readily agreed and supported her candidacy, though he had offered to drive the bike. She had protested at first, believing it easier for one person to disappear than two, but he had the final say.

"Drone is tracking," Jarak notified. "We have target lock on the third SUV. Good work, Agha."

"My pleasure," Basira said as she began packing up her position, having lost sight of the convoy in the tight city streets.

"Forward team, the target is en route to your position. Stand by," Jarak said.

Laila unslung the small duffel bag from around her shoulders and rotated the bag to the orientation she desired.

Then, she took a deep breath.

27

General Dudka, the Commander-in-Chief of all Ukrainian armed forces, stared at De la Vega as he waited for the American to answer his question. It was a question of great breadth, Dudka knew, and invasion was not news to him. As De la Vega's expression grew even more serious—the lines on his face deepening as he prepared to answer—Dudka smirked, twisting his mouth toward the left side of his face, before looking down at his lap. The action confused De la Vega and gave him pause.

"Red Horse Global is an asset of Anderson Stovall, no?" the general suddenly asked.

De la Vega fought to hide his surprise, but he failed, and the Ukrainian commander chuckled again. De la Vega glanced at the driver and the aide in the passenger seat in front of him, but Dudka waved his hand.

"Do not worry about them. They have been thoroughly vetted," he said. "You claimed invasion was imminent, and unlike our President, I know the deeper things of how the world works, and such tidings are not to be taken lightly given recent events."

"What recent events?" De la Vega asked. The SUV felt as if the interior was shrinking. *What has Stovall gotten me into?* he thought.

"I shouldn't expect you to know or perhaps even care," Dudka replied, "but I do suspect, since you are in Stovall's employ—despite however far removed you may be—that you have vital information regarding this invasion."

Now, De la Vega truly did not know where to begin or even how. Though still furious with his employer, he was a loyal man, and therefore, he had no intention of betraying any trust Stovall placed in him.

Trust. De la Vega mulled over that word before he sighed and dragged his hand down his face.

"Take your time," Dudka encouraged, seeing the turmoil within the CEO.

De la Vega thought of the only question he felt he could ask. One that would give him insight without compromising his employer, and one that just might reveal Dudka's intentions and allegiances. He thought of his lunch with Natalie Shaw, and her words came screaming back to his memory: *What if I told you that Stovall is complicit in a global conspiracy that extends beyond national borders?*

He remembered clearly his own reply: *I'd believe you.*

With another deep inhale, he turned his gaze toward Dudka and asked, "General, do you know of a Sofia Vitori?"

Laughter bellowed from the reserved man and startled De la Vega. He watched in bewilderment as the general slapped his thigh several times through his laughter. It was odd, and De la Vega felt odd, unnerved even.

"Everything makes so much more sense now," he finally said. As quickly as laughter had burst from his lips, they flattened into serious stoicism. "Yes, I know Ms. Vitori. She and I were once colleagues."

"She was Ukrainian military?" De la Vega asked.

"No," the general curtly replied. "I believe she is Italian, but I'm not sure, perhaps Slovenian. I suppose that is more likely given her draw to the Brotherhood."

"The Brotherhood?"

"Yes," the general replied.

"What are you talking about?" De la Vega asked, wary now for his own safety. Not from Dudka, but the kind of danger that emerges when one knows too much about something they shouldn't.

"Because you are here, and not here by accident. In truth, I had hoped that you would be more informed. In hindsight, perhaps it would have been better had I not said anything, but alas, here we are, and I need answers."

"About the invasion," De la Vega reasoned. Dudka nodded gravely. "I hate to disappoint you, sir, but I have no actionable intelligence other than I've been assured it is coming."

"And coming soon at that," Dudka replied.

"How do you know?"

"Because you are here. Ms. Vitori has made several attempts on my life, and she now controls what is likely the most dangerous criminal and intelligence enterprise in the history of the world, rivaling your CIA," Dudka explained.

"This Brotherhood, you said you were a part of it," De la Vega countered, realizing he was sitting next to a criminal.

"I *am* a part of it. Do not think your own nation does not have its like."

"Stovall," De la Vega muttered.

"Precisely," Dudka confirmed.

Alarm echoed through De la Vega's mind as he processed the severity of this information. Having Natalie's accusation, Stovall's manipulation, and now Dudka's confirmation, De la Vega's world spun, and he felt his bile churning uncomfortably in his stomach. His anger against his employer soared to new heights at the realization that he was simply a pawn in Stovall's game.

"What is his goal?" De la Vega dared to ask.

"Stovall's? To rule the world," Dudka replied as if the answer was common knowledge.

"And Vitori's?"

"The same."

"And yours?" De la Vega asked, his eyes cold and hard as they bored into the general's, but Dudka only smirked. De la Vega ground his teeth as he fought through his rage. "What if I told you that Stovall and Vitori are potentially in league, that this invasion might be their doing for the sake of profit and enterprise?"

"I would not be surprised," Dudka replied. "It is the only explanation that fits the narrative."

"What narrative?"

"The Czar is dead. The First Arab has joined him," Dudka answered. "When men such as these are killed, chaos fills the void until a new party can take the mantle."

"By force," De la Vega stated.

"Yes, most often, but this is different. Something like this has not happened for centuries, not since Napoleon, I think. The power vacuum is far larger than ever before, and the calamity could destroy the world as we know it."

"You said *killed*. Kill by who?"

"Have you heard of David Shaw?"

It was now De la Vega's turn to laugh as all became clear. He shook his head and exhaled his disbelief.

"Last year. The raid in the Gulf of Finland. That was your Czar."

"Yes," Dudka replied. "And now Vitori has taken his mantle, a mantle that should have gone to me."

"Why?"

"Because I would have brought order and strength, not this chaos. Not war. Never war."

Before De la Vega could reply, he noticed the SUV had come to a stop. He looked through the windshield but only saw the stopped vehicle in front of them.

"What is it?" Dudka asked his driver.

"I don't know," the man replied in English for their guest's sake. He scooped up the handheld radio on the dash and called out in Ukrainian. The reply quickly reported back.

"Well?"

"There's been an accident just ahead," the driver answered.

A flash of black to his left, beyond the general's window, drew De la Vega's attention. He watched a motorcycle lurch to a quick stop. The rear passenger dropped a bag on the roof, producing an unusually heavy thud, before the motorcycle sped away.

Stressed voices echoed from the radio mounted on the dashboard as a wide-eyed De la Vega sprang toward the general. Seizing his shoulder and jacket, De la Vega wrenched him onto his lap before reaching for the door handle and throwing his weight into the door.

"IED!" he shouted as he fell outside the SUV, pulling the general with him.

The ensuing explosion erupted upward with impressive force, shattering the windows of the buildings on each side of the road and rocketing dust off the concrete buildings as fiery black smoke coiled into the air, rising high above the rooftops.

As illuminating lampposts heralded the coming evening, Laila gripped the bag tightly while Troske rolled slowly forward amidst the city traffic. Tall buildings rose on either side of the street, and people began to fill the sidewalks as their workdays ended. Laila glanced left and right, taking count of the number of pedestrians and praying for their safety as her fingers strengthened their grip on the nylon duffel.

"Forward team, execute," came Jarak's command.

At the intersection ahead, the Škoda Octavia sedan lurched forward from its street parking to make the light before slamming into a random vehicle and blocking traffic in the intersection. Troske slowed the bike to a stop, angled the wheel left, and braced the weight of the bike with his left foot while waiting for Jarak's orders.

"Command, forward team, green light," the sedan driver said, his voice shaky.

"Copy, forward team. Kinetic element is a go. Execute," Jarak echoed in the entire team's earpieces.

Laila squeezed the bike tightly with her legs as Troske gunned the throttle and surged into the empty lane now blocked by the staged accident. With no oncoming traffic, Troske and Laila sped forward rapidly to clear the cars in between them and the convoy. Counting up three SUVs, Troske hit the brakes hard, which lifted the back wheel off the pavement enough to provide Laila with the height clearance to drop the bag onto the roof of the SUV over General Dudka's seat.

As the rear wheel returned to the road, Laila slapped Troske's shoulder twice. Receiving the signal, he gunned the throttle again, accelerating rapidly toward the intersection before weaving around the wreck. Once back onto the right side of the street, he punched the motorcycle into a higher gear.

As they crossed the intersection, Laila glanced backward just as the explosive over the SUV detonated, its blast surging skyward. The shockwave, minor as far as explosions go, swept toward them, and Laila felt the sudden force roll over her back and press her into Troske. As quickly as it had come, the sensation vanished, and screams and echoing car alarms followed in a chaotic cacophony.

I don't know how to give you a bigger signal to follow, Natalie, she thought.

Troske piloted the bike into a privately-owned underground garage not far away and specifically chosen for its lack of video surveillance and security. The two ditched their vehicle and stripped their helmets and jackets as they moved back toward the entrance. In a matter of seconds, Laila appeared on the street with her red, curly hair bouncing around her shoulders and over the high collar of the dark green overcoat she had retrieved from her backpack. Troske now wore his signature brown leather jacket.

They mirrored the activity around them, donning fearful expressions, while joining crowds of pedestrians fleeing northward.

28

Langley, Virginia

Natalie frowned, and Lincoln sighed as they waited for Mari Sosa's response to the video circling the world of the explosion in Kyiv, Ukraine. After Lincoln's sigh, a dreadful hush fell on the conference room until Natalie broke the silence.

"There's a C-17 at Andrews preparing a flight for Germany. I've got a detour order drafted and ready for it to take us to Kyiv. I just need your signature," she said. Sosa only nodded, and slowly at that, causing Natalie to cut her eyes toward Lincoln, who met her stare with grave concern.

"Are you telling me that Laila Malik conducted this attack?" Sosa asked. Her voice held a sternness that teetered on the brink of anger, and Natalie knew the internal battle that waged within the Deputy Director of Operations.

"This wasn't an attack," Natalie corrected, "but a message." Lincoln again sighed and scratched his cheek.

"This is bad, Natalie," Lincoln cut in. "You can't spin this differently." He directed his gaze to his boss and said, "Yes, we believe it was Laila."

Sosa nodded again and finally broke her gaze from the monitor mounted to the wall at the end of the long, empty conference table. The stark Virginia sky flowed in brightly from the tall windows behind Lincoln, silhouetting his broad shoulders. Finally, Sosa looked at Natalie.

"You have two minutes, Mrs. Shaw."

Natalie, in full control of the monitor, replayed the video in slow motion.

"Look at the denotation," she began, her voice crisp and eager. "The majority of the blast is directed upward and away from the intended target. Look here," she continued, pacing quickly toward the monitor. "See this?" she added, pointing to a portion of the explosion as it erupted frame by frame.

"What are you pointing at?" Sosa asked, not seeing whatever Natalie was pointing to.

Lincoln suddenly chuckled when he recognized it.

"It's molten slag," Natalie answered excitedly. "The bomb was placed upside down on the target. This should have cut through the roof of the vehicle and killed the target, but instead, the blast and slag were directed upward and away, ultimately causing little damage."

"Could she have made a mistake?" Sosa asked, but Natalie was already shaking her head. "Scott?" Sosa queried, turning to face her associate director.

"While it's possible," he answered, "I don't think it's likely. Not Laila."

"What of the intended target? Did they survive?" she asked.

"Yes, with only minor injuries," Natalie answered. "General Ihor Savych Dudka, the Ukrainian commander-in-chief."

"Why would Laila do this?"

"Maybe she's working on behalf of the Russians. After all, Rykov was Russian. If it's his network that has her doing this—knowing as we do that their allegiance leaned toward Russia—it's not hard to draw a larger motive here. We've been warning the Ukrainians for months now of a credible invasion threat," Lincoln suggested.

"I don't think that's the case," Natalie stated. "Though I do believe invasion is imminent. As I said, I believe it's a message. She's under duress, and she's doing what she can to control the situation. If she wanted Dudka dead, he would be. She lit a beacon using what she had at her disposal, and we've been tracking her since."

"I thought we were already tracking her?"

"She couldn't have known we were. We have no way to contact her, and regardless, she's still in the situation she's in," Natalie explained. "Also, there's more. Much more," Natalie added, aware of the timeframe Sosa had given her.

"Continue," the director said, clearly intrigued though still troubled.

"General Dudka wasn't alone in the vehicle," Natalie began again. "The CEO of Red Horse Global was with him, and it looks like he was the one who pulled the general away from the explosion."

"De la Vega?" Lincoln pressed, astonished.

"Yes," Natalie answered. "As far as why? I don't know yet, but I believe Anderson Stovall has something to do with all of this."

"Explain," Sosa ordered sharply.

Natalie proceeded to share all she had collected and unearthed about Stovall's enterprises, his control over defense companies through various trusts, venture capital, and holding companies. She briefly detailed her recent interactions with Diego de la Vega, who all but confirmed knowing Stovall personally.

"War is no longer a catastrophe to be avoided. It's an enterprise to be exploited," Natalie said gravely.

Sosa chewed on her words as she gazed at the frozen video of the explosion. She curled her fingers into her palm repeatedly as she thought.

"I wouldn't have believed you a year ago," she admitted, dropping her hand to the table and looking up at Natalie. "Still, we have an Agency asset who just conducted an assassination attempt on an allied nation's highest military commander. If word of this gets out, I'm afraid of the damage it could cause. We've had enough of that in the last year, and we're still not even close to getting ahead of it."

"I understand, but what makes Dudka a target?" Natalie asked. Sosa and Lincoln hadn't yet thought to ask the question. Seeing their expressions, Natalie continued, "We know that Troske kidnapped Laila in Istanbul after a scheduled meeting with Reza Afshar. We know that he knew Laila, which suggests he was part of Rykov's enterprise with her. I believe Laila was put to this assignment against her will by a remnant of Rykov's cabal. So, either the cabal is working on behalf of the Russians to eliminate key obstacles to their invasion plans, or there's conflict in the vacuum."

"What?" Sosa asked, but Lincoln chuckled again.

"Now that makes more sense," he said. Sosa glanced at him, then back to Natalie.

"Rykov's death left a vacuum, and we were warned that that vacuum would cause conflict we couldn't imagine. Kormann referenced World Wars One and Two as examples. Similar to how ISIS rose to power in Iraq and Syria," Natalie explained.

"Okay," Sosa said, the word long and drawn out as she tried to grasp what Natalie was saying.

"I think the more likely scenario is that Dudka is one of the parties vying for power in this vacuum. I think if the Kremlin wanted him dead, they would have used more traditional means. This is different. This is not subtle. The former KGB men in power now would not want to draw this much attention.

"But a rival who needs to eliminate an opposing threat to one of the most coveted seats of power in the world would certainly employ a skilled assassin like Laila to achieve their goals and do so with flair as a warning to anyone else thinking of resisting the new regime," Natalie finished.

"That is compelling," Sosa agreed, bewildered and in awe of Natalie's capacity and thoroughness yet again. "Who then is the other party?"

"I believe it is a woman named Sofia Vitori," Natalie answered.

"And who is she?"

"I don't know yet. I've not been able to find out anything about her, just traces," Natalie answered.

"Just like Rykov," Lincoln noted.

"And Barakat," Natalie added.

"How do you know about this Sofia Vitori?"

"A trusted informant who is no longer with us," Natalie answered. Lincoln eyed her suspiciously as he attempted to hide the smile playing at the corner of his lips. "Based on his information, she may have already filled Rykov's seat at the table."

"And you think Dudka was perhaps the last remaining holdout opposing her," Sosa reasoned.

"I do," Natalie replied.

"And only Laila can confirm any of this," Sosa said with a sense of finality. She sighed and rubbed her forehead. "Why would this Anderson Stovall want to start a war between Ukraine and Russia?"

"I believe, that in this vacuum, powerful parties are attempting to take advantage of an unprecedented opportunity. I know that Stovall and Rykov sat at the same table. The power struggle has been disrupted with Rykov's death, and Stovall is likely aiming to broaden his reach," Natalie answered.

"That still doesn't answer the question," Sosa replied.

Natalie looked at her, pressing her lips flat as she weighed her response before saying, "Stovall *is* the United States military industrial complex. If he can get NATO to invoke Article Five, the wealth coming his way could be unfathomable."

"That very well may be the case, and if that's the case, it's not in our wheelhouse to do anything about it. Our Agency alone has a history of doing similar," Sosa admitted, as much as she hated to.

"You're right, but it *is* my wheelhouse, and like Rykov, Radi, and Barakat, I intend to do something about it," Natalie stated boldly.

"What do you want us to do?"

"Give me room to play."

Sosa stared at her for a long moment before nodding, her brown eyes filled with trust. She had earned it.

"Fine. Specifics."

"I want an MQ-9 out of Câmpia Turzii Air Base in Romania over Kyiv, and I want my team deployed to Kyiv on this C-17 to get Laila out of there."

"Done." Sosa turned to Lincoln. "Scott, see to it." She turned back to Natalie and received the document she held out for her, quickly scribbling her signature and handing it back.

"Ukraine isn't going to welcome a drone over their skies," Lincoln countered.

"It flies at 50,000 feet and has some of the best stealth technology in the world. I don't think it will be a problem," Natalie countered.

"But best not test diplomatic relations. We'll claim it's in support of the Red Horse contract," Sosa explained. "It will have to go in without munitions, though. I'll alert our personnel at the embassy of the situation and see what intelligence or support they can offer."

Natalie blew out her displeasure at the statement but agreed.

"I don't want to be that guy," Lincoln began, "but this is a lot for someone who isn't an American citizen. I get that we need to protect sources and methods, of which she knows plenty, but we've done far less for our own..."

"We owe her, Scott," Natalie snapped. Lincoln looked away, scratching his temple with one finger.

"I got this pushed through," Sosa said, sliding a folder toward Lincoln. He looked at it, perplexed, before he scooped it up. Opening it, he chuckled his disbelief.

"Well, this certainly changes things."

"What?" Natalie asked.

"Turns out, Laila might be our newest citizen," he said, turning the folder around and showing Natalie a State Department Certificate of Citizenship. The slight closed-mouth smile on Laila's face brought a grin to Natalie's lips.

"That clear things up for you, Scott?" Sosa said, a tad condescendingly.

"Yeah, I'm good. Let's get her out of there. Natalie, you sure you can get that bird to Kyiv squared away for us?"

"Us?" Natalie echoed.

"You didn't think I wouldn't go, did you?" he retorted, almost offended.

"Never doubted you," Natalie scoffed.

"Right. When are we leaving?"

"Three hours," Natalie answered.

"Can your boys be ready by then?" Lincoln asked, raising an eyebrow.

"My boys are always ready."

29

Laila cautiously entered the apartment lobby, but not before risking a peek at the security camera that covered the front door. Her eyes were pleading, and she hoped Natalie could decipher accurately all that was happening around her.

"Come on, quick!" Troske urged, nearly pushing her inside.

The two made their way to the apartment on the upper floor and, after issuing the correct knocking sequence, were allowed inside. Laila immediately pulled the earpiece from her ear and relished the vanishing irritation.

"Mission success!" Troske called, exuberant and suddenly more relaxed upon entering the sanctuary. He knew they would need to vacate the city as quickly as possible, but he never passed up a moment for celebration for a job well done.

As he strode to the kitchen to regroup with his two men and grab a drink, Laila moved toward Jarak and Basira, who stood together, watching Laila with concerned eyes.

"Any word?" Laila asked, pretending not to notice their disapproving stares.

"Why did you do it?" Jarak asked quietly, his voice a faint whisper filled with disappointment and condemnation.

"Do what?" Laila asked, feigning ignorance.

"Laila," Basira pleaded. Laila shook her head and willed her eyes to show confusion.

"Is the target alive?" she asked. Jarak gripped her arm tightly, and she didn't dare fight him, which might alert Troske.

"You placed the bomb upside down," he accused.

"What?" Laila retorted, blinking her eyes in offense.

"Let her go, Zdenko," Basira said quietly. With a scowl, Jarak dropped his hand.

"Do you not think Vitori will notice?" he hissed. "Did you consider how this might affect the rest of us?"

"Hey!" Troske called from the kitchen, "what is it?" His voice was light and euphoric as he reveled in his success.

Jarak glanced at Laila and saw the pleading in her blue eyes.

"Nothing," Jarak scowled, turning away. Troske's brow furrowed, and his lips pursed in consideration. He set his freshly opened beer on the kitchen table before he passed through the small archway into the living room, the old shag carpet muffling his footsteps as he left the tiled kitchen.

"Doesn't look like nothing," he pressed, licking his lips.

"Well, it is," Jarak shot back, but Laila knew right then that he had messed up.

"Come on," Troske said, his voice smooth and cool. Laila knew him well enough to see the gleam in his eyes. "We're all family here. Tell us." He shifted his gaze from Jarak to Basira, and she quickly looked away. Troske scoffed and ran his tongue over his front teeth. Laila saw the offense flash across his face. Troske's eyebrows furrowed deeper when no one answered him. He turned back to his men. They met his look with a shrug; having executed the wreck, they didn't know any more than he did. They had seen the explosion, had run like everyone else, and had assumed mission success.

Now deeply suspicious and angry, Troske strode over to the drone operator—a man named Tsikhamir Lojka from Belarus—and ordered him to show the feed. Lojka glanced at Jarak, who only inhaled as the situation grew more dire.

"Show me!" Troske roared. The small-framed man complied immediately, and Troske viewed the recording, his fingernails clawing into the wooden table as he watched the explosion rip upwards. He spun around, jittering with fury as his eyes fell on Laila. “What did you do?” he hissed.

“I did as I was told,” she snapped back, raising her chin in defiance. Troske’s eyes grew wide with rage, and his jaw slid sideways so as to misalign with his skull, creating a ghoulish image of insanity as he exposed his bottom teeth.

“Easy, Stefo,” Jarak said, but Troske received the words as a threat, causing him to laugh. He never took his eyes off Laila.

“You placed the bomb upside down,” he accused.

“I didn’t know,” she began.

“*Sranje!*” Troske shouted, cursing in his native language and calling her bluff at the same time. Laila remained as steady as stone as Troske raged before her. He jabbed a finger toward her while stomping forward. “Why?” he roared.

Both of Troske’s men lingered in the kitchen, but they too had put down their drinks, their hands gripping the openings of their jackets as they watched the encounter unfold before them.

“As you said, Stefo, we are all family here,” Jarak interjected.

“Don’t!” Troske growled, shifting his finger toward the seasoned operative. Jarak gritted his teeth in response, his beard hiding the act. Troske spun back toward Laila.

“Why?” he demanded of her again.

“I made a mistake,” Laila replied, trying to disguise her anger as fear, but Troske shook his head without taking his hard eyes off her.

“The Spider of Kandahar doesn’t make mistakes,” he retorted. He watched as Laila’s expression hardened into iron, and for a moment, he felt afraid before his anger reclaimed control.

“No more lies,” Laila said boldly.

“No...” Troske replied, shocked and bewildered. The sudden realization short-circuited his restraint. “Traitor!” he growled as he reached for the pistol hidden in a holster under his jacket.

But Laila sprang forward, covering the distance between them with blinding speed. She leaped upward, leading with her left knee before shifting her hips mid-flight and driving her trailing knee forward into Troske’s face. The flying knee slammed into a quick guard Troske had thrown up, though not entirely in time. As she came down, Laila smashed her elbow into the crown of Troske's head, and a jolt of numbness raced up her forearm and tingled in her fingers.

Troske's eyes pressed closed, and a grimace passed between his gritted teeth as his brain rattled painfully in his skull. He stumbled backwards, and then the room erupted into chaos. Troske caught and reoriented himself as he collided into the sheetrock behind him, denting it inward. However, Laila was upon him, delivering blow after blow as she sought an opening.

As Troske endured the onslaught, putting up an impressive defense while he sought his own advantage, his men, pistols drawn, advanced toward Laila.

"Don't! Drop them!" Basira ordered, her own pistol raised and pointed at the two men. Troske's men paused, glanced at each other, then to Troske and Laila before returning their gaze to Basira.

"Laila, stop!" Jarak cried, but she refused to withdraw, and he dared not move forward between Basira and Troske's men. He knew if he didn't regain control of the situation, Vitori would have his head.

Dipping and striking, Laila knew she couldn't keep Troske at bay for long. She had tried to end it quickly, but he was fast and his defense too well constructed. For a moment, she thought of making a run for the door, but she knew if she relinquished her assault even for a moment, he might shoot her.

"Do something!" Troske roared to his men as Laila's quick, sharp blows continued to daze and frustrate him while he tried to grapple her. With that order, the two men committed forward. One turned on Basira, the other on Laila.

In a split second, Basira had to choose. She adjusted her aim and fired several times. The bullets caught the man advancing toward Laila in the side, and he stumbled into the wall, but before she could transition her sights, Troske's other goon engaged. His pistol barked loudly and sharply as it sent its payload hurtling toward Basira.

She screamed as the rounds punched into her body, and she crumpled to the ground with frightening speed. The gunfire made everyone jump and shout in alarm, their ears ringing with startling pain. Laila's flow faltered, and she blinked rapidly to fight off the agony in her ears.

Troske, not expecting the gunfire, lurched and turned his back toward the sounds as he appeared to skip away from the noise, all the while reaching for his own weapon.

Jarak let out an enraged howl as he charged the gunman, and Laila, eyes wide and processing everything, located Troske's fallen man. She leapt for the pistol, his fingers attempted to still manipulate even as his body shut down.

More gunfire pounded through the small apartment as Laila scooped up the pistol. She snapped the weapon left and engaged Troske's gunman at the same time he opened fire on Jarak.

His body jolted right, and he gasped in pain, but his shots fell true. The first bullet caught Jarak in the throat, causing him to gag and stiffen before his head drooped forward. The second round thundered through the top of his head as his body continued toward the floor.

"No!" Laila shouted, but she couldn't hear her own words. Enraged, she adjusted her aim as the man spun toward her in a last-ditch effort to prevent his looming death.

Laila was quicker and fired a single shot, the slug boring through the man's forehead just above his left eye and blowing out the back of his head. Blood and brain matter splattered the kitchen in a wash of dusky crimson.

She spun back towards Troske, her eyes leading her pistol. Seeing him produce his own firearm, she fired as she dove into the kitchen to avoid his deadly response.

Mobility is survivability, she reminded herself as she darted around the corner of the kitchen, cutting off her view of the living room where her friends lay dead and dying. However, Troske fired through the wall, driving Laila to the floor. She rolled onto her left side and fired through the cabinets in front of her, hoping the 9mm rounds could punch through.

On the other side of the wall, Troske hopped from one foot to the other as Laila's rounds tumbled indiscriminately by him. Retreating to the exit, Troske watched Lojka crawl toward Basira's downed body.

He's going for her gun, he thought. Without hesitation, he sent two shots through the Belarusian's ribcage, which produced immediate shrieking and shuddering. Annoyed and frustrated more than any other time in his life,

Troske couldn't bear the young man's cries; they only increased his agitation. Taking careful aim, he fired a final shot into Lojka's left temple.

Instantly, silence permeated the space, though Laila and Troske wouldn't have known the way their ears rang.

"What's it going to be, Laila?" Troske shouted, louder than he imagined, as he reloaded his pistol. "You already got your friends killed."

Laila pushed back the terror that encroached upon her. Her previous wounds throbbed from her exertion, and she was convinced that she had ripped open some stitches. In that brief pause, her grief mounted. She was no stranger to suffering, and so she permitted it to pass over her and through her, facing her fear head-on.

She knew she didn't have as many bullets as Troske, and she wondered how she might construct an ambush; however, she knew she couldn't wait for him—time wasn't on her side. Eventually, he would start shooting through the wall again, and she knew it wasn't hard to calculate the angles needed. He would get lucky eventually.

"It doesn't look like Basira has much more time," Troske stated. "You surrender, and I'll see to it that she gets the help she needs. She might just make it, but that depends on you. I didn't want any of this."

"But how do I know you won't just kill me?" she asked, her worry for Basira causing her to consider his offer.

"How do I know you won't just kill me?" he countered.

Laila had thought about it. It would be easy to agree, round the corner, then shoot him before he could react, but she knew he might be the quicker one.

"Basira!" she called out, but the wounded woman did not respond.

"Time's ticking, Laila. What's it going to be?" he yelled again. He crept forward slowly and quietly to the edge of the foyer, where it cornered the kitchen opening. If Laila decided to run the rabbit, he resolved to be ready for her.

He silently dropped to a knee and attempted to acquire as large a view of the kitchen as possible, taking in the small wooden table and chairs in an otherwise plain, drab space. He thought of speaking to her again, but knew that if he did so, he would compromise his new position.

Basira managed a groan that carried softly across the room. Though her ears hurt, Laila heard it easily enough.

"Hold on, Basira," she called back. "Alright, Stefo," Laila agreed.

Troske tensed and strengthened his grip on his pistol to fight against the sweat compromising his hold.

While mustering her courage, Laila processed her situation. She didn't regret her decision not to kill Dudka, but she regretted how things had evolved to this point.

I should have tried to escape before all this, she lamented to herself. Everything in her screamed for her to continue the fight, to kill Troske, and to try to save Basira herself, but she knew that Basira's best hope was for multiple hands to try and save her. The same was true for any of the others.

She looked at the back of her hand, her blue eyes falling on the pink scar given to her by Natalie. *What would they do?* she pondered, but she didn't have to wonder long. The answer came to her swiftly, as if on the wings of the divine.

"If I come out, I have your word on the Brotherhood that you will save Basira?" she asked.

"You have it," Troske called back, his mind racing with how much time they had until Ukrainian authorities arrived. "Throw your gun where I can see it."

Laila inhaled deeply, trusting this new way of life she had borne witness to, ready to make the sacrificial play for Basira's life. After all, she knew she was responsible for what had happened. With a forceful exhale, she tossed the pistol through the archway.

"I'm coming out," she said.

"Keep your hands where I can see them. You try anything, and I will shoot you," he threatened.

Laila walked forward with her hands spread wide from her body. She closed her eyes and inhaled one last time before she faced Troske, preparing herself to see her family once more. Even after so long, she saw them clearly in her mind's eye, smiling as they waited eagerly to embrace her. They looked happy, no trace of the terror she had last seen on their faces all those years ago.

For a brief moment, she wished Troske would kill her, but the thought fled as quickly as it had arrived; for, as soon as she rounded the corner, a biting pain erupted on the side of her face, sending her sprawling to the floor. She didn't need to touch the wound to know that blood was flowing freely.

"*Kučka*!" Troske swore at her. Laila grunted through the shock and paralysis that accompanied the strike as she writhed on the floor. The room spun, and her brain throbbed with a horrible pounding that radiated down her spine. Troske stood over her, seething. He pointed the gun at her head, but tore it away after a brief moment, knowing he could not return to Vitori empty-handed.

Better for her to take the fall, he thought.

"Basira," Laila groaned as she tried to crawl toward her friend, but Troske kicked her hard in the stomach, his foot barely missing her ribs. Nausea engulfed her as she gagged on the pulsing pain. She felt Troske roll her over, but he easily defeated her sluggish attempt to repel him.

Using a set of stiff flex cuffs, Troske bound Laila's hands together and hoisted her to her feet. He half-carried, half-dragged her toward the door.

"Basira," she moaned, as her consciousness receded from her control. Between blinking eyes, she saw Basira, blood on her lips, weakly reach out her fingers.

Tears filled Laila's eyes before her vision blurred and the darkness took hold.

30

Special Operations Forces Headquarters
Kyiv, Ukraine

"I want answers now!" General Dudka roared as he stormed into the main situation room used to observe and monitor special operations missions conducted by his forces.

"General, I must insist..." cried a staff doctor who followed with a suture kit. Blood wept from a deep cut on Dudka's scalp. The crimson poured down the side of his face, drenching the collar of his white dress shirt and giving a ghoulish gleam to the right side of his face and neck.

De la Vega, dusty and bruised, watched the ordeal alongside Ricochet and the rest of his team, who stood among Dudka's concerned entourage.

"Please, General," the military doctor insisted. "You have refused to go to the hospital, at the very least, permit me to care for your wound."

Huffing in his anger, the general bore all stares and frightened with his enraged countenance. Who De la Vega had first thought looked like a peaceful farmer now held a wrath that fit his standing as a criminal cabal leader. De la Vega watched as Dudka relented, took a seat, and allowed the doctor to examine the gash on the crown of his head.

"Mr. De la Vega," Dudka called as he sat rigidly still and allowed the doctor to proceed.

De la Vega strode forward with Ricochet tight on his heels. As they neared, Ricochet cursed under his breath as he watched the doctor drive the first stitch through Dudka's flayed scalp. He quickly looked away, feeling queasy. He could handle blood and guts, but not needles and certainly not needles puncturing through bloody flesh.

"Yes, General?" De la Vega asked, answering the summons.

"You are here to advise, yes? Then advise," he ordered harshly, sweeping his hand over the situation room to all the wide-eyed military intelligence officers dressed in Ukrainian combat uniforms. "Who do you think did this? Is this the start of the invasion you speak of?" Confusion mixed with a rising dread spread across the room as the officers and enlisted personnel heard their commander-in-chief speak seriously of invasion.

De la Vega remained silent as he stared at the general, not appreciating his tone but also not blaming him. At the very least, he expected gratitude for saving the man's life, which he had yet to receive. For a moment, he considered taking his men and leaving.

To hell with the contract, he thought.

Seeing De la Vega's expression, Dudka relented. Again, he extended his hand, but this time toward De la Vega, and in a much kinder voice said, "Please."

De la Vega sighed and nodded.

"Do you believe this to be the work of the Russians?" Dudka asked.

"While possible, I think it's not likely. In my experience, they prefer more intimate methods," De la Vega replied.

"Intimate," Dudka echoed with a smirk. He showed no pain as the doctor continued to stitch his wound. His uniform was wrinkled and covered with gray and black dust, much like De la Vega's face and clothes. "So a terrorist attack then?"

"That is the most reasonable assumption," De la Vega answered. Dudka's thin lips scrunched as he attempted to nod, his face finally showing a trace of pain. "If I had to guess based on the method, I would guess Quds Force, but as to why, I haven't a clue," De la Vega added.

"The Iranians," Dudka muttered. He laughed for a moment and tilted his head in the process, drawing a deep and frustrated sigh from the doctor.

"General, please remain still," he urged. Dudka scoffed at his request.

Based on the general's tone, De la Vega thought that Dudka disagreed with his assessment. The sharp look Dudka cut back his way held what appeared to be a dose of accusation, and De la Vega fought the urge to take a step back. He sensed Ricochet's stance widen, his center of gravity dropping slightly, ready for action.

"Clear the room!" Dudka suddenly shouted. His voice was not angry, but forceful and firm.

While all realized it would have been much less of a hassle for Dudka and De la Vega to vacate the large situation room, no one dared voice protest, and they all funneled out quietly and obediently, save for a select few who somehow seemed to know the order did not apply to them.

Ricochet and the rest of the Red Horse operators didn't move, and De la Vega wondered if he should command them otherwise.

"Your men, Mr. De la Vega," Dudka urged respectfully.

De la Vega heard Ricochet take a solid step forward, and he turned to look at the short man. His powerful arms bulged even from underneath his loose flannel, stretching the wool fabric to its limit. He nodded the command and watched Ricochet sigh and drop his gaze.

"We'll be right outside," Ricochet voiced, his tone holding an air of warning and gravitas.

"Your doctor?" De la Vega asked, pointing at the thin, uniformed man.

"He's with me," Dudka answered.

De la Vega only nodded, not offering an objection.

"Earlier, you laughed when I mentioned David Shaw. You know this man?" Dudka asked once the doors had closed behind the Red Horse team.

"I've met him once," De la Vega admitted.

"Not since the assassination of Archduke Ferdinand has one man unknowingly wreaked such havoc on the world," Dudka said with a sigh.

De la Vega's face twisted in obvious confusion, drawing a chuckle from the Ukrainian general.

"The world was on a path, and, while not perfect, it was stable. Humanity as a whole has never known such prosperity. While some peoples lag behind others, there was progress, and four pillars maintained this stability—four men, powerful men who understood that which the masses could not hope to."

"And what's that?"

"Man must be ruled. Man longs to be ruled. It is our natural state as a population," Dudka answered, his voice full of conviction and passion.

"Millions of Americans, both alive and long dead, would disagree," De la Vega shot back, a bit harsher than he intended, but Dudka only laughed.

"Mr. De la Vega, you touch the trunk of an elephant and call it a snake. For one so close to the truth, you remain blind."

"Open my eyes then," De la Vega snapped, his anger brewing. Dudka grinned, almost devilishly.

"The pillars—the powerful men—did not direct the future of humanity collaboratively. Through conflict, they kept each other in check. The threat of utter annihilation, of complete mutual destruction, created a system of contentment. *Contentment!*" he roared, banging his fist on the desk beside him, as if in awe of that state of being which clearly eluded him. "Can you imagine such a thing? Of being content? Content *only* because you toed the threshold of your destruction?" He shook his hand, all his fingertips pressed together, to stress his point and embellish his wonder.

De la Vega remained silent. For all his ambition—war fighting at the highest levels of the United States military, building personal wealth beyond his imagination, and networking in circles of the most powerful people in the global military industry—he had never considered what the general was now sharing with him.

More was always on the horizon, just over the next hill, an objective to be secured. He could barely wrap his mind around Dudka's wonder and the completeness of this epiphany which he now shared with him.

"And you're saying David Shaw disrupted all of this?"

"Yes!" Dudka exclaimed, excited by De la Vega's interest. "One man, an insignificant pawn, brought down not one, but two empires. And with two legs of the foundation destroyed, the walls cannot stand. The structure buckles in on itself, creating calamity beyond scope and destruction that cannot be repaired."

De la Vega's brow furrowed as he found the weight of Dudka's statements both unnerving and impossible to readily believe. A million questions assaulted his mind. Was Dudka insane? Based on his position in the Ukrainian military, De la Vega very much doubted it. Was Stovall one of these four pillars or was he subject to one like Dudka and himself?

He thought of his lunch with Natalie Shaw and began to believe that Stovall was indeed one of the pillars, as Dudka had said in the car. First, Natalie Shaw—a capable and credible intelligence operative—and now the commander-in-chief of the Ukrainian armed forces was telling him that Stovall ruled a portion of the world, and without oversight at that. The reality that he was connected and even favored by one of the most powerful men in history did not sit well with him.

The last of the questions proved most troublesome. Was Shaw responsible for the coming calamity? Had he started all of this? Did that make him an enemy to the highest degree? De la Vega couldn't say, and his brain hurt just trying to wrap his mind around the idea of it all.

Seeing the troubled look on De la Vega's face, Dudka dropped his chin and stared at his guest with great severity. His dark eyes gleamed from underneath his prominent brow line as he waited for De la Vega to meet his gaze. When he did so, the general said, "I find it no coincidence that on the eve of war—whether today, tomorrow, or next week—you have come, a red horse."

"I'm not bringing the war!" De la Vega blurted, his usual stoicism unraveling. He knew as well as anyone the inspiration for Red Horse Global's name and motto.

"No, no, you are not," Dudka quickly whispered. Though quieted, his voice seemed to thunder with the weight of knowledge, of understanding beyond De la Vega's. "It is he who *rides* the red horse that brings the war, who takes peace from the earth so that people should slay one another."

In a sheer moment of clarity, De la Vega fought against the panic rising in his chest.

"Stovall," he whispered, his eyes wide as they stared into Dudka's. The general nodded his admiration of De la Vega's conclusion, taking deep satisfaction in bringing the man to this higher understanding of the world.

"And Vitori," Dudka added. "I suspect it is she who is behind this," he said, pointing to his scalp just as the doctor—unnerved by the conversation and sweating—finished his work. "So, you herald a new era of war for Europe, Mr. De la Vega. I have a feeling it cannot be stopped, only mitigated." He sighed and stood before reaching out to De la Vega and grabbing his shoulder in a way much too familiar for De la Vega's liking. "Thank you, Mr. De la Vega. For saving my life and for bringing warning and counsel that will not go unheeded, at least not by me. Help me mitigate this coming war."

De la Vega didn't know how to respond. He reminded himself that though Dudka was the commander-in-chief of the Ukrainian armed forces, he was a high-ranking leader in an international criminal cabal that his countrymen had disrupted. How could he trust such a man to tell him the truth? If it weren't for his previous conversation with Natalie, he would have written the general off and left with his men, but now?

He didn't know what to do.

"It is getting late. We will discuss this more in the morning," Dudka said, turning away.

"What of the assassins?" De la Vega asked, still bewildered.

"Oh, we will not find them," Dudka replied as if with humor and admiration. "My rage blinded me before, but now I see it all too clearly. I made myself too vulnerable and am reminded of the penalty for even the slightest of oversights and carelessness. In truth, it is because of our conversation that the realization dawned upon me. For some reason, when you said Quds Force, I was reminded of an assassin within the Brotherhood, a sister, if you will, who might be the culprit. And her life is too precious to seek to end."

De la Vega thought that was a very odd and unusual way of thinking of one's would-be assassin.

"Major Rybak will see you and your men to the accommodations which have been prepared for you," Dudka said. He turned toward the major—who De la Vega knew had to be part of this Czar's Brotherhood—and said something in Ukrainian. The major strode forward and extended a hand, directing De la Vega to the exit.

When Major Rybak and De la Vega exited, Ricochet breathed easier. He unfolded his arms and removed his weight from the wall upon which he leaned. All the Red Horse operators perked up at their CEO's emergence.

Once clear of the door, Major Rybak issued another order, and the staff funneled back into the situation room.

"What was that all about?" Ricochet asked quietly as he eyed Major Rybak suspiciously.

"You don't want to know," De la Vega muttered.

"You know that just makes me want to know more, right?"

"Trust me on this, Paul," De la Vega said with great conviction. He placed his hand on Ricochet's shoulder. "Come on, the major here is going to get us some chow."

31

Joint Base Andrews,
Maryland

"Man, it's starting to feel like I live here," Bray joked as the team of Invictus operators, who had carpooled, pulled into their designated hangar.

"I hear that, brother," Pikari replied as he piloted the SUV. McEwen glanced at Bratcher, both men wearing serious expressions.

"You don't get called up this last minute for lunch with the Queen," McEwen muttered as his eyes found Shaw, Natalie, and Lincoln engulfed in conversation and standing around a monitor situated on a chest high frame. "Let's see what all this is about," he added once the vehicle parked.

"Hey, team!" Shaw called, trotting toward them as they opened their doors. "Get over here! We're wheels up in ninety mikes!"

"Why the rush?" Bray asked as he followed McEwen with Pikari and Bratcher behind him. Reeves followed with Aston and Rakestraw at a brisk pace. Roman walked obediently at Aston's side, his breath wafting in a thick mist as he took in his surroundings.

"We're hitching a ride on an Air Force C-17 that's been delayed for us. They're not thrilled about it," Shaw answered.

"Hitching a ride to where?" McEwen asked, *hitching* sounding odd with his heavy Scottish accent.

"Kyiv. Come on, we'll get you guys briefed," Shaw said.

"What's the op?" Bray asked.

"Extraction of a US citizen."

"In Ukraine?" McEwen probed, not enjoying the lack of clarity.

"Yep, let's go," Shaw insisted, leading the group of men towards his wife and Lincoln.

The group gathered around the monitor as Shaw took his place next to Natalie.

"Hey, Scott," Reeves greeted, shaking hands with his former director. "You seeing us off?"

"No, I'm tagging along this time."

"No kidding? It'll be like Switzerland all over again," Reeves said, joking. Lincoln did not look amused.

"Let's hope not, but, yes, in more ways than one," Lincoln replied. The smile vanished from Reeves' face.

"What do you mean?"

"I'll let your new boss fill you in," Lincoln chided. However, before Reeves could rebuke him, Lincoln grinned and slapped him on the shoulder.

"Gather up!" Natalie called out, spurring her team to action.

"Ma'am," they all said in turn, starting with Reeves.

"Good to see you, boys, and sorry to drag you out here last minute. We've got a priority operation to extract a CIA clandestine officer who has been abducted by a criminal element called The Czar's Brotherhood."

A bewildered curse shot from Reeves' mouth as she said the name.

"Sorry, ma'am," he quickly said upon seeing her disapproval. "But, come on, are we still dealing with these guys?"

"I'm afraid it's worse than that, Rick. It's Laila," Natalie shared. Reeves rolled his lips inward to suppress his anger while shaking his head. Natalie turned toward the rest of her team as an image of Laila Malik appeared on the screen. "This is Laila Malik, an Afghan national and recent US citizen. Some of you may remember her from Istanbul last fall."

"How could I forget?" Bray whispered to Pikari, who kept his arms folded across his stout chest.

"No kidding," the Māori whispered back, both men enamored with her beauty.

"Callsign Firefly and exact location currently unknown. We're prepping a UAV out of Romania for support, and in the meantime, Agency personnel on the ground are working to locate her and her captors. We had a bead on her location, but lost surveillance not an hour ago."

"Who specifically are her captors?" Reeves asked.

"We believe an individual under the alias The Macedonian. His real name is Stefo Troske, former North Macedonian Special Forces," Natalie answered.

"And part of the Brotherhood, I take it?" Reeves asked.

"Yes, that is confirmed. Laila was taken in Istanbul while meeting with Reza Afshar. We found her in Kyiv twenty-four hours ago."

"Was the explosion her doing?" McEwen asked. "Her being the Spider of Kandahar and all that?"

"We believe so, but the target, General Ihor Dudka, was not killed, nor anyone for that matter," Natalie answered.

"That doesn't sound right," Bray interjected.

"We believe she intentionally botched the operation in order to draw our attention. Also, I think she is attempting to operate within the code of conduct to which she is held as an employee of the Central Intelligence Agency," Natalie explained.

"Got to give her props for that," Bray replied. "CIA isn't exactly known for a code of conduct."

"This Macedonian," McEwen began again, "what kind of support is he working with?"

"We don't know, but based on our past dealings with this organization, you can expect well-trained and dedicated resistance," Natalie answered. "We'll be receiving updates in real time from Agency staff in Kyiv and the UAV once it's in the AO, so we'll be constantly updating METT-TC until we're active on the ground. Any additional questions?"

"What toys are we bringing to play with?" Pikari asked.

"Glad you asked," Natalie said. She turned to her husband and gave him the floor.

"I want full combat loadouts. Armor, NODs, everything," Shaw said. "I want us to be able to conduct sustained firefights if necessary." He watched Bray's hand shoot up into the air.

"That seems like a lot for an urban op like the one we pulled in Turkey last fall," he said.

"Or Bahrain," Pikari added.

Shaw nodded and inhaled. The team immediately realized there was more to the story.

"I won't sugarcoat it for y'all. The last time we tangled with the Brotherhood, things went south fast. We can always scale back, but I want us to be capable of rolling out our full strength if the situation calls for it." He turned to Rick. "You agree?"

"One-hundred-percent," the bald, bearded man said without hesitation. The younger and newer team members, though all in their thirties with years of special operations expertise at the highest levels, glanced at each other. They weren't nervous, but they couldn't shake the natural feeling of unease that comes when things don't match up with known experience.

"Any other questions?" Shaw asked. The team was silent, and Shaw nodded. "Associate Director Scott Lincoln from Ground Branch will be joining us in an advisory capacity," he added, directing a hand toward Lincoln. "He was with us in Zürich and has as much experience with the Brotherhood as we do. So, if he says something, listen to him. Rah?" The operators nodded. "Alright, let's get to it."

Laila awoke slowly, and grimaced as the searing headache assaulted her waking senses. She moved to touch her head but suddenly became aware of an awkward stiffness and strain in her muscles. Her hands did not obey her commands. They felt restrained, restricted, though eager to fulfill their orders. It was like a dream, a haze her mind couldn't penetrate.

What happened? Where am I? Basira!

The startling clarity snapped her upright, and she realized her hands were bound to a handle on the ceiling. She was moving, but at the same time not moving. *I'm in a car.* Laila oriented herself into a more comfortable position, and, though her head still throbbed, her muscles relaxed, grateful to be relieved of their unnatural stretching due to the way she had been slumped in the seat with her hands bound above her.

Troske sat behind the wheel, and his dark eyes snapped up to the rearview mirror to meet Laila's vengeful gaze. He was too angry to capitulate to his snarky nature and thus suppressed any desire to speak to her. She had killed his team—his *entire* team—and had purposefully sabotaged their mission. Vitori was not going to be happy, and he felt at least a little relief in being able to deliver the culprit and avoid Vitori's wrath himself. Though still wary of Laila's ability and wishing she had not awoken, he returned his gaze to the road.

The darkness around them told Laila they were no longer in Kyiv. She felt the cold seeping through the window despite the car's heat audibly blowing. Her feet felt warm while her right side felt much colder. Using her chin, she attempted to rub some warmth back into her shoulder, but she wasn't successful. Finally, she looked at Troske again.

"Is Basira dead?" she asked, her voice low and mournful.

"Probably," he replied. His tone was calm, though not apathetic.

"You lied to me," she accused.

"Look, don't blame me. I didn't start any of that. You did," he scolded as he wrung his gloved hands on the wheel. Laila's anger soared, and she lashed out, kicking at him. "Stop it!" he rebuked, not angrily, but annoyed and tired, like a father disciplining children on a road trip taking far too long.

Laila didn't relent. Better for him to wreck.

"I said stop it!" he voiced more firmly, turning to slap at her feet. His gaze snapped back and forth from the road to Laila before he pointed a finger in warning. "Stop it," he urged, calming his voice. He was too tired and emotionally drained to fight back, though his anger still dominated his overall state.

Laila relented, seeing him lift his pistol into view. There was no honor in dying now.

"Where are you taking me?" she asked.

"Following the extraction plan," he mumbled back. He looked at his watch, and seeing the movement, Laila stole a glance at the digital clock on the dashboard, glowing brightly in the darkness.

11:34.

"Worried we're not going to make it in time?" Laila asked, her voice turning cold.

"We'll make it," he replied confidently, but Laila swore she heard an unfamiliar unease in his voice. After a long pause with only the constant low hum of the automobile filling their ears, Troske said, "I should have just let you walk away in Istanbul." Laila didn't reply. The lament was the sincerest she had ever heard him speak, and, though her anger still burned against him, she kept quiet, seeing the finality in the statement.

Laila kept adjusting her shoulders and arms to relieve the discomfort from their prolonged suspension above her head. She resettled her body in every way she could think of to dissolve the persistent, localized irritations that just wouldn't abate. After an hour, she grunted out her frustration in a forced exhalation, drawing Troske's eyes from the rearview mirror.

She met the gaze with simmering anger, but the man did not smile, smirk, or even raise his eyebrows. The utter apathy, though expected, angered her further.

"How much longer?" she asked before blowing a lock of tight, natural curls from her face.

"We're here," he replied. Laila glanced out the windshield, noticing a growing light in the distance.

"An airport," she scoffed. "You think you can get me out of the country that way? Like this?" But Troske didn't answer. Infuriated, she raised a leg and slammed her foot hard into the side of his seat. He spun toward her with a flash of rage across his face, his countenance seeming to glow for a brief moment. Laila held her ground, staring defiantly at him.

Laila watched as he pulled a small device from his inside jacket pocket. Keeping the device low and out of sight, he finally took his attention off Laila to stare at it for a few moments.

"Who are you contacting?" Laila probed, a hint of concern in her voice.

"Our extraction," he answered. He finished sending his message on what Laila could only assume was a satellite messenger.

"What happens now?" she asked.

"Now, we wait."

"You really think you're going to get me out by airplane? I'll make sure you're detained."

"No, you won't," Troske said, his confidence shaking her own.

"And why's that?"

"Because the invasion is about to begin."

PART III

HOSTILE EXTRACTION

32

Special Operations Forces Headquarters
Kyiv, Ukraine
0452
February 24, 2022

De la Vega lurched awake in the wing of the barracks in which he and his men had been offered accommodations. For a split second, he thought the concussive blast had only been part of his dream—a firefight years ago in Ramadi—but the blaring alarm shook the last holds of sleep from his eyes. The siren wailed loudly, an unfamiliar tone, but De la Vega knew its meaning well enough.

The invasion had begun.

Before he could jump from his bed, his body surged upward and to the left before smacking into the corner where the wall met the ceiling. His ears rang, and pain erupted throughout his body as he fell.

Battered and shocked from his collision with the ceiling, his mind whirled with panic, but he still expected to hit his bed or the floor any second. However, to his horror, the walls buckled around him—starting with the far right wall—which dropped the ceiling. He only outpaced the collapse in his descent due to a head start on his fall. A thick cloud of dust billowed upward from beneath him, and his bare arms and legs flailed widely as he descended before he smacked his side on a toppling dresser and tumbled into the dark, gaping maw beneath him.

He cursed loudly and repeatedly as he fell with the building crumbling around him. Dressed in nothing but a pair of Ranger silkies, the CEO plummeted downward and slammed hard onto the bottom floor of the two-story barracks building. His breath blasted from his lungs with such force that it paralyzed him. White splotches stole his vision, and he heaved for air, unable to move. The dust choked him, but, in his paralytic agony, he couldn't even cough to find relief.

But he heard it all.

And for the first time in a long time, he prayed, short and quick, as he thought of his wife and children before the thundering wave of concrete and steel crashed atop him.

Ukrainian Airspace
0452
February 24, 2022

David Shaw blinked groggily and raised his right hand to rub the lingering sleep from his eyes. After lying on the floor of the cargo hold of the C-17 Globemaster, his left arm was numb from the shoulder down. He glanced left to see Natalie snuggled up against him, breathing softly, her head pinning his upper arm to the hard floor. Though they had tossed and turned throughout the flight, both had plenty of past experience stretching out on the floor of the gigantic military aircraft to catch what sleep they could.

Shaw glanced around to see his team bundled and snoring in different positions and locations throughout the hold. He smirked when he noticed Bray sprawled across the top of their pallet of gear. It became clear to Shaw now why the former SEAL had arranged their large Pelican cases on the pallet with space in the center of the top row. Bray had formed a little nest for himself, and Shaw found it both fitting and amusing.

Shaw checked his watch, having synced it to local Ukrainian time before they left, as had all his men, and groaned a quiet complaint at the time. His body ached in a couple of places, his buttocks, hips, and surprisingly, his calves—which he didn't quite understand. Still, he remained where he was while arcing his feet to alleviate the stiffness in his legs.

Out of the corner of his eye, he watched the Air Force loadmaster jump up from his seat near the rear cargo door and rush toward the nose. The urgency of his pace concerned Shaw, and so he called out in a firm, yet hushed tone, "Hey, Staff Sergeant, what is it?"

Natalie stirred next to him before sighing and growing still again. The airman paused and searched for the source of the question among the snoozing individuals. Though the aircraft could easily accommodate just over one hundred troops, this one was packed with war-fighting supplies bound for Ramstein Air Base in Germany. There, it would equip and support combat training missions throughout the United States European Command. There had been just enough room for the Invictus team and their gear.

Shaw waved his right hand to draw the airman's eyes, and the man nodded when he found the source of questioning.

"It's probably nothing, sir," the young man answered. He was maybe twenty-eight or so. "There's some air activity just over the border in Belarus that the PIC wants to brief the crew on."

"What kind of air activity?" Shaw asked, lifting his shoulders and disturbing Natalie. She rolled over with a groan, freeing Shaw's arm entirely. He shook life back into it as he stood.

"Probably just normal exercises," the staff sergeant replied, finding it curious his passenger was so interested.

"Alright," Shaw said, relenting. The airman nodded and continued on his way while Shaw rose to his feet and stretched his arms high. He knew they still had over an hour of flight time, but he decided he'd wait for the report from the loadmaster before settling back down again.

When the loadmaster didn't return after a few minutes, Shaw's nagging gut prompted him to action. It wasn't that something didn't feel right; he just couldn't ignore the need to find out what was going on.

The constant drone of the engines grew louder as Shaw made his way forward, picking his route through the cargo. He passed Aston. Roman's head shot up from his lap, and the Dutch Shepherd made eye contact with Shaw as he passed. Shaw grinned at him and continued on his way before the canine resettled his jaw back on Aston's thigh.

As he neared the nose, Shaw squeezed by the dark green Stryker M1296 Dragoon Armored Personnel Carrier, but his pace quickened as he caught the pilot-in-command's agitated voice. He was talking to someone, but Shaw could only catch every other word on account of the engines until he got closer.

"This is a United States military aircraft," the pilot urged forcibly. "Stand down. I repeat, stand down."

"What's going on?" Shaw asked, alarmed. The loadmaster jumped at the unexpected intrusion.

"Sir, please return to your station," the loadmaster stated, turning slightly and raising a hand to Shaw's chest.

"I've got men on this bird, Staff Sergeant," Shaw countered. Even in the soft mix of blue and green light emanating from the systems around them, the loadmaster could see there was no forcing this man back. But before he could receive an answer, the co-pilot's voice drew all attention.

"Pegasus Command, this is Pegasus Seven-One, we have two bandits at our six o'clock. I repeat, two bandits at six..." Before he could finish, his eyes popped wide. "They've got target lock!" A high-pitched, uninterrupted tone filled the cockpit, and the blood drained from Shaw's face. "Spiked, six o'clock!" the co-pilot suddenly yelled.

"Taking evasive maneuvers," the pilot-in-command shouted as he wrenched on the controls. "Deploy countermeasures!"

Shaw gripped the edges of the steel doorframe as the colossal aircraft lurched upward and starboard.

"Missiles in the air!" the loadmaster called to Shaw. "Get back to your station!"

Shaw didn't have to be told a third time. He raced aft, stumbling down the stairs and slamming against a pallet of weaponry as the aircraft climbed and yawed. He staggered as he found his footing and continued, shouting, "Everyone up! Look alive!"

If the sudden maneuvers hadn't already awakened the sleeping team, the thunderous snaps of the deploying countermeasures startled them from sleep.

"What's happening?" Aston shouted as he leapt to his feet before tumbling into the fuselage as the plane suddenly pitched and dove.

"We're under attack!" Shaw shouted back, not stopping. He reached Natalie, and her fearful eyes wrenched on his heart. With the loadmaster right behind him, Shaw turned to face him. "We need chutes, now!"

"Right here!" the frightened airman called, though his voice cracked with fear. He opened an emergency panel and began handing out parachutes to everyone.

"We're still over thirty thousand feet!" Bray exclaimed as he received his chute, but no one replied. Shaw worked furiously to fix Natalie in her harness, and she trembled as she attempted to help.

"Just stop," Shaw scolded as he fastened the buckles.

"Sorry," Natalie said. She fought against the rising fear, having never faced a situation like this. She knew there was nothing she could do, no way to fight her way through, and, as a result of that revelation, her resolve faltered.

"Check!" Shaw shouted.

"I got her," Lincoln urged as he took Shaw's place and checked his work while Shaw fastened his own parachute.

The team worked efficiently, falling back into countless repetitions and muscle memory. Their bodies felt light, more floating than standing, as the plane descended rapidly. Another round of countermeasures deployed, and the team waited, counting and staring off as if to see through the hull of the aircraft while Aston worked to rig Roman to his harness. Though calm, the canine twitched subtly, aware of the danger and the fear emanating from his handler and those around him.

The deafening explosion from beyond the aircraft shook the plane, jolting its occupants. Most kept their balance, but a few fell into the crates around them as curses rang throughout the interior.

Natalie clutched Shaw tightly as he stared up at the ceiling, his mind racing with what to do before another echo of countermeasures disrupted his thinking.

"Twenty thousand feet!" the airman called out. "They're still on us!"

"Who?" Bray shouted back.

"I don't know!" the airman replied.

The noise was deafening as the pilots did their best to avoid the incoming missiles, but shouts echoed in the cargo bay as a burst of cannon fire cut through the aircraft. Natalie screamed, and Shaw wrapped her up and drove them both to the ground. The cold air whipped through the cargo hold from the numerous gaping holes punched into the aircraft.

"Everyone okay?" Shaw shouted.

"I'm good!" Pikari answered first. The rest echoed the same.

The loadmaster stood in disbelief, and his courage faltered as terror overwhelmed him. Natalie wasn't any better off. Shaw met Lincoln's gaze, and though wide-eyed, he nodded confirmation that Natalie's harness and chute was cleared good. Shaw nodded back just as the pilot-in-command's voice clipped over the C-17's intercom system, saying, "We've lost two engines from that last run. Bandits still have lock. Prepare to bail out."

"Bail out?" Natalie cried. She had never jumped from a plane before. Though they conducted that training at The Farm, it was prioritized for those in paramilitary operations, not intelligence.

"It'll be alright," Shaw comforted. He turned back to the loadmaster, who remained frozen in fear. "Staff Sergeant!" Shaw barked. The man jumped, and Shaw seized him by the shoulders and forced eye contact. "Prepare this ship for bailout!"

"Yes, sir," the airman shouted, louder than he intended. He staggered and fought for his balance as he rushed to the rear cargo hatch controls. Before he reached them, the countermeasures discharged again, and the team, preparing for the emergency jump, waited for the explosion of the incoming missile.

A blast of heat tore away the rear of the fuselage, the airman shrieking as he was sucked out by the frozen, whirling wind.

"David!" Natalie screamed as her feet left the ground. Her body tumbled, head over heels, as the pressure change dragged her after the airman. The frigid air immediately stole the breath from her lungs, and unimaginable fear filled the emptiness within her.

"Natalie!" Shaw cried, jumping after her without hesitation. Another explosion jolted the aircraft, slamming Shaw's team into the pallets of cased equipment as the plane dropped rapidly.

Shaw barely cleared the jagged rear edge of the damaged plane before it swung by his flying form. His eyes, watering from the buffeting wind, quickly searched the darkness for his wife, and his ears strained to pick up any sound of her. The darkness and the roar of his own fall drowned out his senses.

33

"Natalie!" Shaw screamed, though the action left him dizzy and disoriented. He knew it was a fruitless gesture, but he had to try. Though he heaved with his mouth to take in what little oxygen there was, his chest pulsed with short, shallow breaths. He was colder, colder than he ever remembered being, and his skin prickled painfully as he plummeted at frightening speeds. He kept forcing his eyes open in search of his wife, despite the tears freezing on his temples.

The wind tore at his clothing, and he only heard the roar of his plummeting. He surged downward, accelerated by the force of gravity, slicing smoothly through the top of a cloud. Shaw felt his clothes moisten as his free fall disrupted the condensation in the mist. Droplets pelted him as he passed through the dense covering, and he counted the seconds until he cut through the cloud, his teeth chattering as his extremities grew numb.

Thunder suddenly grumbled around him, generating quick alarm, but the cloud silenced and remained quiet as he punched through the lower seal. He found it easier to breathe as he fell farther and farther, and his mind grew clearer and clearer with the additional oxygen he was able to take in. The clearer his mind grew, the more focus he possessed to ignore the cold and locate his wife.

On the dark earth below, bright flashes of yellow and orange drew his gaze as what could only be missiles detonated. Whether they found their targets or not, the result looked the same to the falling man.

Thunder again cracked above, shaking his bones as an errant bolt of heat lightning surged above him. Shaw shifted his gaze just slightly left as the lightning arced eastward. Getting struck by lightning was not a risk he took lightly.

With the dark earth rising to meet him, Shaw continued to search frantically for Natalie. He'd yet to see an open chute, causing anxiety to spike within him.

Another flash of lightning illuminated the sky, and he caught sight of something falling, failing, and spinning not far beneath him. Shaw twisted his torso and slapped his arms to his side, forming a missile to intercept the falling object. He knew he was running out of time, but he had to get to her.

As he neared, blinking away the moisture crystallizing at the corners of his eyes, he recognized Natalie. She fell without form or focus, and, to his horror, Shaw realized she was unconscious. He knew he had only one chance, and so he piloted himself as best he could, having never been exceptional at aerial maneuvers.

He plowed into her harder than he anticipated and wrapped her up with all the strength he could muster, hoping to God she was still alive.

"I've got you!" he shouted, but she did not reply.

Doing his best to orient her into a safe deployment posture, he kicked out a leg in an effort to rotate them so that his back faced the ground. The orientation unnerved him, but seeing his wife steady in his grip, he yanked hard on her ripcord, looking over her shoulder to confirm good chute deployment.

"Good chute!" he cried, releasing her just before the opening canopy fully expanded and jerked her limp body upward.

Shaw quickly spun over and reached for his own ripcord, pulling hard and opening his chute as he threw his arms wide. In the darkness, it was impossibly difficult to judge the distance to the earth, but he knew he had to be cutting it close.

The wait felt like a lifetime before the jerk on his body pinched uncomfortably in too many places. He grunted as he decelerated far too quickly, and his head spun from the temporary shift in blood flow.

Suddenly, the roaring in his ears stopped, replaced by a faint ringing before the sounds of explosions and gunfire reached him.

"My God," he muttered to himself upon seeing the scale of the conflict. The Russians had, indeed, invaded. That was the only explanation he could think of. *They must have shot down the plane*, he reasoned, anger filling him. With a deep and grateful breath, he reached his hands upward to find the controls, steering himself downward, fighting the growing wind as he attempted to keep his eyes on his wife, and doing his best to predict her route to the ground.

He tried to keep his mind off the fact that he was landing in a war zone without weapons or equipment of any kind: just his wallet, a watch, a small fixed blade from Primitive Woodsman, and his company-issued encrypted cell phone.

Anticipating his wife's path to the ground, he piloted himself that way, landing in an open wheat field bordered by shallow tree lines. He hit the ground harder than he would have liked and grunted as the chute dragged him across the frozen dirt before he shifted his feet under him and wrestled the canopy under control. His skin burned not only from the cold, but from the beating the ground had just given him.

He grunted through his pain as he fought the buckles while transitioning his attention quickly from the task to the sky. His fingers struggled to obey as they worked the buckles. As soon as he was free, he hurtled after Natalie's descending chute just as a gust of wind pushed her into the trees. He wanted to call out to her but knew better than to do so. He didn't know where the Russians were, much less where he himself was.

As he sprinted, his lungs burned from the frosty air. He shivered, and his teeth chattered, but he ignored all discomfort. He watched Natalie's chute descend with her unable to direct or control her landing. The wind led her into the trees, her parachute catching on higher boughs and snagging. Shaw worried she might be impaled by a sharp branch, but, as he neared, his fears subsided, and relief flooded him when he found his wife hanging not three feet off the ground, swaying gently.

Thank God!

When he reached her, he worked her buckles, grateful they were all within reach. Within a few seconds, he caught her and pressed deeper into the trees while cradling her against his chest. The sounds of the war, though distant—maybe a few miles away—did not comfort him.

Locating a cluster of thick overhead canopy and dense underbrush, Shaw barreled in and found a small opening under a fallen tree where he laid Natalie and checked her for injury.

He sighed a grateful sigh when she awoke. He watched her touch her head, and he placed his hand over hers.

"David?" she groaned softly. "What happened? Where are we?"

"If I had to guess, somewhere north of Kyiv," he replied, smiling tenderly at her. He felt his gratitude well into his throat, choking him for a moment. Natalie sat up on her elbows and looked around.

"My head is killing me," she said.

"Yeah, me too. We didn't have too much air up there. Listen, I need you to wait here for me. Can you do that?" Even in the darkness, she could see his concern.

She nodded and said, "Yeah."

"Okay, I'll be right back. I've got to see if the boys made it and guide them in," he said.

Natalie nodded again and closed her eyes to fight against the pain throbbing at the base of her skull. When she opened them, her husband was gone. It was then that she became chillingly aware of the chattering of distant gunfire and the steady cadence of explosion after explosion.

34

Bray's eyes scanned the ground far beneath him as he surveyed what he now knew was a battlefield. He couldn't believe it. He truly couldn't. He was parachuting unarmed into a hot combat zone. As he watched his boots dangle beneath him, he thought of his grandfather, who had jumped into Normandy on D-Day in 1944 for Operation Boston as part of the larger Operation Neptune to secure an Allied foothold in France. For that brief moment, he felt elated at this connection born between himself and his deceased grandfather, whom he had never known.

He laughed briefly at the thought of it all until he noticed a small light piercing the darkness far below. Unlike the yellow bellows of flame concentrated to the south, this light was sharp white, almost blue, and pulsed in a cadence that Bray quickly recognized.

Shaw!

He steered that way and soon found himself wrestling his chute to the ground. Staying low, he rushed toward the treeline where the flashing light emanated. Though pointed skyward, he could see it clearly enough in the darkness.

"Shaw?" he called in a forceful whisper, projecting his voice as far as he dared.

"Here," Shaw replied in kind.

"It's Bray."

"Glad you made it, Owen. You link up with anyone else?" Shaw asked as he continued to manipulate the flashlight on his phone toward the sky. It was a risk, but he needed his team if they were going to make it out of this.

"No," Bray replied, crouching in the underbrush next to Shaw. "I don't even know who made it out of the plane."

"Alright, try to get comms up and see if you can get a bead on our gear. We're going to need it," Shaw instructed.

"On it," he replied, pulling out his own encrypted phone and accessing the Iridium network.

In the darkness, Shaw saw a group of chutes descending toward him. Within seconds, they had touched down, doffed their harnesses, and sprinted toward Shaw and Bray, knowing the flashing, emergency sequence could only belong to their team commander.

The pad of multiple feet drew Bray's attention left, and he jumped briefly as he beheld the eerie glow of two translucent orbs racing toward him. He settled when he recognized Roman, accompanied by Aston, Bratcher, and Rakestraw.

"Good to see you, boys," Shaw greeted. "Eyes on anyone else?"

"Negative," Aston answered, panting and not enjoying the frigid ache in his throat nor the shivering from the cold descent. Even Roman shook as he lay obediently next to his handler, who crouched among the tall, brown grass.

They waited several more minutes with Shaw continually flashing the signal by leveraging his phone's built-in flashlight. It was bright enough to see straight on, but it didn't project a beam like the flashlight in his pocket would. Honestly, he was amazed he hadn't lost anything during the unexpected freefall.

Bray continued to try to triangulate the position of their gear pallet, using their GPS software—if the pallet survived the fall. While he focused on that, Bratcher, Rakestraw, and Aston kept a vigilant watch all around, all feeling very naked without weapons, though grateful for their alert and lethal fur missile.

Shaw stopped his signal and turned toward the three men, his heart heavy for the potential loss. This was truly devastating, but he knew he had to push forward. His wife and his men were counting on his leadership.

So was Laila.

This just got way more complicated, he thought.

Shaw suddenly sighed as chills radiated across his skull in response to the oppressive cold. He knew they needed protection from exposure. Their street clothes just weren't enough, and the sudden urge to check on his wife overwhelmed him.

"Come on," he said, trying to push the defeat and anguish from his tone. None blamed him. They knew this was as bad as it got. At least they had made it, and they held onto hope that the others did as well. They followed him, careful to step silently, rolling their feet from the outside in, though they doubted their footsteps would be heard over the war raging around them.

When Shaw returned to his wife, he found her sitting cross-legged with her phone pressed to her ear. She looked up, and even in the darkness, she saw the concern in her husband's blue eyes.

Who's that? he mouthed.

"Solid copy, Rick," Natalie said into the phone, answering Shaw's question at the same time and bringing him great relief.

Reeves is alive. Thank God, he thought.

Bray cast an encouraging glance Bratcher's way, but the Englishman didn't notice, fixated as he was on Natalie's call. In response, Bray returned to his own phone and attempted again to locate the GPS tag inserted into each of their equipment cases. He went device by device, hoping one had survived the crash.

"Copy, rendezvous at the crash site," Natalie answered, but Shaw was shaking his head.

"The Russians will be all over that," he said.

"We can't leave those pilots," Natalie shot back. Shaw sighed, knowing she was right. Still, they may not have survived.

"That's if they survived," Aston blurted. Shaw nodded solemnly and turned to Bray.

"Bray, sit rep."

"Nothing yet. I don't know if the GPS trackers survived the impact from that height...wait! I've got one!" he exclaimed in an exuberant whisper.

"Where?"

"Northeast, two clicks," he answered.

For the first time since landing, Shaw grinned.

"Rick said he's with Scott. They landed near the crash site and are Oscar Mike that way. They're going to see if they can locate the loadmaster and the pilots as well as salvage what weapons and gear they can from the C-17," Natalie explained.

Shaw was surprised the plane had landed so close to them, and he hoped the pilots had been able to put her down mostly intact.

"Alright, we get our gear, we get to the plane, and then figure out our next step from there," Shaw said, making eye contact with all present. "We stay low, we stay together. Tyler, you're on point with Roman."

"Roger that," the Southerner replied. "Come on, boy," he said to Roman, who perked up immediately.

The group made their way northeast, and in less than fifteen minutes, they arrived at the location Bray had indicated. They halted short, and squinting through the darkness, they noticed forms moving about the site. Straining, Shaw noticed they were carrying weapons, and he exhaled his frustration and concern.

"Could it be Tāne and Rowan?" Natalie asked, crouched behind him. The winter wheat was barely a few inches high, and so they relied on the blanket of dark clouds above to keep them in near total darkness.

"I don't know," Shaw whispered back.

"Do the Russians have night vision?" Aston muttered, his voice teetering on panic.

"I don't know," Shaw replied, alarmed.

"Because these guys do," Aston whispered.

"Everyone down," Shaw hissed, dropping from a crouch to his belly. Everyone followed suit, none more terrified than Natalie.

She tried to wrestle control, to recall her courage in Yemen, the Congo, and Zürich, but she failed. There was a literal invasion raging around her, the fog of war all too real on account of the situation in front of them. One wrong move and they would die, unable to defend themselves. Even an honest mistake by a frightened and enraged Ukrainian soldier would be enough.

Natalie knew the odds were low that Russians or even Ukrainians had found their gear. It was dark with a looming rainstorm. Both parties likely had more pressing concerns than checking out an unmarked and unknown drop of what was likely damaged or destroyed equipment.

"Shaw?" came a call from the darkness ahead. No one moved, though they knew it was impossible for anyone other than their team to know of their existence. Also, the accent was unmistakable.

"Tāne!" Shaw called back quietly, immensely relieved to see the man alive and that he was not a Russian soldier. The group rushed forward, and Natalie, tears in her eyes, let out a long sigh. It did little to ease the tension, but it helped.

Pikari wore his full combat loadout, having flipped his night vision up and away from his eyes.

"Man, are we glad to see you," Shaw said, grinning as he gripped Pikari by both arms.

"We released our kit when we knew the bird was going down. We were the last out, Rowan and me," Pikari explained.

"Thank you, Tāne," Natalie said. She hugged him, and the Māori didn't know how to react. He patted her gently on the shoulder until she let go.

"You're welcome, ma'am," he said quietly. He greeted the others, embracing Bray with gladness and relief.

"How's our gear?" Shaw asked McEwen as the two men shook hands.

"Cases are busted to hell, but they did the job. Can't say if our weapons maintained zero, but everything's here. Night vision works, as well as comms," the Scot answered.

"That's a relief," Shaw muttered as he searched for his case. Finding it, he popped the latches, but when he raised the lid, the back brackets failed. The lid fell off the base, but Shaw didn't care. He searched frantically through the jumbled gear, hoping it was there. When his eyes fell on the pistol seated securely in its Safariland holster, he sighed with deep relief.

He scooped up the Alchemy Custom Weaponry Quantico 1911, relishing the tactile feel of the grip checkering in his ice-cold hands. Performing a quick press check, Shaw confirmed the condition of the weapon and couldn't help but smile as the slide glided smoothly as if on ball bearings. Shivering, he returned his gaze to the rest of his kit, grateful he had thought to pack some cold weather gear. He turned around to observe those who had landed with him going through their own cases.

"Alright, gear up," he urged.

35

Reeves and Lincoln moved in coordinated fashion, sticking to the wooded areas when they could, and sprinting across open areas when they had no alternative. They paused often, straining their ears to hear anything nearby, anything unnatural. Though the sound of the war ebbed and shifted through the duration of their trek toward the downed aircraft, the two men feared that at any moment they might stumble upon a Russian advance.

The explosions echoed to the south, and both men understood the crucial importance capturing Kyiv was to the Russians. They feared that the Ukrainians might not stand a chance at repelling and breaking the siege. Even if they could halt the Russian advance, they would still have to contend with a front far too close to their capital.

"Zürich seems like a walk in the park compared to this," Lincoln whispered as he joined Reeves at the edge of the narrow wood. They had reached the end of their cover, and both men sought their courage as they prepared to cross another expanse of cold earth. They shivered almost uncontrollably, keeping their elbows pressed tightly into their sides and their hands close to their chests.

"You can say that again, bro," Reeves replied gravely. He knew that even if they made it to the downed C-17, which he hoped would increase their odds of survival, they still had an impossibly low shot of making it back home. "You ready?" Reeves asked after checking his watch-mounted compass once more. Having kept situational awareness as he parachuted down, he'd watched the plane fall in its steep glide before cutting a wide swathe through a field to the southeast. He glanced up to locate a landmark, but it was too dark.

"Yeah," Lincoln whispered back.

"Let's go."

The two men again sprinted forward, keeping low and alert, until Reeves stumbled, his hands flying out to catch him as he fell. Lincoln hobbled and skipped in an awkward dance to keep from falling as well, the ground having suddenly dipped drastically underfoot.

Reeves cursed as he slid down the steep embankment of fresh, moist dirt. His slide evolved into a full body roll until he slapped into the mud at the base of the shallow gorge.

"What the hell?" he mumbled to himself as he pushed up from the ground, his fingers sinking into the cold, wet earth. The dirt, not quite mud but certainly not dry, clung to the side of his face in large chunks that he wiped away with a hand. Hearing a muffled cry of alarm, he glanced back, his heart in his throat, just in time to see Lincoln lose his footing before smacking into the dirt next to Reeves. Having landed hard on his rear, the force of the impact coiled up his spine, bringing a wave of bruising pain up to the base of his skull.

Reeves couldn't help but laugh at Lincoln's tumble, even though he had done the same himself.

"Shut up," Lincoln groaned as he rolled off his rear onto all fours before pushing through the pain and standing. "What is this?" he asked, glancing left and right. Though dark, he could see the dirt had only recently been moved, and a lot of it. "It can't be a trench," he said. "Not this soon." He sniffed the air, taking in the thick notes of exhaust before coughing it back out.

"I think this is from our plane," Reeves reckoned, standing.

"Better than a rocket or a missile," Lincoln replied.

Reeves checked his compass again and lined up his orientation in the direction of the crater. He smiled and pointed his right arm, all fingers bladed together in the designated direction.

"Southeast," he said proudly. "Come on." He took off down the shallow gorge, and Lincoln hurried after him, wishing he had night vision as he stumbled over the broken earth.

After a minute or two, the fumes grew thicker, though neither man saw flames. They knew the pilots would have jettisoned all fuel before a crash landing to reduce the threat of fire.

The two men continued on, knowing they were getting close, and soon the jagged and damaged rear of the C-17 loomed in the darkness like the gaping maw of a slain dragon. Both men felt incredibly small as they cautiously approached. Not only were they concerned with the crash's volatility, but they didn't want to be shot by scared airmen either. Still freezing and wary of investigating forces—either friendly or hostile—Reeves and Lincoln picked their way through the debris and entered the plane.

The first thing the two men noticed was that their pallet of gear was missing in its entirety, but the pilots appeared to have done the best they could. Reeves guessed neither individual had ever experienced aerial combat before. Why would they have?

"We likely don't have much time. I'm going to check on the pilots, see if you can find us something to get warm and fight with," Reeves said to Lincoln.

"Sounds good," he said, shivering.

Reeves left him to sift through the remaining equipment while he made his way to the nose. He readied himself for what he might find, and as he passed by the Stryker, he wondered if they might be able to leverage the armored infantry carrier. As quickly as the thought came, he pushed it aside. He reached the ladder and called out softly, "Friendly coming up." As he climbed the steep stairs, sounds of war still raged in the darkness outside.

Greeted by faint lights, Reeves paused at the top of the stairs and called out again, "Friendly coming in." He inhaled and waited, hoping the two men weren't dead.

"Identify yourself," came a harsh, commanding whisper from the cockpit, followed by the unmistakable ratchet of a pistol's hammer.

"Master Chief Rick Reeves, former Navy SEAL, and current Deputy

Director of Operations with Invictus International. You can put your gun away, sir," Reeves said calmly.

"Oh, thank God," the man groaned as he decocked the hammer on his M11 pistol. Reeves then materialized in the doorway, the pilot recognizing him.

"You boys alright?" Reeves asked.

"A little banged up, but yeah. We're alright," the PIC said. Reeves looked at the co-pilot who clutched his M11 pistol tightly against his chest.

"Still using the M11s? Nice," Reeves said in an attempt to lighten the mood.

The PIC—Pilot-in-Command Captain Carey Coffey—glanced down at his pistol, sighing and nodding before glancing back up at Reeves. Compared to the former SEAL, Captain Coffey appeared tall and lanky, even though seated, with a head of short blond hair, a fair complexion, and light blue eyes.

"Do you have a plan?" Captain Coffey asked.

"We're working on it," Reeves assured him. "First things first, we need to scavenge what we can here to increase our chances of survival. Do you have comms?"

Coffey shook his head and said, "It's all dead."

"Alright, no problem. A portion of our team made it and is heading this way. I need your help to get this Stryker up and running."

"We don't know the first thing about that!" the co-pilot protested, not opposition but fear.

"Will you put your gun away?" Reeves told him, seeing it still in his hands. The co-pilot's nervousness made the former SEAL anxious.

"Yeah, sorry," the co-pilot stated, fighting embarrassment.

"Get whatever you need from here and meet me down in the hold. If you have a jacket, I recommend it," Reeves said before turning and leaving. The pilots readily grabbed their flight jackets and followed after Reeves.

When they set foot in the cargo hold, Reeves continued forward past the Stryker and regrouped with Lincoln, who now had a basic M4 slung across his chest along with an Army-issued parka.

"Here," he said, handing one to Reeves who quickly slipped his arms inside. A red headlamp glowed from Lincoln's forehead.

"Thanks," Reeves replied, immediately relishing the protection, though the jacket was cold.

"And look who made it," Lincoln added, pointing to the Air Force loadmaster who also had an M4 slung across his chest. "Staff Sergeant McCrae."

"Glad you made it, brother," Reeves stated. "You got one of those for me?" he asked, pointing at the rifle.

"Got a whole crate," the Loadmaster replied. His voice was shaky, and Reeves could only imagine the fear the young man experienced. He knew they were all scared, but having everyone focus on one problem at a time would help.

"It's good he showed up," Lincoln muttered. "He knows where everything is."

"Lucky. Let's hope it holds," Reeves replied. "Wish I had my own gear though. You know we can't stay here long. I was wondering if you knew how to drive that Stryker."

"You sure that's a good idea?" Lincoln asked, his headlamp preventing his eyebrow from raising. His forehead scrunched in too many wrinkles, but Reeves didn't pay it any attention.

"I know it may draw attention, but it'll be good to transport these guys around in," Reeves stated quietly. Before Lincoln could answer, they all jumped as an explosion echoed far too near. They felt the rumble in the ground and plane.

"That was close," Lincoln said gravely.

"We need to stick around until Natalie and the others get here. They're on their way," Reeves said. "If we don't have our gear, that Stryker might be the best option we've got. I haven't checked to see what armament it's got, but it's definitely better than these," he said as McCrae returned with a carbine for Reeves.

The SEAL took the weapon, removed the magazine, and felt the cartridge alignment with his index finger before reinserting the magazine and racking the charging handle.

"Thanks," he said. He turned to the pilots and asked, "You boys know how to shoot?"

"Yeah," Coffey replied.

"Have you shot since basic or your annual qual?" Reeves asked.

"No," they both said. Reeves inhaled deeply and looked at Lincoln.

"See what I'm saying?"

"Yeah," Lincoln admitted. The pilots knew better than to take offense. Without these men, they knew they'd be on their own, and it had been years since either had attended SERE training. It's why they had remained in the cockpit, trying to remember all they needed to do.

"Alright," Reeves said, taking command. He turned to McCrae. The young airman stared back, his dark eyes wide and waiting. "I need food and water, enough for a week for thirteen people. Got it?" The airman nodded. "Good, get after it." He turned to Lincoln. "You're on getting that Stryker squared away, good?"

"Oh, how things have changed," he muttered with a chuckle.

"Advisory capacity," Reeves replied with a grin, reminding Lincoln of his role. "Go on." Finally, he turned to the pilots. "You guys are on watch. Don't shoot anything that moves. We're expecting friendlies. If you think you see something, you come get me. Got it?"

"Yeah, what about you?" Coffey asked.

"I'm going to prep as much ordnance as this bird is carrying. God knows we'll need it."

36

Shaw, Natalie, and their men moved silently, bounding in teams when gunfire sounded close and patrolling in a standard formation of two wedges when the war sounded distant. Both formations consisted of a point man, two riflemen on one side, and a gunner or grenadier on the opposite side. The trailing wedge held a formation opposite to the lead wedge to ensure maximum firepower should the team be ambushed or engaged from either flank.

Aston led the lead wedge with Roman not far in front of him. Shaw, carrying Reeves' MK46 light machine gun, paced a few meters behind and to the right, responsible for engaging threats from their three o'clock. Opposite him marched Bray and Pikari, separated by the same distance at an angle that completed the wedge from Aston's point position.

Behind them, Natalie led wedge two—perhaps the safest position in the entire formation and one usually reserved for the team commander. To her right and trailing behind Shaw but mirroring Bray's and Pikari's formation, walked Bratcher and McEwen, each with their rifles—the former carrying his Knights Armament M110 Semi-Automatic Sniper System (SASS) and the latter carrying his Daniel Defense M4A1 he had outfitted for the Radi mission. Opposite them, Rakestraw, with his M203 grenade launcher, patrolled in formation. Though not ideal, Shaw felt the arrangement best complemented Bratcher's designated marksman capability and kept his wife the safest he could manage.

They had diversified Lincoln's and Reeves' gear between them, and all still had not recovered from the frigid exposure. Even though they now wore their combat uniforms and supplemental cold weather gear they had thought to pack, it wasn't nearly enough. With the continued cloud cover and occasional thunderclap, Shaw did not want it to rain.

Rain always brought complications, and he did not need additional difficulty; however, he knew a storm might prove advantageous to their mission and assist with infiltration.

After a couple of clicks, the downed plane emerged into view, highlighted by their advanced night vision binoculars. The NODs—leveraging the latest in blended thermal and night vision technology—amplified ambient and ultraviolet light while highlighting heat signatures in an orange outline. It was cutting-edge technology that all were grateful to have at their disposal.

Shaw keyed his PTT in a pattern that signaled the team to halt their advance. The team all knelt, each member facing outward to cover all sectors in 360 degrees. Shaw again engaged his radio and said quietly, "Nectar, let's get them on comms."

"Copy, Philo," Natalie replied. Hearing his old callsign brought a wave of emotion Shaw hadn't expected, but taking McEwen's advice, they had implemented an individual user choice policy for their employees. Shaw had wrestled with his own callsign selection. He easily could have said it didn't matter, and in a way it didn't, but he couldn't shake the call from beyond the grave.

To remember.

To never forget.

Though he had retired Philo team to a place of honor, opting for the callsign Invictus, Invictus had become something far bigger than he had originally imagined, and he didn't want to lose sight of why he and Natalie had taken this path. Philo brought him back to the start, and though he could never call another team by that name, he could bear the name proudly to honor those he had lost and avenged.

Natalie had opted to keep Nectar, mainly on account of Shaw liking it, and her previous personal callsign, Ozark, was randomly assigned by her CIA station supervisor. The others had grown interesting and somewhat out of control. Certain vetoes had to be implemented, particularly with Bray.

McEwen had selected Vagabond, which all had liked and thought fitting. Reeves had opted for Matterhorn, which was equally as popular. Rakestraw had chosen Haystack since it was his callsign in Special Forces. Pikari chose Riptide, Aston Romulus, and Bratcher Beowulf. After Shaw and Natalie had vetoed Star Lord, Boba Fett, and Muad'Dib—of which Shaw was quite fond, but Natalie had pronunciation concerns—Bray had finally settled on Strider.

"Rick, we have eyes on, approached from the northwest," Natalie said quietly once her encrypted satellite phone connected with Reeves.

"Copy, glad you could join us," he replied.

"See you in a second," Natalie replied before hanging up. She pressed her PTT and said, "We're clear to move."

"Copy," Shaw replied. "Romulus, lead us in."

In just a few minutes, Invictus team was reunited with handshakes all around. Reeves and Lincoln were both unbelievably relieved and grateful to have their personal gear brought to them. They quickly donned their equipment and readied their weapons while MREs and US Army parkas were distributed to the newcomers.

"What else have we got to play with?" Shaw asked Reeves and Lincoln.

"Aside from the Stryker, the next most valuable asset we've got are a batch of Stingers," Reeves said, "but Air Force over here isn't keen on us using gear he's responsible for." Shaw almost laughed at the absurdity.

"The pilots?" he asked, but Reeves shook his head.

"The loadmaster," he confirmed. Shaw shot the young staff sergeant a glance over Reeves' shoulder.

"Well, I don't think he has much say," Shaw remarked. Reeves and Lincoln both agreed.

"What's the plan? We still trying to get to Laila?" Reeves then asked. Shaw sighed, and the former SEAL knew what that meant.

"We've got to find her first," Shaw replied. "Natalie's working on that, and we can't stay here too much longer."

"You got that right," Reeves muttered, fighting through a series of chills.

"Scott, what are your thoughts?" Shaw asked. With the rest of the team pulling perimeter security around the downed aircraft, they could talk freely about their operation and their current situation.

"It'll depend on Sosa," Lincoln replied. Shaw nodded; it was an answer he expected.

"Rick?"

"I'm not for leaving without what we came here for," he answered, his tone serious. Again, Shaw nodded.

"David," came Natalie's quiet call from deeper in the plane. Receiving a nod from Reeves, David turned and joined her at the base of the ladder leading to the cockpit.

"You get through?"

"Yeah," Natalie replied with a sigh. "UAV entered the AO just as we went down. They were going to withdraw, but now they're tasking it to guide us to friendly lines."

"Do they have a bead on Laila?"

"Yes, local staff tracked her to Antonov International Airport in Hostomel, about twenty clicks south of us."

"How far have the Russians made it?" Shaw asked.

"Hard to know, but Mari says they haven't breached Kyiv with conventional forces, though Russian special operations are attempting to take key locations within the city," Natalie explained.

"So, Laila's on our way?" Shaw asked.

"Appears so," Natalie replied.

Shaw looked Natalie square in the eyes, and she sighed yet again, the cold air on the inhale jarring her to keep her focus.

"I know that look," she said quietly. Shaw now sighed, knowing better than to deny what she saw.

"This is bad, love," he whispered as he checked her plate carrier, having refit it over the bulky winter parka. His fingers were still numb despite the gloves he now wore, but he was satisfied with her work. He was suddenly grateful he had ordered all his men to pack their full combat loadouts. He was even more grateful that the C-17 carried food and water in addition to heavier armaments.

"We've been through bad before," she assured him, feeling much warmer now. Though the additional layers inhibited her mobility in ways she hadn't ever experienced, she was grateful for the warmth, and the cold air wasn't as painful to breathe.

"No, this is different. This is a real war. We're not equipped for this, and though we know where Laila is, an airport is going to be a major strategic asset for the Russians to prioritize. They're going to swarm the place," he countered, his voice still a whisper. He glanced back to view Lincoln and Reeves standing next to each other, hands in their pockets, watching them. "The fact that we were shot down by Russian forces changes everything," he added, returning to her gaze with stout conviction.

"We can't abandon Laila," Natalie shot back, a little too loudly. Shaw dropped his gaze and nodded.

"I'm not saying that," he said softly. "There's the pilots, there's the loadmaster, and there's..." he paused, his voice strained.

"There's me," she finished for him. She watched his short nods and understood his internal dilemma. He had already lost his son, and she knew he couldn't handle losing her, too.

"We're in a war zone. If I have to choose between you and Laila, it's not even close. I can't lead you right into the hands of the Russians. I've got to get you out. If I don't, and something happens..." he trailed off again, but Natalie understood. She had already reasoned that out for herself.

"If we don't get to Laila, if we don't get her out, we'll lose our only lead to stopping Stovall and Vitori," she pressed back. Shaw sighed and looked away, but Natalie drew his gaze back with her hand. "If we don't do this, if we can't curb this war by exposing their hand in it, they'll work endlessly to ensure our men and women in uniform are deployed here to die for their profits. You went after General Weber for this exact same thing," she said, stressing those last three words with hard emphasis. "*This* is the risk we take; *this* is our duty." The fire behind her green eyes seemed to push back the darkness around them.

"That same duty applies to these downed airmen, too," Shaw countered.

"David," she began again, frustrated for the first time by his protective nature. "If we don't get Laila, no one will be able to prove what's really happening here. Once Stovall catches wind that the Russians shot down a US Air Force plane, he's going to have all he needs to convince the administration, the intelligence community, and the military to commit troops to this fight. Thousands will die!"

"But they did shoot down this bird," he countered. He again glanced toward Lincoln and Reeves, who still stared at them, processing their exchange. He turned back to Natalie and added, "We can't change that, and if that's cause for Article Five, then so be it."

Natalie wrung her hands in front of her face toward her husband. They moved to her forehead as she tried to press out her frustration.

"And we're now wasting time. Once you're safe and out of this hellhole, I'll try to find a way to go back for Laila."

"But there's no time for that!" Natalie argued, her cry again louder than it should be. Shaw rapidly threw a cupped hand over her mouth and pressed close to her at the same time. The action only enraged her further, but she knew she had messed up.

"This is my world. If I have to treat you like a grunt to get you to do what I need you to do, I will. Understood?" he said, his tone hard, ruthless even.

Natalie had never heard him talk to her that way before. Why would he have? Now, with their circumstance more dire than ever and death reaching for them from the darkness, she couldn't blame him, though she was angry. Her eyes showed as much, and Shaw knew they would have to work through this later. However, now, he just needed her to obey. He gently removed his hand but kept his gaze stern.

"I see it, Nat. I really do, and I'll do my best to get Laila out, but the priority is you. You're not a soldier, and I need to get you out of here. Even if we were to extract Laila, the damage is done. There's no going back from this. There's the guys to consider. This is not what they signed up for. I can't just walk them into a firefight with a near-peer enemy."

"But this is what Stovall wants," she hissed, drawing another sigh from her husband. "You think *you* have the final say? I've got Laila's location, and I'm going to save her. If you want to keep me safe, you're going to have to come along."

"And if you get hurt?" he said, his voice pained.

"We'll deal with it as we've dealt with everything else," she replied strongly. Her imagination swirled with the ways that might happen, and then her heart sank as she thought of her husband as the one wounded or killed. The thought sobered her immediately, having nearly lost him on more occasions than she was comfortable with. She thought of the CIA team she had led in Yemen, who all had perished on account of her commitment to her mission. Would the same happen now?

As Natalie and Shaw wrestled with their fears, McEwen approached Lincoln and Reeves. The rest of the team, still on watch, patiently waited, submitting to Shaw and Natalie's leadership. Only McEwen struggled with the uncertainty, having only recently doffed the mantle of leadership for his position at Invictus. It was a trade not made lightly, but one he had peace with.

"We going to get a move on and save Firefly or what?" he asked Reeves and Lincoln, through their encrypted radios that ran to their helmet-mounted ear protection.

"Yeah, what are we waiting for?" came Bray's contribution.

"She can't have that much more time with this invasion," Pikari added.

The words from their men broke the struggle between Natalie and Shaw, and they looked at each other, both realizing their roles in the world and the sacrifices they were willing to make for the greater good.

Still an impossible choice, Shaw pushed past his fear, allowing it to go through and beyond him, reminding himself that fear is the little death that brings total obliteration.

Remembering the lesson from one of his favorite books, he relented, seeing his decision for what it truly was—between courage and cowardice. He was afraid to face his most dire fear, and in relinquishing control, he found the way forward, unified with his wife. However, the truth of the situation remained with him, bubbling deep in his gut.

If he failed, he knew he would likely lose his wife, perhaps even his own life, the lives of his men, and potentially doom a generation of American and Allied soldiers in a war born solely of greed and ambition. He knew he would need all his focus, all his cunning and wit, and all his training and experience. Still, he figured it might not be enough.

Shaw inhaled and met Natalie's gaze with a resolution that drew a smile to her lips.

"There you are," she said.

Shaw raised his hand, slid his fingers over her left cheek, wrapped them around the back of her neck, and pulled her in for a kiss, canting his head to clear his NODs.

When they parted, Natalie's mind spun from the subtle yet intense passion behind his kiss. Shaw didn't say another word to her. He just stared into her eyes as he pressed his PTT and said, "Invictus, mount up."

37

Washington, DC

From his estate in Kalorama, Anderson Stovall sipped his Scotch while watching the breaking coverage of the Russian invasion. He checked his watch. It was just after 10:00 p.m.

"Later than you said, Sofia," he muttered to himself, displeased, but knowing it to be of little consequence. Though alone in his lounge, he felt the eyes of the world on him as they watched with bated breath his handiwork. He wondered if Rykov had done anything this ambitious and grew immediately sour as he figured he had. Had the Soviet Union fallen on account of Rykov's work? That was far more than he was accomplishing here.

For now, at least, he thought.

He recognized that his work now could destroy, rebuild, and remake Russia into something far more beneficial to the world, something he could control. He thought of the untapped opportunity that existed in Siberia, the fresh water that undoubtedly would become a coveted resource in the coming decades.

Decades...

Though faced with perhaps his greatest opportunity, Stovall couldn't shake his looming mortality. He had always considered himself middle-aged, or at least he had for the last twenty years, but now, he recognized he was entering his golden years, that he was becoming an old man whether he liked it or not. He likely only had three more decades, maybe four if he really focused.

"I've built a legacy with no one to leave it to," he said out loud with an accompanying chuckle, as if the thought had just occurred to him. However, he had been struggling with that reality for weeks now. He knew he could have women presented to him of the finest pedigree, as perfect genetics as possible, to be the mother of his heir. He knew he could even undergo multiple attempts with numerous candidates to groom the perfect heir and discard the rest. They would be cared for and provided for, no doubt, as money was merely a trifle to him, but they would not inherit his most coveted possession, his greatest legacy.

His power.

Though he thought of the many ways he could sire that coveted heir, he kept coming back to the same problem: though genetically superior, he could not ensure the mother's commitment or values would align completely and unfailingly with his. That was the frustration that confounded him. He could take all the steps to sire his heir, only to have him coddled and weakened by a doting mother. No, he needed strength and ambition in the mother to rival his own.

The clarity that struck him in that moment made him laugh out loud again. He shook his head as he drained his dram, smacking his tongue to accent his epiphany.

I've been looking at her all wrong, he thought.

Viewed previously only as an asset to leverage, to tempt with power in order to achieve his own goals, he now saw that Sofia Vitori could be more, much more.

A child born of them both would have the cunning, strength, and ambition worthy of the legacy Stovall had built. He wouldn't have to concern himself with harmful doting, as Sofia had the strength he saw when he looked in the mirror. She valued the cause, the legacy, above all else.

Yes, he told himself.

He couldn't deny his arousal as he initiated a call through their proprietary, encrypted communication channel, and he waited impatiently for her to answer.

"Anderson, what a pleasant surprise," Sofia replied, her voice sounding silkier than ever.

"Sofia, yes, I wanted to congratulate you on a successful launch," he said. "What are you doing now?"

"I'm taking a bath," she said, adding a short laugh that stirred his loins for her.

How quickly things change, he thought, not for the first time.

"I wish I was there," he said, knowing he was sharing too much.

"Who says I want you here?" she shot back, but the statement only made him yearn for her even more. "How is the media campaign faring?"

"It just launched, so far everything is going according to plan. How is everything on your end?"

"Well, General Dudka is still alive and in opposition to me," she replied curtly. "Saved by your man no less."

"My man?"

"De la Vega, your Red Horse man."

"Diego is in Kyiv?" he asked.

"I thought you knew," she said.

"I didn't," he replied, troubled.

"Well, I had to take drastic measures in the last hour to ensure things remain under control," she said.

"What kind of drastic measures?"

"When my assassination team failed, I had my men target Dudka's base of operations. I'm still awaiting reports, but I must say that your Red Horse men might be collateral damage."

Stovall was silent for a moment, and Sofia didn't care if she had overstepped or not. Dudka needed to die, and having members of her Brotherhood throughout the ranks of the Russian army only aided her ability to direct fire where she needed it. She doubted the Kremlin even knew the location of Dudka's headquarters, but she did. Launching the missile barrage to target the base was part of the original plan, and now she hoped the Russian paratroopers inbound could finish the work if the missiles had failed.

"Pity," Stovall finally said, his tone carrying a certain nonchalance. "But this is what we planned for. After all, nothing enrages America more than a dead hero. I'll work on seating his replacement ASAP."

"There's more," she said. "I had one of my men shoot down a US Air Force cargo plane bound for Kyiv. I believe the Shaws were on board."

"I've not yet received word of this," he said, barely containing his jubilation. "The Shaws are dead?"

"I don't know yet, but the Russians targeting and shooting down an American military aircraft gives your call to war stronger legs upon which to stand," Sofia answered.

"This is wonderful news!" Stovall exclaimed.

Sofia was surprised by his response. She had been angered and frustrated by Troske's failed attempt. Though the Brotherhood filled the ranks on both sides of this new conflict, each escalation she leveraged risked her exposure more and more. Too much meddling, and she knew she might endanger herself. Pulling strings was one thing; directing the show was something altogether different.

"I need to see you," Stovall said quickly.

Sofia was taken aback by his forwardness. Though she had resolved to push harder to exert her control over him, she had not yet been able to implement those plans. What had happened since their last meeting that had brought this new desire? Her ignorance of it made her wary.

"I don't know when we can make that happen," she probed. "There is still too much to do."

"The details will take care of themselves," he urged. "I can meet you in Paris. I have business there next week."

Sofia thought for a moment as she extended a soapy leg from the cloud of bubbles covering her. Her dark, slender eyebrows furrowed, revealing tentativeness and concern through her expression.

"Please," he said, his voice tender with longing. Sofia bit her bottom lip as she tried to discern his intentions.

"Okay," she said.

"Wonderful, I look forward to meeting again," he said.

"The feeling is mutual," she replied.

38

North of Hostomel,
Kyiv Oblast

The armored Stryker's massive eight wheels churned through the frozen earth of the Northern Ukrainian countryside as the team inside felt nearly every bump. They were crammed, exceeding the Stryker's capacity by two, but they were all thankful for the heat that swirled around the space. Rakestraw drove, and all were grateful he had driven one as a lowly Ranger private. He and Lincoln were really the only individuals on the team who had any operational experience with the system, having worked with the vehicles in the 75th Rangers during early GWOT. However, Lincoln—a former Ranger captain—had never driven one. He was going back and forth with Reeves about it until Rakestraw mentioned his experience. All were relieved. This, however, did not mean Rakestraw was a proficient driver. He was long out of practice.

"Sorry," he called out as the vehicle careened through a drainage ditch at the edge of a field before bouncing over a dirt road and continuing onward. Lincoln sat behind the turret fire controls, keeping his eyes on the multiple sensors and cameras that provided maximum external observation. It had taken him a minute to get his bearings, but he was now confident he could leverage the weapon systems to the desired effect should the need arise.

Natalie sat in Shaw's lap as they both kept their eyes on the ATAK devices strapped to the top front of their plate carriers. They not only kept tabs on what the overhead UAV broadcast around them but also on their target destination, the airport at Hostomel.

Before departure, the team had taken what supplies they knew would be valuable. In addition to food and water, they had secured Stinger Man-Portable Air-Defense Systems, Claymore mines, and extra ammunition while also outfitting the pilots and loadmaster with as close to a standard fighting loadout as possible. Afterwards, they had leveraged a pallet of C4 to destroy what they could of the aircraft and supplies, even though they knew it would draw attention to their location. They didn't feel right leaving the munitions for the Russians to leverage, and now they were putting as much distance between the wreckage and themselves as they could.

Everyone was aware that the Stryker's armor would only protect them from small arms fire, shrapnel from artillery, and maybe mortar fire, but a direct hit from an enemy fighter or tank would end their lives. They had weighed the options before them—of leveraging the infantry carrier or moving on foot—and had decided that the carrier was best for the situation, not only for the added armor, but for the firepower. With its Kongsberg unmanned turret and MK44 Bushmaster II 30mm cannon, this newer Dragoon variant simply provided firepower they couldn't afford to abandon.

"Do we know where Laila is being held at the airport?" Shaw asked Natalie. Her weight, though light on account of her athletic frame, still generated a stiff discomfort in his thighs. He kept shifting his legs back and forth with the movement of the vehicle to keep the blood circulating.

"This hangar," Natalie said, drawing Shaw's gaze to her own ATAK. "I'll mark it," she added, tapping the screen. Shaw looked back at his own device to see the blue box superimposed over the structure.

"I've got it. We're sure she's there?"

"As sure as we can be," Natalie replied.

"Doesn't look like the Russian front has advanced this far south yet," he said, "but it's impossible to know. I heard gunfire to the south."

"They likely are deploying paratroopers to take key points in the city," Natalie reasoned.

"Makes sense and certainly complicates things," Shaw muttered, keeping his gaze on the ATAK.

"Nectar, this is Hummingbird. How copy?" came the long-awaited voice in their headsets.

Mari Sosa's voice sounded deep and groggy and was void of its usual sharpness. The Deputy Director of Operations hadn't been asleep for thirty minutes before she received the call about the Shaws' current predicament. Now, in an ops room at Langley with an equally tired team—including Kara Bivens and Regan Pompeo—she nursed a hot coffee, preparing for what she knew would be a long night.

"We read you, Hummingbird, thanks for coming to play," Natalie replied.

"Not my idea of play," Sosa retorted before taking another sip. "We don't have much time before everyone knows about your downed plane. SecDef isn't going to take kindly to losing a bird to Russian forces."

"We need to keep this quiet until we can figure out what's going on," Natalie replied.

"Figure out what's going on?" Sosa shot back, harsher than she intended. Natalie glanced at Shaw, who only raised his eyebrows. "Don't tell me you think a particular someone is behind this?"

"I do," Natalie said with an air of certainty. She imagined Sosa sighing and pinching the bridge of her nose.

"Understood, Nectar," Sosa replied, her tone frustrated.

"Just trust me," Natalie urged. "Keep this quiet until we extract Firefly. She'll have the information we need to put everything together."

"You have eight hours," Sosa replied.

"Roger that."

39

Special Operations Forces Headquarters
Kyiv, Ukraine

"Zorro! Zorro!"

The calls were faint, distant but audible through the surrounding rumble of shifting and falling rubble. But there was something else, a familiar, muted popping that eluded recognition.

"Zorro! Can you hear me?"

De la Vega coughed, and the dust caking him shot upward with the action, though in the complete darkness, he couldn't see it. He blinked rapidly and brought his fingers to his eyes even as the movement coursed agony throughout his body.

Where am I? Am I blind?

The sudden panic surged with terrible force, but the seasoned special forces operator beat it back with honed will.

Easy, Zorro. Focus, De la Vega told himself. He fought to clear his mind of fear and confusion, both assaulting him with unwavering zeal. He reached out with his hands and found a firm barrier on either side of him sloping upward and over him like a triangle.

"Zorro!" came the call again.

"Ricochet!" De la Vega replied, surprised at how weak his voice sounded. His throat burned from the dust, and he coughed again.

"I hear you, brother!" Ricochet shouted back, relief evident in his tone. "We're going to get you out!"

Before De la Vega allowed the solace to wash over him, new, louder pops reached his ears.

"Contact!" he heard Ricochet shout before the thundering of automatic gunfire sounded just feet away, though muted.

"Ricochet!" De la Vega shouted, fearing for his friend. *Contact? How? Where? Who?* The gunfire continued as additional weapons opened up, and De la Vega heard the snaps and cracks of bullets chipping into the debris around him. "Come on!" he urged himself, reaching out with his hands again to make some sense of his orientation and the space around him. He was acutely aware that if he moved, bumped, or dislodged the wrong piece of debris, he could bury and crush himself.

He shimmied on his bare back, feeling new scrapes and cuts open up, but he ignored them all. Ricochet was in trouble.

The gunfire continued as De la Vega squirmed his way along the tented structure that had saved him from being crushed. He could only assume that it was part of the walls having collapsed inward over him, only to be held in place by the other. He didn't have to crawl far before faint stars glowed ahead—small pinpricks of light guiding him as the seafarers of old.

He found enough space to roll onto his stomach and crawl faster down the prism toward the stars. Though grateful he had not lost his vision, he feared for his men, for Ricochet.

As he neared the stars, he reached out for them, feeling the dense debris of twisted rebar, crumbled concrete, and coarse grit. Probing with his fingers, De la Vega gently tested the integrity of the mound while drawing his legs up as close to his torso as possible. If the tented concrete collapsed, he didn't want to be stretched to his full length.

He tested one of the small openings and pressed his fingers through the gravel, pushing out a handful and widening the hole. As he did so, sound funneled through with unexpected force. Gunfire, sirens, explosions, all filled his ears. The thundering disoriented him for a moment, but his resolve quickly took back control.

Cautiously, he widened the hole by pushing out more gravel and then waited as the gunfire continued.

It's got to be the invasion, De la Vega reasoned, his anger against Stovall reaching new heights. *Did he send us here to sacrifice us?* Surely not, but De la Vega couldn't shake the feeling. *Get out. Fight. Survive. Then get to the bottom of this.*

Again he widened the hole. The firefight was right on top of him. A form fell over his hole and startled De la Vega.

"Man down!" he heard Ricochet shout as the gunfight continued. The figure blocking De la Vega's path jerked several more times as it took additional rounds.

The Red Horse CEO pushed the limits of his comfort and began pulling handfuls of debris toward him in an effort to clear a way and join the fight. After one large handful, a dead man's face materialized, but De la Vega didn't recognize him. Grateful the soldier wasn't one of his own, he continued to work toward digging to locate the man's rifle.

Having cleared enough to crawl out, De la Vega pushed against the body, rolling it slightly to expose the composite stock of an AK-74. He struggled to free the weapon from under the man's weight while he still remained concealed in his tunnel. Finally wrestling it free, De la Vega checked the chamber and magazine to confirm condition before pushing again on the body with his left hand while presenting the rifle forward with his right.

The cold air stung his eyes as it washed in from around the body. Bracing the rifle on the back of the corpse, De la Vega took in the battlespace with wide eyes already adjusted to the dark. The muzzle flashes in the darkness provided easy targets as he took aim and engaged the enemy combatants firing at Ricochet.

Ricochet heard the gunfire to his right as he leveraged the cover provided by the destroyed building. It stung his already ringing ears, but he welcomed the addition. He had already lost both the Ukrainians he had teamed up with—one killed from the first shots and the other just a few seconds ago. He was glad to know that he wasn't alone, and gladder still to know that the only person who could possibly be on the other end of that gun was Zorro.

"Just like old times!" he shouted as he locked in a new magazine on his borrowed AK-74 carbine.

"What times are you talking about!" De la Vega retorted as he carefully placed his shots, one at a time.

Dressed in silkies and an old chest rig, Ricochet's pale skin gleamed in the darkness. Even with most of the lights blown out from the initial strike, he knew he was still an easy target and needed clothes to conceal his easily identifiable silhouette.

First, win, he reminded himself as he engaged another target. Knowing that mobility meant survivability and that Zorro couldn't free himself from his hold without exposing himself to the enemy, Ricochet formed a plan in his mind. He had to flank—at worst to draw their fire to give Zorro the breathing room to extricate himself, at best to end the fight.

"Moving!" he shouted out.

"Move!" came Zorro's response as he increased his firing cadence.

Ricochet darted left, deeper into the damaged barracks and toward the impact zone. He tripped over debris and the laces of his untied boots, but he pressed forward, scraping his arm on a piece of exposed rebar. Clambering down into the crater, he raced across and climbed up the right side, his feet slipping on the loose gravel. Upon cresting the rim, he glanced left, straight ahead, then back right toward the firefight.

Clear.

He bolted from the crater, across the street, and into the alley on the other side. The windows of the building had been blown out by the blast, and part of the exterior wall was crumbling. Though he hurried down the alley, he kept vigilant with his rifle ready to engage any threat. Coming to an intersecting alley, he neared the right side wall and pied the left corner as far as he could see.

It looked clear. Backpedaling briefly, he moved to the left wall and, his shoulder rubbing against its concrete surface, he pied the right corner, peering as far as he could and knowing in that direction stood the force he needed to engage. He didn't know their numbers, but he had to do something to give Zorro a chance. Eventually, the force would be able to skirt Zorro's field of view and either put a grenade down his hole or approach to engage point-blank.

After working through the puzzle of the fatal funnel, Ricochet decided to commit to the right where he knew the threat lay. He flowed forward, keeping his rifle high and ready while skirting the intersecting alley all the way to the far side. Once his left shoulder made contact with the far wall, he stole a glance back over his shoulder.

Clear.

Doing this alone sucks.

He inhaled deeply.

Embrace the suck.

He exhaled and pressed forward, his eyes on the end of the alley and focusing on how much of the street he could see. The gunfire grew louder as automatic fire ahead threatened to deafen him. Gritting his teeth, he zigzagged down the alley to keep as much situational awareness on the street as he could.

Ricochet didn't stop moving as an enemy combatant breached the alley opening, his attention focused on Zorro's hide. Picking up his iron sights, Ricochet squeezed the trigger, and the soldier stumbled sideways in an attempt to regain his footing, but another shot dropped him to the ground.

Chaos erupted through the Russian paratrooper team as one of their teammates unexpectedly fell from what could only be a flanking element. The squad leader directed half of what remained of his ten-man squad to address the new threat to their three o'clock while the rest continued on the threat ahead.

Though they had landed in the base as planned, they had overshot their landing zone and were separated from the rest of the company. Based on the radio chatter, his squad wasn't the only one to have missed their mark. The entire company was spread thin, and all platoon commanders were urging their troops to regroup in order to take the base.

Sergeant Popov fought against fear as his men dwindled around him. He was down to six, including himself.

"There were only three of them!" he growled as he fumbled his reload on account of his rising frustration. He realized now that the men he had engaged were far better trained than his own, and he questioned the decision to send only one company to take the base. He knew other paratrooper companies were working to secure other important objectives, with the highest being the capture/kill of the Ukrainian President.

Popov watched another of his men fall, and panic rose from his toes, stifling his movements and causing him to sweat, even in the frigid, early morning cold.

"*Otstupat'!*" he cried, his sharp Russian accent cutting through the air.

Upon hearing the command to retreat, his remaining four men turned and sprinted back the way they had come. To Popov's utmost horror, he watched them fall one by one as they turned their backs on their adversary and ran without considering the open alley and exposing themselves to the flanking element.

Popov attempted to salvage the situation by providing a burst of cover fire toward the ruined building ahead, but he staggered backward as something slammed into him. He didn't register the pain at first, just the difficulty breathing. As he gasped for air, the fire slowly spread and radiated from underneath his clavicle. Choking followed as his blood filled his trachea, and no matter how much he tried to cough, he couldn't manage to clear his airway.

Wide-eyed, he reached out for one of his men, who stopped to render aid only to be cut down a second later. His blood splattered Popov's face, and the dying sergeant's reflexes still jerked in response to the horror. Out of the corner of his eye, he caught sight of a pale form, a ghost emerging from the alley.

Baba Yaga...

As Popov's reason fled in the midst of his death throes, his vision faded, though he tried to focus on the apparition advancing toward him.

"*Nyet...nyet...*" he managed through his gurgling, over and over again, until his breathing ceased and his eyes stared blankly at the sky.

"We're clear," Ricochet stated, breathless, as he raced up the rubble toward De la Vega. His adrenaline surged through him, but he managed strong control after an entire career of gunfights, though he could say that was likely the most disadvantaged he had ever been.

Grateful was an understatement.

Ricochet crouched and reached into the hole, gripping De la Vega's forearms and pulling gently. Both men were aware that they needed to vacate the area, establish comms, and group up with allied forces. Once free, De la Vega inhaled deeply and shook away the lingering claustrophobia.

"I can't tell you how glad I am to see you," Ricochet stated, unusually emotive. De la Vega nodded back at him.

"Where's the rest of our guys?" he asked, but Ricochet's sorrowful exhale answered the question. "No," De la Vega murmured. Ricochet nodded gravely, looking toward the impact crater.

"Had to be a missile. Hit right where we were bunking down. I was on the other side of you, and you must have been just clear of the blast. They're all gone, Diego," Ricochet answered.

"It's just us?" De la Vega asked, bewildered in his rage. Ricochet's nod nearly sent him over the edge.

Stovall!

De la Vega couldn't help but blame the man. He felt all of this was too coincidental not to be planned.

"How did they know we were here?" he asked, more to himself than Ricochet. The short, white-bearded operator furrowed his brow.

"What are you talking about?" Ricochet asked.

"I need to find Dudka," De la Vega quickly said before crouching and further equipping himself from the dead Ukrainian at his feet.

Ricochet did the same from the second soldier he had teamed up with, taking radios, load-bearing equipment, and, despite hating every second of it, their clothes. With their adrenaline waning, both Americans began to shiver in the cold.

"Alright," De la Vega said, still feeling chills sweep over him. His feet slid around in boots too large for him, and the camouflaged uniform hung loosely on his stocky, yet lean frame. "Let's go."

40

Antonov International Airport, Hostomel, Ukraine

Though Natalie gave them the all clear, the Invictus operators remained conscious of the rattling of distant gunfire, artillery, and airstrikes as they gathered under the security of the nearby evergreen canopy. Having disembarked from the Stryker, Shaw and his men prepared their infiltration. Of their eight-man team, only Rakestraw remained behind to operate the infantry carrier for their exfiltration.

The seven remaining men split into two teams, one led by Shaw and the other by Reeves. They kept their attention outward as Shaw and Reeves consulted within the tight circle.

Bray surveyed his sector, which extended beyond the wood and across a field, his night vision searching for any orange blips to indicate a thermal presence.

“Man, I’m definitely living a childhood fantasy right now. This is straight out of *Saving Private Ryan*,” he muttered to Pikari, who paced next to him.

“In more ways than one,” the Māori replied quietly.

"No kidding, this is wild," Bray said in eager excitement as he crouched among the sparse, late winter undergrowth.

Pikari shifted his gaze east, his dark expression grim and stern as he observed the plumes of smoke that accompanied the distant roar of artillery and heavy armor. To his right, he could see the lights of Kyiv glowing faintly to the south. Sporadic flashes of bright orange indicated the battle for the city raged onward.

It was clear to the team that the forest had taken its fair share of recent damage. All around them, trees lay in unusual ways, their trunks splintered by great force. The craters in the fields around them told the men all they needed to know. The airport just to the south was, indeed, a prime target of the Russian invasion strategy. If the artillery that caused all this damage had ceased, it meant that ground troops were on their way.

The continued rattle of distant gunfire and consistent artillery bombardments only added to the reality that they were conducting an operation in a newly war-torn European nation. The rising intensity suggested that Ukraine was finally responding.

The rain slowly began, pattering through the naked branches above before falling on the seven men below. Within seconds and following a thunderous roar, a light rain fell, misting more than raining. The water collected on their gear and tickled their faces, but the professionals only exhaled their annoyance.

Shaw flipped the Nav Board down from his plate carrier to access his ATAK, viewing their GPS location and the secure UAV feed that focused on his team. He gathered his bearings and confirmed their location on the advanced tactical software.

"Nectar, this is Philo, how copy?" Shaw muttered into the microphone hovering over the left corner of his mouth, which connected to a secure radio strapped to the left side of his plate carrier.

"Copy, Philo," Natalie replied from the security of the Stryker. "We've got you on ISR."

The CIA's stealth unmanned aerial vehicle flew high above the storm, its advanced sensors penetrating the darkness, and its technology keeping it hidden from Russian radar and aircraft.

"This section of the oblast shows no activity, but I don't think it will be for long. You're good to circumvent the airport and wait for us to the south," Shaw said.

"Copy, Philo. Hummingbird estimates Russian forces are northwest of you, advancing from Dymer. This invasion isn't Baghdad fast, but they're not wasting any time," Natalie replied.

"Good copy, Nectar. We're Oscar Mike toward the target." Shaw transitioned his attention to his team and nodded toward Aston and Roman. "Lead us forward."

Aston, with Roman taking point, rose and moved boldly south, keeping his rifle ready and his head on a swivel. The rest followed, maintaining a loose line as they moved through the small wood.

War in Europe was a different game, they all knew. These weren't ill-equipped insurgents; this was a near-peer enemy, and one the operators had not faced before. However, that uncertainty had no effect on their focus, lethality, or eagerness.

Thunder roared again, lightning flashed, and the rain toyed with them —thinning and thickening randomly as the seven men, keeping to the forest, paralleled a dirt road.

The small city of Hostomel lay farther south, and the team kept their pace through the haunting woods slow enough to stay alert and silent but quick enough to put distance between themselves and the advancing main Russian force. Each was glad their boots kept their feet dry and their socks warm as they sloshed through the new growth of wet ferns at their ankles.

As they neared their target location, the tension grew. Although experts in their field, each man couldn't deny the anxiety that clashed with excitement within their guts.

Reeves firmed his lips as he took in the scorched civilian vehicles littering the road. Had the Russians targeted civilians? The thought angered him, but he was not so naïve to think otherwise.

"It's like coming into Fallujah all over again," Reeves muttered quietly to Shaw as they kept a slow, tactical pace together.

"Yeah, except this is Europe. Can you believe it?"

"I honestly can't, brother," Reeves replied as he shifted his grip on the highly customized, suppressed MK46 squad automatic weapon.

The eerie whistle of the wind and the light drumming of rain manifested a severe sense of isolation among the seven men. They slowed as they passed a farmhouse not far on their left. It was clear to the men that it had taken a shell, whether intentionally or errantly, they couldn't tell.

An unnatural rustling rose from their left, picked up by the hearing amplification of their headsets. Each man spun quickly, weapons high and ready as their eyes rapidly located the source. With fingers on triggers and safeties off, each man let out a slow exhale as they steadied themselves, wrestling back control of their readiness to kill.

The blonde girl, no more than twelve and dressed in ripped and soiled clothing, stood motionless among the trees, paralyzed with fear. The men lowered their weapons and suppressed the adrenaline surging through their bodies.

"Bro," Bray said softly to no one in particular, bewildered by her presence. It was one thing to have seen Iraqi and Afghan children in that exact situation, but for some reason seeing a little girl, with the same complexion as his own assaulted his psyche.

"Hold up," Shaw said as he moved to Reeves' back. He unzipped the man's pack and produced two MREs—the brown packages each containing a heavy caloric load as well as packaged water. He turned and urged Reeves to fish out two of his own.

Shaw and Reeves set the light brown packages on the ground at their feet, and Shaw touched his fingers to his mouth in a signal to the girl, telling her what it was. She nodded but did not move until Shaw and his team continued on their way. Shaw glanced back as the girl raced forward, scooped up the packages, and disappeared into the dreary haze, reminding him of a stray dog.

The ordeal affected him more than he would readily admit, but he continued to put one foot in front of the other, trying to keep his mind off the emotions the little girl had stirred within him.

Focus, David.

Emotions like that will get you and your men killed.

You would know.

As they neared the airport, Shaw paused in the shadows offered by the forest to survey the target location. Half hidden behind a tree, the team leader took in the information before him. The airport showed clear signs of significant damage with multiple hangars having suffered direct hits from some type of large munition. Though difficult to discern clearly through the haze, Shaw thought he saw several commercial aircraft dotting the airstrip.

He witnessed little movement as he planned their infiltration. The airport, oddly, seemed mostly quiet.

"Which building is it?" Reeves asked. Shaw pulled a monocular from his plate carrier and studied each structure. He saw the challenge the open-air compound presented, and that only stressed the need for accurate intelligence. The longer they were there, the more likely they were to be discovered.

"Makes sense that Ivan would want this place," Reeves added.

"Yeah, but just from our limited time on the ground, this does not look like a well-executed invasion," Shaw countered. Reeves had been thinking the same thing. Perhaps their near-peer enemy wasn't as near-peer as their government believed. Time would tell. "Intel puts Firefly in the main hangar on the northwest side of the tarmac," Shaw continued.

"That doesn't help," Reeves muttered as his eyes focused on the bare landscape before them. New gunfire and explosions clattered not far to the west, serving as a reminder that the Russians were indeed advancing.

"Alright, I'll call it in," Shaw said as he turned his body away from the airport and again accessed the ATAK on his Nav Board. As he got a read on their position from the UAV feed and surveyed the scope of the facility before them, he reviewed their original infiltration route and pressed his PTT to engage with Natalie. "Nectar, this is Philo. We're in position on the north side of the airport. We've got eyes on the target building, requesting confirmation, how copy?"

"We read you, Philo. Target building confirmed. We've seen no movement. We believe the main contingent of Russian forces is still to the northeast of you. Be advised, expect armed resistance. Current surveillance shows no indication of a change in the intel. Firefly is believed to still be on the premises," Natalie said, her voice clipping in Shaw's headset.

"Understood, Nectar. Any new intel on why Firefly is here?"

"Nothing, but I assume that there is some kind of extraction plan in place. My guess would be Russians, probably special operations."

"Copy, we're Oscar Mike on infil route one," Shaw answered.

"Good copy, Philo. Stay safe," Natalie said. Shaw heard the concern in her tone, but he didn't want to think of the outcome if they failed. He had been separated from her once against his will, and he had no intention of allowing that to happen a second time. He took one last look at the UAV feed before closing the device into his plate carrier and turning again to assess the airport. It was small compared to American standards, perhaps like something he'd see in a rural town.

"Beowulf, assessment?" Shaw asked, maintaining his commitment to hear from his men, even more so now that he commanded those who had chosen voluntary employment.

Bratcher peered through his riflescope.

"Not much I can do here for you," he said in his rugged Geordie accent, his low tones making the accent more muddled than usual. "Can't see anything on the southern side, on account of those smaller hangars there, and even with this seven-six-two, I'd still like to be a bit closer than we are now."

"Good copy, I feel the same," Shaw replied. "What if we get you on that rooftop there?" Shaw asked, pointing to a larger cluster of buildings to their southwest.

"That'll work, though I'd like some company," Bratcher replied.

"I wouldn't leave you up there alone," Shaw answered with a smirk. "Alright, we'll move south and clear the hangars and drop Matterhorn and Beowulf off before advancing through those structures there to get us to our target hangar; minimizes exposure, how copy?" Shaw glanced down the line, looking at each man, save the two pulling rear security, and heard their rounds of agreement. With a nod, he rose to his feet and led his team onward.

The seven operators emerged from the dark wood as specters from another plane of existence. They moved with perfect efficiency, their bodies rigid yet somehow their movements smooth. They appeared as floating torsos with heads too big for their bodies and eyes that jutted forth in disturbing proportions.

Many an adversary had fallen before the capable hands of the Allied warfighter, and with their confident movements, the men of Invictus showed that that boldness and resolve had only strengthened over the last twenty years of war, refining their capability beyond any other warrior in the history of humanity. Handpicked for immeasurable lethality and teeming with moral integrity, there was likely not an adversarial force on the planet that could match them.

Still, each man had lost friends to a lucky shot from an enemy combatant, and those painful lessons were always kept close at hand.

41

Shaw and his team hunkered down in the ruins of a charred building. "We've got eyes on the hangar," he said into his radio for Natalie, Lincoln, and Rakestraw's sake. The bellowing of the distant gunfire had grown louder and louder as the team had pushed into the perimeter of the airport.

The five men, having left Bratcher and Reeves in an overwatch position on the buildings behind them, observed little movement as they planned their approach to the hangar that held Firefly. From their angle, Shaw and his team couldn't see anyone, threats or otherwise.

A few windows in the terminal building emitted a dim glow, but most were bathed in blackness. Shaw and his team waited and readied themselves in case they were unknowingly compromised. The team scanned their options.

"Everything looks good," Aston noted with Roman crouching on his right. "No alerts from MPC."

"We just going to stroll right in?" Bray asked. Shaw studied the hangar from under the glow of his night vision. His stomach turned. Something felt off, but he couldn't quite place his finger on it. Regardless, Firefly needed them and needed them now. Shaw licked his lips in silent tactical consideration. Making up his mind and trusting his instincts, he pressed his PTT to initiate team-wide comms.

"New plan. We're moving north, around the fuel center, and will flank the hangar from that direction. Invictus Overwatch, lead us in," Shaw said.

"We've got you, Philo," Reeves replied. He trained his machine gun on the opening of the hangar.

Shaw patted Aston's shoulder, and Aston issued Roman the corresponding command. The canine, silent and steady, moved forward at Aston's side. Bray and Pikari followed, then Shaw and McEwen. Each man moved with unmistakable aggression, ready to engage any threat the moment it presented itself. They trudged through the mud as they stacked up against the cinderblock wall that formed the perimeter of the small fuel depot.

"Hold," came Bratcher's command. The team froze. "I've got two helos inbound from the north. They'll pass right over you."

"Invictus, be advised: we have confirmed two helicopters inbound on your position. Assume hostile," Natalie said, her voice concerned.

"Copy, Nectar," Shaw muttered. He turned to his men. "Into that shed, move," he hissed, his urgency driving his staff to action. The men didn't have to be told twice, the fact not lost on them that they finally faced an adversary with aerial combat capability. Recent events suggested they had already used up their luck reserves. "Invictus Overwatch, find some cover," Shaw muttered.

"Already ahead of you," came Reeves' reply.

"Wait for them to pass," Shaw whispered. Thunder rattled the airport as a loud crack resounded from the heavens, the roar continuing as the helicopters took over the sky. *They're flying low,* Shaw noted.

"Philo," Natalie began.

"Go ahead, Nectar," Shaw replied.

"The helicopters have stopped over the runway, looks like they're deploying forces via fast rope," she said, her tone now even more serious.

"Solid copy, Nectar." He didn't need to brief the team; they had all heard.

"What's your call, Boss?" Bray asked quietly. Shaw felt his heart thump at the word *Boss*. His mind whirled back to Afghanistan, of saving Reyes, only for him to die just a couple of weeks later alongside the rest of Philo

Team. He thought of Wyatt, who had perished in a Congolese mine. He shook his head to clear his thoughts.

Not now.

"You alright?" Bray asked, seeing his commander's stoic expression from his side angle view. Shaw barely heard Bray before regaining command of his thoughts.

"Invictus Overwatch, you have eyes?" Shaw inquired.

"Affirmative," Reeves replied.

"Alright, ready the Stingers, we'll hit them both at the same time and continue toward Firefly."

"Bold," Reeves shot back. "I like it."

"We'll have to move fast," Shaw replied. "It'll grab the attention of every Russian in the vicinity."

"Good call then on bringing the MANPADS," Reeves replied.

"I had a hunch," Shaw answered back. Though they were long, heavy, and cumbersome, the Man-Portable, Aerial-Defense Systems—the same weapon system that had taken the lives of nearly everyone on Saber One and Two over a year and a half ago—were now to be used as intended, and Shaw gained some satisfaction in that.

As they left the shed and rounded the northwest corner of the fuel depot, Pikari and Bray prepped their FIM-92 Stinger surface-to-air missile system that Bray had carried on his back.

"Count twenty Ivans on the tarmac under the helicopters," Bratcher whispered into his mic.

"Copy," Shaw replied as they headed east, nearing the opposite corner of the fuel depot.

"Awaiting your command," Reeves said into his radio. He turned his head slightly to glance at Bratcher and said quietly, "As soon as you let that rip, they're going to know exactly where we are."

"I'd say so," Bratcher replied, wearing an excited smirk. In his fifteen years of special operations, Bratcher had not once participated in the destruction of an enemy rotorwing, and he couldn't wait to start the show.

He trained his Stinger's sight on one of the pilots of the nearest Russian-made Mi-8 helicopter but didn't activate the targeting just yet. He would wait for Shaw's command, which would give the helicopters the shortest window to evade once their systems alerted them that they were being targeted by a lethal payload.

Shaw swapped places with Aston at the front of the line and peered around the corner of the fuel depot. His sight was bathed in pale green as he focused through his night vision binoculars.

A small muddy path led south from their position, through sparse trees and over a small field littered with craters. On the other side of a narrow road that bisected the field lay the hangar just over one hundred meters south. Shaw pressed his PTT and said, "Romulus, Vagabond, on me, Riptide, Strider, get ready to take down west side helo. Overwatch, take east side helo. Matterhorn, I want effective fire on Ivan at engagement. On my mark."

With a wave of his hand, Aston and Roman took point with Shaw following and McEwen taking up the rear. The three men moved through the trees slowly, Aston keeping tabs on Roman for any alerts. Behind them, Pikari and Bray took a position with a clear sight of the eastern helicopter.

Shaw continued around the north side of the hangar and proceeded down its length. Pausing at the corner of the entry, he once more checked his ATAK and observed the new positions of the Russian contingent that had just arrived. Though it was unexpected, Shaw felt it hardly set them back.

"Nectar, we're in position to engage," Shaw whispered into his microphone.

"Good luck, Philo." Shaw turned back to face McEwen, who gave him a stoic nod. He patted Aston on the shoulder twice as he keyed his PTT.

"Mark."

42

Lieutenant Colonel Dima Kuznetsov remained proud and tall despite the wet cold annoying him greatly. Having fast-roped down from the lead helicopter, he exuded every bit of Russian pride he felt. The Spetsnaz commander couldn't pass up the opportunity to secure the favor of his superiors at the Kremlin, and the opportunity to deliver such a prize demanded that he facilitate personally. Additionally, seizing the important facility for the invasion effort only added to his hope for continued advancement and recognition.

The GRU officer had every confidence in his men who hurried behind him as they prepared to defend the airport from any Ukrainian counterattack. He knew he only needed to hold long enough for the main ground forces to arrive, and thus, he was not overly concerned. His men were highly trained, some of the best the Motherland had to offer, and the invasion plan to take Kyiv in three days held his full confidence.

He kept his strides long and purposeful, desiring to leave the mist behind, though he knew the cold would remain in the hangar. However, his heavy brow furrowed as he saw the unexpected shadow manifest around the corner of the structure. Kuznetsov's eyes widened in surprise and fear as a blur of fur rocketed toward him faster than he could possibly react, its titanium-capped teeth gleaming from a sudden flare of lightning above.

Kuznetsov shouted his alarm, but his helicopters deafened all sound as they shredded apart, crashed into each other, and spiraled into the ground. The ensuing explosions swallowed up a contingent of his troops. Then the breathy chirps of silenced rifles rang faintly amidst clamor, and a muted bellowing echoed from the north as American bullets cut through Russia's finest.

Roman snarled as he raced down his prey. He leapt into the air, his sharp canines targeting Kuznetsov's neck. The Spetsnaz officer raised his rifle, but he was not quick enough. Roman struck true, his teeth tearing and slicing into the man's neck. He jerked the Russian's body back and forth as he drove the man to the ground, ignoring his shrieks. His deliberate thrashing and steadfast hold ripped through Kuznetsov's throat as he tore at his jugular. The Spetsnaz officer's screams faded into a sickening gurgle as Roman left him to engage the next threat: a group of Russian soldiers taking position inside the hangar.

The light rain splattered Kuznetsov's face—the drops smacking into his wide eyes—as his blood pooled around him, mixing with the standing water and spreading far too quickly. Finally, his eyes closed, and he lay still, his ambition and pride having failed him.

43

Shaw remained loose, his muscles performing actions ingrained from over two decades of training and application. He moved upright, balancing the weight of his combat and sustainment gear, as he pivoted his torso at the waist to provide the most stable shooting platform while on the move. Moving into the hangar alongside Aston, he opened fire on the scrambling Russians who appeared as shocked and disoriented as they should have been.

No one had expected the helicopters to be shot from the sky. Even as some retreated and others fought back, they all wondered who these men were who had so violently and successfully assaulted them.

Reeves continued to lay down effective fire in steady bursts, leveraging the light machine gun to maximum effect. Behind the weapon, he could only describe his emotions as pure elation at overcoming a force so numerically superior.

Bratcher, back on his rifle, dropped the last Russian in view among the wreckage of the two downed helicopters.

"Bloody hell, that was awesome," he celebrated with a laugh. "Haven't had that much fun in...well, ever."

A stillness set on the tarmac even as the thunder echoed. Bray and

Pikari had joined the fight and now fanned out toward the hangar, each man killing two Russians while helping to secure the tarmac.

Within a matter of seconds, the engagement had ended. Roman sniffed around for a moment until a quiet call from Aston brought him obediently to his side.

"Clear," McEwen called into his radio after dropping the last Russian inside the hangar. He suddenly wondered if any of them had even fired a shot.

"Clear," Bray echoed.

"Clear," came Pikari's assessment.

"Clear," Aston replied.

"Clear," Shaw added with confident finality as he swept the interior of the warehouse with his M4A1. "Invictus Overwatch, how are we looking?" Shaw asked.

"Clear," came Reeves' reply, "but we won't be for long. Get a move on."

Satisfied, Shaw and his assault team moved deeper into the hangar, their weapons high and ready. They walked silently around various crates as they searched for Firefly. With the ground floor clear, that only left the small enclosed office at the back of the hangar, but the team ceased all forward movement when a lone man appeared at the only window, holding Firefly tight in his grasp with a pistol trained on her temple.

He shouted, his fear clearly evident. He wasn't dressed like the others, and Shaw suddenly recognized the man from images shown at Langley.

Stefo Troske.

Shaw, facing Troske from straight on, didn't have a clear shot, nor did Aston to his right. Cutting his eyes at McEwen on the far right flank, Shaw discreetly keyed his PTT with his fire control hand.

"Vagabond?" he asked.

"I got it," came McEwen's confident reply. Shaw moved his fire control hand out wide, showing his open palm toward Troske as he lowered his rifle. He made eye contact with Firefly, and even through the pale green of his NODs, he witnessed her firm resolve, though he noticed the fresh blood on her face.

From his angle, McEwen inched farther left, which opened up his target. As soon as Troske dropped his elbow, McEwen depressed the trigger.

His rifle chirped and recoiled lightly into his shoulder. The round snapped Troske's head rearward and to the left, and both he and Firefly dropped to the ground faster than anticipated.

"Good shooting, Vagabond," Shaw replied as he advanced toward the office door. Though he had watched McEwen's bullet strike Troske, he could not deny his concern for Firefly.

Stacking up on the door with Aston and Roman across from him, Shaw threw open the door, Aston gave the command, and Roman bolted inside with vicious intent. The two Invictus operators followed him closely.

"Clear," Aston said.

"Clear," Shaw echoed as he stowed his rifle behind his back and crouched to check on Firefly.

"Laila, it's me, David," he said calmly as he lifted his NODs from over his eyes. Laila fought against the tears that rimmed her blue eyes as she leapt into him. "You alright?" he asked. She pulled away, and although blood ran down the side of her face—partly hers, partly Troske's—she nodded and steadied herself with a deep breath. "We've got to go. Can you walk?"

Laila Malik firmed her jaw as Shaw helped her stand.

"Alright, you're good," he said. He pressed his PTT once more, "Nectar, this is Philo. We've got Firefly and are Oscar Mike toward exfil."

"Good copy, Philo," Natalie replied, relieved and elated.

"Aston," Shaw called off the radio. "Let's get Firefly a gun." As Aston moved to the nearest downed Spetsnaz soldier, Shaw checked Laila's head, his eyes searching through the blood to find the wound just forward of her temple.

"What happened here? You alright?" he asked.

"Yeah, I'm fine," Laila replied. She shivered, not from the cold, then turned to look at Troske. Her blue eyes found the bullet hole. "I told him I would kill him," she added.

Shaw glanced down at the man sprawled unnaturally on the floor of the small office. His head lay on his fanned out left arm, and his right leg bent at the knee in what looked an uncomfortable way. His dark eyes, void of any recognition, stared at the far wall.

"He's Troske, isn't he? The Macedonian?" Shaw asked. Laila nodded and hugged herself as she stared at him.

She hadn't expected to feel a sense of remorse looking upon his dead body, and it confused her. Was it because she hadn't been able to kill him? She thought it odd if that were the case. Maybe it was the usual shock of seeing someone you knew dead. It was one thing to kill his men; she hadn't known them, but, even if for ill, she had known Troske. Perhaps long ago, she might have considered him a friend, or at the very least a friendly acquaintance.

"We've got to go," Shaw urged her, taking her gently by the elbow.

"Yeah," she said, not resisting and allowing him to lead her to the main floor of the hangar to meet McEwen and Aston, who stood offering her a suppressed AK-105 carbine. He himself had one lashed to his assault pack, as did Bray. Shaw looked at him questioningly.

"You know how rare a real Russian AK-105 is?" he answered. Shaw scoffed.

"If you want to carry it," Shaw relented with a smirk. He turned to Laila. "I assume you know how to use one of these?"

Laila nodded, tied her blood-flaked copper hair into a low ponytail, and accepted the rifle from Aston. She slung the weapon over her shoulder, pulled the charging handle back just slightly to check its condition, and released it, slapping it with her palm to ensure proper chambering.

"Let's go," Shaw urged, guiding her toward the door. When they exited the office, Bray approached and offered Laila one of the Russian helmets and NODs he had salvaged for her.

"Thanks," Laila replied as she donned the equipment and adjusted everything quickly to her liking.

"Wow, you know your stuff," Bray complimented.

"You don't know the half of it," Laila answered. She gave Bray a playful wink before moving past him. Pikari, having watched the exchange, chuckled, which drew Bray's attention.

"I think I'm in love," Bray admitted.

"Yeah, I'm pretty good looking," Pikari replied before blowing him a kiss and following after Laila, Shaw, McEwen, and Aston.

That's not what I meant, Bray thought as he proceeded after them.

"Invictus Overwatch, we're coming out with Firefly now," Shaw said.

"We've got you," Reeves replied.

He and Bratcher watched as the team escorted their principal back through the route they had come before they packed up and reunited with them on their exfiltration from the airport.

"Nectar, how are we looking?" Shaw asked once the team had exited the airport and followed Roman south through a cratered field.

"Skies are clear," Natalie replied, her heart still in her throat. Though they had rescued Laila, a two-kilometer trek remained ahead of them before they regrouped with the Stryker. Then came the race to beat Russian forces back to Kyiv. Even once in Kyiv, extracting themselves from the country would not be easy, and if the Russian advance did succeed in taking or even encircling Kyiv, how would they hope to escape?

It'll be alright, Natalie told herself as she watched her husband and his team head her way with Laila centered among them. *We'll be alright.*

44

Special Operations Forces Headquarters
Kyiv, Ukraine

Moving slowly as a two-man tactical element, Ricochet and De la Vega made their way to Dudka's command building, where they had last seen him. Each funneled their rage to keep their grief at bay. The men of Operational Detachment-Mustang were some of the best Red Horse had to offer, some of the best America had to offer.

Though Ricochet channeled his fury against every Russian trooper the two men came across, De la Vega was plagued by a much deeper wrath, anger laced with betrayal and pain. As he put one foot in front of the other —his years of habitual execution propelling him forward—he thought of nothing but Stovall's announcement in his DC home weeks ago, celebrating the expected war in Europe and the riches coming to all of them.

De la Vega would have traded all the riches in the world to have his men back.

Using their superior tactics and training and realizing how disorganized the Russian assault on the military base truly was, the two former Green Berets made short work of any confused Russian squads they came across, eventually grouping with a contingent of base security and leading them in effective fire and movement despite the language barrier.

They had understood one word: *Dudka*, and like the Americans, they were keen to find and defend their commander-in-chief. However, en route to the headquarters building, the Ukrainian soldiers under their de facto command stopped all forward movement and burst into celebration.

De la Vega and Ricochet knew that could only mean one thing.

The base was theirs.

They had repelled the Russian assault.

For now.

"Dudka!" De la Vega turned and ordered. He had little time for celebration, and he needed to speak with the general immediately. If anything, he needed comms access.

Then, he thought of who he would call. If Stovall had orchestrated all of this, he couldn't call his headquarters. Those communications would surely be compromised. Troubled and frustrated, he cursed, drawing Ricochet's gaze.

"What is it?"

"You remember that thing I said was better you didn't know about?" De la Vega replied.

"Yeah?" Ricochet replied, puzzled.

"It's that. I need communications."

"To HQ?" Ricochet asked, but De la Vega shook his head.

"I need to speak with Natalie Shaw of Invictus International."

As Ricochet followed his CEO into Dudka's headquarters building—his rifle dangling across his chest and his oversized pants bunched around his boots—he couldn't understand why Zorro had to talk with their competition. Sure, there were countless private military companies all over the world, and Red Horse Global wasn't even the biggest, but Invictus had cut into their area of expertise in a way Ricochet had never expected.

Having provided services beyond security and executive protection, Red Horse was one of the first in the space to compete with the CIA in recruiting former Tier One and Two operators for high-stakes missions. Invictus had emerged out of nowhere and dominated the small market that was specialized mission execution. Why Zorro needed to talk to their CEO was not only troublesome but borderline traitorous.

But Ricochet knew he was overreacting on account of his highly competitive nature, but the entire situation troubled him. Red Horse's weren't the only casualties of the day, but Zorro's secrecy was upsetting. Even if it was for his own protection that Zorro kept him in the dark, he didn't like it at all.

"Mr. De la Vega," General Dudka greeted when the two men entered the command center. "I am sorry about your men."

"They were murdered, General," De la Vega stated matter-of-factly. Dudka offered him a slow nod.

"The Russians have murdered many of mine as well, and I fear they will continue to do so," he replied.

"No, my men have been betrayed. I need comms, ASAP," De la Vega snapped.

Ricochet watched Dudka warily, the Ukrainian's expression hardening as his eyes narrowed.

"If any of what you told me is true, we don't have time for this. I need comms now," De la Vega urged.

Dudka relented and nodded, turning to one of his staff and ordering him in Ukrainian.

"Who do you wish to contact?" he asked.

45

Laila stayed shoulder to shoulder with Shaw as the team moved south toward Kyiv. They maintained a five-meter spread in wedge formations as they moved through the fields with Roman in the lead. The misty rain persisted, and its dampness began to wear on the men, though they were grateful for the cover the fog provided. Shaw knew both the Russians and the Ukrainians would attempt to press any advantage the weather brought them, but what he had seen of Russia's finest revealed they likely did not conduct this war with the precision with which he was familiar.

"You didn't tell me how you ended up in Russian hands," Shaw muttered as he kept his gaze eastward.

"You didn't tell me how you landed the op to rescue me," Laila shot back with her usual wit. Shaw smirked and glanced her way. She wore the body armor from one of the deceased Russians as if she had been born in it.

"How'd you get captured? What happened?" Shaw asked her again.

"I figured you already knew."

"Seriously, Laila," Shaw said off air, his tone firmer. "How did you end up here? What's going on?"

"Might be easier if you told me what you already know," she began, returning her gaze forward. "I can then fill in the gaps."

"Did you intentionally botch the Dudka assassination?"

"Wait, you don't know?" Laila asked, stopping in her tracks. "I thought you were just messing with me."

"Hold," Shaw called into his radio. The team immediately paused all forward movement and each man dropped to a knee, rifles ready as they scanned the woods around them. "What don't I know?" Shaw finished, lifting his NODs off his eyes to stare at Laila's face. He could barely see her features, but his gut nagged at him in a way he knew too well.

"It was the Brotherhood. They rolled me up and..."

"Wait, are you saying that The Czar's Brotherhood is still *fully* operational even with Rykov gone?"

"Yes, it's being led by a woman named Sofia Vitori," Laila answered. "You didn't know this before you inserted?"

"We didn't insert. We were shot down," Shaw replied.

"Shot down?" Laila repeated, astonished. "By the Russians?" Shaw's nod gave the answer.

"We need to keep moving," came Reeves' voice in Shaw's headset.

"Yeah," Shaw answered. "Let's move."

Though the war grew steadily louder the farther the Russians advanced toward Kyiv, the team rendezvoused with the Stryker and once more crammed inside.

"You can sit here," Bray joked to Laila, patting his thighs as he sat down across from Shaw and Natalie. To his surprise, she approached and nestled into his lap without another word. His wide eyes and frozen expression showcased his shock. She adjusted herself more than she needed to, driving her rear deeper into his lap. Laila removed her ill-fitting helmet and twisted her torso faster than Bray expected, her hair tickling his face as it swept by him. She met his gaze and said, "Thanks," before winking at him again.

His heart leapt into his throat, and he fought the urge to reach for her hips, knowing he could justify it as steadying her. He wondered if she would even mind.

Best operation ever, he thought.

"She's just playing with you, brother," Pikari said, leaning over and speaking quietly into the speaker of Bray's electronic hearing protection.

"She can play with me all she wants," he said back with a contagious grin.

Laila didn't pay Bray any more mind as she turned her attention to Natalie and Shaw.

"Laila, I'm glad you're alright," Natalie said, her tone serious, yet holding a hint of compassion. Hers was an interesting relationship with Laila, and she doubted they would ever actually be trusted friends, but she knew they were dedicated allies to one another.

"Thanks, Natalie," Laila replied.

"Lincoln's here," she said, directing her eyes to the gunner seat ahead. Laila met Lincoln's gaze with a nod.

"You alright, kiddo?" he asked.

"Yeah, thanks for coming for me," she said.

"You're welcome, but this was hardly the plan," he retorted. "Alright, Rakestraw, get us to Kyiv."

The Stryker lurched forward, and Bray instinctively shot a hand to Laila's right hip to keep her from falling off his lap. Her hand shot to his and stayed there for a while, driving Bray's heart into his throat.

"Can you fill us in?" Natalie asked Laila. "Everything you know, starting with Afshar?"

"Afshar is compromised," Laila stated with firm certainty. "You already know who Troske is, so I'll skip that. He's been feeding Afshar intel on behalf of Sofia Vitori."

Seated in her husband's lap, Natalie exchanged a grave glance with Shaw.

"How far back does it go?" Shaw asked.

"El-Shahan was the proof of concept, as I understand it. I believe she was looking for a way to leverage you against her enemies," Laila explained. "When I was discovered and taken, her plan unraveled, and she gave me no choice but to attempt to assassinate General Ihor Dudka."

"Yeah, we got your message," Natalie said. "Dudka's alive. Red Horse Global was with him. Do you know anything about that?"

"I found out they were here, but not the reason," she answered.

"What about Anderson Stovall?" Natalie asked, but Laila shook her head.

"I don't know that name," she admitted. The disappointment on Natalie's face alarmed her.

"Dudka is Vitori's only rival. He has considerable influence within the Brotherhood and might be the last to oppose Vitori's claim. The rest are either dead or allied with her," Laila said.

"And you spared him?" Natalie asked, her stare showing her deep disapproval. Laila grew confused.

"I was under the impression that wasn't how we did things," she said, meeting Natalie's green eyes.

Bray and Pikari exchanged skeptical glances.

"We're not assassins," Shaw interjected. Natalie, receiving the subtle rebuke, cooled her anger and reminded herself they acted out of self-preservation. Dudka had done nothing to them.

"It's disheartening to know that the Brotherhood is thriving," Natalie said, "that's all."

"I understand," Laila replied with a nod.

Shaw's mouth firmed as he considered the implications of this update. Though he doubted, with the war in full swing, that they would face any trouble with this Dudka or the Ukrainians over Laila, he could not rule it out. However, he did not fancy the idea of being labeled a co-conspirator to assassination, nor did he like the thought of the implications it might bring against his company, the CIA, or the American government. It was precisely the sort of thing Stovall would want.

"Does Dudka know it was you?" Shaw asked. He watched Laila sigh and shrug.

"I think he could figure it out," she replied.

"Invictus Actual, this is Hummingbird, do you copy?" came Sosa in their headsets.

"We read you, Hummingbird. Go ahead," Shaw answered.

"Word just came down from the upper levels," Sosa began. "I'm being ordered to end this operation and cut all ties to Firefly for the attempted assassination of an allied military officer."

"How could they know that? Did you tell them?" Natalie shot back.

"No," Sosa replied. "I don't know for sure, but I have my suspicions."

"Stovall," Natalie reasoned.

"The upper administration is worried about the international optics should word get out that Firefly is employed by the CIA," Sosa said.

"But she's an American now," Natalie protested.

"This is bigger than that, Natalie. I can stall as long as possible, but eventually they will remove me and pull the plug," Sosa informed.

"They'd abandon us?" Natalie scoffed.

"Yes," Sosa replied gravely.

"And Lincoln?" Natalie pressed.

"Listen, *I'm* not abandoning anyone," she said fiercely. Her outburst caught even her by surprise, and she rubbed her eyes to quell her desperation. *How could this be happening?* The implications could prove disastrous to any joint Ukrainian-American relations, and even worse, if America was seen as aiding the Russians in their unlawful invasion...she couldn't begin to think of the fallout.

Sosa watched as all eyes in the stations in front of her turned to regard her. Sosa suddenly straightened, steeled herself, and said, "I need everyone looking into this right now. I need to know the best options for getting our people out, and I need it now."

"We can't stay out here with the Russians closing in," came Shaw's voice over the radio, "but I also don't want to walk my team right into a bunch of Ukrainians who may have an order to put Firefly down."

Pikari glanced back at Bray, whose attention remained fixed on Laila.

"We know Diego de la Vega is in Kyiv, and that he was with Dudka," Natalie said. Shaw recognized when his wife's wheels started turning. Natalie kept her PTT depressed as she continued speaking, "He might be able to provide the intel we need, not only to put the remaining pieces of this puzzle together but for our extraction, too."

"De la Vega is Stovall's man," Shaw countered.

"The consequences could be severe," Natalie said, immediately reading Shaw's mind, "but I don't think we have a choice."

"It'd be easy to chalk it up as blue on blue," Shaw replied, referring to potential fratricide.

"Not really even blue on blue," Natalie replied gravely. Shaw saw the validity in her observation.

"If Stovall is powerful enough to start this war, he's powerful enough to cover something like that up," Shaw added. Natalie nodded as did Sosa from a world away. Lincoln and the rest of the Invictus operators listened to the exchange, nervous for their predicament.

"Boss, I'd put us up against Red Horse any day," Bray chimed in. Shaw smiled sadly. He appreciated his enthusiasm, but in his mind's eye, he saw the young operator dead in the dirt at the hands of their enemies.

"If we don't find a way to get the truth out, we risk the lives of countless US service members in a war based on a lie," Natalie stated. "Our downed plane is more than enough rationale to justify Article Five." Natalie looked at the pilots and the loadmaster scrunched between her staff. Laila nodded her agreement even as they all bounced in the personnel compartment of the Stryker.

"Do we risk it?" Reeves piped in, cutting through the contemplative silence. Shaw inhaled deeply as he thought.

"Those who took Firefly are dead, the risk of contacting De la Vega outweighs any reward. We head west, make for Poland," Shaw said.

"We can't make it all the way in this," Natalie countered. "We only get what? One hundred miles, give or take?"

"We can leg it. It won't be easy, but if we outpace the Russians, we should be in the clear. I can't help but feel we've been outplayed yet again. There are kings and pawns in this world, and I suspect we're all pawns right now," Shaw replied.

"But you know better than anyone that a pawn can take a king, and at the end of the game, both pawn and king go back into the same box," Natalie answered. Shaw smirked.

Natalie knew, even though the concrete details eluded her, that this war was the work of Stovall and Vitori. All the pieces were in front of her; she just hadn't yet placed them all in the right positions. Vitori had infiltrated their intelligence chain through Afshar—a matter that still needed to be addressed—and after capturing Laila, she had forced her to assassinate General Dudka.

However, Dudka was accompanied by the CEO of Red Horse Global—Stovall's man, and that suggested the two elites were in conflict with one another. Natalie, though, was certain this was an illusion, a ploy to trick the world into action.

"Stovall can't directly deploy US troops anywhere, right?" Natalie said.

"Not that anyone is aware," Sosa replied. Natalie nodded quickly.

"But who *can* he deploy? Who *can* he leverage as battlefield casualties to spark outrage over the loss of American lives, American war heroes specifically?"

"You don't have the evidence for that," Sosa replied.

It did seem like grasping at straws, but Natalie had learned through all her dealings with the elites at this level—starting back with Silva—that the outrageous was often the truth. Both she and her husband had danced enough in the underdark of the world's elite to know and recognize their scheming.

"If De la Vega has caught wind of this, it just might be enough to bring him to our side. If we can get him to spill what he knows, as I said before, it might be the missing pieces we need to finally confirm all that we suspect," Natalie explained.

"You want to turn him?" Shaw asked.

"I think I may have done so already," she replied.

"If he's still alive," Sosa countered.

"If he's still alive," Natalie confirmed.

There was a long silence from Langley, causing Shaw and Natalie to exchange concerned glances. Natalie then looked at Laila. There was an apology behind the Pashtun's eyes, saying sorry for not having more information, for them risking their lives for hers, though she had nothing they had hoped. Natalie wondered if she was just seeing things on account of her own disappointment in the limited intelligence Laila possessed. Then she wondered why she had originally thought Laila knew more than she did.

Hope, she reasoned. She had hoped. Though always a gamble, she took comfort in expecting what she needed was just around the corner—just one more step—that Providence would reward her diligence to stop the evil persisting in the world.

"Invictus," came Sosa's voice again through the radio. She sounded surprised, flabbergasted even. "You're not going to believe who I have on the phone."

46

Bucharest, Romania

Sofia Vitori sipped her tea as she waited for the sun to rise over the medieval city she had come to love. Even in the early hours, the city glowed warm from the streetlights, the light rising from between the buildings as modern skyscrapers clashed with the antique architecture of the surrounding smaller structures. Through the apartment's expansive windows, she relished the city's full majesty.

She waited patiently for news of Troske and kept fighting off her anger, choosing instead to focus on her triumph. Kyiv was within reach, and though Laila and Troske had failed, in just a few days, she would have Dudka's head. If Rykov had taught her anything, it was contingencies upon contingencies.

With her plans for Paris secured, she wondered at the change in Stovall's enthusiasm. Was he simply aroused by the start of the war or was there something more? Sofia had to assume there was always something deeper, and she didn't mind so long as she advanced her own power and influence. Already, her alliance with Stovall was paying dividends beyond expectation, and those were only bound to increase once NATO began funding the Ukrainian resistance.

With Russia's stubbornness and their fear of appearing weak to the rest of the world, Sofia knew she was in for long-term profits. Through the members of the Brotherhood who staffed the Kremlin, the Main Intelligence Directorate (GRU), and the Federal Security Service (FSB), she held power over the highest levels of Russian military and intelligence. What Rykov had built was truly astounding and the loyalty unparalleled. Though the cause was a sham, she knew, the members of the Brotherhood still lived for the world Rykov had promised.

That was what made Dudka so dangerous. He was a true believer, fully deceived by The Czar's vision. In his blissful ignorance, he could unwittingly unravel the very structure Rykov had built, relinquishing the power without even knowing it.

If the world thought Russia could influence elections in America, they couldn't begin to fathom what the Brotherhood could orchestrate, what Sofia could control. Just the thought of having someone as disillusioned as Dudka take her throne was unbearable; thus, he had to die. But she never imagined it would be this difficult.

I had to start a war just to keep my throne, she thought. Then again, so had countless rulers who preceded her.

However, unlike those former kings and emperors, Sofia had Stovall—a peer to manipulate the actions of her proxy opponents. Together, they could push the war where it needed to go for the sake of their own advantage, and likewise, pull it back when it equally suited them. Their goal was not devastation, but opportunity, and she knew they could compose the movements of a grand symphony that mesmerized both sides, inflaming passion for glory and ego for increased commitment.

It was perfect.

Eliminating the Shaws was an unexpected and surefire opportunity she couldn't let pass her by. If they had extracted Laila, Sofia believed they surely would have come for her, and she did not fancy fighting the same war both Rykov and Barakat had lost.

She checked her watch, expecting an update from her subordinates in the Russian GRU regarding Troske and Laila's extraction, but the minutes dragged on, and so did her frustration. Her agitation soon gave way to concern, and concern quickly gave way to alarm until the encrypted and secure tablet in front of her alerted to an incoming call.

Inhaling and forcing herself to relax, Sofia answered the call, wearing a smile she knew would not put the caller at ease.

"General Baranov, it is good to see you. I trust the GRU is performing well? How fares progress on the ground?" Sofia asked the director of the GRU. She was constantly amazed at how Rykov had secured the loyalty of such men that her ascension was mostly uncontested.

"We have lost contact with the team sent to extract our people," he confessed, his tone firm yet tired. Sofia remained silent, her smile flipping into a stout frown that seemed out of place on her slender face. Seeing this, Baranov's expression animated suddenly, and he continued, "We can no longer track the helicopter squadron. We are attempting to uncover why."

"And Dudka?" she asked. She watched the GRU general scratch his thick cheek.

"They have repelled our initial assault. We have no information on General Dudka's current status."

"This is unacceptable, General," Sofia stated coldly. She had purposely kept the true reasons for the war close to her chest, sharing with very few, and as far as General Baranov was concerned, they were expanding the Brotherhood's power and influence in a way that was also strategically advantageous to his own country. "Based on your intelligence and your expertise, what do you think happened to our extraction team?"

"I am inclined to believe there was some type of mechanical failure with the helicopters. We've seen this happen with advancing ground forces too regularly," he answered, now beginning to sweat.

"Not simply a communications failure?"

"The likelihood that all communications systems on both helicopters and in the possession of our team to fail is unlikely," Baranov replied. Sofia nodded as if she had already discerned as much. The Russian general felt he was being led to some conclusion, and he didn't care for the process. He wished she would just tell him directly, but thus far, that had not been Sofia's way.

"Since communication failure is unlikely on account of the numerous avenues to maintain that communication, we surely would have heard something from them regarding a mechanical failure, and what are the chances that both helicopters would have the same failure, rendering both unavailable?"

"It would be extremely unlikely," he admitted.

"And if they were engaged in flight by Ukrainian forces, it is understandable to assume that we would have received some hint of warning from any who had access to these numerous communication systems, yes?"

"That is a fair assessment," he replied, hiding his annoyance.

"So there is only one likely explanation then," Sofia said.

"They were ambushed," the general reasoned, his stare flat and unamused. Sofia tilted her head like a mother expecting more from her child.

"The odds of such a thing must be impossibly low, correct?"

"I would have to concur," he replied.

"Thank you, General. It is imperative that you find out who did this and hunt them down. Failure will not be tolerated. Am I clear?" she stated with finality.

"Yes, Your Grace," he replied quickly, bowing his head in submissive obedience.

"I expect an update within the hour," she said before terminating the video call.

Sofia slumped into the leather chair and shielded her eyes with her hands. She did not mourn the potential loss of Troske and Laila; however, she was concerned with the nature of their disappearance. She shivered as she considered the implications. A name pestered her thoughts, and regardless of how unlikely, she couldn't deny the fear.

Shaw.

Had they survived the plane crash? If they had, could they eliminate an entire GRU Spetsnaz troop before they could contact headquarters? If they could, would they leverage what Laila knew to come after her?

The questions frightened her more than she dared admit.

"Paris," she muttered to herself before deciding to accelerate her departure.

47

North of Kyiv

"Nectar, this is Zorro. Do you copy?" came Diego de la Vega's voice in Natalie's headset after Sosa briefed him of callsigns in use and patched him through.

"I read you loud and clear, Zorro. Go ahead," Natalie replied.

"I'm breaking all sorts of etiquette and protocol, but I don't know where else to turn," he began. She noted his upset tone. He then spilled everything: Stovall's declaration at his DC residence of the coming European war, his meetings at the Capitol where Stovall informed him he was to deploy Red Horse staff to Kyiv, and the tragic fate of his men.

"I'm sorry for your loss, Zorro," Natalie said sincerely.

"You said that Stovall might be part of some council, and I said I would believe you," he stated, ignoring her sympathies. He was still too angry.

"I remember," Natalie replied.

Shaw listened to their exchange in his own headset, concerned and bewildered at the same time.

"You're confirming what we already believe," Natalie continued, "that Anderson Stovall is in collaboration with a Sofia Vitori to orchestrate..."

"Wait, did you say Sofia Vitori?" De la Vega interrupted.

"Yes, do you know something?" Natalie asked, her heart skipping a beat at his recognition.

"I met the woman in DC," he said, his mind whirling with how everything was clicking into place.

"Where specifically?"

"At Stovall's residence," he answered, barely believing that all this could be happening. "When he announced the upcoming war in Europe."

Natalie glanced up at Laila, celebrating in her own way the facts that De la Vega had confirmed for her. Though it was possible Stovall was merely capitalizing on an opportunity, his connection to Rykov and now Vitori confirmed for Natalie that he was playing a much larger role in this conflict and that he was instigating the entire war.

Before Natalie could continue, an alert signaled through the Stryker as a new, but familiar, voice cut in, "Unidentified aircraft bearing two-four-four on intercept approach to your location," Kara Bivens informed once obtaining the near instantaneous information from their drone pilot in a separate facility at the George Bush Center for Intelligence.

"Lincoln!" Shaw cried.

"I see him!" the former Ranger captain called back from his forward-facing gunner's seat. He cursed as he manipulated the unfamiliar controls. It had been so long, and when he was in the battalions, this Stryker Dragoon variant wasn't even a twinkle in the Army's eye.

"Lincoln!" Shaw roared again.

"I'm working on it!" he shouted as everyone found the nearest handhold for support.

"Deploying smokescreen!" Rakestraw announced from his driver's seat. One of the pilots sat crammed in the channel leading to his seat, and now the interior had become quite stifling from all the bodies.

The Dragoon's smokescreen launchers popped as they deployed the dense fog to cover the vehicle.

"Aircraft is still on approach," Kara warned.

Natalie's eyes dropped to her ATAK, and she focused on the small screen projecting the feed from the MQ-1 Predator UAV above. Though a dense cloud covered the Stryker, they were still visible through the green square the software overlaid on the vehicle.

"I need to know what that aircraft is," Natalie barked. She engaged the radio that connected her to De la Vega. "Zorro, we've got an unidentified aircraft en route to our location. How copy?"

"Copy, Nectar, but what's going on?"

"We're in Ukraine, north of Kyiv. Long story," she replied.

"You're in Ukraine!" he called.

"We had to extract a friend," Natalie answered, trying to keep her cool.

"Alright, I'll try and find out if the Ukrainians have a bird in your AO," De la Vega said, his tone adopting a firm professionalism.

"We're sitting ducks in this thing!" Bray called out. They all knew he was right, but Shaw knew they were vulnerable regardless. There was nowhere to hide, and Shaw figured, even with the smokescreen, the jet already had a bead on them.

As if on cue, the fighter jet screamed overhead in a low pass, and Invictus team instinctively ducked as the roar rolled over them.

"That's a SU-25, Russian," Kara exclaimed as the jet passed under the drone's feed as it cruised at 50,000 feet.

"Invictus Actual, bogey is Russian. I repeat, the aircraft is Russian CAS," Sosa cried into the radio, alerting the team to the jet's close air support function. Shaw's gaze shot toward the two Stingers resting on the floor between their seats.

"Incoming!" Natalie shouted as she watched the jet on her ATAK. Seeing its approach, she snapped her gaze toward her husband. He met her eyes with a steely concern as they heard the turret above them groan and whine as it oriented toward the threat.

Lincoln opened up with the Dragoon's main cannon, but he knew he would have to get lucky. The jet was advancing on them too rapidly; nonetheless, the quick cadence of the turret's cannon thundered through the passenger compartment.

Everyone inside flinched violently as the jet's autocannon bellowed from above. It passed overhead before its payload thundered across the ground, cutting through the smokescreen, and shooting plumes of mud and dirt high into the air.

48

Bucharest, Romania

Sofia took the call from General Baranov as she climbed into the rear passenger seat of the charcoal Mercedes SUV. She fanned her hair over her left shoulder as she settled in the seat.

"Yes, General," she greeted just as her vehicle pulled away, bound for the airport. "I trust you have an update?"

"Yes, Your Grace," he began, sounding reverent. Sofia lifted her chin as she awaited the rest of his sentence. "We believe you were right in your assessment. Our force sent for extraction was eliminated at the Hostomel airport. Both helicopters were shot down, and we suspect there are no survivors."

"Was it Ukraine?" she asked stoically, though fearing his answer.

"We cannot be sure, but I do not think so. As of now, there are no Ukrainian forces in the area, and I believe they would have remained to defend the airfield," he answered.

"That is a fair assessment," she replied, agreeing. At the same time, she felt her stomach drop. "You said you are tracking the believed culprits?"

"Yes, Your Grace. An SU-25 flight has located them and is currently engaging what appears to be an American armored personnel carrier. Our intelligence suggests that the Ukrainians do not have possession of these types of vehicles."

"Could the intelligence be incorrect?" Sofia asked.

"While it is possible, it is very unlikely," the GRU general replied. "We are sending in another Spetsnaz troop on gunships to clean up and identify."

"Very good, General. I await your updates."

"Yes, Your Grace."

Special Operations Forces Headquarters
Kyiv, Ukraine

De la Vega lowered the headset that connected him first to Langley then to Natalie. He turned to face General Dudka, who, with his arms folded over his chest, stared at him with pensive interest. He had changed out of his service uniform and into a set of combat fatigues and boots. The green camouflage appeared darker and busier than America's Multicam pattern, sporting a digital pattern similar to the Navy or Marine Corps fatigues.

"Well?" Dudka probed, dropping his chin and staring at De la Vega from underneath his hooded brow. He had a war to fight and really couldn't be bothered with anything the American might need; however, De la Vega had saved his life, and that afforded a certain courtesy.

"Do you have air support north of the city?" he asked the general.

"We're lucky to have air support anywhere," Dudka replied. "We've scrambled all squadrons. I would assume the answer is yes."

"There are Americans in the field. I need to get them to safety," De la Vega insisted. Dudka sighed.

"I cannot help you there," the man said, turning.

"They know about Vitori, about Stovall!" De la Vega cried, stopping Dudka in his tracks. He turned back slowly to regard the shorter Latino. His dark eyes narrowed as he contemplated this new development. "If there's anyone in the world who can end this, it's them," De la Vega added boldly, driving his index finger toward the floor to stress his point. The exchange drew all eyes despite the chaos raging throughout the city.

"Stepanenko!" Dudka called, turning to face a soldier nearby. De la Vega drifted his gaze toward the special operator. "*Teper vy zvituyete pered misterom De la Vega. Robit', yak vin kazhe.*"

"*Tak, Heneral!*" the soldier responded with fervor. De la Vega returned his confused stare to General Dudka, who smirked.

"What does that mean?"

"Chief Sergeant Stepanenko and his men are yours to command."

49

Shaw shook his head to clear the ringing in his ears from the impact against the Stryker. Even with his hearing protection, the assault against them had rattled his equilibrium.

"Haystack, get us moving!" Shaw shouted into the radio when he realized they were stationary.

"We're dead in the water!" Rakestraw called back. "I've got nothing from the engine!" They all heard the uncharacteristic whine of the turbo diesel engine.

"Everybody okay?" Shaw heard Natalie call out.

"He's coming back around!" Lincoln shouted, watching the aircraft through the Stryker's sensors.

"Get the back door open! Everyone out! Make for the trees at our three o'clock!" Shaw shouted. Having never received fire by air, the entire team didn't have to be told twice.

"What do we do?" Captain Coffey asked Natalie, worry deep in his eyes.

"Just stick close," she replied. However, she really didn't know herself. She placed her faith in her husband's ability and in the capable men around her.

As the rear door lowered, the Invictus operators, keeping their fear under control, funneled out as orderly as possible, though the cramped space made fluid movement difficult. No one wanted to fall or trip up a teammate and be the reason someone was injured or killed.

"Haystack!" Shaw called back to Rakestraw, who initiated the lever to recline the seat fully. Laden with his kit and cold-weather gear, he struggled to climb through the narrow tunnel from the forward driver's seat to the rear passenger compartment. "Lincoln!" Shaw shouted next.

"Go!" Lincoln cried back as he continued to operate the turret controls. With the rear door open, the concussions from the 30mm cannon pressed through them, jarring their insides.

"Don't be a hero!" Shaw protested.

"I'll be right behind you!" he promised, but Shaw saw the lie for what it was. He patted Rakestraw on the back as he exited just after the airmen, and cursing Lincoln's stubbornness, Shaw leaned his head out the rear of the Stryker to see his team legging it fast toward the treeline. He caught Natalie's gaze as she looked back for him, and her expression opened in alarm at seeing her husband with half his body still inside the carrier vehicle.

Shaw watched her slow, and he keyed his PTT and urged her, "Keep going!"

Torn and frightened with the roar of the jet's engines increasing as it lined up its approach for another gun run, Natalie obeyed, turning and sprinting with Laila and Bray toward the dark forest.

The Stryker's cannon continued to fire as it slowly moved to track the incoming jet, its tracer rounds searing through the night like bright red lasers. Shaw disappeared back inside, racing to Lincoln's side.

"Everyone's clear! Let's go!" he shouted, grabbing his friend's upper arm and yanking hard. Lincoln shot him a glance in frustrated anger before relenting.

Natalie tore into the treeline and, once hidden among the underbrush, turned and peered through the darkness toward the Stryker. Her night vision binoculars suffered from the lack of infrared illumination, and she dared not give away their position by using the illuminator on her rifle.

"Come on, Philo!" Natalie urged through the microphone hovering over the left side of her lips. The entire team heard her fear.

"Let's get these stingers up and running," McEwen and Reeves said, nearly in unison.

"Missile's in the air," Natalie heard Captain Coffey shout as he pointed toward the sky, recognizing the audible signature.

"Philo, Rail-Splitter, move!" Natalie called, strengthening her tone in an effort to ward off the spiking fear. Then she saw them, highlighted in orange by their thermal signature, as the two men stumbled out of the back of the Stryker and raced her way just before the missile slammed into the vehicle behind them.

The ensuing blast launched both men forward as the Stryker erupted into a ball of flame, the heavy turret thrown from its housing before crashing back down on top of the vehicle as it burned from the inside out.

Natalie started forward, but Bray gripped her arm, keeping her in place.

"Let go of me!" she shouted.

"Just wait!" he urged, pulling against her.

"It's coming back around," Coffey cried, fighting down the panic rising from his stomach as his keen, pilot eyes trailed the jet by the glow of its burners.

"Get up!" Natalie called to her husband as Bray fought to keep her in the forest.

"Get those stingers up!" Reeves exclaimed as he pushed through the brush. Low branches tore at his clothing and gear as he pressed onward. "On me!" Reeves had fallen fully into his element, commanding men in the heat of battle the likes of which he had never experienced. Though his conscious mind did not register the sensation, he felt as his enemies had always felt, outgunned and alone.

He cut along the border to the forest, directing Bratcher and Pikari to advantageous positions along the treeline. The two warfighters surged with a mix of excitement and dread, but they both operated at the highest level, performing their duties with unconscious competence.

"Here!" Reeves shouted, directing Bratcher and Pikari to an opening in the trees. "Stagger your shots! Catch him in between his countermeasures!" McEwen, supporting Bratcher as he hefted the shoulder-fired aerial-defense system, checked his immediate surroundings.

"Clear," he shouted before patting Bratcher twice on the head. Without waiting, Reeves moved to Pikari's side, who had set up not twenty feet to the right. Bratcher's stinger issued a low whine as it tracked the Russian jet across the night sky. Just a second later, its breathy surge propelled the munition from its tube before the missile's propellant ignited and sent it screaming into the night.

"Hold!" Reeves cried to Pikari, his arm outstretched toward the Māori as he watched the first missile rise toward the incoming jet. The aircraft tilted on its axis and banked left as it discharged its countermeasures in a crackling display of brilliant light. "Fire!" Reeves ordered, dropping his hand.

Pikari's stinger whined before launching its own munition toward the jet. It soared toward its target with deliberate force, and as Reeves had predicted, the aircraft's countermeasures could not respond in time after an immediate discharge. The missile drilled into the belly of the aircraft, ripping it apart in an explosive display of force.

"Good hit!" Reeves congratulated above the hoots of his team.

Natalie tore from Bray's grip and bolted back onto the field toward her husband. Cursing, Bray sprinted after her, leaving Laila and the airmen hidden and nervous in the shadows of the tall pines. He kept his rifle in high port as he ran after her.

Before she got to them, Natalie watched her husband slowly rise onto all fours, shaking his head as he recovered. As she neared, she felt the growing heat of the burning Stryker not far behind them.

His head throbbing, Shaw crawled to Lincoln, who lay on his stomach next to him. He ran his hands down the back of his legs, checking for blood before moving up his rear and back. He then examined his arms from the armpit down to the wrist.

"I'm alright," Lincoln groaned. His voice was light, still raspy, but dazed.

"Come on, let's go," Shaw muttered, his own words sounding tired and forced. He inhaled deeply but found he just couldn't quite fill his lungs to satisfaction. He didn't feel any pain, but he knew adrenaline could mask even a lethal wound.

Weaving an arm under Lincoln's armpit, Shaw helped hoist him off the ground. The world spun for both of them, and, rising to their feet, they both stumbled forward for their first few steps before Natalie and Bray caught and steadied them.

"Invictus Actual, we've got two rotorwings inbound on your position," Sosa said gravely, cutting the team's celebrations short.

"We're out," Bratcher said solemnly as he dropped his Stinger onto the ground, but everyone already knew, having kept a mental tally of how many missiles they had taken from the C-17. The Stingers were large, cumbersome, and heavy, and difficult to reload in the field. Their remaining two Stingers from the C-17's pallet of six had been fastened to the exterior of the Stryker, which they could not remove in time.

Shaw, Lincoln, Natalie, and Bray returned to the forest, and all checked their ATAK devices to locate the inbound helicopters of which Sosa had warned.

"I told you not to be a hero," Shaw scolded Lincoln as he observed the inbound Russian rotorwings.

"Yeah, yeah," Lincoln replied, still breathless. He stared at his own screen, calculating an estimated time on target. They all still heard the faint drumming of war to the south as the Russians continued to besiege Kyiv.

"Let's move. They don't see us yet, and maybe we've given them a second thought in coming after us by downing their jet. We need to stay ahead of the main advance," Shaw said, before meeting the gaze of his wife. He glanced at Lincoln and Bray just as Laila approached, followed by the airmen, who palmed their M4 carbines nervously.

Shaw nodded toward Captain Coffey before starting his way. The pilot sidestepped as the former Marine Raider approached, allowing him to pass and press deeper into the woods.

"Romulus, on point," Shaw ordered after pressing his PTT. Aston and Roman hustled forward to take point position ahead of Shaw. "Invictus, fall in."

Assuming their usual wedge formations, the team advanced after providing some direction to their airmen, who formed a loose, three-man wedge with Staff Sergeant McCrae leading. All he had to do was follow Lincoln and keep the appropriate distance. Lincoln led the next wedge up in the formation with Natalie and Laila flanking on either side. In the lead wedge, Reeves stalked in front of Laila, and Shaw opposite him in front of Natalie, with Rakestraw offset and behind to his seven o'clock. Pikari, McEwen, Bray, and Bratcher took up the rear.

"These guys must have been searching for us after the airport," Bray said into the radio for all to hear.

"Yeah, mate," Pikiri agreed, "we must have killed someone important."

"Or they really want Laila," Natalie chimed.

As the team moved south through the forest, Sosa's voice echoed in their ears, "They're almost on you. Hide!"

The airmen, not privy to the radio communications, watched in fear as everyone around them scurried to a hiding place, most pressing close to the trunks of trees still sporting foliage. They quickly did the same.

"Nobody move," came Shaw's command.

The team held their breath and kept their gazes skyward as the Russian helicopters thundered overhead, encircling the perimeter and searching for their prey.

"They know we're in here," Reeves muttered, a determination present in his voice.

"You got that right," Bratcher replied with a hint of eagerness.

"Hummingbird, what are our options?" Shaw whispered into his radio as he watched the helicopters through the canopy. He refused to check his own ATAK for fear of its light drawing the enemy's attention.

Sosa inhaled deeply as she felt the cortisol pump through her body. She stared at the monitor, ignoring the pleading and grave glances Regan and Kara gave her. Even now, she felt the clock ticking on when her superiors might barge in and cut the operation, leaving her friends stranded and at the mercy of Russian forces.

"We'll find our way out of this," Sosa replied as she fought against the assaulting desperation. Shaw smirked gratefully at her use of the term *we*.

"How long before they drop troops?" Bray asked.

"I give them five mikes," Pikari replied. Shaw heard Natalie inhale next to him, and he turned and placed a hand on her shoulder.

"You alright?" he asked.

"Yeah, been a while since I've killed anyone, and I'm just developing a tic," she whispered back. He suppressed a laugh and patted her twice on the shoulder in approval. She had nothing to prove; Shaw had beheld her prowess firsthand.

His mind returned toward their situation, and he knew he needed to risk a glance at his ATAK. While he could rely on Sosa's dictation, he needed to see for himself. He rolled toward the ground to hide its light signature, folded down the device, and watched the UAV feed in real time, observing the position of the two helicopters to seek a tactical advantage as his team lay hunkered down in the brush.

"They're looking to close us in from the south and north," Reeves noted as he moved his gaze across the forest in the same direction. They all easily heard the helicopters positioning around them.

"Which side is going to flush us out?" Shaw asked.

"I'd wager south on account of driving us back to their territory," Reeves reasoned. Shaw agreed.

"The gunships will cover the east and west," Shaw added. "Would you push on us?"

"Absolutely not," Reeves said. "I'd call in an airstrike or, at the very least, destroy this place with the gunships before conducting a BDA."

"So, are they stupid or just stretched too thin?" Shaw asked.

"Maybe both," Natalie piped.

"Or they want to take us alive," Shaw said.

"Nae chance," they heard McEwen say, his Scottish accent giving the ultimatum a certain weight. Everyone agreed.

Shaw studied the ATAK screen for a moment longer. "The minute we return fire, those gunships will open up on us," he continued. "Hummingbird, we're looking for a way out here. What is that south-south-east of our position?"

"Looks like some kind of creek bed," Sosa replied, her heart beating in her throat from concern for the team she didn't feel she could help. *How can they get out of this?* She began to prepare herself for the worst, but Shaw sounded quite calm given the dire circumstances, and she steadied herself from his strength.

"That's exactly what it is," Shaw replied, seeing it clearly now that Sosa had identified it. "Looks much deeper than it should be, though. More of a small gully." He turned slightly to Natalie and said, "Think we can sneak into that?"

"It's a long shot," she replied.

"Better than staying here," Shaw responded. Natalie tilted her head and raised her eyebrows as she considered his proposal.

"We're showing gunships deploying a contingent of hostiles north and south of your position," Sosa alerted. *Get out of there, Invictus.*

"We see them," he returned calmly through his radio. "Alright, team, let's leave some welcome gifts for our friends and leg it south-south-east. There's a gully running south from the woods that we'll make for."

"Copy," came a round of replies. Though the situation was grim, the team had formed a bond of trust over the last several months of global operations. Shaw had proven himself a capable commander and Reeves a trusted team chief. As the minutes passed, Shaw kept tabs on the Russians as they prepared to enter the woods while his team finished setting their traps.

If you're not cheating, you're not winning, Shaw reminded himself. He figured the claymores taken from the C-17 would draw the attention of the gunships and thereby increase their chances of escape.

With one last glance at the ATAK, he folded it away and checked the condition of his rifle and the barrel-mounted M203 grenade launcher. Satisfied, he glanced around at his team, and receiving nods, he pointed Aston and Roman southeast.

50

Invictus team slipped into the gully one by one before clearing the forest as the Russian gunships offloaded their soldiers via fast rope.

"Stay low," Shaw muttered from his kneeling position at the lip of the deep creek as he urged his team forward while keeping an eye on the southward helicopter. Though shrouded by the night and the oblong shape of the tightly packed forest of evergreens and hardwoods, Shaw still faced the real threat of his enemy's night vision and thermal capability.

He cued Reeves forward, who, staying low, planted his left hand on the ground at the edge of the embankment and propelled his legs over the lip and down into the narrow gully. He quickly put distance between himself and the forest, legging it to Aston, who, keeping a low profile, kept his carbine ready and his body positioned south toward the Russian soldiers preparing their advance into the wood. Roman lay poised and ready next to him.

Rakestraw crouched next to Shaw to await his cue while Shaw checked the feed on his ATAK again.

"Go," he urged, patting him on the shoulder. The warfighter followed the same route Reeves had taken just a moment ago and raced beyond Reeves' and Aston's cover positions.

Though pleased the gully was deep enough to hide a man at full height, it was damp and wet from the light rain that continued to sprinkle down around them, and that did make Shaw slightly nervous.

Regardless, it appeared as their only way out.

With the Russians apparently none the wiser, Shaw ushered the next group forward while Bray, Pikari, Bratcher, and McEwen pulled rear security.

"One at a time," Shaw quietly told Captain Coffey, whose gloved fingers nervously flexed around his rifle's grip and quad rail. "Follow the gully until you pass Aston. Reeves will give you instructions from there. Good?"

"Yeah," Coffey whispered back, mobilizing his courage and inhaling deeply.

"Your boys will be right behind you. Stay low and quiet," Shaw urged. The pilot nodded repeatedly, then gingerly eased himself down into the creek bed.

"We've got to speed this up," came Reeves' quiet warning in Shaw's ear.

Without responding, Shaw turned back to the other two airmen. He ushered them forward with a wave of his hand before pointing toward their senior officer. They nodded, and one at a time, climbed down into the gully. The copilot slipped, and the raking of his boots against the hard bank as he attempted to catch himself tested the nerves of all present.

Staff Sergeant McCrae helped the pilot to his feet, and the two men, hunched low, made their way down the natural trench. Lincoln moved up next.

"Make sure they don't die," Shaw commented. Lincoln couldn't help but smirk, though he didn't reply. He hopped down into the moist creek bed with relative ease.

"I'm staying with you," Natalie said, dropping to a knee beside him as Laila climbed down after Lincoln.

"No, you're not," Shaw replied sternly. "Get down there."

Laila was already moving southeast toward Aston's position. Natalie knew better than to protest. The sooner she had cleared the forest, the sooner her husband would join her. Still, her mind played the recent scene of Shaw barely making it out of the Stryker in time. She huffed her frustration and climbed down before moving briskly after Laila.

"Alright, boys, you're up," Shaw instructed, glancing back at his rear security.

"You go ahead, Boss," Bray said without taking his eyes off his sector.

Bray's continued use of *Boss* rattled Shaw, but not unexpectedly. As he looked at his new team—men he had come to love, men for whom he felt responsible—he saw the faces of Philo Team, of Beasley, York, Reyes, and Wyatt. He quickly shook his head, his helmet's momentum straining his neck, but the ghosts faded away.

"Negative, Strider. Get over here," Shaw ordered harshly, though his voice remained barely a whisper.

His tone startled Bray, and he found himself obeying before he realized he was. Shaw patted him on the back as the former SEAL dropped beneath him.

"Riptide," Shaw then ordered, but it was unnecessary. Pikari was already moving his way. The team bounded in perfect order from their security positions, leaving McEwen as the last man who had posted up nearest the threat yet closest to the gully. Shaw patted Bratcher as he climbed down, then turned back to McEwen. "Alright, Vagabond." Without a word, the Scot, keeping low, turned fluidly and raced forward, cradling his carbine in a way that freed his support hand to aid in his descent.

Once McEwen had passed the exposed roots Shaw had been using as a reference point, Shaw dropped himself into the gully, but as he primed his legs to follow McEwen, the Russian gunship banked from hovering at his three o'clock to his twelve o'clock. His eyes cut right in time to see the helicopter clear the trees as his mind rapidly processed a response. Shaw immediately fell backwards and scrambled while on his back, pushing with his heels to drive his body deeper into concealment.

He lay unmoving among the exposed roots as the yellow and green camouflaged gunship paused, hovering directly over the gully. The downward force from its spinning rotors assaulted the trees and undergrowth, making them sway and clash into each other as Shaw lay still beneath the forest's groans.

His eyes focused on the chin-mounted 30mm autocannon, and he inhaled deeply to steady his nerves. That weapon alone, not even considering the wing-mounted rocket pods, would devastate the entirety of the small forest that currently concealed him.

"Philo," came Natalie's worried voice as she watched his predicament unfold on her ATAK screen. She swallowed her fear and continued, "Counting twenty-four tangoes advancing on your position. They're closing in from the north and south." Shaw looked left and right, but the creek bed's high walls concealed all enemy movement.

"I can't see them," he muttered in reply. He stared back at the gunship, wondering if they had the ability to see him. Was the pilot guiding the foot soldiers to his position? Or did Shaw's uniform and equipment make him practically invisible to the helicopter's near-infrared capability—if it possessed it at all?

As the Russians advanced warily into the forest, Shaw considered his tactical disadvantage and the options available to him. As if reading his mind, Reeves' voice spoke through Shaw's headset.

"Give me a sitrep, Philo," Reeves said as he trained his light machine gun on the helicopter hovering just ahead of him. Further on, the gully cut sharply south, providing the Invictus operators with a fighting trench of sorts that put cover between them and their enemies.

"It's not good," Shaw replied, his voice barely above a whisper. "Nectar, Hummingbird, somebody find me a gap," he urged.

Natalie, her heart pounding in her ears and her trachea constricting from the stress and the cold, pored over her ATAK, watching the glowing forms of Russian soldiers converging toward the center of the forest.

"Think you can slip under the nose of that Hind?" Reeves asked.

"That thirty mike-mike is making me second-guess that option," Shaw replied. He craned his neck to look through the boughs above and watched the Russian gunship steadily hovering above him, his blue eyes falling upon the autocannon. From the angle, he wondered if the pilots could see him, but he wasn't up to date on the Hind's blind spots.

Realizing his only option was what Reeves had suggested, he moved into a crouch, his suppressed M4A1 ready, as he kept his back to the tangled roots jutting into the gully where it shallowed and rose behind him. On the balls of his feet, he readied himself to move as soon as Natalie gave him an option or the Russians stumbled upon the trap they had laid for them.

"Your best bet looks to be what Matterhorn suggested," Natalie informed after evaluating the situation further. "I think you could beat the pilot's reaction time." Shaw let out a long exhale.

"That's quite a gamble," he replied. "And if I'm spotted, we'll have one hell of a fight on our hands." Natalie felt her heart drop at Shaw's statement, realizing immediately what he was thinking. "I can buy you some time," Shaw added.

"No," Natalie pleaded, shaking her head as her voice broke.

"You can get Firefly out," he reasoned, realizing the weight of his predicament. His heart thundered loudly from his chest, but he saw no other way. "If they see me, it endangers everyone. Just go. I'll try and catch up if I can."

"Philo, that's a no-go," Reeves quickly interjected, his deep voice commanding.

"Get them out of here, Master Chief. That's an order," Shaw replied.

"This isn't the military, brother," Reeves countered.

"We don't have time for this," Shaw snapped. "Go."

"That's going to be a no from us," came Bray's opinion.

"We're not leaving you, mate," Pikari confirmed.

"The mission," Shaw protested.

"Forget the mission," Laila retorted. Shaw smirked and, moved by their loyalty, reconsidered his position. Honestly, he was glad for it. Though willing to make the sacrificial play, he didn't want to.

"Nectar, we've built quite the team, haven't we?" he muttered. Natalie had never felt more grateful for a group of individuals in her life.

"I was getting kind of bored with the idea of running from these blokes," Bratcher added.

"The Russians are going to trip your traps in just a few moments," Sosa informed. Shaw glanced back toward the zone where they had deployed their improvised anti-personnel mines, but he couldn't see over the rise of the creek bed. The mix of claymore mines and fragmentation grenades—bound to tree trunks with paracord serving as makeshift trip wire linked to the pins—were arranged in such a way to deliver maximum damage based on the topography.

"Alright," came Shaw's whisper. He honestly liked this plan better, yet he did not like the idea of further endangering his team if they could slip away unbolted without him. "I'm going to go for it once Ivan sets off the trap."

"Good copy," Natalie replied, greatly relieved.

"We'll cover your move," Reeves answered. Shaw remained absolutely still as a Russian soldier passed just three meters behind him, dropping into the head of the creek where it shallowed before climbing up the other side.

"Hummingbird, count us down," Shaw dared.

Feeling the weight of his trust in her, Sosa nodded, tracked the movement of the Russians, and evaluated their time to target.

"Three," she began, counting down the Russians' approach to the traps.

Shaw turned toward the gunship.

"Two."

Reeves tucked his cheek harder into the stock of his machine gun, ready to fire upon the helicopter if needed once Shaw was clear.

"One."

51

The rolling, consecutive explosions thundered through the forest, cueing Shaw forward. He rounded the roots, his carbine in football carry, as he sprinted down the trench, his feet slipping off wet rocks. As he planted his right foot, it slipped on a patch of wet mud, and he stumbled before catching his footing and hurrying forward. Injuring himself would only jeopardize his team, so as he ran, he focused on each footfall, though it was extremely difficult under the haze of his NODs.

He passed right underneath the gunship, never before feeling so vulnerable. The screams of wounded and dying Russians finally reached him as he raced down the trench.

"He's seen you!" Natalie cried as she watched the helicopter shift its nose on a route toward the creek bed, but Reeves opened up with his light machine gun.

The sudden peppering of too many rounds panicked the gunship pilot, and, as several bullets struck the bulletproof cockpit glass, he jerked his controls in unrestrained reflex. The rotors ate into the forest, quickly deteriorating against the hard tangle of bare limbs, and the helicopter yawed too far to the left before it tumbled into the trees with a deafening roar.

"Did you see that!" Reeves cried, overjoyed at the unexpected success. Shaw didn't look back, but kept pounding forward down the stretch of gully, aware that he was horribly exposed. He breathed easier once he rounded Aston's security position at the end of the corridor.

"Let's move," was all Shaw said once reunited with his team. Natalie exhaled her immense relief as she continued to monitor the Russian forces on her ATAK.

Invictus team hurried through the gully—weapons high with deliberate focus—while the remaining gunship rose over the forest and surged toward its downed comrades.

"They don't know where we are," Shaw reasoned quietly into the microphone hovering over his lips. "Let's keep it quiet." Before the team could respond, a shrill buzz filled the air.

"What is that?" Reeves called, his eyes darting upward.

"Invictus, we're tracking a small UAV inbound on your position. Looks like a commercial style drone," Sosa informed.

"Copy all, Hummingbird, we hear it," Shaw replied, his eyes searching the night sky for the new intruder. The unit soared over them at over one hundred miles per hour.

"That thing's going to give us away," McEwen stated as he watched it bank and head back toward them. It paused overhead and hovered as it seemed to study the group.

"Somebody's watching us," Bray muttered gravely.

"But who?" Pikari replied.

"That's the question," McEwen answered.

Shaw, unnerved by the unexpected technology, dug into the pocket high on his right sleeve and pulled out a folded wad of silk. He quickly unraveled the bundle, revealing a small American flag with only forty-eight stars. His grandfather had carried the flag in the jungles of Guadalcanal, and thus Shaw had carried it on every one of his combat deployments. He held it up to the drone, and it slowly descended as if getting a better look.

"Someone ready to shoot this thing down?" Shaw asked.

"On it," Bratcher replied, already having his rifle trained on the small drone. Before he could pull the trigger, the drone shot upward with blinding speed, the team losing view of it.

"Invictus, that gunship is coming around, and ground forces are sweeping southeast. They're entering the creek bed now," Sosa informed.

She watched through the UAV feed as one of the Russians wounded by the trap motioned to his head with his hand. One of his companions nodded, raised his rifle, and discharged a round into the head of the wounded man. The entire intelligence floor jumped, unnerved by the sight of voluntary fratricide.

"Copy all, Hummingbird," Shaw replied. "Beowulf, lock down that corridor behind us," Shaw instructed. Bratcher hurried back down the trench, and falling prone—keeping most of his body behind the southward bend—he trained his rifle down the earthwork, ready to engage the new targets in his sights as they stumbled through the gully.

"Now counting twenty-one tangos," Hummingbird said as the gunship hovered protectively over the ten who advanced over open ground.

Shaw hurriedly set up their defensive position as he planned to catch his foes in an L-shaped ambush. He left Reeves, McEwen, Bratcher, Bray, and Pikari at their current location before he led Lincoln, the airmen, Aston, Natalie, and Laila farther along the gully, moving into a channel that turned westward. Turning right, the group and their Dutch Shepherd hurried forward and set up an overlapping field of fire.

"You three, stand here," Shaw instructed the airmen, pointing out a quick line. "Guns that way. You boys are about to get more combat experience than most of the Air Force combined." The three airmen mustered their courage. Though they trembled—none having fired a weapon since requalifications months ago—they reminded themselves that they still wore the uniform and were expected to do their duty. Besides, if they survived, what a story to tell.

"Matterhorn, we're in position," Shaw informed, once he had lined up alongside Aston, his wife, and Laila. He had positioned the three airmen in such a way farther west that when the shooting began, even if Shaw's team pushed to flank, they were not at risk of friendly fire.

"Good copy, Philo," Reeves replied. "On your mark." Shaw flipped open his ATAK one more time to gain additional situational awareness provided by the MQ-1 Predator UAV that soared above them at 50,000 feet.

His eyes found the little drone as it hovered a greater distance away, as if observing. *What are you up to?* Shaw thought. He refocused his attention on the advancing Russians. The gunship was his primary concern. He knew they had gotten lucky with the first one, but he simply doubted they had the firepower to take it down. *Maybe at best, we could force a retreat*, he reasoned.

"On my mark," he began, finding a good foothold on the bank that he could use to climb over the top if necessary. "Three, two, mark."

His team opened up their violent hate as automatic fire from Reeves' light machine gun cut across no man's land with utter apathy. The others picked their shots with accurate fire, and without hesitation, the gunship raked the firing line with heavy rounds which smacked into the earth, raining chunks of dirt and splatters of mud down upon the Invictus operators.

Shaw launched a 40 millimeter grenade from his M203 into the midst of a group of Russian soldiers who had fallen prone. The gunship returned fire with a barrage of rockets whose flames leaped high into the night sky, shaking the entire creek bed. Sections of the gully caved inward, spilling dirt into the bed and immobilizing McEwen and covering Bratcher.

Shaw fell as the concussive force threw him backwards; Natalie and Laila hit the ground hard as well. The two women shook their heads to fight against the ringing disorientation in their ears, before stumbling back to rejoin the fight.

"Concentrate fire on that gunship," Shaw called into his radio as he staggered back to his firing position. The shockwave from the barrage had penetrated his hearing protection and left his ears ringing.

Sosa watched the entire gunfight with a hand over her mouth and tears streaming down her cheeks. She cursed herself for not taking Natalie's advice to arm the UAV they had sent into Ukrainian airspace. All she could do was watch helplessly as her friends fought for their lives. She focused her attention on Lincoln as he fired from his position within the gully.

Come on, she urged, hoping they would prevail, and yet feeling utterly useless to advance her wish.

The gunship continued to fire even as Bratcher, having dug himself free, reengaged the Russians still advancing down the trench. Shaw reloaded his grenade launcher and took a wild shot at the gunship, but the grenade glanced off its curved hull and detonated off target. He tried again, aiming for the rotors, but he was not hopeful, yet there was nothing more to do save for pepper the armored helicopter with small arms fire.

The night suddenly illuminated brightly as the gunship ripped apart in dazzling brightness before it spiraled into the ground. The hulking craft smashed down on top of its own soldiers as its rotors churned up the earth.

"What was that?" Reeves cried.

In like surprise, Sosa had started forward toward the screen before realizing she wasn't actually there. She choked on her own relief but didn't dwell on it as she watched Shaw climb from the gully just as a jet screamed overhead in a low pass.

"Push!" Shaw shouted as he vaulted the wall and advanced toward the scrambling Russians.

"It's the Ukrainians!" Natalie cried, her relief bubbling out as laughter.

Aston and Lincoln quickly matched Shaw's stride as they too climbed from the natural trench. With weapons raised, they engaged any remaining Russians attempting to fight back. The airmen, seeing even the women to their right climb up and follow the three operators, found a sudden fire burn through their hearts. This unexpected courage caused them to shout as they climbed and followed the lead of the more experienced warfighters.

The Russians attempted to fight back, but with their air support burning around them and their comrades dead and dying, they crumpled under the advancing aggression Shaw and his team unleashed upon them.

Shaw's rifle snapped from target to target, though there weren't many left, and he fired several times, seeing also that his team did the same. Each individual enemy soldier took more rounds than necessary as Invictus sought to end the fight. With his upper sectors clear, Shaw adjusted his attention northward toward the gully as he raced across no man's land with Aston and Lincoln flanking him. Natalie and Laila followed behind with the Airmen who had caught up with them.

Keeping their carbines in low ready, the three operators and their canine neared the lip of the gully section they had first followed from the forest. With their rifles pointed down on the surrounded Russians, they engaged only those who lifted their weapons. The sudden and unexpected violence overwhelmed the Russians, who immediately dropped their weapons and surrendered while gazing fearfully up at the men above them, each appearing as a colossus as they towered over them. Shaw, Aston, and Lincoln, all professionals, held their fire and commanded them out of the trench.

Of the ten in the trench, only four emerged; the rest lay dead from Bratcher's precision and McEwen's support.

"We're clear," Shaw called to his team while keeping his rifle trained on his prisoner.

"Clear," came Reeves' reply.

"Invictus, this is Hummingbird," Sosa chimed. "Be advised. We're tracking several vehicles approaching from the south. They appear to be Ukrainian."

52

Standing in no man's land on the north side of the creek, Invictus team and the airmen, with their prisoners kneeling on the ground before him, watched the column of dark green, Ukrainian-built Kozak infantry mobility vehicles tear through the countryside as they approached. They resembled the MRAP, which Shaw and his team were familiar with, marking them as not Russian. However, Invictus team still maintained a posture of readiness, with weapons held in a nonthreatening, but ready position.

Captain Coffey and his crew shook as their bodies became aware of the adrenaline affecting them in the wake of the intense combat. Though still scared, they floated as if in a dream, not fully comprehending how they had made it through. In their minds, they couldn't help but replay the firefight, unaware that it differed slightly each time. None of the three could say with confidence how much they had contributed, if they had actually endangered their allies, or if they had actually killed any enemy combatants.

In some way, Coffey was grateful he couldn't be sure. Having never flown combat missions, this was his first taste of death in the field, and he and his co-pilot could confidently say that they preferred the air.

Staff Sergeant McCrae, on the other hand, teemed with energy as he shivered from the adrenaline. He no longer felt the cold, and the silence settled on him with a measure of discomfort. He had never felt more alive. The air even tasted fresh on his tongue in a way he had never before noticed. He glanced right, down the line of men and past his fellow airmen, his gaze settling on David Shaw.

Even the way the man stood inspired him, and in that moment, he knew he wanted to be more than he was. There had to be something in the Air Force he could do beyond his current job. Maybe as a Pararescue Specialist or a Joint Terminal Attack Controller. There had to be some avenue where he could become like the men whom he had just fought alongside. After all, he was only twenty-seven.

Natalie stood to her husband's right, still breathing deeply from the exhilaration of combat. It was her first time doing anything like it in full kit with a rifle, and she thought of their last stand on that Yemeni beach before SEAL Team 3 and Special Boat Team 20 arrived to extract them. Then, she had only had a pistol and had not conducted any tactics other than holding her ground. Even in the previous gunfights in which she had fought alongside her husband in the Caribbean, Switzerland, and the Gulf of Finland, he had led, and she had followed. In most of those situations, she hadn't even fired her weapon. This, indeed, was different, and she felt relieved to have employed her skills towards the victory they all shared.

She shared a glance with Laila, who stood to her left, and the woman produced a smile that inwardly startled Natalie. She reminded herself that taking life had been common to Laila since her childhood, and for her to so quickly return to a place of calm contentment shouldn't unsettle her. But it did. Laila was a constant conundrum, a frustration even, and yet, at the same time, a wonder. Natalie briefly thought of the way she had teased Bray in the Stryker, and though she didn't approve, she found herself fixated on how the young woman lived fully in every situation despite all she had lost and suffered.

That last thought brought the image of her son to mind—his impossibly small, pink body and tiny hands. Though he had never drawn breath, Nathanial was the most precious sight she had ever seen. Natalie had never known such love, such devotion, and the agony of having that ripped away from her was still overbearing.

Her expression contorted in a mix of rage and grief that no one saw. She endured those emotions in the cold of Ukraine alone, even though surrounded by people she trusted and loved. Glancing back at Laila, whose smile had firmed into a plump line as she stared at the approaching convoy, Natalie sniffed and sourced her inward strength, knowing Laila had much to teach and held much to be admired.

She needed her. This was not over.

"How do you think this is going to go?" Reeves asked Shaw, his voice coming through all their headsets. He stood to Shaw's right and kept the barrel of his MK46 hovering over the left shoulder of his kneeling prisoner, who muttered his hatred harshly in his native language. "Shut it," Reeves barked before he slammed the muzzle of his machine gun into the back of the kneeling man's helmet.

After recovering, the Russian trooper sucked on his front teeth to simmer his anger. He did not want to die, and after what these men had done to his own, he didn't question their ability, capacity, or willingness.

"I hope well," Shaw answered, his voice low in the cold stillness of the coming dawn.

They had lost connection with De la Vega after he said he was marshaling assistance, and Sosa had confirmed that keeping comms connected between them all was simply too varied and complicated to make work. Shaw understood that well enough. Communications, if anything, were tricky, and all who worked on them professionally in the military held a healthy superstition surrounding the equipment and operating procedures.

Shaw didn't blame them. The wrong comms could result in unintentional fratricide. The wars of history had confirmed that time and time again.

"You think Zorro is with them?" Natalie asked him.

"I don't even know if they are the help he said he was working on," Shaw admitted. "This firefight could have drawn the attention of Ukrainian forces in the AO." He glanced up at the drone that still circled around them. He figured it was ensuring the area was clear of additional Russian forces.

With the sky brightening with the rising sun to the east, Shaw flipped up his NODs as the lead Kozak rolled right up to the edge of the creek and stopped before doors opened on either side.

"Ukrainian," the lead man shouted, patting his chest as he emerged upward from between the door and the vehicle's frame. "You American, yes?"

"Yes, we're Americans," Shaw replied, stepping forward. The Ukrainian soldier, moving toward the edge of the trench, laughed and clapped his hands together.

"Americans!" he shouted as he turned back toward the convoy and raised his fists into the air in an obvious display of excitement. He turned back toward Shaw and continued in his broken English. "We have found you."

"Found us?" Shaw echoed.

"Yes," came a different accent as another man emerged from the back seat of the second vehicle. He was dressed in a Ukrainian military uniform and carried an AK-74 with black, polymer furniture but no optic. Shaw couldn't help but smirk as he laid eyes on Diego de la Vega, but he was not without his concerns and reservations.

"Was that you guys?" Shaw asked, pointing toward the sky, referencing the fighter jet that had saved them.

"They're calling him the Ghost of Kyiv. Apparently, he's already downed a few Russian aircraft, and this war is only getting started," De la Vega replied. He pointed to a short, pale man with a stark white beard puffing out oddly from his helmet's chin strap. "This is Ricochet. He's with me."

"We are all with you!" the lead Ukrainian stated proudly, remembering his orders from General Dudka. Shaw strode forward, stowing his rifle at his side. He extended a hand, and the Ukrainian shook it from across the narrow trench. De la Vega approached and reached for Shaw's hand. Shaw was not too proud to return the gesture.

"Thank you," he said.

"I am Chief Sergeant Stepanenko, Ukraine Special Forces. We originally thought you were orcs," the noncommissioned officer introduced himself.

"Orcs?" Shaw echoed. Stepanenko laughed and pointed at the Russian prisoners.

"Orcs," he repeated.

"So, the drone was yours?" Shaw asked. Stepanenko looked at him with a wide smile, clearly not understanding. Shaw flew one hand into the palm of his other and pointed at the sky. "Drone?"

"Yes, yes!" Stepanenko said excitedly once realizing what Shaw was asking. "Was Sergeant Lyashko's idea. Your...uh...your..." his eyes darted back and forth as he sought the right word in English.

"My flag?" Shaw offered.

"Yes! Flag!"

"It's good you had that on you," De la Vega interjected.

"Yeah, no kidding," Shaw replied.

"Let's get you all loaded up," De la Vega said, looking over Shaw's shoulder to his team. Seeing Natalie shocked him. He inclined his head toward her and said, "Mrs. Shaw, you sure are full of surprises."

Approaching, Natalie replied, "Thanks, Zorro. Appreciate you coming through for us."

"It appears we have a lot to talk about," he said.

"Yes, we do," she responded, wearing a relieved grin.

"Ivan here has pissed himself," came Bray's voice over the radio. His tone held a comical yet concerned tone. Shaw turned to look at the young Russian at Bray's feet, who sobbed and shook horribly. The others scowled and barked at him for his cowardice, but their captors quickly silenced them with muzzle thumps to their helmets. Seeing the young Russian's fear, Shaw realized immediately what fate awaited them at the hands of the Ukrainians. He sighed and turned back to Stepanenko.

"What will you do to them?" he asked, stepping aside and pointing at the kneeling Russians.

"We kill them," Stepanenko stated firmly, his brow furrowing. De la Vega's lips rolled inward. He lowered his chin and did not remove his gaze from Shaw's.

"They are our prisoners and are protected under the Geneva Conventions," Shaw replied calmly.

"No Geneva here," Stepanenko replied, shaking his head. "Orcs rape, murder, and invade our land, and not for first time. It why we call them orcs."

Shaw bounced his head in solemn nods before turning to meet the gazes of his team. They had all turned up their night vision binoculars, and, in the faint morning, he could see their conviction. He offered them a grateful smile.

"These men are under our protection," he said, doubling down. He returned his attention to Stepanenko, widened his stance, and fought the urge to place his hand on the pistol grip of the M4A1 that hung across his chest. The Ukrainian chewed on his lips as his expression soured. "We need to get out of Ukraine. Can you help us? We will take them with us and turn them over to the CIA." Stepanenko's narrowing eyes moved from Shaw to the Russians to Invictus team and then back to Shaw. Shaw noticed in his periphery as Ricochet tensed, gripping his AK with what looked like supportive resolve. Finally, Stepanenko shrugged and rose his palms upward in apathy.

"Make no promises to you. General Dudka have final say. We would like you to stay and fight with us," Stepanenko said.

"We cannot stay," Shaw replied.

"Must ask, you understand?" Stepanenko replied with a laugh. "Come, come," he added, waving his hand and calling them to cross the trench.

"Can we trust these guys?" Bray asked.

"Don't have much of a choice," Pikari replied as he hoisted his prisoner and prepared to cross the trench.

53

En Route South to Kyiv

Shaw, Natalie, Laila, Lincoln, De la Vega, and Ricochet, accompanied by the Ukrainian vehicle crew, conversed as their Kozak rumbled south toward Kyiv. Natalie's nose and cheeks burned from the cold, but she ignored the discomfort and focused on De la Vega.

"Do you think you can take off with things the way they are?" Natalie asked De la Vega, but the man only shrugged.

"The Ukrainians would need to have secure control of the airspace for me to even consider it," De la Vega answered. "So long as the Ukrainians can halt the Russian advance and secure airspace, we can try. But Natalie, we need to talk about Stovall."

"I know," Natalie replied.

"You know?" De la Vega responded, surprised. He glanced at Shaw, who kept a stern, stoic expression. The Red Horse CEO turned back to Natalie.

"Let me fill you in," Natalie said firmly. De la Vega nodded, leaned forward in the confined space, and gave Natalie his undivided attention.

She explained everything she knew, bringing both De la Vega and Ricochet up to speed on who Laila was, her involvement with Vitori and The Czar's Brotherhood, as well as their mission to extract her from the situation. De la Vega couldn't believe what he was hearing, though he didn't doubt her in the slightest. Now, he worried how Dudka would react to the presence of the assassin who had attempted to take his life.

However, when Laila explained in more detail, De la Vega recalled Dudka's words on how precious the life of his would-be assassin was—if she was who he thought she was. When he relayed the information, Laila seemed to relax in her seat. Still, Natalie and Shaw were not comfortable chancing the situation, but at Laila's insistence, they relented.

"He can help us," she said. Natalie and Shaw exchanged glances.

"But do we want his help?" Natalie countered. Shaw nodded his agreement. If he was anything like Rykov, he wanted nothing to do with the man, and he feared he might even want to kill him, especially if he had anything remotely close to do with Wyatt's death.

"He needs to know the truth, and only I can tell it to him," Laila insisted, keeping secret the fact that it was Dudka's men who ambushed them in Zürich at Rykov's orders.

De la Vega quickly realized that he knew very little of the history and depth of the entire narrative. For being so close to Stovall, he chided himself for not understanding better how this elite community functioned. *Am I really so blind?* he wondered.

Even more so, Ricochet couldn't believe his ears, but he resolved to let the information enter one ear, pass through his mind unmolested, and exit the other without another thought. *Zorro was right. The less I know, the better*, he reasoned. "Zorro, just point me in the right direction here. Tell me who to shoot, and I'll shoot him. I don't need to know all this other stuff. Freaks me out, if I'm honest," he said to De la Vega.

"I get it, brother," De la Vega replied. Natalie couldn't help but smile at Ricochet's perspective. Some part of her wished she could adopt the same, but she and her husband were too deeply embedded in the muck to escape it so easily. There was only one path forward, and both she and Shaw knew what had to be done.

They'd done it before.

Though they couldn't say with certainty that it had improved things.

However, they also couldn't say it hadn't.

"What a world we live in," Natalie remarked.

"You can say that again," Lincoln chimed.

"So, what's the plan?" Laila asked, her soft, accented voice holding an admirable determination.

"We get out of Ukraine and stop Stovall before things get worse," Shaw voiced. Natalie nodded. He wanted to say, *and stop him from spilling American blood in Ukraine,* but by the looks of De la Vega and Ricochet, he might already have.

"Easier said than done," Lincoln admitted.

"General Dudka will help us," De la Vega voiced. He watched Shaw sigh and shake his head.

"We would still have to find Stovall before news of our crash gets ahead of us," Shaw said.

"It's likely he already knows," Natalie replied. "We have to assume he does."

"Then we need to get Sosa on this," Lincoln stated.

"We do," Natalie confirmed. "Though I fear there isn't much she's going to be able to do."

"What about your friend Reggie?" Lincoln asked.

"Maybe, but I think we all know there is only one way to end this threat," she replied.

"Like Weber?" Lincoln probed. He watched Shaw nod, his eyes grave.

"Like Roark, Rykov, Radi, and Barakat," Natalie stated, daring him to question her.

"So Barakat was you," Lincoln replied with a chuckle. "That was a mess, and you guys certainly get around. Should I be worried?"

"We're all still on the same side," Shaw responded. "Nothing has changed." Lincoln nodded, but Shaw didn't think he was convinced. He understood and wrestled with the same dilemma. Every pull of the trigger was justified, but it never seemed to end; the world never seemed to grow safer for those living in it. Even now, Ukrainians faced death and tyranny, and Shaw couldn't help but feel that he was partly responsible. If Rykov was still alive, would this have happened?

You can't live on 'what ifs,' he reminded himself, even as he inhaled deeply.

"Wait, are you going to kill Stovall?" De la Vega asked. Natalie met his gaze with unflinching resolve.

"That is the plan."

"Then you'll have to get in line," he shot back before smiling. Natalie returned it and looked at her husband, who stared at De la Vega.

Not six months ago, the Red Horse CEO had approached them with a buyout offer and threatened to shut them down if they didn't agree. *How the tables have turned*, Natalie thought. She found that she trusted De la Vega, perhaps not to the extent he trusted her, but circumstances have a funny way of rewriting relationships, and Natalie was not one to let access to Stovall slip by. If De la Vega could get her to him, then perhaps, he had just become their most valuable ally.

Special Operations Forces Headquarters
Kyiv, Ukraine

The column of Kozaks roared through the streets of Kyiv as the sun took full ownership over the darkness. With Ukrainian Air Force pilots contesting the skies, the convoy rolled southward into the city unmolested.

Kyiv was mostly quiet now, though the sounds of war waged to the north as the two opposing forces, Russian and Ukrainian, met now in conventional contest. Each passing second, Shaw grew more and more aware of the lives being lost on both sides. He had never experienced war like this, and yet he understood the calamity for what it was and the new era it brought to warfare. The last twenty years of war in the Middle East produced new technologies; how much more so would a larger conventional conflict? He knew he couldn't permit Stovall to manipulate events and world leaders to evoke Article Five. He knew the clock was ticking.

Once on the military base that housed Ukraine's special operations headquarters, the convoy came to a stop at Dudka's command building, and all funneled outside. Given the recent attack, none were asked to relinquish their weapons.

"I'll stay out here with these guys," Ricochet stated, throwing a thumb over his shoulder toward the Ukrainian soldiers behind him.

"Alright," De la Vega replied.

He, the Shaws, and the rest of the Invictus operators, as well as the airmen, Laila, and Lincoln, all followed Sergeant Stepanenko inside. Within minutes, they all stood before General Ihor Dudka, who wore a subtle smirk before he reached for and gripped De la Vega's hand. The two shared a quick pump before De la Vega turned to introduce those he had departed to rescue.

"General, this is Natalie and David Shaw," he said, offering a hand their way.

"In the flesh?" the general stated with an air of surprise. "You did not tell me that these two were among those you departed to bring back."

"Hopefully, there is no problem," Shaw said sternly, his brow furrowed. Dudka laughed.

"No, no problem at all," the general replied. "It is an honor to meet you both. Your infamy is admirable."

"Infamy?" Natalie echoed, her slender eyebrows raised.

"Brother Dudka," Laila stated, drawing all eyes. The unexpected greeting furrowed Dudka's brow in what Natalie could only perceive as brief confusion. Both she and Shaw tensed, concerned for Laila's safety. Though they trusted her discernment, they did not like the situation in which she had placed herself. However, they knew their options were limited.

"Deep down I suspected," Dudka replied. His hard face softened somewhat as his eyes fell on Laila. She removed her helmet, revealing the fullness of her identity, and Dudka's smile appeared unexpectedly endearing. "The Spider of Kandahar. It is an honor," he added, inclining his head. Laila forced a smile of her own. "I suppose gratitude is in order. Thank you for flipping the charge."

"You know?" Laila asked, surprised.

"I have reviewed the footage," he said. "Come, sister, you must explain everything to me." Dudka reached out his hand, as a father inviting a daughter, and Laila complied.

Natalie and Shaw watched uncomfortably as Dudka led Laila out of earshot, and Natalie's eyes bored hard into Dudka as she watched the two converse.

"She's alright," Shaw whispered, leaning close but also not taking his eyes from the two. "She knows what she's doing."

"Yeah," Natalie replied quietly, allowing herself to be assured.

Turning to his men, De la Vega, and Lincoln, Shaw asked, "Is there a way we can get some chow? You know, save our MREs in case we have a long drive ahead of us?"

"Sergeant?" De la Vega asked Stepanenko.

"Yes, no problem," he replied, in his heavy accent. "You can follow me."

"Can we have it brought to us?" Shaw asked, drawing Natalie's gaze from Dudka and Laila. Shaw pointed his forward slightly toward Dudka and Laila, and Stepanenko understood.

"Yes, no problem," he said as identically as before. He departed, and all eyes returned to Dudka and Laila. Natalie noticed that Bray was quite uneasy and that his hand had not yet left the grip of his carbine, which hung loose around his chest, ready just in case. Natalie imagined his thumb on the safety lever, and she hoped it wouldn't come to that.

Stepanenko soon returned with staff carrying trays of a reddish stew with a side of grilled meat and potatoes. No one asked what it was but took their portion and ate greedily, ignoring any unpleasant flavors solely for the calories. Despite being heated by the food, none doffed their gear to cool off. Instead, they kept everything close, rifles slung, even the airmen, who Shaw had checked on twice already as they ate circled together in plastic chairs. As he kept tabs on Laila, he also processed the buzz of Dudka's command center as staffers, both enlisted and commissioned, responded to the invasion as ordered. However, to Shaw, there appeared a lull in the excitement as the Russian advance seemed to stall in the north.

It was a good sign.

All perked up as Dudka and Laila rose, and all relaxed as they watched the two embrace. Laila started back toward the group first, followed by Dudka. He offered Shaw, Natalie, and De la Vega a nod before saying, "Sister Laila will update you all. I've taken quite enough time away from urgent matters to clear things between us. You have my full support. No more lies."

Natalie's eyes widened in surprise at his words before they darted to Laila, who wore a satisfied expression.

"Thank you, sir," Shaw said for them all before Dudka took his leave to continue his oversight of their resistance.

"Well, things seem good," Lincoln said as he approached.

"Yes," Laila said, relieved.

"Tell us," Natalie urged, taking a step closer.

"He credits me with saving his life, and after I filled him in about Vitori, he was most willing to help us," she explained.

"The conversation seemed longer than that," Shaw said. Laila looked at him.

"Yes, he had me relay everything about Rykov's demise, so I started at the beginning," she answered.

"He knows about us and Rykov?" Natalie asked.

"Yes, I told him," she replied firmly. "No more lies."

Natalie only nodded.

"Seems to have worked out," Shaw admitted. Again, Laila nodded.

"Once I shared about Otakar's betrayal and why, he understood, even saying that he had suspected for years that Rykov was hiding something from us all. The clarity, oddly enough, caused him to capitulate his ambition for the Brotherhood. He says all influence he has retained will be directed toward the defense of Ukraine. However, he insisted that Vitori be dealt with, and I told him we would take care of it. With your track record, he agreed."

"If only they were all so easy to turn," Natalie said, hardly believing the news.

"It's a win," Shaw said. Laila grinned. "Thank you."

"Thank you," Laila returned.

"The only thing left to do is find Stovall and Vitori," Shaw said. He turned to Lincoln, "We can't ask you or the CIA to accompany us any further, considering what we plan to do. You are free to walk away, as is anyone here."

"I appreciate that, David," Lincoln replied, without providing an answer.

Shaw turned to De la Vega and said, "Do you know where Stovall is?"

"I can find out," he responded.

"Good," he said as he turned toward his wife. "We need to get out of here now before things get worse."

"General Dudka has arranged transportation for us to the airport," Laila said. All eyes fell on De la Vega, and he tilted his head.

"All it would take is one missile," he warned. "I don't think I have to tell you all that."

"I bet the roads to Lviv and Odessa are packed with refugees already," Natalie said. "If Dudka can provide an escort, we should make the attempt. All other options delay too long."

"We'd likely be the only non-military bird in the sky," Shaw noted.

"Oh, I wouldn't say my plane's 'non-military,'" De la Vega interjected. Again, all eyes fell on him. "With a fighter escort, we could make it."

"Do we have a fighter escort?" Shaw asked Laila.

"The general said he would provide anything we needed in order to stop Vitori," she said.

"It's the only way out for me," De la Vega insisted. "I've got men in the field who I need to get home."

"I understand," Shaw replied. He turned to Laila. "Did you mention to Dudka our prisoners?"

Laila sighed and nodded. "I'm sorry, he isn't allowing them to leave the country, but he said they would be detained and interrogated."

"Tortured, you mean," he countered.

"I can't say," she replied.

"There's nothing we can do for them," Natalie hurriedly interjected. "We've already done all we can by sparing their lives in the field."

Shaw huffed his displeasure, but nodded, understanding and relenting. "Alright, fine. Let's get out of here."

PART IV

THE COURT OF THE COMMON MAN

54

Suite Impériale,
Ritz Carlton,
Paris, France

Anderson Stovall dabbed the corners of his mouth with the black, cloth napkin before gently replacing it in his lap. He looked down at his plate, at the remaining crumbs from his croque monsieur delivered to him from Les Deux Magots, an establishment Stovall adored for its long history and notable patrons, including Ernest Hemingway and Pablo Picasso. But sometimes, he just craved a toasted ham and cheese sandwich with fries.

He couldn't say why. Perhaps it was the ham and cheese sandwiches his mother made him during his childhood, especially on their annual beach vacations to the Florida panhandle. Regardless of the history, the sandwich from Les Deux Magots was one of his favorites in the entire world. Were there better sandwiches in the city? Probably, but Stovall often leaned into certain anchors that kept him centered.

Everyone has their quirks, he reminded himself as he resisted the temptation to scoop up one more fry.

Seated in the spacious hotel suite, he checked his watch, counting down the hours until Sofia landed. The fact that she was arriving early only excited him, and he wondered how she would respond to his offer.

Everything is coming together, he thought excitedly as he inhaled deeply. With Rykov and Barakat gone and Oza retreating like the coward Stovall had always assumed him to be, the world was finally his. Soon, he and Vitori would merge their empires into something the world had not seen since Genghis Khan or Julius Caesar. Maybe the British Empire in its days of glory, but no predecessor could possibly imagine the wealth and influence Stovall was coming to possess.

Though his empire wasn't measured in leagues or borders, his media campaigns and businesses influenced billions of lives. He could now place whoever he wanted in whatever position of power he wanted them in. Not all because of Ukraine, but because of the opportunity for expansion afforded by his colleagues' disappearances. Only Oza remained, but Stovall would deal with him. It was only a matter of time before he fell beneath the combined might of his and Sofia's authority.

Despite all this, he didn't feel invulnerable. Far from it, actually. But knowing that the Shaws had died in a plane crash in Ukraine gave him a sense of peace, though he mourned the loss of opportunity. Regardless, he would shore up his defenses and ensure his legacy could not be disrupted. The additional security that milled around the hotel, both overt and covert, brought greater confidence, but where more security existed, so too did the reminder of Stovall's own mortality.

I have to pass on what I've built, he thought, teeming with excitement for Sofia's arrival. However, he was keenly aware of all the work that still lay ahead. Without his constant oversight and involvement, he knew the war would not yield the desired results. Without pressure on lawmakers and national leaders, it would remain an isolated conflict, void of any real revenue.

Stovall knew the longer the war continued and the higher the stakes grew for both the West and the East, the more profit he could extract. Even on this first day, outrage was higher than expected. America had yet to fully wake, and the media—per Stovall's influence—ran rampant with coverage, diving into Russia's intentions, Ukraine's defensive reaction, and the capacity of NATO's responsibility.

It should have overwhelmed him, being the grandest endeavor yet undertaken, but he exuded a cool confidence, as was his usual state of existence. He reached for his sparkling water just as his chief of staff, Ross Barton, entered the room, holding an encrypted phone presented outward in his right hand.

"Mr. Barton," Stovall said, setting down his glass and rising from his seat.

"You have a call, sir," Barton said, inclining his head respectfully. Stovall never carried a phone or any technological device that could be bugged, no matter how unlikely.

"Ms. Vitori, I take it?" he asked as he dropped his cloth napkin on his plate.

"No, sir," Barton replied, his tone strained. "It's Mr. De la Vega."

Surprise flashed across Stovall's face, but he still reached for the phone. He deactivated the mute feature and placed the phone on speaker.

"Diego, to what do I owe the pleasure of your call?" Stovall greeted.

"Mr. Stovall, I'm in Ukraine."

"My God, man, what are you doing in Ukraine? Haven't you seen the news?" Stovall jabbered, feigning his surprise.

"I felt I needed to accompany the team with all that was happening. I'm the only survivor," he lamented.

"Oh, Diego, I'm so sorry. Is there anything you need?" Stovall asked, mustering compassion with a bit of difficulty. He wondered if De la Vega saw through the facade. Stovall knew De la Vega wasn't stupid, though he was a bit aloof when it came to the activities happening around him. It was part of the reason he had been such a good fit for the CEO role at Red Horse. He had the pedigree and background in Army Special Forces, something Stovall admired, but he was obediently loyal, never questioning his orders or intent.

However, Stovall wasn't a fool. He knew just about anyone could connect the dots. Better men than De la Vega might blame him for his men's deaths.

"I'd like to meet," he answered.

There it is, Stovall thought.

"Of course, anything you need," Stovall said. "I'm in Paris. Do you need transportation?"

"No, I can get there," De la Vega said.

"Good, good. I'm staying at the Ritz here in Paris. I'll be expecting you."

"Very good, sir," De la Vega replied. "I'll be there within 24 hours. Though I will need to stop for a change of clothes."

"Nonsense, I'll have my tailor prepare clothes for you. Come as you are. You're what, a forty-eight regular, thirty-two-thirty?"

"Yes, sir," De la Vega replied.

"Wonderful, I await your arrival eagerly."

"Thank you, sir," De la Vega replied.

Stovall terminated the call and rolled his lips inward as he stared at the phone. He turned sharply, his bright blue eyes finding Barton.

"Sir?" Barton probed, knowing an order was coming.

"Double current security," he commanded.

"At once, sir," Barton replied, ignoring the concern rising in his throat.

"And where's Mr. Scalco?"

"Nairobi," came the reply.

"Recall him here, ASAP. Tell him to bring his best."

"His best, sir?"

"If De la Vega is planning something against me, I want to be prepared."

"You think he would do such a thing?" Barton asked, startled by his employer's train of thought.

"Hard to say, but too much is at stake to forgo certain precautions, and there is only one way to find out."

"I understand, sir," Barton replied, "but can you not just take Mr. De la Vega someplace secret and interrogate him there? Why risk yourself here?"

Stovall chuckled. "Because if I'm wrong, and Diego is still loyal, I would have to then kill him. He would never forgive such a thing, and I'd rather not lose him if I can help it. He truly is the perfect fit for Red Horse CEO. Who would I replace him with? Scalco?" He laughed as he said it. "Could you imagine Scalco with that kind of power? No, I need Diego's humility and loyalty; it is too valuable to lose. With Scalco here, I can assure my protection while also giving Diego the honor he is due. Should he, in fact, have traitorous intent, Scalco and his men will be here to deal with it."

"Seems like a risk, sir," Barton replied.

"Anything worth having in life takes risk. I will not dishonor Diego on account of any fear or suspicion I may have. He's earned at least that, and I never intended for him to go to Ukraine."

"Very well, sir," Barton replied before bowing slightly and turning to take his leave.

Stovall dragged a hand down his mouth before planting both palms on his waist, elbows out wide. He inhaled, held it, then exhaled.

You're probably overreacting, but it's best not to take any chances. You're doing the right thing.

55

Sikorsky Kyiv International Airport
Kyiv, Ukraine

"How'd it go?" Natalie asked De la Vega once he lowered the phone from his ear.

"He's in Paris," he answered. Natalie nodded. Though the war still raged to the north, the sounds were distant enough for the seasoned operators to realize there was no ground threat to the airport. The Ukrainian forces had repelled Russian paratrooper assaults across the city and now secured critical infrastructure, like the airport. Fortunately, the airport in which the Red Horse plane had landed lay situated on the southwest side of the city, far away from the current ground fighting.

The sun, hidden behind a low cloud covering, illuminated the tarmac in a mystic orange haze. The roar of several jet squadrons pierced the mist as they flew constantly to keep the Russians at bay—landing, refueling, rearming, and deploying over and over again all morning. They had only lost two planes, and one of those had been a fratricide incident after air defense systems in Kyiv misidentified the Ukrainian Su-27 fighter. Natalie didn't know if the pilot had survived or not.

The team, along with Ukrainian assistance, had finished loading the sealed, aluminum containers containing the bodies of De la Vega's and Ricochet's deceased teammates. After promising to assist Ukraine in whatever way Red Horse was able and promising to return double all that was given, General Dudka's staff had given De la Vega all he had asked for concerning the bodies of his men. It was Ricochet who had led the effort to dig out the deceased, but they had only recovered two bodies, the rest having been obliterated by the missile impact.

Both De la Vega and Ricochet had quickly realized how lucky they were to be alive. Dudka had assured them that any remains would be handled with honor, preserved, and kept until such an opportunity arose to return them home.

Though De la Vega hated the idea of leaving men behind, he felt confident in his BDA that no additional bodies remained intact, but he knew from history how complicated and complex a cleanup like this one could be. For days, the Ukrainians would continue to clear the space, and though he couldn't be there, he hoped for some dignity for the dead—that at least a few more bodies had been preserved—but he seriously doubted it. The entire situation weighed on his psyche, and he wondered if he would be able to exercise self-control upon seeing Stovall.

If Stovall even lets me see him, De la Vega thought.

"Alright, time to load up," Ricochet shouted as he jogged toward Natalie and De la Vega.

With all their gear already stowed on board, everyone mustered their courage and climbed the stairs into the private plane. In silence, everyone found an open seat, quietly prayed, and waited as the engines spun up and the plane advanced down the runway.

"Red Horse Flight, you are clear for take off," came the call from Wolf Three-One, the flight commander for their fighter escort.

"Affirmative, Wolf Flight, we are taxiing now. Stand by," the Red Horse pilot-in-command replied.

Natalie's hand shot on top of Shaw's as the husband and wife pressed back into their joined seats, keeping their heads against the headrest. The aggressive takeoff shook the entire aircraft until it rose from the tarmac.

"Red Horse Flight, you are clear," Wolf Three-One stated, his accent thick.

"Copy, Wolf Flight, we are clear," the Red Horse PIC replied. He kept his voice stoic, though on the inside he shook with terror. Jets flew fast, but missiles flew even faster. His only confidence lay in the cloud covering and the chaos of the battle around them, essentially hoping that any Russian fighters were otherwise occupied than to direct their attention to their plane. Still, they would keep low, not breaching the stratus layer, and rely on their instruments to guide them far away from the battle. He did take some comfort in the plane's fully charged countermeasures should they be needed.

"Red Horse Flight, we are falling into formation at your three and nine o'clock," Wolf Three-One informed.

"Copy, Wolf Flight, we see you," Red Horse PIC replied as he peered out the window to his right to see the MIG-29 on his wing. "Never thought I'd be escorted by a MIG," he remarked off-air to his co-pilot.

"You got that right," came the quiet, yet very nervous, reply.

After an hour of tense silence with nothing but the faint roar of the plane's engines filling their ears, the crew and passengers relaxed as the pilot's voice echoed throughout the cabin.

"We've cleared the primary hostile airspace. Our escort is turning back, and we are clear on to Poland. We'll leave Ukrainian airspace in approximately thirty-eight minutes."

Shaw and Natalie looked at each other, Natalie having kept her eyes either closed or out the window the entire time, though there wasn't much to see through the fog. Their hearts quieted and resettled into their chests, but neither they, nor anyone else, celebrated the milestone. They would not fully relax until they reached Poland, but that did not mean they couldn't make use of the time.

With Ricochet watching over the airmen who were made to don noise-cancelling headphones and listen to music, the rest of the group did their best to face each other and formulate their plan. Though curious, the airmen understood that they were not privy to what they figured was a classified briefing, but little did they know that Natalie, Shaw, and Lincoln only wished to spare them from the hard truths and decisions they now faced.

Even Natalie and Shaw were concerned for how their team might respond, knowing the line they walked between the light and the dark.

They hated it, perhaps even hated a part of themselves for it, but they knew they couldn't forsake their path. To do so would jeopardize countless lives, to say nothing of those already affected who cried out for justice, some from beyond the grave.

"We have to assume Stovall expects Zorro to betray him," Natalie began once all were focused and the airmen settled forward in the cabin.

"Who's Zorro?" Bray asked, his eyes focused and hard underneath his light brown eyebrows.

"I'm Zorro," De la Vega replied.

"Ah, okay," Bray said, though Natalie saw that he hadn't made the connection between De la Vega's callsign and its origin.

"Did your parents name you after him on purpose?" Reeves asked, putting two and two together.

"They did," De la Vega admitted.

"Nice," Reeves replied. "For those of you who are confused, we'll watch the movie once all this is over. Office pizza party and all that," he said, winking at Natalie. She couldn't help but smile back.

If only it were that simple, she thought.

"Back to matters at hand," Shaw said firmly. Grins dropped off the faces around him as the serious nature of their task regained focus. "Nat, go ahead," he added.

"As I was saying, we have to assume Stovall expects De la Vega to betray him."

"Why?" Bray asked. Natalie sighed but offered the young man a smile.

"Hey, zip it," Reeves stated, staring at Bray. Bray rolled his lips inward sheepishly as he nodded. Laila, seated next to him, grinned and nudged him with her body. He blushed and couldn't hide his smile if he tried. Reeves just shook his head.

"Because," Natalie began again, "you have to understand the level at which Stovall has seated himself. There is no one higher, and his plans are coming together in a way that he probably never imagined. When we eliminated Rykov and Barakat, we opened up an opportunity for a power grab. We were forewarned, but we were already too far invested to pull back. Stovall isn't going to risk anything," she explained.

"And with his alliance with Sofia Vitori, who has taken control of Rykov's cabal, he's only opposed by one other power," Shaw added.

"Who's that?" McEwen asked, his gruff, low vocal tones matching his rugged appearance as he leaned over Natalie's seat back.

"Vayun Oza," Natalie answered. "We don't know much about him other than he is part of this council that has crumbled apart."

"The short of it is that Stovall is a tyrant, the likes of which the world has probably never seen," Shaw said. The gravity of his statement fell on all present, and none questioned him.

"And like all tyrants, he will be concerned with two things: his legacy and protecting himself," Natalie added. "The fact that he so willingly agreed to meet with Zorro in the first place after knowing what he lost in Ukraine, even urgently summoning him to his current location, suggests that Stovall not only questions Zorro's loyalty but needs to discern it for himself immediately. He would lose too much to force Diego's replacement at Red Horse."

"And we wouldn't go for it!" Ricochet interrupted. "But sorry, I'm not supposed to be part of this meeting."

"You're proving my point," Natalie replied. "Thanks, Ricochet."

"No problem," he replied as he sipped his sparkling water.

"Why would that be the case?" Reeves asked, trying to keep up.

"Because I control the majority of his private army," De la Vega stated. He had never thought of it quite that way before, but now he knew how eager Stovall was to play soldier with them all for his own gain.

"But here's the deal, we're not going to be able to take Stovall guns blazing," Shaw said. "If he's suspecting treachery, he'll boost his security and maybe even abduct you, Diego."

"I'm prepared for that, so long as you have a plan," De la Vega replied. "And that plan can't involve a war in the streets of Paris."

"Noted and accounted for," Natalie replied. She rotated in her seat to look up at McEwen. "I'll need you to contact a friend." The Scot scoffed.

"Don't know that I'd call her a friend, but sure, why not," he replied. "It'd help if we knew what you're thinking."

Natalie smiled and laid out her plan before them, step by step, providing numerous contingencies based on the different ways she suspected Stovall might react. She relied on De la Vega to either confirm or reject her analysis of their target, and she relied on Laila to add her input concerning any standard security measures or procedures she might be familiar with, having lived in that world for so many years.

Everyone asked questions, testing and probing Natalie's plan for any weakness that might result in catastrophic consequences. Though they all recognized that much relied on certain conditions that needed to be met, they felt confident in her planning, and it only increased their reverence for her all the more.

"Any final thoughts?" Natalie asked.

"Even if we're successful, it won't stop the war," Lincoln said.

"No, it won't," she agreed, "but it may shorten it or keep it from escalating. We can't sit back and do nothing. This is no different from the others. If Stovall and Vitori are successful here, what comes next? Will they orchestrate an Asia-Pacific war next? China and Taiwan? Pakistan and India? You know I've been chasing this for almost a year now. These people are ghosts, and if we don't stop this now, in the immediate, we may never have another opportunity again."

"This is different, though. This guy is an American," Lincoln protested, though not forcibly.

"So was Weber," Shaw said, his voice stern yet pained.

"And Stovall is infinitely more powerful, infinitely more influential, and infinitely more dangerous than Weber ever was. There's only one way this ends," Natalie inserted, staring hard at Lincoln.

The rest of the team looked at each other.

So, it is true, Reeves thought, his blue eyes bearing hard down upon Shaw.

"Yeah, alright," Lincoln replied, defeated and looking down at the floor.

When Natalie turned back to her team, a lump formed in her throat. They all stared at her husband, and she couldn't quite place the expressions they held. Was it contempt? Judgement? Disdain? Whatever it was, she knew it was not positive. She heard her husband inhale deeply.

"I'm not at liberty to discuss Weber or answer the questions you all have right now," he said. "I'm legally bound by a non-disclosure agreement."

"From who?" Reeves asked, his voice icy.

"The Office of the Director of National Intelligence and SOCOM," Shaw answered. The answer raised some eyebrows. They looked at Natalie, who nodded.

"Me too."

"And me, for what it's worth," Lincoln added.

"You don't have to explain anything to me," Bray stated, meeting Shaw square in the eye.

"Or me," Pikari added, offering Shaw a nod.

"I'm not even American," McEwen joked, reaching down and patting Shaw on the shoulder. "I owe you my life. My family owes you. I'm your man until I die or you find someone better."

"I'm in it to win it," Bratcher stated with a grin.

Reeves sighed and tugged on his long, red beard. His transparent blue eyes remained on the floor and only looked up once Shaw exhaled.

"It was Weber who got Sotelo and Adara killed," Shaw said. Natalie cut him a disapproving look for breaking his NDA, but Shaw didn't meet her stare. "Don't ask me to share any more. I like being a free man," he finished. Reeves only nodded, his expression changing from concern to gratitude. Shaw, his lips pressed firmly together, returned the nod, a sacred understanding passing between the seasoned warfighters. Shaw then glanced around, meeting the eyes of everyone, including Laila. "Rakestraw? Aston?"

"You kidding? This is like straight out of a Jack Carr book," Aston replied, as he excitedly patted Roman's ribcage. "I'm totally in."

"We're all brothers here," Rakestraw began, his dark hazel eyes serious. His angled, sculpted face contrasted sharply with his bald head and wide-flared ears. "We've split blood together, suffered together, there's an ethos there not easily broken. I won't be the first to do so."

"Thank you, Eric," Natalie said, moved by his serious commitment.

"Thank you, boys," Shaw said, his voice cracking slightly, which he tried to hide with a forced cough. Recovering, he said, "We all know best laid plans don't survive first contact with the enemy, so when that happens, we'll pivot and do what we do best."

56

VIP Terminal,
Paris Charles de Gaulle Airport,
Paris, France

Sofia Vitori descended the steps of her private jet, wearing a dark, silky fur coat made from Russian Sable. The garment was hemmed at her calves, and she kept the collar clutched tightly around her neck with her hands warmed inside a pair of chestnut-brown, Italian leather gloves lined with fine vicuna. Her shiny black hair draped down her back in a straight fall from a Cossack hat made of the same fine fur as her coat.

As she stepped onto the tarmac, her advanced security enveloped her as they escorted her to the waiting column of five vehicles. The center vehicle, a dark olive Rolls-Royce Phantom, idled waiting for her, end-capped by four black Range Rover SUVs. A contingent of Stovall's security greeted her respectfully, keeping their eyes from making contact with hers.

Once settled in the car, she smiled warmly at a familiar face, though one that gave her an uncertain pause.

"Hello, Ms. Vitori," Josh Scalco said, smiling. Though his presence was unexpected, she did not show her surprise. However, it concerned her that Stovall's chief of kinetic operations personally escorted her. "You look beautiful," he added, his smile widening to show his white teeth. She couldn't help but linger her gaze upon his overdeveloped canines. "Oh, it is natural, I assure you," he dared.

Sofia's gaze rose to meet his, her sour expression showcasing her warning.

"Oh, there's no need for that," Scalco commented as he offered her a glass of champagne.

"We're wasting time," she snapped, her flight having done little to settle her nerves, especially after learning from General Baranov that the force sent to finally eliminate the Shaws had themselves been eliminated. She had never known such fear, and she only hoped that the Shaws couldn't possibly extract from Ukraine before she found security in Stovall's company. From now on, she believed it best if they were never separated. At least until the Shaws could be found and terminated, but how to break the news to Stovall?

She knew he would not receive the update well, and she feared what that might mean for her. She knew he was now powerful enough to eliminate her and the entirety of The Czar's Brotherhood. With his growth in Africa and the Middle East, he was truly the uncontested power in the world. She loved and hated him for it, and it upset her that her strength had not grown as rapidly as his. However, that was never her plan.

Change requires discomfort, she reminded herself.

As she held Scalco's stare, she reminded herself that the goal was always domination over Stovall, to dominate his heart and his mind. Neither could occur without the weakening of the Brotherhood and the advancement of his empire. She had delivered to him that which she had promised, an unparalleled opportunity perhaps never before seen in the modern world. World War I had planted the seeds of industry. World War II had watered and sprouted those seeds, showcasing how such a global calamity could spark unprecedented wealth and opportunity on a national scale. The subsequent Cold War taught political positioning and refined spy craft, while continuing the development of the enterprise of war in Korea and Vietnam. Finally, the Gulf War and the War on Terror defined how the private sector could capitalize on blood for its own gain. Now, all those lessons were being applied to Ukraine, and though early in the war, the engines of enterprise were churning with anticipation for how they would benefit.

Sofia saw it all easily enough; it was her brainchild after all. She had orchestrated everything, prodding Stovall along and using her body to advance her standing in his eyes. It hadn't been easy, but his sudden, overly positive shift toward her and unexpected invitation to Paris either foretold her ultimate victory or her downfall. All signs pointed to the former. Still, she was wary, and Scalco's presence did not bring the needed dose of confidence.

"We'll be underway in a moment," Scalco said as he checked his encrypted smartphone.

"What's the delay?" she asked, hiding her alarm behind her annoyance.

"You are not the only passenger on today's manifest," he said, smiling again.

No matter how often he smiled, or how wide, or how sincerely, it all looked slightly devilish to Sofia. It didn't help that he was a beautiful man. Not in a rugged way, but a refined way that still didn't quite diminish the aura of dangerous capability that exuded from him like early morning fog from a cold lake. The subtlety of it, the confidence of it, was unnerving to her.

"And who are we waiting for?" she asked.

"A friend of yours, I believe. Diego de la Vega," he replied. As capable as Scalco appeared, she recognized he was not one for personal spycraft, for he had overplayed his hand. It was obvious to her as his eyes searched hers, looking for anything that might give him some hint about how much or little she knew.

"I was under the impression that Mr. De la Vega was dead," she said, her face stony and unforgiving.

"It appears not, and as you can imagine, this news creates a certain dilemma for my employer," Scalco replied, seeming to take pleasure in the muted threat. However, Sofia doubted Stovall held any such intention toward her, given the facts she knew.

"I look forward to seeing Mr. De la Vega again. I'm relieved he is well," she said with mock apathy. On the inside, she reeled, her mind churning through second and third-order consequences as quickly as she could.

"We'll see," Scalco replied, frowning. She had not responded in the way he had hoped, and seeing no fear in her took the wind from his sails and ruined any fun he hoped at her expense. "Ah, his plane is landing now."

Sofia only lifted her chin and fought the urge to search through the windows for the aircraft. After several minutes of impatience, Scalco opened his door and exited. Reminding herself that she might be filmed, she remained calm and apathetic on the exterior. All the while, she fought with herself to uncover what De la Vega may or may not know.

Scalco, surrounded by his own staff and Vitori's security detail, watched as the Red Horse Global jet taxied to a stop before lowering its main stairs. Keeping his brown eyes on the opening, Scalco waited impatiently before grinning when he observed De la Vega fill the opening.

Though he had never met the man, Scalco admired and hated him at the same time. His competitive nature surged upward from his chest and tickled the base of his brain, his body teeming with desire to openly confront the man Stovall had called him here to evaluate. He thought of his custom Glock 19 holstered at his waist, under his black, wool peacoat. He kept only the top button fastened in order to reach the weapon quickly if needed.

I wish I could just shoot him here, he thought to himself. The idea of taking his place as Red Horse Global's CEO, though not promised, did fascinate his thoughts. He believed he could sell the proposal to Stovall easily enough, and though he didn't have the formal military experience De la Vega had, he had proven himself above and beyond in the dark places of the world. It was time he stepped into the light, with prestige fitting his service and skills.

As the man jogged over, alone, the stairs to his jet rose and closed shut before the craft continued to its designated hangar. Scalco sighed at this, as he was supposed to search the plane, but as De la Vega neared, all he could think about was ensuring Stovall removed the man. He could always check the plane later.

"Mr. De la Vega," Scalco called out. "Thank you for joining us. I'm Jake Scalco." He extended a gloved hand as the wind whipped his dark hair.

"Mr. Scalco," De la Vega replied flatly, completely unaware of the man's station. He gripped Scalco's palm and squeezed with his usual firmness, catching a flash of offense arc across Scalco's sharp countenance.

Scalco nodded to one of his men, all clad in matching black suits and wool overcoats. De la Vega eyed him warily as he approached, the man raising a hand-held metal detector he had kept discreetly at his side.

"Arms out, sir," he said respectfully. De la Vega huffed his annoyance but did as instructed. Not only was he wanded, but he was patted down as well.

"This is a first," De la Vega said, as the wand chirped over his left-hand pants pocket of the Ukrainian fatigues he had been loaned after losing all he had carried with him into Kyiv. "Should I be worried?"

Scalco interpreted his question more as a threat than a sincere inquiry. He grinned at the challenge, his eyes meeting De la Vega's stern gaze.

"That depends entirely on you," he replied. "What is it?" he asked his man as he lifted the hem of De la Vega's camouflaged parka and reached into his pants pocket.

"Just a pocketknife," he replied, showing off the heavy folder.

"Anything else?" Scalco asked.

"No, he's clean," came the man's reply.

"Not a good start," Scalco said as he took the knife from the man offering it.

"Give me a break," De la Vega muttered.

"We can't allow weapons around our employer," he replied, followed by a series of tsks. "Load him up."

"This way, sir," the man with the wand directed, his tone remaining courteous.

57

Suite Impériale,
Ritz Carlton,
Paris, France

Stovall teemed with excitement at news of Sofia's pending arrival and couldn't sit still. Though annoyed by the unexpected delay and disruption De la Vega's attendance brought, as a businessman, he knew he could not afford to put off the problem De la Vega represented. He was keenly aware of how De la Vega's testimony could advance his efforts in Ukraine. He could be the herald needed to drive the United States people to call for military intervention beyond simply supplying aid.

Once American troops deployed on the ground, the funding and technological advances that would come to support the sons and daughters of America would make him richer than he ever dreamed possible. De la Vega was too important to cast to the side, and the only thing that mattered was whether or not the man was still loyal.

Stovall hoped to find out soon enough.

He heard the footsteps on the hard wooden floors before they were muted upon the ornate red and gold rug. Stovall turned and looked expectantly at Ross Barton.

The younger man, though graying at his temples, inclined his head, ignoring the grandeur of the suite around him. Such sights had become so commonplace, he hardly noticed anymore.

"Sir, they have arrived," Barton stated. "Mr. Scalco is escorting them to the suite now."

"Excellent. Thank you," Stovall replied before draining his dram and setting the crystal on one of the marble-topped, circular end tables that capped the scarlet, velvet sofa.

Within a few minutes, the main door to the suite opened, and, surprising even himself, Stovall's heart leapt into his throat at the sight of Sofia in her fur coat. He didn't bother deciphering the unexpected emotions as he knew already that his destiny lay with her, and possible rejection was unsettling.

"Sofia, you are a vision," he said, advancing coolly with his arms outstretched for her. Wearing a confident smile, she raised her chin before folding into his arms, pressing her body against his with more weight than usual. She felt his warm lips on her cheek, and before she pulled away, she raised a gloved hand to his own, just enough touch to send an affirmative message.

As he dropped his hands, feeling deep satisfaction in their reunion and feeling even more hopeful toward his proposal, Stovall raised his gaze back toward the entry to see De la Vega follow Scalco inside.

"My God, Diego, you look horrible," Stovall exclaimed, mustering a mock concern.

"Apologies for my appearance," De la Vega quickly replied, doing his best to hide his anger.

"It is no bother at all, my dear Diego. My Parisian tailor has supplied a selection of pieces for you to choose from. The second bedroom is available to you, and I'm sure you wish to shower," Stovall replied.

"Yes, thank you, sir," De la Vega replied, adding submissive gratitude to his voice.

Once he disappeared through the bedroom door and closed it, Stovall turned to Scalco. His eyes asked all he wanted to know.

"He only had this on him," Scalco said, handing over the pocketknife, which Stovall took with limited interest. "Otherwise, no issues."

"Understood," Stovall answered, peering at the large folder. He flipped it open with familiarity and relished the heavy clack of the blade locking in place.

"I didn't know you knew your knives," Scalco remarked with a grin.

"Benchmade Adamas. One of the few companies not under my portfolio or influence, and I respect them for that. It's a good knife." Scalco laughed.

"Of all the custom knives you can afford..."

"There is more to this world than the most expensive of things. It would do you well to learn that, considering how much you go over budget every year," Stovall retorted.

"I bring in triple what I spend, and you know it," Scalco replied confidently. Stovall smirked and closed the knife.

"That you do," he said. He turned to Sofia and said, "Now, you and I have much to discuss."

Sofia smiled at seeing his eagerness.

"Let me start with congratulations. I believe a round of Champagne is in order."

However, before summoning the suite's steward, Stovall caught the sudden concern flashing across Scalco's face.

"What is it?" he asked, more curious than alarmed. He then tilted his head as blaring sirens grew louder and louder, coming from outside the tall windows.

"French authorities are converging on the hotel; several vehicles have already stopped outside the lobby," he answered.

"Find out what's going on," Stovall stated firmly. He knew the odds of any action against him were impossibly low, but he didn't want to rule anything out. "Report back to me ASAP."

"Will do, sir," Scalco replied before turning. He pointed at two of his men and said, "Stay here, cover De la Vega's room. You're responsible for Mr. Stovall's security. Understood?"

"Yes, sir," they both replied. They weren't particularly imposing or physically impressive, but their backgrounds in global black operations housed a lethality that their exteriors hid well. The two men quickly took up positions on either side of De la Vega's door and stood casually but ready.

Far from hired goons, these men were some of the best America had to offer, who believed they advanced American interests, knowing that their people slept peacefully in their beds at night only because they and men like them stood ready to do violence on their behalf. The fact that they had been summoned from their operations in Africa to guard their employer was a waste of time, and each man truly couldn't stomach it.

58

Ritz Carlton,
Paris, France

Gisèle LaRue stepped down onto the concrete from the back of the black, armored Nexter Titus. The colossal six-wheeled vehicle loomed imposingly among the flashing lights of the surrounding smaller French police sedans.

Following Gisèle from the armored carrier, a contingent of France's elite Action Division of the Directorate-General for External Security climbed out, dressed in black fatigues, balaclavas, goggles, and helmets. Armed with suppressed HK MP7 submachine guns, the eight-man team and a working canine surrounded Gisèle with an imposing aura as she proceeded before them while police officers cordoned off the area and moved to secure the interior.

"What is the meaning of this!" roared the hotel manager—a short, thin Frenchman—as he stormed across the lobby, but Gisèle remained completely unfazed, confident in her authority.

"We're here on behalf of French Intelligence for a matter of national security; your full cooperation is required," she stated firmly, pressing the blade of her hand into his chest to create space. He resisted until the lead Action Division operator immediately behind Gisèle planted a hand on his chest. Terror shot through him, and he began mumbling incoherently, dumbfounded by such a display of firepower and indifference for his luxurious establishment.

"Anderson Stovall, where is he?" she demanded.

"What you are asking is against our policy," the manager stammered, his temples beginning to sweat.

"You are inhibiting a federal investigation; you are hereby detained," she said calmly, looking away and making her way to the front desk. The lead Action Division operator, still with his hand on the man's chest, tightened his fingers, bunching up the manager's suit, and locking hard despite his protests.

"Wait!" he nearly screamed. Gisèle turned slowly, and despite wanting to smile at the manager, she kept her face stoic. "This way, madame," the manager stammered. The Action Division operator released him and returned his hand to the grip of his subgun before falling in step behind the manager as he led them toward the white marble stairs accented by crimson carpeting.

The guests lingering in the lobby scrambled for their phones before the police officers swarmed toward them, demanding strict compliance and no filming. Fearful, they relented.

"Identify foreign security," Gisèle ordered calmly as she walked, her earpiece picking up the tonal vibrations from up her jaw and transmitting to the entire contingent of law enforcement and intelligence officers on site. Within seconds, officers began questioning each man who fit the descriptions provided prior to the operation. They weren't hard to find, and soon, Stovall's security was not only located but disarmed and cuffed.

Gisèle was surprised by the sheer number of detained individuals but kept her concern from showing in her large hazel eyes. Still, she trotted up the stairs behind the trembling manager.

Scalco burst back into the suite, his expression disheveled and concerned. Once word of the French intrusion came through the earpieces of both Sofia's security team and Stovall's, the suite exploded into motion. A pistol appeared in Scalco's palm as he moved to take Stovall by the arm. The man wrenched free.

"Do not grab me!" he bellowed, but Scalco remained unfazed. "What are you doing?"

"French authorities are rounding up our men posted downstairs," Ross Barton declared after rushing in. He quickly froze when he saw Scalco with his firearm ready in his hand.

"Thank you, Mr. Barton," Stovall said, rattled by Scalco's agitation.

Scalco turned toward the two men guarding De la Vega's room and snarled, "Get him out of there!"

"You think this is because of him?" Stovall asked, disappointment laced in his tone.

"That's the clearest explanation," Scalco replied, just as the door opened and De la Vega strode forward dressed impeccably in a fine wool suit.

"Diego, what's going on?" Stovall demanded. Sofia's four-man security team now surrounded her with weapons drawn.

"What do you mean?" De la Vega answered, confused. He noticed weapons in their hands and froze. He slowly raised his palms outward. "What *is* going on?" he asked, his eyes not leaving the pistol in Scalco's hand.

"French authorities are rounding up our men downstairs and are presumably on their way to us now," Stovall answered, connecting all the dots.

Suddenly, Scalco cursed.

"What?" Stovall asked, more angered than alarmed.

"Air assets are fifteen minutes out," he said, having received the communication through his earpiece. "They won't make it in time."

"No bother," Stovall said, straightening his suit. "Put away your weapon, Mr. Scalco. You are overreacting."

"But..." he began.

"Now, Mr. Scalco," Stovall pressed, his tone hard. He watched as his employee holstered the pistol. "We are not going to engage our allies in a firefight. Are you out of your mind?" Scalco didn't answer, but everything in him screamed to shoot first. "Mr. Barton and I will clear this up, and trust me that heads will roll." Scalco's face showcased his immense displeasure, but he remained silent.

Stovall turned to Sofia, surrounded by her security, and said, "I apologize for this intrusion, my dear. Please retreat to the back bedroom until this is resolved, and please do not engage in confrontation; it will only complicate matters. Civil affronts are much easier to work through than criminal ones."

"And if they are here for me and not you?" she countered.

"I believe that would be highly unlikely," he answered. "Now, if you please," he added, extending a hand toward the bedroom.

He kept command of his rising rage. This unforgivable intrusion would not only cost him important business in Paris but also his offer to Sofia.

Once she and her team disappeared inside the bedroom, Stovall turned back to De la Vega, but before he could open his mouth to speak again, the lock on the main entrance clacked before swinging open. A host of black clad operators stormed inside with weapons ready, which Stovall, Scalco, his security, and De la Vega all met with raised hands.

"What is the meaning of this?" Stovall shouted, his vain attempt to command the situation falling on deaf ears. His eyes widened once he realized these men intended to lay their hands on him. "Do not touch me!" he shouted as the lead operator grabbed at him. Stovall continued his protest until a swift muzzle strike to the sternum careened him to the floor, making him gasp for breath.

It had been a long time since Stovall had experienced such pain, decades and decades. In fact, he doubted he ever had. He wanted to shout at them, to rage, but he couldn't find his voice amidst the pain enveloping his torso.

"You're going to regret this," Scalco snarled as one of the operators hauled him to his feet. However, the operators made no reply, only dutifully carried out the orders of Gisèle LaRue.

Once on his feet, Stovall heaved through the pain, his pristinely styled hair matted and distorted from where his head had been pressed against the rug during his cuffing.

"Anderson Stovall," Gisèle stated, her alluring accent only embellishing her confident presence. At the mention of his name, Stovall's anger skyrocketed as it combated his confusion and fear.

How does she know my name?

"You and those with you are being detained by the *République Française* for crimes against peace and the crime of aggression under international law by the Rome Statute of the International Criminal Court for the incitement of international war to include incitement to war crimes," Gisèle stated calmly.

"This is preposterous!" Stovall growled back, finding both his courage and his voice. "This is some kind of mistake!"

"There is no mistake, Mr. Stovall," Gisèle assured him.

Before Stovall could respond, suppressed gunfire erupted from deeper in the suite, echoed by the startling blast of an unsuppressed handgun and a woman's scream.

"Sofia!" Stovall shouted, tugging against his restraints and fighting against his captor. However, a slap to the back of his head silenced him and drove his gaze to the floor in agonizing humiliation.

I am the most powerful man on the planet! his thoughts roared. Yet why could he not stop this? How had this happened? How had his failsafes failed him? The remaining operators surged toward the conflict, weapons high and nerves on alert, as they funneled inside the bedroom.

Within seconds, Sofia emerged, rattled and disheveled, with her hands pinned behind her back in metal cuffs. A black clad operator guided her forward, but none of her security followed. Gisèle looked concerned, but a nod from one of her men calmed her.

"Take them," she ordered.

They all moved with wariness now that they had met armed resistance to their mission. They had cut down Sofia's four bodyguards, only one clearing his holster enough to get off a shot, which flew errantly into the floor, leaving the operators unharmed.

They marched their captives through the hotel, down the stairs, and into the back of the waiting Titus. Gisèle was the last inside, and as she helped to close one of the rear doors, she called out over the air, "Prime suspects in custody, transporting. Confirm when scene secured."

"Copy all," came the reply from the officer in charge of detaining Stovall's security.

With that, Gisèle slapped the interior wall twice, prompting the driver to initiate the rear door controls and pull away.

Scalco seethed, his eyes wild with hatred as they scanned up and down the row of operators seated in the blue seats across from him, when one suddenly removed his goggles, helmet, and balaclava. His eyes widened in recognition.

"What is this?" he demanded, wrestling against his restraints.

"Did you think you could start a war and not suffer the consequences?" came a woman's voice from the front passenger seat. Her head appeared between the seats, staring at Stovall, who stared back without a glimmer of recognition.

"Who are you?"

"Oh, I've been hunting you for a long time, just like Rykov, just like Barakat," she answered.

Though fear crept along the edges of his psyche, he pressed it away, turning instead toward anger.

"So what, you ally with the French to arrest me? Is that your plan? You can't win here."

"Who said anything about allying with the French?" the woman replied. Stovall cast her a confused look until the horror dawned on him.

Natalie Shaw glanced toward the operator who had removed his mask and said, "I don't think we need to keep Mr. De la Vega cuffed."

David Shaw stood, having to stoop, and turned De la Vega enough to undo his cuffs.

"Sorry about that," he remarked as he returned to his seat.

"You guys sold it well," he said.

"You betrayed us!" Scalco seethed.

"Cool it, or I'll shoot you," Shaw threatened, jabbing the man in the chest with the end of his suppressed subgun. Scalco calmed immediately, sulking and truly scared for the first time in a long time.

"You're Natalie and David Shaw," Stovall finally managed to say. Natalie only smirked but didn't confirm or deny. Barton let out a loud whimper as he broke into sobs. All ignored him, and Stovall looked at De la Vega. "Diego, why?" he asked, staring at the man he would have called friend.

"You killed my men, my brothers," he replied, hatred laced in his tone. He had never spoken to Stovall in such a way. "Sent us to die."

"I didn't send you!" he protested, knowing the fate that awaited him now. He couldn't hold back the fear any longer, not in the presence of the individuals who had killed both Rykov and Barakat. "And it wasn't me! It was Sofia! She planned it all." Anything to not die.

Sofia suddenly laughed and shook her head, knowing how the most dire of moments betrays the deepest of character.

"Sofia, I..." but he didn't finish his thought as he watched her turn away in disgust. He inhaled deeply and turned to face Natalie. "What happens now?" But she only offered him a smile and swung back around. "What happens now?" he shouted louder, beginning to fear for his life.

"Hey, shut up," Shaw stated, his cold blue eyes sapping what little courage Stovall had left. All he had built, everything, his entire life, crashed down upon him, and the despair was too much to bear.

59

VIP Terminal,
Paris Charles de Gaulle Airport,
Paris, France

"Is that his ride?" Gisèle asked, marveling at the white and gold Bombardier Global 6000 as it touched down on the runway in the distance. Natalie smirked and nodded. "Well, it appears he has certainly improved his station in life."

"In more ways than you probably know," Natalie answered.

Gisèle looked at Natalie quizzically, but Natalie only smiled. After meeting Gisèle, she now knew why Romuald Affré was so fond of her. Not only was she beautiful—her dark, cropped hair falling in a delicate curve to frame her slender face—she was strong, cunning, and even a bit ruthless.

"You sure what happened back there won't be a problem?" Natalie asked.

"No," Gisèle replied. She waved her hand whimsically to accentuate the absurdity of Natalie's concern. "This is not America. There are never any questions. As long as my people can eat, drink, and make love, they are content."

"And you're okay with what is happening?"

"Natalie," she scoffed, grinning. "I am French. No people know better than we that certain people deserve the guillotine. After all, it was made for men such as your Stovall."

Natalie didn't know how to respond to Gisèle's casual manner regarding such a heavy subject. She felt between a rock and a hard place, and though she thought it would get easier, she was wrong. She took some solace in knowing the decision wasn't hers alone, and that they still had time to explore suitable options.

"Is Romuald on the plane?" Gisèle asked, before biting her bottom lip. Natalie found her timidness curious.

"He didn't say," she answered. Gisèle didn't reply, only turned to keep eyes on the jet as it taxied toward their hangar. Natalie turned, leaving Gisèle hugging herself against the biting cold, and moved to her husband and her men who stood circled together. They opened up to make a spot for Natalie, but Shaw kept speaking.

"Alright, boys, y'all head back with Ricochet on the Red Horse jet. Natalie and I will take things from here," he finished after explaining the situation, having only provided limited clarity. The men chewed on his words and now looked at Natalie for her voice, but she remained silent.

"I'm not one for bailing on you both," McEwen readily stated.

"It's not like that, Rowan," Shaw replied, shaking his head. They had all changed out of the loaner French uniforms provided by Gisèle and stowed all related gear and weapons in the crates provided. They again wore their uniforms previously soiled from Ukraine, including the parkas taken from the C-17. "I need you all to safely see these airman back to the States," Shaw said.

"It disnae take seven men to nanny a couple of bairns," McEwen retorted. Bratcher snorted his amusement before covering his mouth. When Natalie stared at him, he showed her a palm in apology. "Or are you forgetting they shot us down, too?"

Shaw sighed and dragged a hand down his face.

"I'll go," Reeves voiced. "You know I don't have the stomach for what's happening here, even if it's the only way."

"I'm sorry, Rick," Shaw quickly said.

"No, no, it's fine," he replied. "Lincoln will need the company anyway."

He forced a grin, but Shaw saw the confusion. He felt similarly. It was a suck situation.

Embrace the suck, he reminded himself.

"Look, we'll have more than enough eyes on them, and this isn't a loyalty test. Nothing here has anything to do with bonuses, advancement, or anything. I'm trying to protect you guys."

"The rest of them can go, I'm not," McEwen stated firmly.

"I'm with Rowan," Bratcher said. "I'm seeing this end with my own eyes, so I don't have to keep one open at night."

Shaw sighed and pinched his nostrils together, the cold causing his nose to run.

"When you put it that way," Bray commented.

"Yeah," Pikari added.

"Guys," Shaw labored, his frustration mounting. He sighed again and looked at his wife, who only shrugged in response. She didn't care either way. "Fine," Shaw replied, angry now. "Those who want to go home get on the red plane. Those who want to come with us, get on the white and gold plane. But I don't want to have to say I told you so."

Natalie smirked at his agitation. It was cute, and she needed a dose of cuteness right now.

She moved to Shaw's side, and the two shared a look before heading to the Titus to check in on their prisoners and the two individuals watching them.

"How's it going?" Natalie asked Laila once she and her husband peered inside.

"Fine," she replied. "We headed out?"

"In just a few minutes. The plane will pull in here, and we'll move them with their heads covered," Natalie explained.

"And where are we headed?" she asked.

Natalie glanced at the prisoners, their eyes fearful.

"You'll see."

Baniaan River Conservatory,
Eastern Cape, South Africa

Josh Scalco moved forward as instructed, stumbling and cursing as he tried to keep his footing while marching forward blindfolded with his hands still bound behind his back. His shoulders, elbows, and wrists ached and burned from being bound that way for so long. He had marched for the better part of an hour after a long car drive, and now he felt the ground shift under his feet, sloping downward quite aggressively.

A strong hand found his shoulder, steadying and keeping him from falling. He figured it must be the Scot, as the man had driven him forward for the last hour with short commands and subtle hints toward rocks, roots, or shallow crevasses that could trip him.

He knew Stovall, Vitori, and Barton marched with him, as he heard their occasional protests and pleas, especially Barton. Scalco, himself? He was just angry, waiting for the right time to make his move, to survive or to die on his own terms.

A bone-chilling series of cackling yelps crescendoed around them, louder than it should, and Scalco jumped. He had surmised he was in the southern hemisphere on account of the shift in the air from cold to warm, but now, he knew.

Hyenas.

Lots of them.

"What was that?" cried Barton, panic rising within him. He stumbled, but Bray caught him before he fell.

"Please, you don't have to do this," Stovall petitioned, but his plea went unanswered.

The ground finally leveled off, and after a few short steps, a quick shove high on Scalco's back drove him to his knees. He cursed and tried to ignore the sharp nerve pain radiating up his thigh and down his shin from his kneecap hammering hard on a pointed rock.

His eyes then flashed with quick agony, blinded by the high sun as his hood was torn from his face. He blinked away the pain, hearing the cries from his fellow captives. As the glare lessened, he first made out David Shaw standing just a few feet ahead, wearing a khaki safari shirt and brown pants capped with leather boots. Crowning his head sat a narrow-brimmed, brown canvas field hat rimmed with a leather band. In his hands, he carried a fully kitted, suppressed M4A1 carbine with a mounted grenade launcher. A ranger green chest rig loaded with extra magazines and other pouches stretched across his torso.

Scalco looked around at the sound of more feral yelping, closer this time, and noticed the group of men and two women who all carried similar weapons and kit.

"This is overkill for just the four of us; I'm the only fighter here," he dared.

"Shut yer geggie!" McEwen growled, knocking him sharply on the back of the head with the suppressor mounted to the end of his carbine. Scalco saw stars as his torso slammed into the dust, the side of his face grating against the grit.

"Get him up," came a command. Was it from Shaw? Scalco couldn't be sure, but it held something he didn't expect, a tenderness. Was it pity? The notion only spurred Scalco's anger. No, he realized, not pity. Regret. Remorse.

"If you're going to kill us, get on with it. I don't need your guilt," he muttered, spitting a wad of dusty saliva from his mouth.

"For God's sake, Josh, be quiet!" Stovall hissed. He glanced at Sofia; she appeared empty, her eyes glossy and unfocused, and he felt great shame.

"Anderson," Natalie began, "you know why you are here, but I will spell it out for you. You started this war with Sofia Vitori. We know this because of the testimony provided by both Laila Malik and Diego de la Vega, who are here with us now."

"And where is here?" he asked, sweat beading down his eyebrows and stinging his eyes.

"That's not important. What is important is that you knowingly engaged in activities that threatened the lives of American service members, resulted in the deaths of distinguished special operations veterans in the employ of Red Horse Global, and staged events with the intention to force NATO to invoke Article Five, which would have cost hundreds of thousands if not millions of lives, needlessly, solely for your own material benefit," Natalie explained.

"What is this? Some kind of vigilante court?" Stovall spat, finding his courage in the face of his fate and surprising even himself.

"Call it the court of the common man," Shaw replied, but Stovall didn't understand.

Natalie turned to Sofia, who appeared not to see anything. Though Natalie met her gaze, the woman stared onward, through Natalie, and into the beyond.

"Sofia Vitori, in like manner, you are guilty of all the aforementioned, but I'll add the abduction of a CIA employee, tampering with United States Intelligence sources and methods, and attempted murder on United States intelligence and military personnel," Natalie said.

Still, Sofia showed no sign of recognition or anything for that matter. Natalie stepped back and gave way to her husband.

"This is difficult for all of us here," he said, "but you all know as well as we do that there is no court in the world that can grant justice; there is no other way. Accept that your fate is not taken lightly and that it is evidenced by our treatment of you now."

"Is that how you justify it?" Stovall spat, angry now. "It doesn't change the fact that this is murder!"

"No, it doesn't," Shaw replied calmly. "That's the difficult part." He nodded toward De la Vega, who stepped around Stovall and raised his rifle in line with the kneeling man's heart. "But it's necessary," Shaw added.

"Diego, wait!" Stovall cried with as much firmness as his breaking voice could ally. "Wait, wait, wait..."

De la Vega fired three times, two to the chest before raising his rifle just enough to send a round through Stovall's forehead. The slugs tore through his body, trailing wide sprays of crimson.

"Oh God!" Barton shrieked as he watched his employer fall stiffly backwards on top of his heels, his eyes staring lifelessly at the sky. Barton's bowels loosened, saturating his suit pants with putrid stench. No one seemed to pay it any mind.

"Bastards!" Scalco shouted. "I'll kill you all!" Again, no one gave the man any notice, their solemn expressions showing their displeasure with their task.

"Laila," Shaw said.

Without hesitation, Laila moved forward, raised her carbine—Sofia still didn't show any signs of awareness—and pulled the trigger just once. The bullet cut through Sofia's forehead, and the woman crumpled to the ground faster than expected. Laila then flicked her weapon on safe, turned, and retraced her steps back behind Shaw.

Scalco chuckled, unsure of what had come over him as he tried to reason with his fate. He then broke out into sociopathic laughter, sounding more like the hyenas than any laugh motivated by humor.

Shaw frowned and sighed, feeling the weight of what had just happened. He kept his gaze on Scalco as he said, "We know that Stovall's network is expansive. You have one chance to save your life, and that is to agree to assist in the dismantling and liquidation of his empire," Shaw offered.

"Yes!" Barton screamed, hanging on to any thread of hope. Scalco laughed again, his prominent canines glinting white in the sun.

"I don't think we should let this one go," McEwen warned, his muzzle hovering casually over the back of Scalco's head. "Something's off with him."

"His name is Josh Scalco," Barton blurted, latching on to anything he could to secure the favor of his captors. "He's head of all Stovall's clandestine operations. If you let him go, you will never be safe. I, on the other hand, only manage Stovall's financial assets. I have no connection with his kinetic apparatus, and even if I did, everything is compartmentalized; I wouldn't be able to order a hit even if I wanted..."

"Shut up, Ross!" Scalco snarled.

"He will try to kill me for helping you and all of you! He is relentless! He won't ever stop!" Barton continued, his eyes darting back and forth between his captors. He could see he was convincing them—their expressions perplexed and even hardened.

"Ross!" Scalco pleaded, but then he quieted, chuckling again as he met Barton's fearful gaze. "You know what? He's right," he said, laughing loudly. "He's one-hundred percent righ—"

McEwen's shot cut him off. The bullet cut through the back of Scalco's head and blew out his jaw, flinging bone and flesh in wide arcs as his skull fractured and expanded from the violent impact. His body careened forward and smacked hard into the ground, his blood drenching the dirt around what remained of his face.

"Rowan!" Shaw called out, shocked. McEwen flicked his safety back on and draped his carbine across his chest.

"What?" the Scot replied unapologetically. "You heard the man, and instead of stopping a problem after it's become one, maybe we take some preventative measures, aye?" He glanced around at his teammates, Bray, Pikari, and Bratcher, who didn't seem fazed by his action. "You heard what he was saying, and I'll be damned if I let a threat to my Bonnie and my wee Rob have access to the power this bloke's got."

"Yeah, I'm good with that," Bray quipped.

"Yeah, but still," Shaw chided. "Would it have hurt you to let us all get their first?"

"Suppose not," McEwen replied with a shrug.

Shaw turned to Barton and asked, "How can we trust anything you say?"

"Please, I don't want to die. I've got a wife and children. My oldest daughter is expecting," Barton rambled.

"You realize that you just killed your friend, right?" Bray asked. Barton's mouth gaped open as the horror dawned on him.

I suppose I did, he rationalized. Having been so caught up with preserving his own life, he had sacrificed Scalco's.

"Oh God, what have I done?" he stammered, tears wetting his cheeks.

Shaw looked at Natalie, who sighed. She looked up over the corpses to meet the eyes of Romuald Affré and Rian Mather-Pike, the two standing in stark contrast to one another—Affré with his shorter, lean frame, bronze skin, and honey-green eyes, and Mather-Pike with his tall, broad structure, long blonde hair, and nearly translucent, silver-blue eyes. One a son of France and Morocco, the other a son of South Africa.

"We can keep an eye on him," Mather-Pike stated. Affrè's gaze snapped upward toward his friend, but the South African paid him no mind. "Bring his family here, keep them isolated, supervised."

"Hostage, you mean," Natalie scolded.

Mather-Pike shrugged.

"If you look at it that way," he said.

"You want the profits," Shaw reasoned.

"Is that so bad?" Affré replied. "Look what good we've done with what we already have. Invictus for one."

"We'll put together a committee," Natalie inserted firmly. No one argued.

"That is acceptable," Affré replied.

"Works for me," Mather-Pike added.

"Wait, please leave my family out of this. We can come to an arrangement," Barton blurted.

"Unfortunately for you," Affré interjected, his accent the most dignified of the group, "you have no say in the matter."

Natalie strode over to him, crouched to his level, and instantly regretted it as the vile stench nearly forced her to retch. She brought her fingers to her nose and mouth before exhaling to steady herself as she met Barton's gaze. He whimpered, his brown eyes pleading as he held onto hope.

"Look at them," Natalie said. Barton's eyes snapped to the deceased without thinking through the consequences. He felt his own vomit rise, and he retched onto the ground before Natalie, who backpedaled rapidly as the sticky substance splattered around her. Taking a quick breath of fresh air, Natalie dropped low again, meeting his eyes once more.

"What are you going to do with them?" Barton asked.

"This valley is home to a cackle of hyenas," Mather-Pike answered for her, his voice casual and light. "They'll make short work of them; got jaws that can crush the femur of a Cape Buffalo. Won't be a trace of them by sunrise tomorrow."

"Oh God," Barton whimpered again.

"Look at me," Natalie urged. Barton complied immediately. "If you betray us, I'll feed you to these hyenas while you're still breathing."

EPILOGUES

1

Invictus Headquarters,
Eastern Shore,
Virginia

Sitting on the cushioned patio furniture on the expansive back deck of his new home, Shaw absorbed the serene quiet rising above the peaceful expanse. His breath rose in thick, foggy wisps as his eyes fell on the dormant construction equipment resting at the bottom of the steady slope. At the midnight hour, sounds of gulls had long silenced, and though his scalp prickled from the cold coastal air, he felt refreshed.

He needed it after all he had been through.

Stovall and Vitori were dead, their enterprises collapsing on account of Affré's and Mather-Pike's new effort. Knowing they could not be eradicated without oversight, Shaw and Natalie had relented to Mather-Pike's pledge to see it done. They both knew the amount of money he and Affré were about to rake in, becoming billionaires seemingly overnight; however, Shaw took some comfort in knowing that he could trust them and that Invictus International would become a priority beneficiary to the sum. Additionally, this way he knew another Vitori couldn't rise and start the fight all over again.

There is still Oza, and we don't know anything about him, Shaw thought, fatigued with this ongoing war. He and Natalie both hoped Barton would be able to provide some insight in the way Hasan Salameh—Barakat's Chief of Staff—couldn't, but Shaw had come out from his bed, from his wife's side, for a different contemplation.

Thus, he turned his thoughts toward his first foray into near-peer warfare. He wasn't troubled or overly concerned with his current security; the MK18 carbine, topped with an Aimpoint T-2 red dot sight and an Arisaka Defense 600 series weapon light, gave him peace of mind as it lay propped against the chair next to him. Knowing that he and his team had been targeted in Ukraine kept him on edge though, he knew those responsible were deceased. Still, Roark had taught him that threats come from unexpected places, and so, he was ready.

Shaw glanced down at the object he rotated between his fingers and smiled. He had finally experienced the closest form of combat to that which his grandfather had fought. As a Marine machine gunner on Guadalcanal defending Henderson Field from Japanese offensives, the man after whom Shaw was named had served with distinction in combat during Operation Watchtower and earned a Purple Heart.

As Shaw studied the worn white gold of the Marine Corps ring, his eyes focused on the golden Eagle, Globe, and Anchor set within the large ruby. The ring detailed the raising of the flag on Mount Suribachi on its right side and Tun Tavern on its left. He had never seen the ring off his grandfather's finger until his father had given it to him when his grandfather passed two years prior at the age of one hundred two.

Now, as he held the heavy ring—which was much too big for his own fingers—Shaw reflected on the Russian lives he and his men had taken not a week ago. He also wondered what would become of the four POWs they had been forced to turn over to Dudka. While he knew the horrors of war, he had not experienced that level of hatred between opponents, and he wondered whether his grandfather had hated the Japanese with as much fervor.

He did own a Honda in his later years, so that had to count for something, Shaw thought with a smirk.

Shaw's smile slowly slid off his face as he thought of the reason they had endured the arduous journey to Ukraine. They had barely made it out, and though he had dealt personally with those responsible, he couldn't help but wonder at the state of his own morality.

What had started with Weber as an impossible situation had culminated in more assassinations than Shaw was comfortable with. He was a Marine, a warfighter, not an assassin, and yet now he was. At worst, a murderer with a vendetta, at best a cold-blooded vigilante, and he wasn't sure if there was much difference between the two.

He had tried to consider any other options that might have been available to him, and though he wasn't remorseful—knowing that what he had chosen to do was mandatory for the safety of countless lives—he still felt the check on his own ethics. The more he thought of it, though, the more he knew he had made the right decisions. His lament was less in his actions and more that he had found himself in the position to take them. He knew, however, that he was in none of the places by accident. All of it, every choice, every step, was purposeful.

And even now, he waited for the update that confirmed the death of another life.

Shaw sighed and transitioned his gaze to the silk, 48-star American flag draped over his knee. *I wonder what Grandpa would think*? he asked himself. Though he would have liked to believe that David Joseph Shaw would have supported him, he knew he would not have celebrated the outcomes. He wasn't a salty Marine but a kind man, a loving man, a man of forgiveness and philosophy, a man who had worked as a teacher in Chicago nearly his entire career. He even wrote a play—the only physical copy lost with the destruction of Shaw's first sailboat, *American Rehtor.*

That thought soured Shaw's emotions, and he firmly pressed his lips together as he thought of how he had fed a Cuban hitman to a shark. He sighed and lifted his gaze toward the bay to the west, the moonlight and stars shimmering against the black expanse.

He hoped to have answers but now had more questions.

The sliding door behind him glided open, nearly noiselessly, but Shaw turned and looked up to see his wife, her hair a complete mess, yawning while staring down at him.

"What are you doing?" she asked as the cold sent shivers coursing through her body. "Man, it's cold," she complained, her eyes narrow with sleep. She hugged her arms and rapidly transitioned her weight from foot to foot.

"Just needed to think," Shaw replied, smiling at her, but she saw the uncertainty, the pain.

"David," she replied tenderly, moving toward him.

Taking his grandfather's flag in his hand with the ring, Shaw stood and embraced her, kissing the top of her head as she nestled into him for warmth.

"What are you thinking about?" she asked, the sleep falling from her eyes as concern grew. The last time her husband couldn't sleep, they had lost John Wyatt. She had never seen him so torn up before.

"What we've been through," Shaw replied, wrapping his arms tighter around her. "What we've done."

"What does that mean?" she asked, concerned. She felt him sigh before releasing her. He turned and scooped up his carbine. Natalie looked down at it and raised her eyebrows, but she understood.

"Let's go inside," Shaw said. He didn't need to tell Natalie twice. She spun quickly and hurried inside to escape the cold.

Shaw watched her as he stepped inside the warmth and closed the door. She wore a calf-length black robe with her hair up in a wild bun.

"You want to talk about it?" Natalie asked, before realizing the absurdity of her question.

"No, that's okay," he said. "Let's go back to bed."

"David," she pressed, her eyes growing stubborn and her chin dropping an inch to stress her commitment to solving his problems. Shaw forced a laugh and looked at her with endearing affection. "What do you mean by 'what we've done?'"

"Can I ask you something?" Shaw countered, setting the carbine on the leather lounge chair next to him.

"Of course," Natalie replied. She watched him inhale deeply, and in response, she folded her arms across her chest.

"Are we still the good guys?" he asked.

"What?" Natalie shot back, her eyebrows skyrocketing. "If we aren't, are you saying Stovall and Vitori are?"

Shaw chuckled and shook his head. He looked at her and noted the concern in her wide eyes. "No, I'm not saying that at all. I'm only wondering if we've stayed on the right side of things, if doing what we've done has corrupted us at all, made us different."

"What? Like evil or something," Natalie jabbed, flustered. Shaw laughed. "Stop laughing," she scolded. "Clearly, this is serious!"

"Look, we've assassinated people, executed them because we felt it the best thing to do. No trial. No due process. Nothing. What we just did in South Africa, I never thought I would ever do anything like that, especially not after Weber," he explained.

Natalie saw he was trying to keep a level head and that he had been contemplating this deeply. She thought he had been more reserved the last couple of days, saying less, spending more time alone. She exhaled her frustration with him, realizing for the first time that she, too, had been troubled by their recent action. Not knowing what more to say, she moved toward him and embraced him, pressing the side of her face against his chest.

She relished the strong cadence of his heart, constant and proud.

"I don't know, David," she said, "but what I do know is that we can only make a decision with the information we have at the time."

"Yeah," Shaw replied, dropping his chin gently onto the top of her head as he inhaled her hair. She smelled beachy, like coconut and mango, and it calmed him.

"What I do know is that we stopped evil people from spilling blood for their greed. We eliminated a force that gripped our military and intelligence services too tightly and saved countless lives. With General Wood and Reggie behind us, altering the narrative of the C-17, we avoided Article Five, which you know our current administration would have pushed, especially with Stovall pulling the strings," she said.

"Yeah," Shaw replied again, rubbing her back. "You know the conspiracy theorists are going to have a heyday with this one."

"And they'd be right," Natalie quickly replied, smiling. "We were in a hard situation and did the best we could. If there was no court that could indict Weber and no prison that could hold him, how much more so for Stovall and Vitori."

"Oza's still out there. Are we going to do this all over again?" Shaw asked.

"If we have to," Natalie replied. She looked up at him. "Come on, we've got the Red Horse burials at Arlington tomorrow. Let's get some sleep."

"Yeah, okay," he replied, letting her lead him to their master bedroom.

2

Arlington National Cemetery
Arlington, Virginia

Shaw and Natalie entered through the stone arches that led to the hallowed and revered grounds of Arlington National Cemetery. Shaw, having gone back and forth with whether or not he should wear his Dress Blues, had finally opted for a black, wool suit worn underneath a black, wool overcoat hemmed to his knees. A black, silk tie gleamed against a stark, white dress shirt. Black leather gloves covered his hands.

On his arm, Natalie wore a black, wool pencil dress underneath a long, black, fitted, wool coat with a standing collar. Her hair was neatly pulled into a low bun, her entire appearance solemn for the grave occasion.

They had arrived early and sought out the tombstones of Shaw's old teammates, spending a long moment at John Wyatt's grave, before continuing to pay their respects at the Tomb of the Unknown Soldier. They stood reverently while the Tomb Guard marched his twenty-one steps, paused for twenty-one seconds, turned, and then marched twenty-one steps back the way he had come.

After a silent prayer of gratitude, Shaw dropped his hand to the small of

Natalie's back, signaling they should leave. He refused to check his watch so as not to disrespect the sacrifice paid by those entombed with honor.

Seeing the tents down the slope to their left, the couple proceeded that way, arm in arm, careful to stay on the path and silent as the weight of communal sacrifice weighed on their shoulders.

The wind moved lightly through the trees, though still cold enough to bite. Shaw and Natalie walked in step, their pace measured, neither of them speaking as they approached the gathering already forming near the two gravesites.

They stopped at a respectful distance from the front.

Diego de la Vega stood just off to one side, flanked by two men, one Shaw didn't recognize, but the other was Ricochet. They all wore Red Horse pins on their right jacket lapels while their military mini-medals adorned their left. De la Vega stood upright, stoic, but his hands betrayed him. He kept clasping them together, then separating them again.

Shaw knew the feeling all too well.

He and Natalie waited until De la Vega's eyes drifted their way. He gave a small nod. Shaw returned it, with Natalie offering a sad, consoling smile. Their eyes then drifted to the families of the deceased, seated in the front row underneath the dark canopies erected side by side. The muted whimpers of grief floating on the crisp air, and the sounds tugged at both Shaw's and Natalie's hearts.

"Hey, Boss," came a youthful voice from behind. Shaw's eyes widened for a brief moment, and he spun too soon.

"John?" he called softly, drawing concern from Natalie as she watched him. However, the man approaching from behind, wearing a simple, dark suit, was not John Wyatt.

How could it be?

Shaw quickly blinked away his confusion, pain, and regret. Feeling Natalie rubbing his arm as she kept her other arm woven around his elbow, he met Owen Bray's gaze. Pikari paced next to him with McEwen, Bratcher, and the rest of the team following. Roman walked obediently at Aston's side, wearing a harness identifying him as a veteran military working dog, and therefore permitted onto the grounds of the cemetery.

"Thanks for coming," Shaw replied softly, extending his hand to greet each man.

"Yeah, of course," Bray replied quietly, being the first to grip Shaw's palm.

Pikari nodded as he shook Shaw's hand, then inclined his head toward Natalie and said, "Ma'am."

"Hi, Tāne," she replied, returning his nod. She turned to Reeves and McEwen. "Rick, Rowan," she added in greeting. "Boys," Natalie continued, turning toward Rakestraw, Bratcher, and Bray. Natalie lingered on Bray and asked, "Did you make a decision about DEVGRU?" His eyes popped wide.

"You knew about that?" he stammered.

Natalie smirked and nodded. "We're friends with the commanders of JSOC and SOCOM, of course, we knew, but we didn't arrange anything if that's what you're thinking."

"No, no, ma'am," Bray replied. The thought had never crossed his mind. "But yes, I did make my decision."

"And?" Shaw pressed, curious and hopeful.

"I turned them down," he replied. At this, Pikari clapped a hand on his shoulder, and Bray smiled sheepishly. "We're doing stuff here that the guys at Six wish they were doing. I can't trade that, and I'm grateful to you both."

The unexpected sincerity surprised them all, and Shaw mirrored Pikari in gripping Bray's shoulder with appreciation and affection.

"We're glad to hear it, Owen," he said.

Before any conversation could continue, a quiet voice rose behind them. "Thank you for coming. Shaw and Natalie turned to see De la Vega approaching.

"We're sorry for your loss, Diego," Shaw replied quietly with reverence for the honored dead.

De la Vega's mouth tightened at that. "Thanks," he said.

No one said anything more. They stood together, feeling the pressure to live well, a call from a million ghosts in olive drab, in brown khaki, in blue and gray, rising from their rest to beckon them onward.

A hush moved through the crowd as the service began. Shaw and Natalie stood shoulder to shoulder as the chaplain spoke. The words were familiar, shaped by repetition, but they carried grief and comfort.

When the bugle raised its haunting melody over the downs and the rifles fired their salute, Shaw did not flinch. He stared ahead, jaw set hard, reliving his own losses.

The service concluded, people lingered, and conversations began softly, as if no one wanted to be the first to leave.

Natalie stepped aside as others passed, finding herself next to a man she had not noticed earlier. He stood alone, hands clasped loosely behind his back, gaze resting on the headstones beyond the ceremony. The breeze lifted the lapels of his dark wool overcoat and tousled his dark hair threaded through with streams of silver.

After a moment, he spoke without turning to her.

"Did you know the deceased?" he asked, his accent dignified, more Queen's English than the Indian he obviously was.

"No," Natalie replied, mustering a kind smile. "I didn't. You?"

He turned then, his expression open, thoughtful. "No."

She considered him before responding, noting his wrinkle-capped eyes that appeared to glow with wisdom and kindness in equal doses. "May I ask why you came then?"

"Only if I may ask the same of you?" he countered, smiling warmly.

"I'm here supporting friends," Natalie replied, her smile widening to the point of faint endearment.

"Ah, to stand with friends," he began, looking down briefly. "A rare and noble thing these days. I, too, am here to stand with friends...and to mark an ending."

"An ending?" Natalie asked, suddenly intrigued.

"And a beginning," the Indian added.

Natalie paused, pensive. The sounds of quiet conversation drifted around them, subdued and respectful, and her smile waned as she studied the man.

"May I ask," he suddenly continued, "if you know Mr. De la Vega well?"

"Well enough," Natalie replied, "not as well as some, but maybe better than others."

"Ah, a good answer." His gaze flicked briefly toward Shaw, then back to her. "Your husband?"

"Yes," she replied, her tone growing unconsciously wary.

The man chuckled, seeming to notice before she did. "I am honored to be in your presence, Mrs. Shaw, and that of your husband."

The words tightened in her chest, and she inhaled sharply through her nose, the cold air irritating her nostrils.

"How do you know my name?" she asked firmly. Hearing the sudden shift in her tone, Shaw turned, towering over her and taking in the situation with wary, cutting eyes, his attention sharpening as he read the shift in her posture.

"I know a great many things about you both," the man continued, still smiling disarmingly.

"Who are you?" she asked sternly, her tone uncompromising. At this, her team fanned behind her, all attention on the man.

The man inclined his head and laid his hand over his heart as he bowed. "I am Vayun Oza, at your service."

Natalie's chilled trachea constricted further, and she attempted to swallow what little moisture her drying mouth held. Every instinct in her told her to fight, to strike first, yet the seasoned restraint held her in check. Was there a sniper on a building ready to end her life if she did so? Perhaps her husband's or one of her men's? Months of grueling hunting, years of being hunted by men like him, nearly paralyzed her with the suddenness of his introduction.

"I have looked long and hard for you," Natalie managed.

"I am quite aware," Oza replied quietly. "And I know who you fear I might be." His eyes darted up toward Shaw, a man he knew he could never overpower or hope to fend off. "I trust my presence highlights certain risks I have undertaken and yields a certain ethos to this conversation."

Natalie never took her eyes from Oza's, even as his passed between her and Shaw.

"What do you want?" Shaw demanded, his tone an odd blend of cordiality—on account of the hallowed grounds—and menace.

"I spent years trying to do the very thing you accomplished in mere months," he said.

"So you can rule?" Natalie shot back, louder than she intended, but Oza chuckled, like a grandfather with his grandchild. The act confused her.

"Why here?" Shaw asked, fighting the urge to scan for threats.

"Because this place leaves little room for deception," Oza answered. "And because these men who died in Kyiv were casualties of a war that no longer needs to continue."

The reply shifted something inside of Natalie, like a lock finally opening after too many attempts with a pick. She had looked into the eyes of Rykov, Stovall, and Vitori—into the eyes of Silva, Weber, and Roark before them. This man had eyes similar to McCoy's, and she reminded herself that that did not make him peaceful.

"You are not like them, are you?" she dared carefully.

"No," Oza agreed, a flash of relief in his voice. He chuckled again as he patted his thighs over his coat. "Not Stovall. Not Barakat. Certainly not Rykov. They believed power was something to hoard. I believe it is something to steward." He paused, then added, "Your actions removed obstacles I could not touch without becoming what they were."

Natalie exhaled slowly. "You're thanking us."

"I am," he said simply. "And inviting you to speak with me as equals rather than adversaries, which we never were, should you be so bold as to believe me."

"You could have stopped them," Natalie tested.

"No," he replied with an unexpected laugh. "I assure you, no. The balance has shifted. The world now has its first chance at freedom since before World War Two. It does not mean it is safe, but I hope that, together, we can try to make it so."

Shaw and Natalie studied him in silence. He seemed sincere enough.

"How can we trust you?" Natalie added.

"I don't like this, Boss," Bray whispered from his position just behind Shaw. The entire team stood tense and ready, eyes alert and scanning, looking for anything out of place. None of them were armed, and they were now all acutely reminded of that unsettling fact.

"I would say that if I wanted you dead, you would be, but you and I both know that is unlikely to be the case. It is more likely I would be the one winding up dead, given your track record. But, I could never beat them; I could only hold out against them. To beat them, I would have had to become them, and that is something I could never do," Oza replied. "So, I invite you to dinner, or rather invite myself to your dinner. You can accept, and we can learn more about each other and find a way to collaborate for a better, freer world. Or you can decline. There is no ulterior motive, and, unfortunately, nothing I can actually do to convince you otherwise. This is my best play, to show up here, alone, to meet you both. You should have heard the protests of my chief of staff."

"And where is he?" Natalie asked.

"Singapore," Oza replied. "Where else should he be?"

Natalie raised one eyebrow before turning to look up at Shaw, even though her body demanded she not take her eyes off Oza. She met her husband's eyes, searching them, then received his short, subtle nod. She felt it, too, a sudden freedom, the weightlessness of a vanishing problem always too large to solve.

"I have a few conditions," Natalie said.

"I would be offended if you didn't," Oza replied with a grin, his dark cheeks pulling with age. "I have not made any reservations or plans. Please, you make the selections, and I am more than willing to accompany you in your transportation. I am assuming you will be armed."

"Aye, you can trust that!" McEwen blurted

Oza smiled genuinely. "Excellent. It has been many years since I have travelled without security."

"You don't have any security?" Bray interjected.

"They stayed with the plane at Reagan. I took an Uber."

"You took an Uber?" Bray repeated, dumbfounded.

"Uber Black, of course," Oza replied, smiling. "Now, I wish to pass my condolences onto the families and Mr. De la Vega. Then, shall we depart? I'm quite famished." He bowed before turning and heading toward De la Vega where he joined the diminishing line of those waiting to greet the families.

Shaw broke the silence first. "Well," he said quietly, "that is unexpected."

Natalie never took her gaze from Oza. She couldn't believe what had just happened, and her brain processed everything in rapid succession, weighing the legitimacy of their interaction. No matter how many times she ran it, or how differently she considered the angles or intent, she couldn't arrive anywhere other than Oza's genuineness. Everything else just didn't make sense.

"Let's go," she finally said, taking her first step toward Oza and De la Vega, just as Oza cordially shook hands with Ricochet.

3

Istanbul, Turkey

Reza Afshar preferred the hours just before midnight, when the city softened and tension from business faded for the day. From his cushion near the rear of his tea house and hookah lounge, he watched smoke rise lazily toward the carved ceiling and dissipate into the dark wood beams. The hum of conversation blended with the low pluck of an oud playing through hidden speakers, a sound meant to soothe rather than entertain.

His body felt unusually heavy, and he couldn't quite place why. He had smoked more than usual, and the business was unusually specific and complicated. However, he had stopped caring about operations, his attention now focused on his protection.

Afshar shifted on the cushion, adjusting the way his weight pressed into the velvet, and dabbed his lips with a napkin before reaching again for his tea. The sugar settled on his tongue, comforting and familiar, but doing little to undo the fear that hovered over him.

Natalie Shaw.

Her threat loomed in his mind, and as a result he had already relocated his family. Though he was not confident the Shaw woman would have followed through to kill innocents, he still performed his due diligence. He hoped his evening's entertainment might settle his nerves, but he doubted it. Previous evenings of similar excitement had yet to do so.

He noticed her immediately as she entered alongside the rest of the harem. She seemed to draw all focus, and the men around Afshar kept resettling their gaze on her as the group of young women shed their coats to reveal their sequined bedlahs, which exposed the full lengths of their midsections.

The dancer drawing the most attention had a curve to her torso that shamed the other girls. Her waist appeared impossibly thin when compared to her hips and bosom, and her dark skin seemed to gleam in the low light. Even the way she moved conveyed an alluring expertise and confidence.

Conversations shifted to her presence, with many of Afshar's guests pointing subtly at her and whispering adoration of her to each other. Jealous of this, Afshar kept his attention on her, even waving away one of the girls who was previously a favorite. Her face was composed, her expression relaxed, and her eyes sparkled with mischievous allure.

Afshar watched as the music started and she took centerstage before him, ringed by her fellow dancers in the room. When her eyes met his, she did not look away. She smiled seductively, her teeth hidden behind thick mauve lips, as her hips bounced with the quick rhythm echoing throughout the lounge.

Afshar exhaled through his nose and leaned back, the smoke from his hookah curling past his cheek as he watched the woman dance before him. Beauty invited risk, but risk was something he managed daily. He had survived worse than temptation, and he allowed himself to be mesmerized by her hips, her belly, and her breasts. All the while, her painted eyes tugged at him, stirring his loins and desires in a way he had not experienced before.

Suspecting that his trusted guests and companions wanted to bed her made him desire her all the more.

He licked his lips and nodded toward her, his jaw dropping in a rolling dip to encourage her closer. She obliged, moving with the beating music until she danced solely for him, and everyone knew it.

When the music ended and praise erupted through the lounge, Afshar extended a plump hand to the cushion next to him. She readily obliged, just enough to move things forward but not so much as to disrupt her elusiveness.

Up close, her honey eyes, steady and alert, maintained consistent contact with his and made Afshar feel as if she only saw him, that nothing else in the world existed.

He spoke quietly to her, though not well, and he wondered what spell she had placed on him. His words came out jumbled, though he spoke quietly enough to hide such from his other guests.

The dancer listened well, her attention undivided, her posture open, and Afshar couldn't help but drop his eyes to the way her legs curled behind her at her hips, focusing on her smooth, flawless thighs. His blood heated at the thought of her atop him. She giggled at his jest, touching his wrist lightly, the contact brief and warm. Afshar felt the familiar loosening in his chest, the sense that tonight might offer something uncomplicated, new, and exciting.

"You are a very important man," she said gently, studying him as if she could see beneath the layers he had spent years constructing.

He only smiled, unsure how to respond, and in that moment, he grew tired of waiting.

"Come," he whispered, even though the words came out thick and breathy. He thought of his chambers upstairs, quiet and private. He rose with effort, feeling a faint pressure behind his eyes, and extended a hand toward her, which she took in a delicate way that nearly made him dizzy with desire. Even the way she rose from her cushion—eyes downward, movement fluid—caused him to swoon.

He led her to the stairs, holding her hand atop his, high so all could see his prize. Then, he directed her up ahead of him.

The room above was dim and cool, lit by only a few lamps that softened shadows rather than banishing them.

Afshar closed the door carefully and turned to the dancer, his smile ravenous. He reached for her, his breath heavier than he expected after his climb. His vision swam slightly, partly from exertion, partly from desire. He frowned and steadied himself against the door.

"Are you well?" she asked, her voice still calm.

"Yes, yes, my dove. I just need a moment. There is tea to be prepared in the cabinet just over there. Please prepare some for us," he said. She inclined her head before turning quickly, her outfit jingling. Again, Afshar licked his lips as he watched her rear. Finding his strength, he lifted himself off the door and made his way to the divan near the rear of the room, shedding his outer garment and seating himself on the edge. The mattress and frame protested, but he hardly noticed, watching instead the dancer prepare his tea. Even the way she moved in its preparation—slowly, her eyes low and subservient—eroded his patience. He looked away, inhaling deeply to steady his racing heart and control the sudden, unexpected shaking produced by his lust.

When was the last time I felt this way? he wondered, his exhilaration and anticipation reaching thresholds forgotten since his youth.

She approached with the tray of tea, setting it on the end table of the divan. She pressed a hand against his chest as she straddled him, sitting on his thighs. The dancer then reached for the tea, handing him first his cup, then taking her own. Afshar raised his shallow cup in salute to her beauty and poise before taking a sip, but she refrained.

Pressure in his chest intensified suddenly, gripping his ribcage and crawling upward into his throat. He swallowed, finding his mouth dry. His hand trembled as he released his hold on his teacup, spilling its contents on himself and the divan. With bulging eyes, he stared at the dancer as she, smiling knowingly, slowly poured out her tea on the rug below.

No! his thoughts shrieked. He had tried to say the words but found he was unable. He gagged sharply, and the dancer retreated from his lap, her chin dropping slightly as she took in Afshar's dilemma.

His heart hammered erratically, each beat uneven and painful. Panic rose up his spine, bursting into his brain, sharp and unfamiliar. His eyes burned as they reddened with weeping blood. His nose soon followed suit, and finally he tasted the sharp iron on his tongue.

The dancer stepped closer as Afshar fell sideways onto the divan, her face now stripped of warmth, certainty filling the void. Her honey eyes held his without cruelty or apology.

"You were warned," she said quietly.

Who? he wanted to cry, to ask before the coming of death. Even in his agony, he wondered if this was the doing of the Shaw woman, the Supreme Leader for his role in Radi's failure, or some other third party, perhaps the Macedonian. *Tell me!* his thoughts roared, but the dancer's stoic face revealed nothing.

Finally, he sagged onto his back, breath coming in shallow yet violent bursts. His vision narrowed, the edges darkening as the room tilted. He understood then, not through logic but through inevitability. This was consequence, arriving at last. It didn't matter from whom.

The dancer watched him until the tremor left his hands, and his chest fell still. She reached for his wrist, the radial pulse absent. Satisfied, she finally turned away, approached the nearest window, and slipped out unnoticed, retrieving a stash of clothes and supplies—a drop made days earlier—and disappeared into the dark alley.

Istanbul, Turkey

Laila waited near the waterfront where the lights of the last passing ferries traced pale lines across the water. The night smelled of salt and diesel, the air alive with voices drifting from late-night cafés and the scrape of chairs being stacked for closing. She leaned against the stone railing, her reflection fractured in the dark surface below.

When Basira Agha emerged from the side street, Laila felt the shift in her surroundings, turning her head just enough to notice the newcomer without revealing she did so.

Basira walked without hurry, her hands stuffed into the slanted pockets of a taupe wool overcoat. Her expression appeared light and composed. Her luscious, dark hair lay restrained by a cream, wool headband that covered her ears and the top of her sloping forehead, which—oddly to Laila—made the beautiful woman's nose look bigger.

Basira stopped at Laila's side, standing upright compared to Laila, who braced her weight against the stone sea wall. She inhaled the salty air. Her slender shoulders rose with the action before resettling with her exhale.

Laila offered her a closed-mouth smile and rose from her position as the two started forward together along the quay, passing vendors packing away their carts and couples lingering over final cigarettes. Laila watched Basira from the corner of her eye, noting the way she breathed, the way her gaze lingered on nothing in particular.

"This one didn't feel any different," Basira said at last, calmly, unburdened, keeping her honey eyes forward.

Laila did not answer immediately but smirked. She watched a ferry pull away from the dock, its wake breaking the reflections into pieces. She thought of Kyiv, of the hospital ward where she had finally found Basira lying pale and furious beneath white sheets. General Dudka had located her for Laila after the shelling had stopped and Kyiv was secured.

That was over a month ago.

"I'm surprised you expected it to," Laila finally replied. "He didn't notice your wound?"

"No, the silicone scar sheet did its job. He didn't notice, but the dancing hurt like hell," she answered with a quick laugh.

Laila grinned, still finding it odd how casually they talked about killing. She wondered if she would ever look at it differently. It was clear Basira had.

"Look, Basira," Laila said, pausing her stride. "The act always feels the same. The dirt never quite vanishes, regardless of the means or cause. It's the results and motive behind it that feels better, lighter even. The Shaws are good people, and Invictus is doing good things for the world."

Basira glanced at her, her expression tightening slightly in surprised contemplation as her slender, dark eyebrows rose.

"Good things," she repeated pensively, clearly not yet buying into Laila's words. "If you say so," she added with a chuckle.

Laila grinned at her, grateful the woman had survived the shootout in that Kyiv apartment.

"When I came back to Kyiv to find you," Laila began, her tone adopting a heavier seriousness. "You asked if I was free."

"I remember," the Algerian replied, keeping her gaze forward as they walked.

"I am, and now you are, too. No more Brotherhood, no more Czar. You'll understand the difference soon enough."

“When will that be?” Basira asked, intrigued.

“When no one asks you to betray yourself,” Laila replied.

The words stopped Basira cold. She wondered if she had ever considered her own personality, desires, or ethics as a factor in her duties. What did who she was have to do with anything she was ordered to do? It was almost frightening to consider. There was no end, no walls or railings to rein in action or thought. What did that endlessness produce? Basira wasn’t sure she wanted to find out.

“That’s the freedom I’m talking about,” Laila said, seeing her friend’s conundrum as it spread across her face.

“I’m not sure I’m here for it,” Basira replied, smiling nervously.

“You’ll soon desire nothing else in the whole world than what you’re feeling right now,” Laila countered, returning the smile, only hers was sure, confident.

“If Invictus is all that you say,” Basira said, “then I want to see it.”

“You will,” Laila replied, “but you have to promise me one thing.”

“What’s that?”

“You stay away from Owen,” Laila teased.

Basira’s eyes lit up, and her smile widened considerably. “Is he handsome?” she asked.

“No,” Laila replied quickly.

“Oh, you’re lying,” Basira shot back.

“Hey, you owe me, I tried to save you,” Laila said quietly, but Basira laughed.

“For the thousandth time, I know. But if I remember correctly, you started the whole thing, and I saved you!” she said, laughing and weaving her arm through Laila’s, tugging her forward. “Come on, I’m starving, and I want to see a picture of this Owen.”

The Second Directive
David Shaw #6

Saving the city was the mission. Getting out alive is something else entirely.

Kinshasa is days from falling. A rebel force four times the size of its defenders is massing at the gates, a desperate call for help has gone out, and only one team answers. Shaw arrives with six operators and an AC-130 gunship. They hold the line. They drive the rebels back. The siege breaks at nightfall.

The trap springs at dawn.

The attacking warlord was never the real threat. The UN peacekeepers patrolling the city answer to a different authority entirely — and the woman Shaw came to protect is at the center of it all. The city turns against his team, the embassy locks down, and somewhere in the chaos, a Chinese powerbroker with a personal score to settle is waiting.

Shaw has always found a way through. But he's never walked into a war designed specifically for him to lose.

ABOUT THE AUTHOR

Harrison is ardently committed to story and narrative, that a good narrative is driven by believable and compelling characters whose struggles are sincere, difficult, and meaningful. Story has spurred humanity into the greatest of endeavors, and valuable contribution is made to the larger human narrative with the telling of a good story.

Inspired by the great stories of Tolkien, Pressfield, Dumas, and others, Harrison strives to build on the foundation of humanity's story to inspire to action, provoke to thought, and call to integrity all who choose to read his work. His gratitude to you is sincere and deep.

Harrison lives in Alabama with his family.

Sign up for the reader list at
severnriverbooks.com

www.ingramcontent.com/pod-product-compliance
Lightning Source LLC
Chambersburg PA
CBHW010344130726
48054CB00025B/198

9781648758560